★★★

GHOST PATRIOT

BY

MICHAEL L. STICKLER

★★★

★★★

Disclaimer

Any references to historical events, real people or real places are used fictitiously. Names, characters, and places are all products of the author's imagination.

ISBN: 978-1-951648-04-6 (Hardcover)

GHOST PATRIOT— by Michael L. Stickler

For Worldwide Distribution
Printed By Ingram

★★★

★★

Dedication

I gratefully dedicate Ghost Patriot to my wife Kim who graciously
shared forty years of life, encouragement, and love with me before
passing into the arms of Jesus.
I am the man I am because of her.

★★

★★

Acknowledgements

<u>Special Thanks:</u>
Executive Editor Jerry Brewer who encourages me in every written
word.

<u>My Editorial and Design Team of Leadership Books:</u>
Art Ritter, COO of Leadership Books
Michele Smith, Managing Editor
Faith Burns, Proofreader
Violet Giovannini, Creative Director

<u>Advance Readers:</u>
Larry Nelson, Esq. (ret.)
Steven Buckley
Vincent Easley II

★★

Table of Contents

Introduction

When the Government decides serving itself and its own interests is more important than serving its citizens, the foundations of the Republic are in the utmost peril, as it begins to crumble away.

Ghost Patriot is a compelling fictional account, torn from modern headlines about the usurping of people's freedoms, rights, and civil liberties by those who are sworn to uphold those same Constitutionally protected laws. It is the story of America, and how citizens rally to save her.

Follow this unforgettable story of four Patriots and a news reporter who through extreme circumstances were providentially forged to become a unit, who together would restore liberty to the people of a great nation and inspire the rising of her citizens to stop the never-ending destruction.

Ghost Patriot is a fast, action-packed page-turner that every reader will enjoy from start to finish while appreciating the detailed research to bring the story to life.

If you've ever wondered what could happen if no one stands up to tyranny and corruption, this eye-opening new book will give you one prediction.

GHOST PATRIOT

Chapter 1

Forever Wars Cost a Man and a Country

Josh, call sign "Sleeper" was Paul's spotter on this tour. New to the Teams, he was the fourth spotter Paul had used in the five years he'd been in. Josh earned the name Sleeper because he would fall asleep at breaks, during meals, and basically anytime he was given the opportunity throughout the intensive five weeks of BUD/S training. When looking for Josh, the BUD/S instructors began calling out, "Where's the sleeper?" So, after graduating – much to his chagrin – the moniker stuck. Thereafter, Joshua Lee Cooper was known as "Sleeper".

"Chance, how are we looking?" came the question with intermittent chirps of static from the COMMS in Paul's earpiece.

"Are we clear to begin?" Paul took one last look up and down the street through the scope of his 50-caliber sniper rifle.

"I'm clear," Sleeper whispered to Paul, confirming what Paul saw as well.

"We're clear," Paul quickly reported.

"Three, two, one," announced the assault team commander followed by, "breach, breach, breach!"

In a military-style single file line, known as "stack formation," the assault team stealthily approached the Mosque's main door. A small explosive was placed on the door by the demolition specialist, followed seconds later by a loud... "KA-BOOM!" The charge ignited the scene in bright lightning sounds, destructively blowing the doors off the hinges flying through the air as the dog was let loose. The Team sent in the finest canine assault team ever, a special breed known as the "hair missile" a.k.a. the Belgian Malinois, making up the fiercest attackers. This particular canine, conveniently named "Rocket" – was trained to viciously subdue any security force or threat that might have been posted at the entrance.

Immediately the breaching team entered the Mosque, one by one. As in all combat assault operations of this type, there was some short radio chatter accompanying the familiar gunfire of the SEAL Teams Heckler & Koch HK-416, their weapon of choice. The "clear, clear, clear, clear" report followed, being shouted out distinctly by each team member, as all the different rooms were cleared.

"Three Tangos in custody, one KIA, one MIA," Sleeper whispered into his radio. *Three out of five, crap,* Sleeper muttered to himself.

"Roger, three in custody, good work," CENTCOM immediately responded. "Your ride is in transport, touch down in five mikes (minutes)."

The assault team tactically placed a two-man security detail just inside the Mosque door to repel any possible counter assault.

"Bag any potential intel and be ready to move in three mikes, we got a ride to catch," the COMMS chirped again, followed by a lingering silence for what seemed like hours.

Chance and Sleeper laid hidden and motionless on the rooftop, ever scanning the streets below in overwatch detail as the roof began to warm with the rising sun. The sunshine provided heat and felt good to warm up, especially after five long nights in one spot. This mission would soon be over and in moments the Teams and captives would board the HELO and head back to the Al Asad Airbase, located about 100 miles west of Baghdad.

Paul's intensity began to fall as he heard that sound he loved: the familiar consistent *'thump, thump'* of the approaching helicopters far off in the distance. From the first day of basic training right up to today, that comforting sound always meant the mission was over and he and his men were returning home. Even if home was back to a base in a country far away from his actual home, wherever that was these days.

"I've got movement," Sleeper whispered as something caught the corner of his eye just to the right of the Mosque.

"Got it," Chance swiftly responded, adjusting his 50-cal site to zero-in on the movement in question.

Just thirty feet to the north of the Mosque, a door opened in what he had thought to be a fully collapsed abandoned building, with only a simple front façade where the door was hung. At first, the

★★

★★★

door opened just a crack, and a little girl tentatively stepped out, before immediately turning and looking back at the door as if she was waiting for someone. Just who she was waiting for became the question on everyone's mind…

Two seconds later, the door opened a bit further, and a woman emerged, immediately following the little girl. It was a woman in a traditional Burqa, fully covered, meaning the sniper team couldn't see her head, face, feet, or anything else.

"Are you seeing this?" Sleeper asked curiously.

"Yeah," Paul promptly replied.

"What is she holding in her arms?" Sleeper asked, with a bit of worry in his voice.

Paul carefully zoomed his rifle scope to get an accurate look. "It looks like a baby," he replied, as discreetly held in the woman's arms he could see the hands and the bundle of a swaddled baby.

"Do you see skin? ... I don't?" Sleeper asked wondering.

"Wait one …"

The woman immediately turned, grabbed the little girl by the hand, and at a brisk pace strolled up the street in the direction of the Mosque.

"We're coming out," the assault team commander squawked over the COMMS, giving notice that the SEAL team was about to leave the Mosque with their captives and the intel they had gathered. The rising sound of the approaching helicopters grew louder and louder.

"Wait one second, we have movement outside," Paul quickly responded. The assault team who were just about to emerge from the door stopped dead in their tracks and instinctively took cover against the high exterior wall inside the Mosque.

Paul continued scoping up and down, focusing precisely on the woman, trying to determine if she was a threat, then focused in on the little girl, —*Emma?* EMMA! *What are you doing here?!* In shock, he couldn't believe his own eyes, as he sighted his own daughter in the streets of Mosul, holding hands with this unknown woman in the middle of his operation! *What the fu…? But, how?* He turned away from his 50-cal rifle scope and rested his head for a brief moment on the gun stock, closed his eyes hard, squeezing out tears and attempted to regain focus.

★★★

★★★

Meanwhile, Sleeper saw a male hand reach out of the shadows from where the woman had just emerged, and in a flash pulled the door closed.

"She's no good, take the shot!" – Sleeper whispered. "Take the shot!" Sleeper insisted, glancing over at Paul who had pulled his head away from his scope.

"Chance, what the fuck is the matter with you?" Sleeper sternly demanded, prompting him to wake up and focus.

Paul returned his gaze into his 50-caliber scope. But once again, he saw Emma desperately holding the hand of this woman. *Wait? Could that be Jennifer, his ex-wife, in the burqa?* Paul gasped, as he watched the scene unfold, frozen with fear.

"That's not a baby, that's an 81-mm mortar round, take the shot!" Sleeper yelled over the COMMS.

The HELO sound intensified as the big birds came in behind them and the rotor blast increased.

Over the COMMS, the CENTCOM commander gives a direct order to fire.

Quickly followed from the assault team commander, "Chance, take the shot buddy."

Barely hearing the second communication with the blasting noise, Chance gathers himself together, takes a deep breath, exhales, and squeezes the trigger.

Paul immediately jerked to an awakened state, having fallen off the bed onto the floor, disoriented, sweating, with adrenalin coursing through his veins. He is in a state of full fight mode. *What the Fuck!* he wondered, as he hastily looked around. *Where am I?* His mind raced quickly, looking around the poorly furnished, dingy room of the Provo, Utah's Budget 8 Motel.

Paul slowly pushed himself up, then reaching out with his right arm pulled himself back onto the bed and rested his elbows on his knees to catch his breath. Heavy sweat dripped off his forehead. He reached over to the bed stand to find his absolute best friend these days. *Good ole' Jack,* he thought to himself, *at least you haven't left me,* as he took a long swig from the half-empty Sour Mash Whisky bottle. Breakfast of champions, he thought to himself, finishing off the bottle and setting it back down. *I'm sure glad that was a dream,* he thought as his heart slowly began calming down.

★★★

The shrill ring of his cell phone jarred him. He picked it up without even looking who could be calling.

"Papa!" came the little voice on the other end of the phone. "Are you coming?"

Paul swiftly focused. "Hi baby, how's my little girl?"

"I'm great daddy, we have all kinds of plans for your visit. When will you be here? Where are you?"

"I am in Provo," Paul replied.

"Where's that?" Emma asked.

"It's in Utah, sweetie."

"Where's that? Is it near Las Vegas?"

"No, not really, but I am closer than I've ever been, and I'll be with you tonight."

"Okay, I can't wait! Here, mommy wants to talk to you," the seven-year-old said excitedly, handing over the phone.

"Paul, where are you?" the woman's stern voice on the other end asked a moment later.

"I'm in Provo. I'll be there in time for dinner."

"Don't let her down again," the woman chastised him.

"I won't, nothing will stop me this time," Paul replied with certainty.

"Are you riding the Harley?" she asked.

"Yep, it's beautiful weather and I have plenty of time. I'll be there soon, and we can start anew."

"Just get here for dinner. The new stuff will wait."

"Okay, I love you," he said.

The phone clicked as she briskly hung up.

Paul took a good look around the dismal room. Instinctively he reached for the bottle of Jack Daniels. Seeing it empty he threw it aside, still not coherent of what had happened and where he was.

Was he simply dreaming of talking to Emma? The little love of his life, and was that really Jennifer, his high school sweetheart and ex-wife who divorced him four years ago? Or was it all a PTSD flashback, the "disorder" the Navy head doctor confirmed he had upon discharge? Well, technically he wasn't officially discharged by the military. He was still running out his leave time, after which the discharge would be official.

He paused for a moment and rethought his decisions. *Should I have left my career? Hell, they offered me $150K for a re-signing* *bonus. No, it was the right decision.* Paul needed to recoup the many years he lost with Emma, and hopefully Jennifer too, although it might be too late with her. *Well, at least I spoke to her and got some words out of her and that's better than I have gotten in years.*

Time to get on the road, I can't be late, Paul thought as he glanced at the clock. "0600 hours? I have never slept so long," he said out loud. "Maybe this civilian life agrees with me or, it was that friend of mine that kept me up all night," he chuckled.

As he slowly headed to the shower, he was struck by how quiet it is here in the U.S. with just some limited street noise outside from cars passing by on the road. Paul could hear the tap, tap, tap, of the maids on the floor below him knocking and saying, "housekeeping, tap, tap, tap, housekeeping." Unlike his experience overseas, he found there is peace here, safety, niceties. *It'll take some getting used to. It's certainly better than my dreams, nightmares, flashbacks, or whatever you want to call them* Paul thought as his head felt the warm water running down his weary body. While he showered, he closed his eyes, trying to wash off the foggy memory of the night before.

As Paul emerged from the motel room thirty minutes later, his eyes gazed upon his dream-ride that had become a reality. His brand-new, jet black Harley Fat Boy, complete with chrome ape hangers and hard case saddle bags. "Damn, she's sexy," he said aloud to no one in particular. He bought it from Sleeper just last month at the end of their deployment, paid cash with the pink slip in hand. Sleeper had rarely ridden her because he was always down range in some foreign land or another. While Sleeper liked the Harley, it was love at first sight for Paul.

Paul planned to kick the Teams to the curb and put as much road between them and himself as possible. *Nothing like the rumble of a Harley and road time to clear a man's head,* he thought. And his head needed some clearing. So, Paul had discharged from NAB Little Creek in Virginia and taken the last eighteen long days riding across the country getting in his road time.

There were just three rules: no freeways, no agenda, and no food chains. His only goal was to eventually get to Las Vegas, Nevada to see his little Emma. Then, to see what happens next. At this time, he was just under seven hours away from his goal to be embraced by the little arms of his only child. And maybe just maybe a reconciliation with Jennifer.

GHOST PATRIOT

Chapter 2

Who Would Hire These People?

Hoover Building, Washington D.C. – 21 days earlier
FBI Director Jim Johnson hated running late for work. Something inside him, the way he was raised or the hard start he had in life had made him almost obsessive about being on time.

"Good morning, Director Johnson," his assistant Kathy declared as he made his way into the foyer of the Assistant Director's private office. He stopped ritually at her desk, picking up the coffee that she had already poured for him. Black and strong, just the way he liked it. The kind of coffee so strong, you might think the spoon will stand up in it.

"Good morning, Kathy, what are my highlights?" he asked.

"You have a new intel report from Homeland, you ought to read and decide if it should be in the briefing you have with POTUS this afternoon," she replied with a smile.

"Why, what's in it," he asked, all the while wondering, *do I want to know?*

"Two Border Patrol agents were killed last night on the Arizona border," she said somberly, almost with tears in her eyes.

Why is this worthy of making my Oval Office briefing later today, he thought, as he gave Kathy a wooden "okay."

"There are some different earmarks to this shooting that they want you to look at," Kathy jumped in, nearly interrupting him.

She's reading my mind again. I was just thinking nowadays this happens all too often, Johnson thought.

"Got it," he replied. "What else?"

"After your briefing with POTUS, I've cleared your calendar for the range."

"Oh, yeah…"

"You must get qualified again; you can't put it off any longer," Kathy interjected.

"I know, I know, I guess with this new 'temporary' responsibility as Acting Director I better follow the rules," he smirked. "Anything else?"

"I'll need to update the Intel Briefing for POTUS by 10 a.m. if you want to add that report to it," she said, pointing to the Homeland report she just handed him. Your detail will be picking you up here precisely at 11 a.m. to head to the White House."

Good, that gives me three hours to review it and make an analysis, he thought, as he began heading into his office.

"Oh! and Director Cornwall is waiting for you in your office."

Jim paused and stared at Kathy. "He set this appointment three days ago, and you told me to fit him in," she replied, justifying her decision.

"You could have let me get this in me before I was faced with him," He smiled, pointing to his coffee.

Kathy just gave him her knowing smile as he turned to head into the office to meet with one of many people he detested in the beltway. *No point in arguing with her I probably did tell her to make the appointment,* he thought.

The newly minted Bureau of Land Management (BLM) Director had just moved into his new position in D.C. He was everything Jim Johnson wasn't. Neil Cornwall was only thirty-two years old and had never held a private-sector job. He first interned with Nevada Senator Lawrence Red, arguably one of the most powerful members in the United States Senate.

Cornwall rose quickly through the ranks on Senator Red's team to become his Chief of Staff. He was a political animal, saying and doing whatever necessary to move up the political ladder. And Senator Red found that admirable.

Though smart and Ivy-league educated, Cornwall was one of the dumbest men Jim Johnson had ever met. The BLM Director came from a wealthy family who used their standing as one of Senator Red's donors to get Cornwall his start as an intern. Now, he sat in Johnson's office as the director of a small department by U.S. government standards, but a very influential department that controlled, managed, and claimed to own about one-third of the Western third of the United States. The funny part - to Jim anyway

– was Cornwall had no land management experience at all. *Hell, he has no useful experience of any kind,* Johnson thought.

Conversely, Jim Johnson came up through the ranks of law enforcement. During a troubled youth, he was rescued by a thoughtful pastor and loving couple who put up with him and the trash he was dishing out as a know-it-all fourteen-year-old. They took him in, taught him a work ethic, held his feet to the fire in school, and introduced him to his faith.

Eventually, Jim got an Associate Degree in history, which led to him becoming a Los Angeles County Sheriff Deputy. He finished his undergraduate degree attending school part-time while working full time, before using the same routine to get his Masters. At forty-eight, he still plugged away at getting a Ph.D., in criminal justice. But he found it hard to keep up that routine.

While serving as a deputy, the FBI recruited him and during the last twenty years he had moved up the ranks to his current position as the Assistant Director of Counterintelligence. He was now the head guy overall domestic intelligence, although lately, he had been filling two roles. Six months into the new president's first term in office, the FBI Director was fired. In Jim's opinion, it was bogus, political retribution against his more traditional views of law enforcement. From the beginning, the old director and POTUS had locked horns over the latter's constant meddling in the daily actions of the FBI. POTUS also used the media to repeatedly criticize the Director, creating a discouraging workplace in the Hoover Building.

Once the Director was fired, Jim Johnson found himself thrust into the role as the new Director. Now, he had two jobs, the role he loved in Counterintelligence and the other, playing politics with the most misguided, confused president he had seen in his lifetime. For now, he seemed to be stuck with it and was trying to be as faithful as he could to what was placed before him. It came back to something Kathy reminded him of as to why the rank and file of the FBI put him forward to be the Interim Director. Jim had integrity, was thoughtful, and a "cops' cop." It was one reason he couldn't stand guys like Cornwall.

"Good morning," Jim extended his hand to greet Cornwall while taking a big gulp from his coffee cup.

"Good morning, it's nice to meet you finally," Cornwall replied as he stood to shake Jim's hand.

Nice to meet you finally? What a moron. I guess he has forgotten we have met what, three times? talked and even discussed the old rancher out in the desert in Nevada. He's really winning me over now.

"I just wanted to stop by and introduce myself since I'm the new guy in the beltway, so we could see each other eye to eye as department heads," Cornwall said with a disingenuous smile.

Now that's funny. He thinks we're equals. I am the Director albeit Interim Director of the premier Law Enforcement department in the world, and he is a park ranger if that. How cute.

"And, as peers, I think it's just good to get the lay of the land and connect on a personal level. Don't you agree?" Cornwall paused for effect.

Director Johnson just gave him a blank stare. For effect. He waited to see if Cornwall broke eye contact, which he did a split second later. Cornwall looked down at his hands.

That didn't take long. I've had criminals hold their stare longer than that, Johnson thought, holding his uncomfortable stare a couple more seconds.

"What can I do for you?" he asked breaking the silence. "I have a meeting with POTUS in a couple of hours and I need to prepare." Jim usually didn't name drop like that, but he wanted to put Cornwall in his place. Letting him know they were not equals, without telegraphing his disdain for the man wasn't easy.

Cornwall shifted a little in his chair and stated his real reason for being there. "I don't know if you have heard about the little problem I inherited out in Nevada?" he began. "You see there is this old rancher that won't sign a grazing lease…"

"You mean, caused, not inherited," Johnson interrupted.

"I'm sorry?" Cornwall responded, flustered by the interruption.

"You caused the conflict, right?" Johnson interjected.

"Ah, well no…" Cornwall stammered, even more confused.

"Sure, you did, and I don't mean the BLM, of which you are now the Director. I mean YOU," Johnson responded, pausing to let his words sink in. Cornwall sat still, waiting.

"I mean it was Senator Red's office that put this whole thing into motion, right? You guys needed to push this old rancher out to pay back all your donors and environmental cronies, right? It was at your direction that his new grazing permit was made useless to him so you could, in essence, steal his right to graze his cattle. Something his family had done for years and years. It was at the behest of your office that the sheriff got a court order to have him evicted, knowing he didn't have the money to defend himself against the army of DOJ attorneys you have at your beck and call."

How much money did your Senator make off this deal? Johnson thought but knew not to say. "So, please do not tell me you inherited this problem. You made it, you, then the Chief of Staff of Senator Lawrence Red's office. Now it's a problem that has fallen in your lap as the new Director of the BLM."

Cornwall was stunned. He had no idea that Director Johnson would have been so thoroughly briefed on this matter. "How do you know…"

"I am the Director of Counterintelligence for the FBI!" *Moron,* Director Johnson thought while simultaneously speaking.

"Besides, we conducted four or five threat assessments on the family, what's their names?"

"Cloyden," Cornwall answered.

"That's right, Cloyden. Haven't you read the assessments?"

"No, I wasn't…" Johnson cut him off again. "Well don't you think you ought to have read them before meeting with me? After all, we conducted those threat assessments at the BLM's request."

Jim decided to pause and let Cornwall catch up.

"Don't you remember talking about this while you were in Senators Red's office?" Jim pressed, seeing how confused Cornwall was.

"Well sure, but…" Cornwall was lying now, so Johnson cut him off.

"I'll ask again, what do you want?"

Cornwall sat for a few moments trying to see how he could get the conversation back to his agenda. His eyes darted right and left as he accessed his memory and reasoning functions, then began.

"I need the FBI's help."

"How?"

"We need help from your HRT," referring to the agency's Hostage Rescue Team.

"Why? Who's been taken hostage?" Johnson responded, playing with him now.

Seeing Cornwall was confused, Johnson decided to give him a respite.

"I'm messing with you. You need a SWAT team?"

"Yes."

"For what?"

"To enforce the court order to remove the cows."

"But, why? These guys are NO threat. If you had read our reports, you would know that!" Johnson responded, feeling the anger rising.

"We have announced operations to start the impounding and sale of his cows and old man Cloyden says he'll 'Do whatever it takes to stop us.' That is a demonstrable threat!"

Oh, bull… that's the kind of thing anyone would say in that situation, Johnson thought.

"What did the local Sheriff say, what's his name. Gillette?"

Yeah, Gillette," Johnson said abruptly, cutting off Cornwall again. "You do realize that under the Federal Land Practices Management Act (FLPMA), you must use the local sheriff to execute legal enforcement actions on public lands?" Johnson reminded him.

"Well, we have our own Law enforcement agency…"

"Yeah, those guys are for enforcing camping fees but don't have the training or resources to conduct a large-scale operation. More importantly, you don't have the federal regulations behind you. Do you even know what FLPMA is?"

"Well, of course, I haven't studied it," Cornwall replied confidently.

"YOU BETTER! It's the Congressional act that brought your agency into existence!" Johnson said, astonished at Cornwall's ignorance. "Look, you need to get the sheriff involved. He is an experienced law enforcement professional who has a significant agency in Las Vegas. He will give you the guidance and resources you'll need."

"But can we count on the FBI's support?" Cornwall pressed.

"Of course, you're a federal agency so we'll support you. But get the Sheriff's leadership."

"Okay, if we need the FBI where do we start?" Cornwall asked, feeling like he was finally getting somewhere.

"Just have Sheriff Gillette's office contact the Local FBI field office in Las Vegas. They work together all the time," Johnson replied, anxious to get rid of his "guest."

"Great! Thank you so much for your support in this extremely important operation," Cornwall stated emphatically, as he rose to leave. The two men headed out together to Kathy's desk to say goodbye.

"Advise my detail that I am ready to leave," Cornwall commanded Kathy, exuding importance.

Kathy picked up the handset of her phone and called the Hoover building front desk in the lobby. "Director Cornwall is on his way down," she told them, pausing to hear the person on the other end of the phone.

"Director Cornwall?" replied the voice.

"He is the Director of the Bureau of Land Management. His driver must be around there somewhere." Another pause. "There must be someone waiting there for him. Look around," she said, hanging up the phone and smiling at Cornwall. "They have been notified," she told the pompous BLM Chief.

"Thanks so much for everything," Cornwall enthusiastically said, smiling and shaking Johnson's hand with vigor. He headed to the outer door with a victorious grin on his face.

Director Jim Johnson turned to walk back into his office. *What a schmuck.* He glanced at his watch and realized he had only forty-five minutes to review the latest report from the southern border and get it to Kathy. *Crap, I hate that guy AND now he's made me late!* Jim thought, disgustedly.

As the elevator doors opened on the ground floor, Director Cornwall made his way into the lobby, where an elderly man in a tan uniform and gun belt approached him.

"All done with your meeting?" the man asked.

"Yeah, where's the car?" Cornwall said curtly, trying to hide his annoyance.

"Oh, it's in the garage where we left it. I was just waiting in the coffee shop while you were upstairs."

Cornwall figured he would have found the old, tired BLM agent who was assigned to him as a driver fast asleep in the car. His driver was just months away from retirement and Cornwall required him to wear his dress uniform, gun and to drive a marked interior

★★★

department vehicle. This was his "Security Detail" even though he didn't really need one. It made Cornwall feel important about the status of the position he held, at least in his own mind.

As he climbed into the back of his vehicle, he jumped on his cell phone as they emerged into the daylight from the underground parking garage. He dialed a Utah number and waited for it to ring.

"Hello," came the voice on the other end. "How did it go?" asked Chuck Dodger, Special Agent in Charge of Law Enforcement, for the Bureau of Land Management's Utah and Nevada Division.

"It went better than expected. We have his full support."

"And the HRT?"

"Them too," Cornwall answered. "You are clear to execute Operation Gold Butte."

Cornwall hung up for dramatic effect. *This ought to make Senator Red well pleased,* Cornwall thought as he blankly stared out the backseat window while his car made its way through the DC Beltway.

Jim settled in to read the high-priority Homeland Intel Report as Kathy brought in a third cup of his favorite strong coffee. He was curious to understand why this file had made it to his desk. It was this investigative aspect of his job that he loved so much.

As he opened the file, the first thing that caught his eye was the grizzly photos of the two slain border patrol officers. Their bodies had been ripped apart by large-caliber bullets, and what appeared to be dozens and dozens of rounds. He flipped to the synopsis, which told him that each body had been hit by at least forty plus rounds, including a double tap to the head.

Geez, somebody wanted to make them dead. Real dead, he thought, grimacing at each graphic and bloody photo.

Then Johnson turned to the narrative portion of the report.

02:48 a.m.: It appears that the victims, Agents Rodriguez, and Porter were on routine patrol when they came across movement in the sagebrush to the north.

Johnson skipped down, past the generalities.

…it appears that the suspects opened fire in mass from two concealed elevated positions, approximately fifteen yards from where they exited their patrol vehicle.

Crap, this was an ambush!
Back to the synopsis, he turned.
One hundred bullets and 127 casings were recovered?
Shit, these guys were lousy shots.
Why didn't they pick up their brass?

Estimated sixteen-twenty suspects from the observed footprints.

Really? And they all had long guns? What kind?
Johnson skimmed the page.

7.62x39mm rounds

That's likely an Avtomat Kalashnikova or better known as an *AK-47. The most mass-produced Soviet assault weapon in the world. Every Jorge, Mohammed, and Harry in the third world has one. But not on this side of the world. They are rare in North America. And here we have sixteen-twenty of them. This likely isn't the Cartels. They usually don't travel in squad fashion and seldom with long guns when they are on this side of the border. But who could they be?*

"Director your detail is waiting. It's time for you to go." Kathy announced as she burst through the door and interrupted his thoughts.

She noticed he was looking at the DHS report.

"There's not enough time now to include that in POTUS's briefing," she said as if redirecting any thoughts he may have had.

"Yeah, I know. I'm not ready to draw any conclusions anyway. I might just verbally report on it during my meeting with POTUS," he replied.

He slowly rose out of his chair and paused.

The investigators also found a shemagh. Wow. That's odd. U.S. Special Operators? They're the only ones who wear those things this side of the ocean. It's a kind of scarf, badge of honor, souvenir, whatever you want to call it, that is worn by the allied military or enemy warriors in the middle east. Humm.

I need to see if there has been some kind of sanctioned or even unsanctioned operation on the southern border that the DHS or FBI has not been told of. Or maybe private security outfits? But none of those guys carry AK's. In fact, they mock anyone who does. AKs shoot like shit. No wonder 40% of the rounds fired miss their mark.

"Time to go, Director," Kathy reiterated, trying to keep Johnson on time.

"Okay," Jim replied, closing the folder.

She traded his coffee cup for his briefing file.

"See you tomorrow," Kathy said with a smile.

"Tomorrow? Are you taking some time off, did I forget?" Johnson, asked, pausing to look at her.

"No, YOU are going to the range after your briefing. Then home. Your detail knows your schedule even if you don't," she answered, guiding him to the door.

"Now, get moving," she said, teasingly, shoving him out into the hallway as if pushing an unwilling pet out the back door.

1600 Pennsylvania Avenue

Jim Johnson, slid across the back seat of his specially designed SUV, exiting on the right side of the vehicle. He had been in deep thought about the report from the southern border and never got around to looking at the agenda for this meeting with POTUS. There was something in his gut, the same feeling he used to get when he was on patrol in Los Angeles County as a young patrolman. "NEVER, EVER, ignore that feeling. It was God warning him of something about to go bad," his Training Officer, Leo Martinez, had repeatedly drilled into his head.

But, what?

Johnson smiled at the Marine who opened the door for him at the West Wing entrance to the White House.

President Molly Mountebank was leaning against the famed Oval Office Resolute desk as Chief of Staff Smith entered. "What's next?" POTUS asked Theodore Smith as he came through the door.

Smith was a young, fit black man from Chicago, who loved his job. He had remained single for all of his thirty-six years so he could keep up with the demanding career he stepped into. When he was hired as a legislative analyst for the Oregon Governor, who was now the President of the United States, there were rumors back in Oregon that he and Mountebank were lovers, something he denied with great vigor. POTUS, however, didn't seem to mind and even smiled when the rumor surfaced.

"It's time for your security briefing," Smith told POTUS.

"Oh, shit I hate this guy. Haven't we gotten rid of him yet?"

"No, we have discussed this, you are stuck with Johnson as your Interim FBI Director until you put forward your replacement for Director," he replied, sounding almost like a husband.

"Well, he's just so much like the old director. They're both so...I don't know..."

"Butch," Smith replies

"No, that's not what I was going to say. They're both such goody-two-shoes. You know, rules, rules, rules, the law says this, the law says that."

"You're supposed to like the Rule of Law. You were the State Attorney General of Oregon after all before I met you. Hell, you're even a "Constitutional Scholar" Smith reminded her sarcastically.

"Yes, I am!" POTUS replied, smiling proudly.

The door swung open and POTUS secretary, Susie Kinum, announced Jim Johnson. "FBI Director Johnson is here for his weekly briefing," she stated in a very matter-of-fact tone.

"Susan, can you have the Steward bring up some finger sandwiches and coffee, or is there something else you would like?" POTUS asked, looking at Johnson as he entered.

Johnson is still inwardly smirking at the statement, "Weekly Briefing." *POTUS hates these briefings, cancels them as often as she possibly can. If I make it once a month, it's a miracle. Hell, the CIA, DHS, and NSA directors don't even bother to come anymore.* He almost missed the question.

"No coffee for me, bottled water would be fine.... And the sandwiches that would be nice." *I haven't had lunch yet.*

I wasn't offering you a sandwich, asshole, the President thought while smiling and motioning Johnson to sit on the couch. *I don't want you to stay that long.*

I hate it when POTUS does that. Referring to the last-minute food order. *The steward always gives me a butt chewing when I don't follow his protocols and give him at least thirty minutes' notice on the food he'll need to have the kitchen prepare. Last time I pushed back, reminding him that he has served four presidents, and this is the way it's done,* Susan thought as she closed the door behind her, feeling put out and unappreciated.

"Ms. President. I have several items on the agenda I would like to review…" Johnson began, hoping to guide the meeting to a more productive outcome than usual.

"What's going on with the White Supremacist in Nevada?" POTUS interrupted

"I'm sorry," Johnson queried, caught off guard.

"Those asshole inbred haters out there in Nevada, you know."

Still, a bit confused, Johnson asked, "You mean the Cloyden family?"

"Yes, yes, those racist squatters on our land."

"Public land," Smith interjected, correcting the President.

"Yeah, 'Public Land'," POTUS giving a snarky reply to Smith for being corrected.

"What about them?" Johnson asked, still trying to figure out where this was going. *I wonder how the Cloydens have come to the attention of POTUS?*

"Senator Red was just here this morning briefing me on the situation out there in…. where is that?" POTUS asked, looking to Smith for help.

"Bunkerville, Nevada," Smith responded.

"That's right, Bunkerville. Senator Red is from there you know?"

"Actually, I am pretty sure he's from Tonopah, not Bunker…" Johnson tried to correct.

"Nevada, Nevada, Nevada! He's the Senator from NEVADA! I couldn't give a crap what backwater town he's from. Wherever the fuck Tonopah is!" POTUS ranted. *This guy is stupid.*

"Anyway, Red was in here this morning, and he asked me to make some god-forsaken piece of dessert out there a National Monument," POTUS said, pausing to let it sink in.

"Three hundred thousand acres of dirt! He wants a National Monument! I mean crap, National Monuments are supposed to be trees and lakes and… well, you know pretty, even scenic," POTUS continued, sounding more female than usual.

"You know what we told him?" Smith asked, jumping in as if he made the decision.

They both stared at Johnson as if waiting for his input.

"I told him to fuck off," the President laughing said, after Johnson didn't respond.

"Yes, you did," Smith said, putting up his hand as if to get a high five.

"I am sorry, ma'am. What are you getting to?" Johnson asked trying to get back on track.

The President and Chief of Staff looked annoyed wondering why Johnson wasn't keeping up.

"I want to know what you're going to do about those Domestic Terrorists?" POTUS demanded as Smith rolled his eyes.

"Nothing."

"Nothing, what do you mean, NOTHING?" the President asked him pointedly.

"There is nothing the FBI can do. As I explained just this morning to Director Cornwall, the law requires…"

"Who?" POTUS interrupted.

"The new Director of the BLM," Johnson began to explain.

"What does Black Lives Matter have to do with this?" Smith interrupted, revealing his ignorance.

"No, the Bureau of Land Management," Johnson said, trying to be patient, while Smith was wishing he could crawl into a hole from embarrassment.

"As I was just explaining to Director Cornwall this morning, he is required to enlist the local Sheriff to assist him in removing the trespass cattle from the range. There is no need for the FBI to be involved."

"But these are domestic terrorists! That's your job stopping terrorists, right?" the President pushed back.

"Well yes, but this simple family are not terrorists. The FBI and other Federal agencies have conducted several threat assessments on this…"

"I don't care if Jesus Christ Himself told you they are wonderful people and innocent as a newborn baby. You need to arrest them. They are terrorists. Their acts of terror are in plain sight. Anyone can see that. Do your job, or I will find someone who will."

I wish you would. I didn't want the Director's job anyway, Johnson thought to himself.

At that moment their tense exchange was interrupted by a knock on the door. Susie entered followed by the White House Steward.

"The kitchen was able to make some nice sandwiches for you," Susie warmly announced, setting the food down on the table in front of the three. Jim reached for a sandwich slice and grabbed a bottle of water.

"Anything else?" Smith asked.

"Well yes, we need to go through the brief," Johnson responded, relieved that they were getting back on track.

"You can just leave that here. I am running out of time," POTUS responded. "You're dismissed!"

You are NOT my Commander and Chief. I have never been in the military, Johnson thought, knowing better than to telegraph his thoughts.

As Johnson began to rise, clutching his slice of sandwich, Smith asked him, "Is there anything not in the report we should know about?" It was a useful question that his predecessor had taught him.

"Well yes, there is," Johnson answered, as he began sitting back down. "Last night two Border Patrol agents were brutally gunned down."

"Oh, how terrible," the President responded, with as much empathy as possible.

Why does the President need to be briefed on this?" Smith jumped in. "I mean cops get killed all the time, don't they?"

"Well, sir, it looks like they were ambushed, by some sixteen-twenty assailants…"

"That's nothing new. That kind of thing happens every night in my hometown of Chicago. I know I lived it!" Smith retorted.

Oh, BS you were born and raised in the Near North Side, the wealthiest neighborhood in Chicago. You even went to a 130-year-

old wealthy private school for the elite of Chicago; the Latin Private School rated the number two private school in the Chicago area, Johnson countered in his head.

"I used to dodge bullets just for an opportunity to get an education. But, my momma, made me take the risk so I could make something of myself...."

Your momma was a drunk. It was your dad who kicked you in the ass to get a good education. I hate that these DC elites need to play a stereotypical role to make themselves out to have overcome hardships, Johnson's internal narrative continued.

"Bottomline it for me," the President interrupted.

"Well, mam,"

I hate it when he calls me ma'am, it's so condescending and misogynist, POTUS thought.

"This shooting is not the typical kind of thing we've seen before at the southern border. Plus, there are some preliminary indications that it might be terrorist-related."

"The Cartels?" Smith asked.

"You mean immigrants, don't you?" POTUS asked, correcting Smith.

"No, it's not the Cartels," Johnson continued, ignoring the stupidity of the last statement. "It may be special operators of some sort."

"You mean like Delta Force or something?" Smith asked, intrigued like a schoolboy.

"No, dumb ass," POTUS said, slamming the aide. "Delta wouldn't be thought of as terrorists. Could it be those self-proclaimed militias who are always 'helping' at the border?"

I hadn't thought of that, Johnson thought. *Something to look into. Many of them are ex-military and some might wear a shemagh.*

"It's just too early," Johnson replied.

"Well, I bet you it's those dumbass militia guys. I dealt with them all the time in Oregon as Governor, always protesting the gun safety laws I was trying to put through. I bet that is it. It's the kind of chickenshit thing they'd do. Murder our boys in blue," POTUS ranted on.

"Green," Johnson responded, not thinking about what he was saying.

"What? I'm sorry. I don't follow," POTUS said.

"Green, the Border Patrol wear green, not blue," Johnson responded, correcting POTUS.

"You're dismissed, Director Johnson," POTUS said, standing up as if to show the Director the door.

It does matter. At least to the boots on the ground. They are very proud of the departments in which they serve.

Johnson stood and headed to the door, still clutching his slice of sandwich and bottle of water as if they were reparation for a wasteful meeting.

As Johnson exited, he stopped at Susie's desk. "Would you mind letting my detail know I am ready?"

"Sure," as she picked up the phone. "Did you and the President have a productive meeting?"

"It always is," Johnson said, lying through his teeth.

Susie suspected as much, responding, "He's an unappreciative prat, but I get paid to put up with it."

"HE? Is there something I should know Secretary Kinum?"

"Not just now Director," she said as she walked off leaving him wondering.

What is Susie trying to tell me? She is way too professional to let something slip.

Director Johnson turned to walk down the corridor of the West Wing and headed for the exit while discreetly trying to gobble down the piece of sandwich. It was three-thirty in the afternoon, and he was starving, mentally noting that he had only had a protein shake and three cups of strong coffee all day. As he reached the door, he saw his detail pull up.

He again smiled at the Marine guard and climbed into the back seat, while a member of his detail closed the car door.

"Here sir, this is from Kathy." The driver handed him a lunchbox of sorts.

"What is it?" Johnson asked.

"She just told me to give it to you after the briefing," the driver replied as the other detail member jumped into the passenger seat.

Director Johnson zipped open the package only to find a roast beef sandwich, celery, and carrots inside. Underneath was a cold can of A&W Root Beer. Johnson began to wolf it all down.

God that woman is brilliant! How did she know?

The driver glimpsed at him in the rearview mirror, "She sent you lunch. She figured you wouldn't have eaten in the Oval."

Throw-up was more likely, Jim laughed to himself, smiling back with a little bit of meat sticking out of the corner of his mouth.

Forty-five minutes later Jim Johnson stood in a lane at the indoor gun range under the Hoover building. The Range Master was a bit perturbed because this was Jim's yearly qualification which should take an hour and a half. The timing meant he would be stuck on the Beltway in the worst of DC's traffic.

What are you going to do? He's the director, the range Master thought to himself.

Jim Johnson has a rote routine that he always begins with as he takes aim.

First, he "clears the mechanism," a phrase he heard when he was a kid about a baseball pitcher, played by Kevin Costner in the movie, *For the Love of the Game.* It just simply means to clear his mind of all thoughts, distractions, and noises. Then, he slows his breathing and aims his weapon.

Finally, he hears the quiet and gentle voice of the man who taught him all the basics of handling a firearm. "Gently squeeze, don't pull the trigger," the voice says.

Bang! The first 9mm round of his Glock 22 is sent downrange. It finds its target dead center. Now that he knows he has sighted his target correctly, three more squeezes.

What a fine grouping, the Range Master thinks to himself. *Two inches in diameter. Maybe this won't take as long as I thought?*

★★

Chapter 3

Whatever It Takes

Bunkerville, Nevada, April 12th
Amos Cloyden half-opened his eyes, squinting, just as the bright morning light began to stream through his window. *Oh my, what time is it?* He can hear muffled voices and the rustling around outside his bedroom door. Reaching across the bed for his wife Colleen, he notices the familiar figure that was normally there, is absent.

He slowly glances at the clock that rests on her side of the bed. It reads 6:06 a.m. Is that possibly right? He lifts his head from the pillow and squints at the analog clock that was his father's before him. *I better get up. I must be tired. I don't know when I ever woke up this late!*

As Amos' feet swing off the bed, he feels the coolness of the ceramic tile floor underneath him. His seventy-one-year-old body is feeling the age of a tattered farmer. His dried and calloused hands pull one, then another sock up his boney feet, as more noises, strange noises quickly come to his attention.

They are quiet voices, male voices coming from right out his window. *Who on earth is outside?* Still drowsy and a bit disoriented, he looks around the perimeter of his bedroom, trying to get his bearings. Then he hears the front door creak open and close, then, the door right outside of his bedroom, the bathroom door, open and close. Then the distinct sounds of a man, urinating loudly into the toilet. *Who is here and why hasn't Colleen woken me if we have a visitor?*

Amos rises to his feet and walks to the window. As he peers out, full conciseness comes abruptly to a full waking. He looks out the window, to see people everywhere outside of his simple two-

★★

bedroom home. The very home he was raised in, the home his father built in the forties, the same home he raised his fourteen children.

There under the picturesque cottonwood trees that surround his simple home, were many men. They looked like military men sleeping dutifully on the grass, and each was slowly beginning to stir. Then, just outside the fence surrounding his yard, there were camping tents, and pick-up trucks, campers, and cars all having someone in or around them beginning to move around leisurely as if they had spent a late night there.

As Amos began to transition from sleep to being fully awake, a phase every human being undergoes, he settles down to sharply focus on where he is and his current situation. As he pulls his pants on and drags his fingers through what little wispy grey hair he has left, he begins to reflect on what brought all those people to his ranch in the arid desert of Nevada.

Ten days earlier, his twenty-one-year conflict with the federal government suddenly began to come to a head. It started in 1992 when his father's ten-year grazing permit had expired. The permit was a contractual agreement between the BLM, who are managers of the public lands, and the ranchers. The permitting process had a long history which had its early roots in the Taylor Grazing Act of 1934, which entitled ranchers to graze their herds ... specifically those who had been traditionally using the vast swaths of virgin land to graze their cattle in those early days when settlers first pushed out from the East into this hard high desert territory of the West, like Nevada.

In time, conflicts arose between ranchers over the boundaries of various pastures and which types of livestock to permit, which resulted in the enactment of this Taylor Grazing Act. The act allowed the ranchers to form local boards, to meet regularly, settle disputes, record settlements for future generations, and eventually provide range improvements, things like new fencing, paved roads, and water access. The ranchers compensated the government for these services through the permitting process monetarily, meaning paying a small fee, not to "lease grass" but to provide needed services to the rancher. It made "cowboy sense" at the time.

Eventually, the federal government began to take a larger and larger role and interest in the process as more and more states were formed. This also made sense to the ranchers, because many of these

★★

large swaths of grazing tracks crossed over state lines. Then along came the big government era, in which the Federal Government seized total control and ownership of the Public Lands through the Federal Land Practices and Management Act (FLPMA) of 1976. It was this act that had birthed the BLM and gave it the sweeping power that put Amos and thousands of other ranchers at odds with the federal government, struggling in a fight for their very lives.

As long as Amos could remember, his family had always grazed on that same sixty thousand acres. Additionally, some neighbors and friends grazed on that same open range as well. Fifty-three in total to be exact. But, at some point in the late 1980's the BLM office in Nevada and Utah established an unofficial policy, which was dubbed "No more moo by 92" meaning that they intended to remove all the cattle from the range with a complete disregard for the rights of the American people.

The policy was so extremely effective, that by the time Amos was presented with a brand-new permit, he was the only rancher left standing in the massive Clark County, Nevada. All fifty-three of his neighbors had been either run out, managed out, or bought out by the BLM, or, by one of the many huge environmental not-for-profit agencies that exist to help lobby and support the BLM's unofficial policy. Some of these agencies employ dozens and dozens of attorneys to litigate these ranchers into submission.

This unconstitutional agenda, along with many other illegal and draconian efforts had caused righteous seething anger from the men and women alike in the west who had lived their whole lives there and considered it their home, but now were wrongfully forced to leave. Many families' heritage goes back a century or more as Amos' has.

It had gotten so incredibly bad that, during the Clinton administration, Government employees had just simply vanished in the rural areas of Nevada. Presumably shot and killed and their official vehicles driven into one of the thousands of uncharted abandoned mines scattered about the state. Never to be heard of again. The apex of the chaos came when a bomb was exploded at the Reno Nevada office of the BLM. These communities were fed up and couldn't take the government's stripping away of their livelihood anymore and began to rebel in desperate ways. They called it the Sage Brush Rebellion.

★★

In 1992 Amos was presented with his new permit, a permit that no longer listed the services that the government was going to provide, instead, it unexpectedly limited the Cloyden's family cattle allotment by ninety percent and also detrimentally limited their usage time to only the months of June through August, the hottest time of the year when there was no feed or water! Making it completely impossible ... because every rancher knew one thing for certain, it was the water that was critically essential, and of the utmost importance in the hard-hot simmering desert of dusty Southern Nevada. And Amos had worked for many years developing miles and miles of a specialized network of cisterns and water troughs from the water rights that he owned and were registered with the State.

The federal government knew unequivocally that if he could not or would not use those water rights, the State of Nevada could and would take them back into the public trust lickety-split. Effectively, putting Amos out of business. So, Amos did what any reasonable person would do, he didn't sign the new contract. He then notified the BLM, that since he now had no more neighbors to dispute with, and since he managed his own range improvements, he no longer needed the services of the BLM. "I fired 'em," he firmly told the reporter in an interview. Which was spun by the bias and dishonest media to say Amos felt the Government had no right on the land. Typical fake news.

But it was no surprise to Amos that the BLM did nothing about him continuing to graze his cattle on the same land his family had always grazed on, that is, until the environmental agencies began to press Senator Red. They had faithfully supported him over the years throughout numerous election campaigns, and now that he had become the most powerful senator in the United States, they wanted some payback. The environmentalists wanted Amos off the land, and in 1993 they had a large enough club to do it with, the Endangered Species Act.

Under this act, the desert tortoise was designated endangered, and now the environmental groups could use this act to pressure Red's office to not just get the Cloyden family off the land but also to cease all the building and land development around the rapidly expanding tourist mecca of Las Vegas Nevada. Just one and a half hours drive from Amos' remote desert ranch, was the boomtown of the 1990's Las Vegas. And, this little reptile, the desert tortoise, was now standing in the way of the wealthy and powerful interests of the entire gaming industry.

By 1998, the court dockets were jammed packed with lawsuits and counter lawsuits over the use of land and the habitat of the desert tortoise. The specific claim by the various environmental lobbyists was that the desert tortoise was nearing extinction because of the encroachment of man on its habitat, by commercial, agricultural, and land development. But in actual fact, the reason was due to the abduction of the animals from their desert home in the 1960s and 1970s as oblivious people would take them home as pets.

In fact, the Nevada Department of Fish and Wildlife had conducted a targeted study on the impact of cattle on the Desert Tortoise and found it negligible. But that study didn't matter whatsoever to the environmental lobby because it didn't fit their agenda nor their ever-manipulating political narrative. So, they kept pressing for a ridiculous policy of zero tolerance, meaning no interaction of man in the Mohave Dessert of Clark County Nevada. If they had it their way all of mankind would be only allowed to live in cities.

This unfortunately put Senator Lawrence Red square in the middle of two powerful groups, the uppity environmentalists, who were impossible to reason with no matter how sound the logic was, and the ruthless wealth-motivated gaming industry, who were completely self-serving without apology. He'd been enjoying the special "perks" of his relationship with both far too long to let either slip away now, just because they were at odds with one another. So Red needed to find an agreeable solution, and of course, figure out how to make money out of it at the same time.

He always figured out a way to line his pockets with a few dollars out of every deal he made. And over time those few dollars added up. He had been a successfully dynamic power-driven politician his entire adult life and, in that time, he had managed to parlay his meager upbringing in rural Nevada, to a financial portfolio of over $100 million. He loved the ever-increasing money and the power of his esteemed position and considered himself a self-made man.

His first solution focused on the bigger problem, the gaming community's desire to grow, build lush green golf courses and support infrastructure for their luxurious casinos. Red creatively came up with a unique land swap plan that allowed the taking of tortoise habitat for commercial purposes, if the BLM would designate land somewhere else in perpetuity for the tortoise. Never mind where that habitat was. Never mind if there wasn't even one tortoise in that designated habitat. There would be no expensive relocating of tortoises, as it was simply just a designation on paper.

The agriculture use issue was by far much easier. He would merely make a quick call to the US Attorney in Las Vegas and demand he enforce the regulations under the Endangered Species Act and close down all agriculture purposes. And that's precisely what he did. In 1998 nearly five years after Amos Cloyden fired the BLM, he was wrongfully served with a lawsuit by the federal government to remove his cattle.

Unlike Senator Red, Amos had very little money, so the resources it would take to defend himself with lawyers in Federal court was not possible. He did the only thing a simple rancher could do. He defended his case as a 'pro se' attorney, meaning he represented himself. Amos was just a farmer and armed only with a high school diploma, he was outmatched by the army of lawyers the government brought to bear.

In short order, the case was ruled against him by summary judgment. He never even had his day in court, the judge simply made his decision based on the legal merits presented by the government lawyers of the Department of Justice. And just like that, a federal Judge approved and ordered Cloyden's cattle be removed immediately.

What happened next was a surprise even to Amos, absolutely nothing. Again, the federal government did nothing, which included never enforcing the judgment. That seemed to be the last he heard from the BLM or the environmentalists. As a result, Amos continued to graze his cattle on the land as his ancestors did before him. And graze they did for years upon years.

Then just one year ago, he received a call from Sheriff Gillette. The Clark County Sheriff and Amos were friendly, not friends, but there was a certain camaraderie about them. Over the years the two of them met several times to discuss Amos's unfortunate predicament. Amos had tremendous respect for Sheriff Gillette, but even more for the position he officially held.

Amos Cloyden was a constitutionalist, which meant he viewed the Constitution of the United States on an equal footing with the Holy Bible, the Book of Mormon, and the Doctrine of Covenants. He soundly believed in the teaching of his church that the Constitution was divinely inspired and brought into existence solely for the purpose of establishing the freedoms it would take for the "True Church" to be restored, the Church of Latter-Day Saints. And, to Amos that meant the Sheriff was the highest constitutionally legitimate law enforcement officer in the County, and answerable only to "We the People." Based on this belief, all other Federal Law Enforcement Agencies were considered by him as usurpers of the Sheriff's constitutional authority and therefore had no legitimate power.

"Amos, I just had a meeting with Charles (Chuck) Dodger, head of the BLM's law enforcement division. He was soliciting my agency's support to round up your cattle and sell them." Opens Gillette frankly and straight to the point.

"Oh," replies Amos, caught off guard, and somewhat frustrated.

"You have some time. I looked over the court order and it's been so long since the judgment was signed that the statute of limitations has passed to enforce it. So, I told him he needs to go back to court and get a new order."

"But why now?" Amos starting to realize the ramifications.

"You and I both know why. They need your land for mitigation, to make a land swap for the solar farms they're building all over the desert around us. Ever since the New President came into office, the government has been pouring billions of dollars into renewable energy. And, thanks to Senator Red, much of it is coming to southern Nevada. Before long, your entire ranch will most likely be encircled in solar panels." Gillette went on. "I am afraid your time is running short."

"Are you going to protect me and my property?" Amos, starting to feel the anger rise.

"Amos, I told them this was a fight they didn't want to take on. Your cattle are making no negative impact on the range. And I told them their plans were way too aggressive. But Dodger is not listening to me. He has a reputation to make or something... I bought you as much time as I could," Gillette trailing off without answering Amos' question.

"How much time do I have?"

"About six to ten months I think at most," Gillette pauses, "What are you going to do?"

"Whatever it takes," Cloyden responds resolutely, then hangs up the phone.

Damn Cowboys, as Gillette realizes Cloyden has ended the conversation. *They're always men of few words, very few.*

In the weeks leading up to this day, Agent Dodger had assembled a team of Federal Agents from all over the country. An army really, of some 200 men and women. They'd leveled and cleared fifty acres in the desert and built a Command Center.

A massive compound really, Command and communication trailers, medical facilities, observation posts, and of course corrals for the soon-to-be impounded cattle. They had rented two hotels in nearby Mesquite and hired for 960 thousand dollars a group of contract cowboys to gather Amos' cattle. They also hired a local in the Utah stockyard to sell the cattle, for which they paid $65 thousand in advance.

In addition, the BLM made arrangements to have the FAA close the 100 square miles of airspace over the round-up operation. No one could legally get air access to the operation, except, of course, the drones that were stationed twenty-four hours a day to give the rangers tactical advantage and to record the operations below. Dodger had even brought in an MRAP, a bomb-resistant military vehicle, used as a sniper base and troop carrier.

During the days leading up to the operations beginning, Dodger would skillfully drill his troops in crowd disbursement procedures, tear gas deployments, and specialized training in making arrests of horseback riders. Of course, the half dozen German Shepard police dogs were drilled over and over again too, just like the troops. Each taking their turn attacking the subjects wearing the kimono bite training suits. Dodger thought it beyond humorous when one of his team had written the names of each of the Cloyden family on the various Kimonos in big black marker, even the children.

Then there were the behind-the-scenes briefings regarding the Cloyden family. Dodger had assembled photos and a dossier on every one of them, including the spouses and grandchildren. Sixty-three dossiers in total.

There was even a dossier on Amos' son Aaron who was in the Philippines on his Mormon mission. They had daily briefings on the intel gathered via the cameras and listening devices encircling the Cloyden home, including their phone conversations and movements. All of which were being conducted illegally without securing the required legal warrants.

Dodger had placed sniper teams in elevated positions around the farmhouse and closed off the entire area, including all the state highways, only allowing a few local farmers to enter into the 100 square mile area where the round-up operation was to occur. To handle the press and potential demonstrators, at the edge of the enclosed areas, they erected two "First Amendment Zones" about fifty square feet each, surrounded by plastic fencing. These areas were there for the so-called "protection of the community," but everyone knew it was really to keep the prying eyes of the American people miles always from the operations.

Amos, called them "pig pens" and the BLM agents were instructed to direct any and all interested parties to the designated locations of these "zones" as the acceptable locations to practice their First Amendment rights. Sounds like something you'd expect to see in a foreign totalitarian state, but in America?

Amos, his family, and his few neighbors felt like they'd been under siege for days. Their movements were restricted and even the grandchildren had been seen with the red laser dots of targeting rifle-sites on their little bodies from the snipers around. He was frustrated, upset, and not sure what he could do.

So, he had his family begin to make calls for support, first to fellow church members, family, and friends in the area, pleading with them to come and protest this government abuse. And they slowly began to come. At first just a few showed, then the crowds grew. They then moved the protest out to the highway where they would get more exposure. Some folks would come and stay the course all day, while others showed only for a short hour or two just to carry a sign.

They called the media, local officials, state, and county representatives, and so the peaceful protest began to build in number. But never more than fifty to 100 protestors. Most were women and children, a few men, as most were working during the day. At night they would have meetings and more rallies in nearby Mesquite.

All the protesters refused to use the First Amendment Zones the BLM had designated for use. Instead, they built a little public stage and hoisted an American flag on a hastily erected flagpole along the highway so every passerby could see the Cloyden's plight. It was about raising public awareness.

During the week there were often small aggravating interactions with the BLM agents patrolling the area or at the checkpoints. Nothing serious, all in all, the protestors were polite and respectful country-loving people. It wasn't until Tuesday things sparked off when Amos' third son was violently arrested by BLM agents for taking pictures of the round-up operations with his personal iPad. The agents had demanded he go to the First Amendment zone and no photos were allowed. His only reply:

"My first amendment rights are wherever I am."

With that, five agents jumped on him, brutally throwing him to the ground while ordering their attack dog on him. With that encounter, he was wrongly arrested and transported to the jail, only to be released one day later, it being determined the BLM agents lacked the power to arrest anyone on the state highway where the incident occurred. The news of this event and then another hostile confrontation the following day began to raise the ire of the protestors. Some were openly outraged.

On Thursday, piercing rifle shots were heard from deep in the mountainous range. Amos became concerned they were shooting his cattle. The contract Cowboys were having trouble gathering the cattle, most of which were momma cows who had just recently given birth. The cows would not leave their babies under any circumstances, no matter how hard the small helicopters and horse-mounted cowboys drove them, the cows would just circle back to their babies. Sheriff Gillette had warned Dodger it was a ridiculous idea to attempt such a round-up during the Calving season. The cows and the cowboys were now paying the price.

After nearly a week of the round-up, they had barely collected 400 of the 900 cows into the corrals to be legally impounded. The BLM was rapidly losing patience, the cowboys were frustrated, and the four-million-dollar operational budget was dwindling and beginning to be exhausted. So, from the round-up helicopter, the mercenary cowboys began to shoot at Amos' cattle. The signed Judicial Warrant the BLM had obtained only authorized them to impound and hold the cattle. Under the judgment, they were in no way allowed to sell, let alone kill Amos' property. This dangerous and illegal action caused the protestors to grow even angrier and rightly so.

Then hearing of a large dump truck pulling a backhoe on a trailer through the desert roads prompted a group of protestors to take it upon themselves to stop the truck and verify whether or not some of Amos' dead cattle were in the back of the truck. They met the truck as it approached the state highway and blocked it with their vehicles and demanded to look inside. Immediately about twenty federal agents converged upon the protestors and things got heated.

Soon Amos' sixty-year-old sister was picked up, thrown to the ground like a sack of grain by one agent. Then out came the tasers and they began to fire them randomly into the crowd, only finding one target, Amos' second son. This only enraged the crowd more, so out of fear they sent their attack dogs in, only to be repelled by the protesters' country boots, as the crowd, all of which had been around animals their whole life, began to kick the dogs senseless and throw rocks.

At the end of what seemed like a long ten-minute confrontation, the agents retreated with no arrests, and the truck was released after the protestors were satisfied that no dead cattle were inside. It was small consolation though because what they did find was the remnants of the many water improvements the Cloyden family developed over years —had now been secretly torn out and taken away. Who on earth authorized that? Where was THAT stated in the court order?

Unlike the arrest the day before, this incident was filmed in totality by a conservative radio host who just arrived from Chicago. He had driven nonstop the last two days to see what the government was up to in this very remote sector of desert. He didn't personally know the Cloydens, he just had an unusually keen reporter's intuition that there was more to the story than what the local news reported. As a result, he came to see for himself. He arrived at the precise moment, of what will later be known as the Battle of

Bunkerville, playing off the historical event known as *The Battle of Bunker Hill* some 240 years earlier.

The reporter knew what he had and knew that once he got it uploaded on social media his audience would eat it up. His instinct was dead right. Within hours of the video posting, it had 1 million views and the numbers were building by the hour.

This one video drew the fervent attention of the Patriot Community. For the uninitiated, the Patriot community is a mix of local and regional Militia groups, gun enthusiasts, second amendment supporters, faith groups, ex-military, rural living farmers and ranchers, and believers in small government, as well as other similar interest groups, mostly from the flyover states. Some have found a voice in the Tea Party Movement, but most feel more and more marginalized.

They have one thing in common, they all fiercely love the United States and its Constitution. All will fight to preserve it without reservation with their very lives. The shadow government watches them with a wary eye and the political progressives label them as racist, violent inbred country hicks, and much worse. The Patriots just simply love their independence and do not understand why anyone would want to live under the dependency and control of any government.

It was this factual video that became the clarion call to the Patriot movement rallying hundreds to the Cloyden family's defense. A call went out across the nation to come and protect the property of the Cloyden family. And, come they did.

Some came as far as New Hampshire, Florida, Idaho, Washington, and dozens of other small towns and communities. They simply, got in their cars or pick-up and headed to Southern Nevada with no other plans but to simply STAND. Answering the call of their hearts to stand with their brother against the ever-growing abuses and overreach of the federal government.

Amos was astonished by the steady stream of people that kept arriving at his ranch, beginning Friday morning, and they just kept coming nonstop. By Friday night there were some 150 people strung all around his property and yet more locals were still arriving. He was completely unprepared. They quickly butchered a cow and started up a BBQ feast to feed the arrivals. In the morning someone drove into town and bought all the breakfast sandwiches they could find.

There came a quiet gentle knock on the door.

"Dad, the sheriff is on the phone. He wants to talk to you," Amos' son declares from the other side of the door.

"Just let him know I am in prayer," Amos replies. He could hear his son swiftly walk away talking on the phone. Amos settles down in the comfortable chair in his bedroom, picks up the book of Mormon.

Then another knock, it's his son again "Dad, the Sheriff says he will be out here at the Ranch at 8:30 a.m. He says he has some good news for you."

"When he gets here tell 'em, I'll meet him at the protest stage at nine o'clock." Whatever he has to say he can say it to "We the People".

Amos was frustrated at Sheriff Gillette, to say the least. He'd asked him in person, begged him to support him, protect him from these usurpers. But the sheriff refused to intervene. Amos expected the Sheriff's department to stand between him and the mass of Federal agents that were trying to steal his cattle. But all he had gotten was an empathetic "I am sorry, but there is nothing I can do."

Then, last night he gets news that a young man is shot and killed by a US Park Ranger on a State Highway because the young man refused to recognize the ranger's authority to pull him over. The dash-cam video from the Nevada Highway Patrol car that pulled up on the scene was on the local TV channel, and you can visually see the Park Ranger pull out his gun and shoot the man. Why? Because he wouldn't obey his commands. Then you hear the Highway Patrolman, clear as day say, "What the fuck did you do that for?" completely astonished at what he just witnessed.

All of this was extremely overwhelming to a normally quiet loner of a man. *All I have ever wanted was to be left alone, grow some melons, and raise a few cows for my community. I didn't want any of this!* Amos picked up his well-worn Book of Mormon and began to quietly read, letting his mind drift from the intense events surrounding him and into the text before him.

This will be an interesting day.

Chapter 4
Tipping Generously

Conservative Political Action Conference (CPAC)
Friday Night

The EMCEE stands smiling confidently before the podium to introduce the keynote speaker of this year's CPAC convention. He waits a moment to allow the packed audience to quietly settle down and bring their full attention to the stage after the dinner break.

"Our featured speaker tonight is one whom many of you are well acquainted, and some have traveled from far across the nation just to hear. He is a man that is a rare find during these difficult times in our nation's history. A man who might just be offering real answers to what ails our country today."

"He gave up a successful career in business, setting it aside to come to our aid, 'We the People' that is. A man who, in the traditions of our founding fathers has come to serve, not be served, nor made famous and wealthy by self-seeking political gain. In fact, by serving you and me he loses an enormous chunk of wealth, every single day. But that doesn't bother him in the slightest, because he feels that keeping our freedoms and way of life is worth sacrifice."

"That's why he diligently served twenty years in the Marine Corps. After his service in both Afghanistan and Iraq in countless combat operations, he retired as a full bird Colonel. Then started a lucrative real estate business in California that now holds nearly one billion dollars in commercial real estate. And he's only very recently returned to public service, first as a state representative in the California legislature."

The crowd moans in disgust just at the slight mention of the state of California. "And now..." The EMCEE pauses for effect, waiting for the crowd to calm, with a pleasant smile.

"And now, he represents the great State of California in the US House of Representatives. It was there he found out that the government systems in Washington DC were broken and corrupted beyond repair and have now strayed so far from the founders' vision they need a drastic realignment. And that's why he is here to speak to us tonight."

"Honorable Mark Fenton is here to reset that vision, a vision our great founding fathers had the foresight to create, yet also knew a season like this would one day come into the life of our republic. A season of desperation and despair, and so they gave us the tools to set it back on the good and proper track it was originally intended. Please give your undivided attention and extend the warmest of welcomes for (now raising his voice louder with every word) Colonel Mark Fenton, the Honorable US congressman from the great State of California!"

The audience rose to their feet in a roar of cheers and thundering applause as Fenton approached the podium. He took a brief moment to shake the hand of the EMCEE and smiled, humbly waved to the audience, which only intensified his welcome.

"Thank you…Thank you."

The audience applauses and cheers, and whistles continued as they remained on their feet.

"Thank you," Fenton continued to smile at the crowd. The sound wave again swirled through the massive room. *Okay, okay, geez.* Finally, a few people started to take their seats. Then slowly more followed.

"Thank you so much for the warm greeting," most everyone is in their seats now.

"Wow, I have never in my entire life seen a standing ovation at the beginning of a speech, thank you." The crowd wildly laughed and began to clap again.

"Alright, alright settle down, I have only been given so much time up here." The crowd chuckles once again.

"Love you, Mark!" comes from nobody in particular. Then the audience begins as if prompted on cue. "U-S-A, U-S-A, U-S-A, U-S-A, U-S-A, U-S-A, U-S-A."

Fenton immediately takes charge, the seasoned Marine commander coming out.

"Alright, –settle down," both his arms now outstretched and lowering as if to tamp down the loud and exuberant enthusiasm.

"Tonight …."

"Tonight, I want to talk to you, my brothers and sisters about the very real and very likely fall of western civilization." Now the crowd was dead still and disturbingly quiet. Mark has a rare and disarming way about his presentation. He was gentle, empathetic, even pastoral as he addressed his audiences. It was not a contrived thing, instead, it came from a place that was genuine and real.

There was a winsomeness in him that exuded an incredible depth. Pundits, from every corner, tried to put their finger on it. Some speculated it was his military training, others said he was given some sort of professional speech coaching or acting class. But it wasn't.

What stood before this audience and television cameras was a charismatic man of fervent principle. It was a principle that was summed up in the Bible, that he was to consider others greater than himself. And he truly did. Mark Fenton begins in earnest now.

"Some of you may not know this, but I was a troubled kid. My dad was abusive. He beat my mom and us kids all too often."

"As I grew up, I didn't handle rejection well and lashed out at umm… pretty much everyone. I felt not just alone but realized I had no place, no identity, no meaning, no purpose. I was constantly in and out of trouble with the law, school, and even at home. I grew up in Ohio in a conservative rural community and though everyone knew about my home life, no one ever intervened."

"Then one day when I had just turned sixteen years old my dad had come home drunk and went into a rage. He started to beat my mom…" he paused reflectively as the memory flooded back.

"At that moment all the rage, all the hurt, all the pain came crashing to the surface. I jumped to my feet, bolted from my bedroom, and leaped on my dad. He pushed me to the ground, and I quickly jumped back up. As he turned again to my mom, I found a hot frying pan on the stove, picked it up, and smashed the side of his face. His ear was burned terribly, the smell of burning hair and his screams were all I remember from that point forward."

"The police told me later I beat him within an inch of his life. He was taken to the hospital and once released, no one in my family ever saw him again. I was charged as a juvenile for assault and battery and was given a suspended sentence if I complied with the conditions of release."

"I suppose the judge took into consideration the totality of my situation in his sentence. The local Sheriff had a lot to do with it. He told the judge I was a good kid at heart and had been in a tough situation my entire life. And he volunteered to look after me if the Judge could find leniency in his heart."

"As a result, I was given a two-year suspended sentence with the conditions that I must graduate high school, have no more trouble with the law, and join the Marines upon graduating. If I did that, my charges would be dismissed. So, that's what I did."

"But my mom had serious reservations she could keep me on the straight and narrow... I was a handful!" Fenton said with an embarrassing smile. "So, the sheriff and my mom sat down and figured out a life plan for me. Then told me I had been 'volun-told'. Mark looked up and smiled. Wondering if the audience got it. 'Not volunteered but told.'"

"The sheriff told me I'd be moving to a ranch he knew that took in troubled kids needing help and direction. I'd be required to enroll at the nearby High School and do anything and everything the ranch owners told me. If not, the Sheriff would personally drive out, get me and return me straight to the judge to be sent to Prison."

"I was scared and apprehensive, but I was willing because I knew he meant it. I was also worried about my mom. I now see she had her hands full raising my brother and sister as a single mom, plus attending to her own healing."

"I was afraid of what this new place was going to be like. Was it some kind of institution or orphanage? But it wasn't. It was just a nice couple who had a BIG ranch and wanted to share their blessings and love with others. Since they didn't have any children of their own, they shared their lives with troubled kids like me."

"There I learned a strong work ethic and respect for my fellow man. There I learned to hunt and fish and what true love is all about. And it was there I was introduced to Jesus Christ and committed my life to him."

"Upon graduation, I straight away went to the local recruiter station and joined the Marines just as I promised. I never saw that sheriff again. I just wrote him a thank you letter after I enlisted."

"In the Marines, at first, I continued my education stateside, but once I got deployed to the war zones of Iraq and then Afghanistan, I started taking correspondence courses while fighting on the front lines. My combat experience combined with the extensive education I received earned me several field promotions and I finished my career as a full Colonel. The Marines gave me the belonging I always needed in my life. Once a Marine, always a Marine."

"Semper fi!" calls out a man from the Audience.

Fenton looks across in the direction to try to meet eyes with the voice. "Oohrah!" Fenton answers back with conviction. Then returns to the audience at large.

"Then came my wonderful marriage to my beautiful and brilliant wife." He gestures toward her in the front row as his eyes affectionately meet hers with an instant grin."

"I was fortunate in business and now I want to return a blessing to this great country and my Lord for the many blessings given me, far beyond my wildest expectations. So, I have returned to public service as a civilian representative for WE THE PEOPLE of my state."

"But unfortunately, what I found when I got to Washington was more discouraging than I could imagine. While there are a few men and women there to truly serve, most are there to just serve themselves. It's a racket, a Ponzi scheme. It's basically a money-generating machine making bartenders into millionaires in four short years. And the longer you stay the more cash you can pocket."

"Simply stated, here is how it works. When you first arrive in Washington, if you want to put a bill forward, you are given a price, an amount of money you need to pledge to your political party to put your bill forward, otherwise, it will die in committee. And, if you want to get something done, you also need to be seated on one of those committees. A seat on a committee costs you money too."

"There is an entire menu to select from, with an approximate cost for each seat, depending on which committee. Staff and office expenses cost additional money in donation pledges as well. Never mind if you don't have any money to pledge because the money is surprisingly easy to come by. You just sell your soul to lobbyists, foreign governments, and/or special interest groups. They're all more than happy to give you all the money you need to cover your pledges, and more, in order to secure your vote that best meets their interests."

"Plus, there is what I call the 'family connection'. Each member can bring a family member in to pedal your influence to make deals; deals that will directly benefit your family member. They become consultants or represent the deal as an attorney or through any number of creative ways secure a position within the deal. And the deals are very lucrative."

"Of course, the representative appropriates a substantial cut to their Limited Liability Company, Foundation or Corporation. It's called plausible deniability. As an example, one of the previous Vice President's sons pulled in a $1.5 billion investment from the Chinese after just one trip to China on Airforce Two. And, then once again millions from the Ukrainian Oligarchs."

"Soon there is so much money coming your way you're not sure what to do with it. So, you find ways to divert it, supplant expenses, double-dip, and pay family members exorbitant salaries or ridiculous consulting fees. Oh, and the bigger, more prestigious committees you are on, the higher price you can demand from all those supporters."

"And once you direct the excess of your cash machine into legal insider-trading on the stock market, you're in fat city. Yes, you heard me right. Congress is completely immune to insider-trading laws. So, as soon as whispered tips and insider knowledge comes your way, it can immediately be utilized to purchase shares in the stock market that can triple your investment overnight."

"It's like playing blackjack with a crooked card dealer who always deals you a winning hand, as long as you tip GENEROUSLY. If you cut them off, they'll immediately begin to deal you bad hands. Then you will lose and lose big."

"Being an elite member of congress for some is like being addicted to crack cocaine. You never seem to get enough, and the high is harder and harder to achieve. This corrupt culture is why Congress hasn't passed many bills since well back into the Bush Senior administration."

"You combine this with the myriad of perks that congress has legislated for itself, gold-plated health insurance, platinum retirement, five-star travel, and housing allowances, and it adds up to a counter-productive disaster, strangling congress' effectiveness

★★

while increasing our national debt. Of course, once they finally do retire, they're all but guaranteed a cushy job on the speaking circuit or an esteemed board member position, working for the companies that employed the same lobbyists that made them rich. This might just be the tip of the iceberg toward the demise of not just the republic, it may very well be the demise of Western Civilization."

Fenton silently pauses again for effect. Let that sink in.

"There is a far-reaching conflict in ideology that permeates western culture today. It's not just a conflict that is brought about by traditional liberalism, now under a new brand name; progressivism, but something much more. Let me explain."

"See, the traditional liberal thinking was that Western Civilization was good, it brings equality and lifts the poor out of poverty and improves peoples' lives. It was based on historical facts. The political differences were mainly found in the delivery solutions, methods, and timings of the programs.

"Conservatives want the delivery of services to be at a minimum which results in a smaller bureaucracy and lighter footprint for the federal government, leaving the majority of needed services for the states to administer. In direct opposition to that way of thinking, is the liberal mindset that believes a centralized federal government can better serve the people, by taking many of the tasks from the states which has resulted in enlarging the federal bureaucracy. This is how it has been since the founding of this great nation. Liberals and Conservatives have always had the best interest of the people at heart but have real pointed differences in HOW to provide those services and best serve the people."

"Then, just under one hundred years ago something drastically changed. There was a rise of socialism, fascism or better described as collectivism. Now it's called Globalism. This socialism continues to sell a utopian idea, that under the watchful hand of a benevolent government there will be peace and harmony for all."

"They believed this truth so strongly that in the first and second world wars they tried to force their ideas upon the world in a violent totalitarian fashion, with guns, tanks, bombs, and through suppression of thought, speech, religion, and association. The message was simply to comply or die. And die we did; hundreds of millions of us died at the hands of fanatical ideologies who tried to force their totalitarian ways upon liberty-loving people."

★★

"And now, in these past sixty years the same ardent cult thinkers have abandoned the direct forceful confrontational approaches of the past and taken to an insurgent approach to the same end; bringing a totalitarian attack on our very way of life, but this time from the inside. Yes, the insurgents have infiltrated academia from the inside, have attacked the family, the home, and marriage from the inside, have attacked the free practice of religion from the inside, have attacked our mind's ability to have free ideas and ultimately think for ourselves from the inside and the insurgents have not only attacked the government and the Rule of Law, but the very idea that western democracies are actually a good idea at all! Don't be fooled, we are at the very brink of the end! And at any time now, everything we know could easily collapse and collapse quickly."

Again, pausing for effect.

"As I mentioned, the old socialism has reinvented itself. Renamed and rebranded as it were. So, let's hang around their neck the label they prefer, **Globalist**. Under this brand of globalism, we see the totalitarianism of the European Union, totalitarian Islamism like ISIS, totalitarian dictators like Kim Jong Un, totalitarian communism like Chinas', totalitarian environmentalism, totalitarian 'enlightened Thinkers', totalitarian socialist, like the Socialist Democrats, totalitarian feminism, totalitarian Black Lives Matter and the totalitarian Arian Nation, not to leave out the many other totalitarian anarchist groups, such as Antifa."

"But in truth, at the end of the day, all these globalist groups pretend, deceive and by design are not what they appear or claim to be. Each has abandoned history, sound facts, and reliable reason for an emotional fantasy that makes them distort and rewrite the truth, and then mollify, or excuse their conniving craftiness by convincing themselves that the ends justify the means. And so, they do anything, say anything, be anything to get their end result ... the installation and establishment of a disastrous and failed ideology, some call — a Reset, A new world order."

"So, what do we do to save our coveted way of life?"

"First, we can no longer trust and depend on our existing government." With that, there was a gasp and rolling murmurs from the audience.

"Hang on, hang on— hear me out," Fenton using his body language to calm everyone down. "I am simply a constitutionalist. I truly believe in our constitution, and I know the answers can be found there. But the reason our government can't get anything done, pass reasonable legislation, pass a budget, let alone balance a budget is not just because of the animosity between parties. That's only part of it. But the real reason they can't resolve any pressing issues is because there is absolutely no incentive!"

"Our nation's leaders are so lacking in character, so self-serving, so high on their own personal style of "Crack" they have no incentive to do the hard work to pass legislation, let alone to amend the constitution. Setting aside the fact there are only three days per week the congress is actually in session, and of those 'workdays' most congressmen only attend one day on average. The biggest reason they don't work or don't care is honestly because they don't want to interrupt the gravy train by angering a lobbyist, special interest group, a foreign government, or any other party member for that matter. Because, if they upset any of these, their funding might get withdrawn, their lucrative deal evaporates and that would ultimately jeopardize the future of their cushy lifestyle."

"Now, don't get me wrong. There are a few sincere, passionate men and women who want to see things get accomplished. But the very nature of our legislative process is to collaborate and compromise to pass a bill. But, when no one shows up to work, and there is no one to collaborate with, then even if they want to do something, they can't."

"My God, back in the day, it used to be that congress would at least do the minimal rudimentary things like pass a budget every year. Even if it was an unbalanced one! But they don't even try to do THAT anymore. Instead, they just pass continuing resolutions to keep things funded every few months and go about their daily agenda."

"That's like you or I applying for a new credit card every month to pay our bills! IT'S IRRESPONSIBLE! And Congress has been doing this for decades!"

"So, what is there to be done?"

He pauses to take a long-needed drink of water.

"As I said earlier, I'm a constitutionalist, and I've discovered that this amazing document has the answers and tools we need to resolve our national catastrophe in the soon to be demised Article V of the U.S. Constitution, giving states the power to hold a Convention of States to propose amendments to the US Constitution. Now, in today's political arena it takes thirty-four states to call the convention and thirty-eight states to ratify any amendments that are proposed. But this convention would enable the states to discuss amendments that "limit the power and jurisdiction of the federal government, impose fiscal restraints, and place term limits on federal officials. The founding fathers unequivocally knew what they were doing when they wrote Article V because these are the key issues we MUST fix if we're going to get our government back on track!"

"Ladies and gentlemen, the hour is extremely late for our constitutional republic. I am not being an overreacting alarmist relying on tin-foiled conspiracy theories, but instead, all one needs to do is objectively look at today's headlines and the endless years of abuse and overreach by the legislative, judicial, and executive branches, to see that they have trampled over the enumerated powers established by the founding fathers and obliterated the constitutional rights secured in the tenth amendment. —The rights that were originally afforded only to the states and its people!"

"It's now time to go on the offensive. We as citizens must restore the original limits of federal power and reign in the out-of-control U.S. Government. Both major political parties have devolved from being the protectors of our liberties to now being the perpetrators against our liberties!"

"And the genius of our founding fathers' original intent is clear and on full display in Article V of our beloved constitution, allowing 'We The People' to continue to preserve and protect the fundamental rights of every individual and keep the United States limited federal Government in check. It's time for the people to take back control of our government, and, for the first time in our history, call a convention of states! Article V is simply set forth: to bring power back to the states and the people, where it belongs."

"Unelected bureaucrats in Washington, D.C. shouldn't be allowed to make sweeping decisions that impact millions of Americans to perpetrate their own agenda. But right now, they do. So, it all boils down to one simple question: Who do you think should decide what's best for you and your family? You, or the Feds?"

"If you've been listening to anything I've been saying, then I pray you take this one thing home with you tonight. You cannot trust the government in Washington DC. It has gone so far off course from its' original design that our country is in immediate jeopardy of extinction."

"I began here today telling my own personal story. I was lost, but now I am found. I had lost my way, my identity, my purpose. In part, this great country helped me find my way back. To set a new fruitful course."

"It's time now that each of us returns the favor and helps our beloved country find its way back. It's lost, and before we lose it forever, I want to try one more time to set it back on its once fruitful course. Will you help me?"

The crowd immediately threw themselves to their feet in wild applause and enthusiastic cheers. There were tears and whistles and more and more applause. It went on and on, But the Honorable Mark Fenton remained standing on the stage. Eventually, he was joined by the EMCEE and another man.

"Folks, folks," Mark began to interrupt them. They took their seats once again.

"Thank you all for listening to me and joining me in this dangerous and mighty endeavor."

"U-S-A, U-S-A, U-S-A…" the crowd started chanting.

"Thank You, Thank You," Mark quickly interrupted them.

"I had mentioned that in my personal life what turned me around was a Judge, a Sheriff, a Rancher, and the Marine Corp. But I also mentioned one other man. It was Jesus Christ. And I think that if we are going to join together to turn this country around, we're going to need His help most."

The crowd nodded in agreement.

"I want to introduce you to my friend and Pastor, Pat Lear. He would like to lead us in prayer together. Pastor…"

"Thank You, Mark, would you bow your heads for a moment and take an attitude of humble prayer." He continued once the auditorium finally became quiet.

"Heavenly Father, there is not a soul in this room who does not recognize your mighty hand in the forming and setting aside this great nation for your purpose. We confess we have been poor stewards in the magnificence of this responsibility. You gave our founding fathers a great and glorious vision for a free and mighty country and yet time and time again we have failed you in its keeping. Yet in those failures, you allowed us to remain your steward.

We beg you now oh Lord, again grant us mercy, do not let this great nation fall into the hands of its enemies. Give us the grace, the courage, the fortitude, and steadfastness to lead our nation back to the purpose you intended it. Help us, Lord, to pass on Your mercy You give to us each day, to those in need, ever mindful of You in every action, every decision, and every prayer in the days to come. Set our path before us and please guide our every step. We beg of you these things in the Matchless name of Jesus Christ."

And in one perfect voice, burst forth "AMEN" from the audience.

Oh shit, I've got a plane to catch. Leah Scrivener reflects, jumping up from her seat in the CPAC convention. As she pushes through the crowd toward the exit, insincerely smiling at the faces in the crowd, *this is sickening,* as she wiggles and squirms trying not to be delayed any further.

"Wasn't he GREAT!" came a familiar voice just in front of her in the foyer. Leah recognized the young barbie doll of a woman in front of her. *It was Carry, or Babbie, Barbie, oh I don't know or care. I didn't think I'd see her again after lunch.*

Leah had slyly invited herself to the woman's table during the lunch break for appearances. She picked her because at first impression she was cute, had an empty seat, and well who knows... *But, Kelly, that's her name,* turned out to be a complete bore and utterly uninteresting. *Not very sophisticated.*

"Just awesome, awesome, awesome!" Kelly exclaimed as she blocked Leah's beeline for the exit door. "Weren't you just INSPIRED?"

"Yeah, it was great," Leah not sure how to answer, and also not sure what she was referring to.

"I think Colonel Fenton was sent here by God," Kelly went on without recognizing Leah's obvious annoyance. "He just hit the heartbeat of us all and he's just so handsome too."

Leah finally catches on. The astute reporter in her kicking in. "You think so? It seemed sort of... out there, I mean all that talk about the founding fathers and the constitution. I mean the government we have now IS in charge, that's just a fact. And they're not really THAT bad, are they? I mean... really?"

Kelly appeared stunned. "If you think that, you may be at the wrong convention."

"Maybe I am," muttered Leah, "I was just leaving."

"Already? There's another whole day to go. It's not over until Saturday night." Kelly lightening up again with a smile.

"Yeah... darn, I'm afraid I'm going to miss it. My boss called and has an assignment for me in Vegas, so I am heading to the airport now."

"Assignment? −What kind of job do you have?" Kelly just being curious.

"Oh, ah... I am a stenographer. I travel all over listening and writing down what I hear," Leah stumbling through her lie.

"Like a court reporter? Sounds boring," Kelly smiles realizing that will be the last she sees Leah.

"It is, but I get to travel, and it pays the bills. It was nice to meet you, thanks for sharing your table." Leah not being sincere.

"It was nice meeting you too." Sticking her hand out in politeness to shake hands.

Leah limp wrists the handshake and quickly turns to get out the door. *I hope there is still a cab,* Leah thinks worrying as she heads for the door through the now crowded foyer.

Two hours later, Leah is sitting on a Boeing 757, in first class, talking to the assignment editor for the Washington Post, "I have a good story for you. I'll file it when I land in Vegas."

"Great, nobody recognized you at CPAC?" came the voice on the other end.

"Oh, hell no. I'm a freelancer, nobody knows who I am. I snuck right in under their radar." Leah Smiles with a slight bit of conflict. *I just wish you'd put me on staff. Nobody knows me because you don't use me enough.*

"Okay good. I'd hate to have paid for all that travel if they just kicked you out of the convention," replies the hardline female voice of the editor.

"Well, I got you the story, just like I always do. And, I have another one for you tomorrow after I arrive in Vegas," Leah pitching her next story.

"Oh, whatcha working on?"

"I am still following Amos Cloyden and his merry band of wackadoo's," Leah trying to sound genuinely upbeat.

"Oh, that asshat, I think that story is well played out. No one out here on the east coast cares a flying fuck about some old curmudgeon hermit in God knows where in the Nevada desert. You can pitch it to me. But really, don't get your hopes up," the editor harshly shutting Leah down.

"I think you're wrong. I can feel it in my bones," Leah still trying to present a convincing pitch.

"We'll see…" Click, the editor hangs up on Leah.

"I'll have the CPAC story to you when I land…" Leah says into the dead phone.

Thirty minutes later Leah's plane is in the air meanwhile she's managed to belt down three Canadian Clubs with just a little 7UP. *Finally, the seat belt light is off. I can start writing my piece on the CPAC convention.* She flips open her MAC PRO laptop and hears that familiar chime all Apple products play. She begins her story…

Once again Colonel Mark Fenton spewed his diatribe of hateful, racist, foolish conspiracy theories to the mindless few at the CPAC convention…

Leah pauses. *Too much? Na, this is for the Washington Post after all!*

Chapter 5

I Just Want the Government to Leave Me Alone

April 12th –Southbound on US Highway 15

Two trucks left Idaho the night before in answer to a call on social media to come to the aid of a helpless rancher in southern Nevada. They didn't know the rancher, and both drivers had a hard time finding the small desert town (if you can even call it a town) of Bunkerville on a map.

The first pick-up truck was a 2016 Ford F-250 Super Duty Crew Cab 4X4, suited perfectly for the treacherous mountain roads in Hayden, Idaho where it departed. The occupants were Kristen Donahue, a Native American in her mid-thirties, beautiful long jet-black hair, and a stocky frame, still carrying some "baby weight" she never seemed to get rid of after her last child eight years ago. In the passenger seat, fast asleep was her most recent boyfriend Patrick Daniels, better known as LT. Not because he was a Lieutenant in the Marines where he served fifteen years, but because he always took command in the III%'ers Militia, where they both were now affiliated.

It was natural for him to take a leadership role in nearly every single situation unless a better leader arose. After all, he was a well-seasoned working soldier, and highly regarded as a top marine gunnery sergeant all his years in the Corps, which were, in his opinion, the best years of his life. Now at forty-nine, he sometimes wonders why he ever left the military. Daniels detested being called LT, but he couldn't get his fellow militia members to stop using it, so he just learned to ignore the moniker.

Many of the militia were "knuckle draggers" or "weekend warriors" who liked guns and just wanted a place to fit in. But for

Daniels, the III%'ers was a place of purpose, a place to use all the training the Marines had given him. A place he could feel normal and highly valued among a community of comrades that needed him as much as he needed them. Besides, he loved the idea of taking a lead commander role in a citizens' group protecting the common man from the constant overreach of the government.

Because to Daniels' way of thinking the militias are part of the checks and balances that the founding fathers had put into the constitution to make sure tyranny would never find its way back on American soil. And also, the second amendment was not adopted into the constitution to give hunters the right to have guns for recreation, which seems to be the argument from the so-called "progressives." To Daniels, the Second Amendment was purposely put there to protect the rights of every citizen to defend themselves from a government gone bad.

The founders of these United States unequivocally knew that our government would grab as much power from its citizens as possible if left unchecked. And that's just what Daniels believed was his primary mission, as a true American patriot now sworn into the militia, to help those who couldn't defend themselves against government abuse, and from what he was seeing in the reports coming out of Nevada, the government was way out of line. So, he felt he had no other choice but to flat-out respond to the call for help from the Cloyden ranch in support of this family and the clear overreach of the Government BLM (one of many 'alphabet soup agencies') that was trying to take their property.

Kristen on the other hand liked the reassuring independence she felt in the III%'ers. She had been in two lousy relationships. The first one she married after she got pregnant. That was simply a mistake. They were both just way too young.

The second, she thought was "the one". He seemed to love her kids unconditionally and her too for that matter. But, by the time he had his third affair while they were still engaged, she at long last came to her senses. It was time to be independent, not reliant on an unhealthy relationship. The III%'ers was without question a perfect fit for her.

As a member, she became physically stronger, more self-aware, and confident. She liked her interactions with the men of the group, who were respectful and honoring, yet appreciated the differences between men and women. To her, the III%'ers were the natural response of the local community's concern, and more specifically a patriotic citizen's dutiful reaction to the terribly wrong direction the country she very much loved was heading.

In her relatively short life, she had watched as a free-fall of moral disintegration, tolerance without boundaries, and a newfound acceptance for modern secular godlessness had slowly permeated the American culture. In just twenty years since graduating High School, she had seen the rights of American citizens trampled upon by a move to globalism, and toward the one world order, she read about in the Bible. It scared her down to her very core. She is not even sure it can be turned around and her beloved country restored.

Nevertheless, she decided two years ago she wasn't going to be a frog in the kettle slowly waiting to be cooked alive. She felt a strong calling to take action, if not for her country, then for her children and grandchildren. So, when the distress call for help went out to come to Nevada, she felt compelled, compelled to come, to live up to a promise she made to herself, her country, and family — - to not just sit idly by and watch one more person lose their civil rights. It was now time to take a STAND!

The second pickup was a fully loaded Dodge Ram, 1500 TRX 4X4 long bed, tow cable with roll bar, roof-mounted night lights, two-inch lift kit for 35-inch Goodyear Wrangler All Terrain tires. It left Challis, Idaho, driven by John McConnel, a retired Army Ranger who heard about the scuffle from his friends in the Oath Keepers. It was his brand-new truck and among the first of the treats, he bought himself in celebrating his retirement.

McConnel, who held a BA in Psychology, was better known as "Joker" to his fellow troops and friends and was well known for his sharp sarcastic wit, which served him well all the many years he spent surviving his army tours in Afghanistan. The Rangers were skillful experts at recruiting local indigenous forces in combat situations. They were required to stay long periods of time in the area of operations and adapt to the local culture. He loved training the Afghanis to take back their own country from the Taliban. It was deeply rewarding to him.

When McConnel eventually retired, he wanted no more war and a little piece and quiet that he could call home away from the craziness of his long career. So, he and his wife found a rustic little cabin near Challis with a tranquil year-round stream passing by the front porch. It was perfect. They were empty nesters.

His one and only son was a busy IT professional in Portland, Oregon, and they seldom saw him or his fiancé. The two had been living together for about a year now and finally had a traditional June wedding planned. The independence from one another was something borne out of years of separation from his long absences away in the tumultuous war zones of the middle east.

He and his son loved each other but were just not close. Something his wife hated as she had raised her son for years on her own and the two of them were very close. McConnel hoped that after the wedding the four of them could forge a new fresh relationship.

But for now, the pain of the empty nest had become dull as this new season of retirement had settled in. It was what they both always looked forward to. Peace.

McConnel, never intended to get mixed up with any Militia group. He always just thought of them as a bunch of fat wannabes that played with guns. And, when he originally moved to Challis, he never considered that he would even come into contact with a militia group. He had a comfortable retirement from the DOD, a nice chunk of savings, and was able to purchase his cabin and truck outright. His immediate goal now was to do some hunting, fishing, and plug into a local church.

It was at church where he first stumbled onto the Oath Keepers. McConnel was new to the Challis Bible Church, a small church of about 350 on a good day. The Pastor loved the Word of God and had a winsome way about him that was attractive to McConnel and his wife Joannie, especially after all the highly charged macho men of the Army.

At first, McConnel thought Oath Keepers was simply a men's group of the church. But after the first meeting, he soon realized they were much more than any typical church group. In fact, there was a strong community and Patriotic feeling about it, which made him instantly feel at home. Also, they were very conservative and pro-constitution. He liked that, but even more, he was curiously intrigued, so when invited to a campout by some of the other men, he quickly accepted.

★★★

McConnel was surprised to find the weekend was more a weekend of active target practice and beer drinking. The men were great! Down-to-earth, smart, and hard-working. He quickly fit in, and when he took ahold of an AR-15 from one of the attendees and demonstrated his skill with a rifle, his excellent marksmanship led to lots of questions about how he became such a proficient shooter.

The next morning the women's group of the church showed up to make everyone breakfast. To McConnel's surprise, Joannie was in the mix of women that showed up bright and early that Saturday. At first, he thought it was a surprise visit by the ladies but soon realized the breakfast was a regular tradition. The ladies were always welcome at the campouts. But they left the men alone on their first night to size up the new guys.

Joannie noticed her husband was now being referred to as Joker, having shared his combat experience in the Rangers with the group, where the guys were hanging on every word, and so, out of respect, the guys call him by his previous handle, more like a sign of honor, because they now knew he was the real deal. A distinguished soldier who had fought for his country, and a true American hero. But there were still a lot of questions they asked him.

As he was barreling southbound down US 15, he remembered back to the five years earlier at the campout:

That's a pretty smart security precaution to quietly test a man alone like that. It was a bit more like a serious interrogation than an informal interview or friendly conversation.

It was only because they'd been infiltrated by the FBI and the nosy media in the past. There were enough experienced operators there, ex and current military, law enforcement to do a good job in assessing a new guy. But that wasn't all they did. They strategically used their national contacts to do a deep background check on every potential recruit to the Oath Keepers. And took it slow, deliberate, never tipping their hand to deeper operations until they were confident that you were unquestionably legit.

Over time Joker came to love the spirited camaraderie of the men and women of the Oath Keepers, coming to accept their solid idea that each in the group as Law Enforcement or as members of the US military had sworn an oath, and had at some time in their lives raised their right hand and swore their allegiance to the United States of America against all enemies, foreign and domestic. They

★★★

all believed that oath was for life, and they had pledged their lives, resources, and sacred honor to such a noble cause.

So, when word came there was a needy patriot in Nevada pitted against a government agency that had gone well beyond their judicial warrant, it was time to take action. Joker was the first to leave Challis from his particular Oath Keeper Chapter. Joker being retired and ready to respond, he was out the door within the hour, knowing the others would follow as soon as they settled with bosses, wives, and responsibilities.

Joannie had kissed him on the cheek and assured him he was covered in prayer. She then went about her daily chores as if she'd said goodbye to a husband who was simply going off to the store for groceries! I guess she's used to it, Joker thought reflectively as he pulled into St. George, Utah, at 6:30 a.m. for breakfast at a crappy little roadside diner he spotted.

After driving all night, I need to stretch my legs and take a piss. Hungry too!

Las Vegas McCarran International Airport

Ding, ding …

The familiar sound woke journalist Leah Scrivener from her all-night red-eye flight from DC to Las Vegas. American Airlines had stopped in Dallas/Ft Worth for a two-hour layover, where she took the opportunity at the massive Admirals Club to finish and file her report on the CPAC convention. Once the second leg of the trip was in the air, she immediately fell sound asleep, not waking until the plane had not only landed but was at the gate and everyone in the plane had already leaped to their feet.

As Leah opened her eyes, she was greeted by the big burly butt of a fellow passenger-only four inches from her nose, standing impatiently waiting for the plane doors to open. She was in an aisle seat and quickly rose to let her fellow seatmates pass to nowhere in particular. Then she plopped back down in her seat to get her wits about her.

Finally, the plane door was opened, and the passengers slowly began to shuffle off the aircraft. Leah decided to patiently sit there and let them pass. *Coffee, I need coffee,* is all she could think of.

Finally, the coast was clear as the very last person passed, except for a mom struggling to gather her children, with way too much stuff to carry. The young mother smiled at Leah as if to say, a *little help, please?* But Leah glanced at her in disdain, *if you can't handle them then you shouldn't have bred them* and kept moving up the aisle leaving the young mother behind, *friggin' soccer moms.* As Leah looked back one more time turning left out the airplane door and onto the jetway, at her feet was a stroller and other baby items placed there by the baggage handlers for the mother.

I really hate kids. Glad I got rid of mine. Referring to her last of three unwanted pregnancies, in a twinge of guilt and justification.

As Leah emerged into the noisy terminal, the familiar sound that is only heard in Nevada. "Ching, Ching, Ching" "Wheel… Of… FORTUNE!" cries one of the hundreds of slot machines greeting a passenger disembarking. Here I am again, in "Lost Wages," the home of everything garish and capitalist. This needs to be the first place to be bulldozed when the revolution comes.

Leah makes a quick stop in the restroom to splash some cold water on her face to wake up. Feeling the urge, she walks into a stall, plops down on the toilet seat. Then stares at her phone. Oh, a message from her editor.

"Great Story about CPAC. We'll run it tonight, your payment will be sent to your account today. Let me know when you have another story."

Leah, replies. "Landed in Nevada, I should have something great on this guy in the desert," Send. Trying to keep her editor apprised and interested. *This guy in Nevada? What the hell Leah — that's all you could come up with? What a clever wordsmith you are!*

Leah grabs a cup of coffee at Peet's Coffee and heads to the car rental area in the terminal. As she takes the long escalator ride down to the ground floor passing all the glitz and glamor of the various shops, she is greeted by a massive high def. screen, with the familiar face and voice of Wayne Newton. WELCOME TO LAS VEGAS! Then Celine Dion, WELCOME TO LAS VEGAS, Then Garth Brooks, WELCOME TO LAS VEGAS! I can't wait to get out of this town. Leah thinks to herself as she b-lines directly to the car rental counter.

Provo, Utah

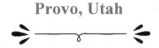

Paul O'Brian firmly swings a leg over his Fat Boy and twists the throttle a couple times. There's something only Harley riders understand about the rumble and deep roar of this bike between their legs. He gives the throttle two more twists without a care of who it might disturb in the hotel complex. On the fifth twist, a little gentler this time, he slowly lets the clutch out as the power of the motorcycle takes control propelling him with the sleek dangerously fast machine forward.

Soon he's barreling southbound down US 15 toward Las Vegas, and closer to being in his beloved Emma's arms. With the early morning sun on his face, the seventy-five mile-an-hour wind tussling through his hair, just cruising down the highway, it didn't take long to get lost in his thoughts of apprehension about his future, and concern that his frightening flashbacks, like consistent nightmares, might never go away.

Bunkerville, Nevada

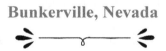

Amos finally emerged from his room into what felt like an ever-growing chaos all around his tiny little ranch house. There were strangers inside, and strangers strung about the immediate area outside. Lots of them. People had been coming all night long.

As he stepped out on the front porch, he suddenly noticed, even more, men, women, and CHILDREN, yes children. It surprised him. They had traveled from every corner of the country, entire families, to his little ranch in Nevada to support him. He was humbled.

Then from just behind him as if on cue, a young woman approached Amos.

"Mr. Cloyden, sir… I just wanted to say hello." The tall brunette woman getting Amos' attention. "You are a great hero to me and my family, and I just want to shake your hand," she thrusts her right hand forward.

"Well, thank you ma... ma'am," replies Amos hesitantly. As he takes her outstretched hand and shakes it firmly.

"I also wanted you to meet my children," then turning says, "this is Jeffery, Susie, and Billy."

Amos bends down to shake the tiny little hands of the three appearing to be between five and nine years old. "Well, howdy partners," Amos extending his hand to each. Each politely standing to attention and returning the handshake, meet Amos' eyes with the introduction, then quickly looking away.

The oldest, Jeffery, responding "It's a pleasure to meet you, sir."

Then Amos' attention returned to the mother. "Children, Mr. Cloyden here is an American hero. One day you will realize what a special moment this is!" The children just politely smiled, as they do when they're really not sure what any of this adult conversation means.

Then Susie interrupts in her most hopeful little voice, "Can we go pet the horses?" The mother looks up at Amos questioning. Amos nods his head in the affirmative and says, "Sure, you can." The kids take off running towards the horse paddock, the last one skipping.

"You got yourself a nice little family there," Amos says with a pleasant smile. "Where did you all come from?"

"We drove in last night straight from Arizona… Tucson. My husband is still sleeping, he drove all night. I'm a little tired too, but those active little ones were up at six, so I decided to get up and feed them. Then to take a little walk and let them stretch. Then I saw you standing over here and I just had to meet you."

"I've been following along with all that's been happening to you, and I just had to shake your hand. It's just terrible what they've done. But 'We The People' have got your back, we're here for you," she said, trying to connect.

"Well, I sure do appreciate you coming all this way, and letting me meet your little ones. Thank you." Amos shaking her hand again to signal his goodbye.

"I had to," she promptly replied.

"Sorry? Had to what?" Amos feeling a little lost.

★★

"Bring my kids, I felt it was important for them to see the purpose of the Constitution, the 1st and 2nd amendment in action. I home-school my kids and make it a point to teach them about the rarity and importance of the Bill of Rights and our Constitution. And here, just a few hundred miles away is an important time in the history of the Republic. A moment that will be written down in the schoolbooks and I wanted my children to have a front-row seat so they could tell their children and grandchildren about it. That's why we came, that's why I brought them. What you're doing here, and all these patriots here is of national interest, maybe even international importance!"

"You think so? I just wanted the government to leave me alone, to live life the way I choose to," Amos solemnly replied. "All of this friction and notoriety has been thrust upon me," sweeping his hand across at the hundreds of people moving around "but I am so amazed by this huge response and yet so very grateful."

"All this here is not just about what has happened to you. It includes ALL the tyranny that has been inflicted on the American people. Our rights have been slowly and methodically taken away from us." Amos nods his head in agreement, reflecting on his fifty-three neighbors who once ranched in the area, and now have been forced out by the federal government.

"What's your name?" Amos asks deciding he likes this young woman.

"Oh, sorry. It's Julia."

"It's nice to meet you Julia from Tucson Arizona. I'm glad we met."

"Just don't let them win," replies Julia with self-assured conviction now.

"What do you mean?"

"I mean, too often the shining lights of Patriots have been extinguished by the federal bureaucrats. Guys, like Robertson in Montana, who they sent to prison for simply building a pond. Or the Hammonds who they charged with terrorism for lighting a backfire on their own property to stop a wildfire the government refused to firefight or the Hages who were told by the 9thCircuit Court that if they wanted to use their water rights they would need to helicopter in each cow, one at a time to the water. And they couldn't use the land that their family had traditionally used for grazing, even though they owned the water rights!"

"Then, there is that crazy attack on the 2nd Amendment in Oregon as the legislature actually tried to ban all guns!" Pausing only to continue.

"Open borders, the legal murder of innocent babies in and out of the womb, sex education for children at five years old! And now they want socialism taught while wiping away our nation's true history. Shall I go on?"

"We're engaged in a battle for the very soul of our country. Our culture and our constitutional rights and freedoms are at stake. It boils down to this. Our American way of life, and our livelihood is slipping away."

"Don't let them win, don't let them extinguish you. Now is the time to stand! Today is the day We the People make a stand!" She stops her impassioned preach and looks into Amos' eyes, still breathing heavily.

I can't let these people down. Amos thinks to himself.

"Well Julia, you have given me, even more, to think about. Thank you for sharing your heart." He leans in to give her a warm fatherly hug.

"Just remember, we are with you till the end, come what may," then lowering her voice in confidence, "and all these people walking around here are risking their very lives to stand with... you," concluding her thoughts and turning away.

"Thank you, Julia, –and take care of those little ones," Amos answers as they part.

"Momma, Momma, that big horse ate some hay right outa my hand!" exclaimed little Susie.

"Oh really? Let's go see the horses," replies Julia. She waves a fond farewell to Amos as they walk away hand in hand toward the horse paddock.

Chapter 6

The Protest

The Protest

Just behind the horse barn slowly waking up to the rustle of footsteps he heard outside his 1978 Ford F-250, Kevin Linfield stretches his sore muscles as he sits up in the cab. Through his groggy eyes, he admires three children giggling in amusement as they extend their hands full of hay to horses through the pipe enclosure. He smiles, as he thinks back to when he rode his first horse at nine years old, just ten years ago.

Kevin had driven all night from Battle Mountain, Nevada, to arrive at the Cloyden Ranch at 3 a.m. Once he arrived, he just parked his truck next to the horse barn, threw out a blanket, racked his hat, and plopped his head down on his rolled-up Carhart jacket. He didn't even bother to pull off his brand new waxy brown and lime 16" Round Toe Buckaroo Western Cowboy Boots.

Still smiling at the kids, he firmly kicked his passenger side door open and swung his feet around to scooch out into the dirt. As he did, he was hit by the strong odor of horse manure and urine. *Yep, that's a horse barn, he thought to himself. It's time to go see a man about a horse.* A phrase he learned from the old Buckaroos he spent his cowpoke days with, in the high desert of Northern Nevada.

Kevin headed straight to the barn slipping his slim body between the pipe corral rungs and into the enclosed stall of the barn. He found a dry corner away from the prying eyes of passerby's and did his business as he'd done hundreds of times at the ranch he now works on. It's ranch etiquette for a cowboy to discreetly use a box stall to relieve himself. For ladies, on the other hand, it's much more complicated.

As he stood straight and swaggered out the barn, one of the little boys who woke him was startled by his appearance. Kevin just gave him a good ole' country boy smile, and said, "hey little buckaroo," and this time climbed over the pipe corral. Jeffery just stood motionless, staring at the oddly clothed man, then after a second or two shyly ran back in the direction of his mom.

Kevin Linfield was a true Buckaroo. A Buckaroo is a cowboy from Northern Nevada, California, Eastern Oregon, and some parts of Idaho. They differ in style and appearance from cowboys you might see in other parts of the world. Their appearance traditionally includes a wide flat-brimmed hat, short chaps or the "chinks" that only extend down just past their knee when on a horse, and suspenders to hold up their britches. Many times, Buckaroo's sport a big bushy mustache that "keeps their lip warm" in the harsh cold winters.

Then there is the trademark "Wild Rag," a long brightly colored silk neckerchief that is double wrapped around the neck and most often tied into a square knot, or sometimes into a friendship knot. This identifying splash of color often tells about the personality of the man or woman. The term buckaroo itself is an Anglicization of the Spanish word "vaquero". The vaquero is a Mexican cowboy who years ago, around the turn of the nineteenth century, dominated the California and Great Basin area of Northern Nevada.

These highly skilled horsemen were revered by the cowboys who had migrated from the other parts of the United States and many of their skills were adopted and made uniquely American. Like the high cantle and slick fork saddles with bucking rolls, and a wide horn or roping post for dallying their sixty-foot-long rawhide-braided ropes called a "Reata." An Anglicization of the Castilian Spanish La Reata which means re-tied rope.

The Buckaroos also wear big rowels on their silver spurs allowing for a lighter touch or cue to the horse. These big rowel spurs jingle as they walk in their western cowboy boots, so, to augment that jingle, buckaroos often added "jingle bobs" –large metal beads that collide with the rowels to make the jingle sound even more pronounced.

But even more significantly, what truly sets a Buckaroo apart from other cowboys is their skill as a horseman. Carefully following the old traditions of the Vaquero, of being a "Horse Whisperer" in more modern terms and using a quite deliberate study of effective communication between horse and human, they've been able to achieve a true partnership, which has been distinctly noted and admired across the world. This highly practiced skill when observed by the untrained eye looks almost magical as the horse begins to adhere to the detailed communications of a man, albeit its trainer.

However, in most other ways a Buckaroo is pretty much like any other working ranch cowboy. Their days consist of docter'n calves, moving cattle from one area to another, feed'n cattle in the winter, fix'n fences, and practicing their traditional arts of braiding leather or rawhide, roping, and even starting young colts. They sometimes carry a side-arm pistol for protecting their livestock against dangerous predators in the wilds. Of course, that means they are very good shots.

In northern Nevada, where Kevin lives and works, it's not uncommon for a cowboy to work on a ranch of hundreds of thousands of acres with just a small handful of other men and sometimes a woman or two. The "Cowboy Crew" works sun-up to sunset six days a week to maintain a cattle and farming operation of that size. Today is Kevin's day off, and once he got his horse put away, chowed down some dinner, and took a much-needed shower, he sat winding down at the computer in the main ranch house to send a couple of emails and stumbled across the call to patriots to come and support the Cloyden family against government overreach.

It was a snap decision for Kevin. He was looking to get off the ranch and do something exciting. He was way too young to head into town because the only thing to do there was barhopping between the three dive bars in Battle Mountain. Besides, that would just land him back at the ranch once again for another boring day off.

This call to action seemed just perfect. He could spend the restful day off in southern Nevada, meet some nice patriotic folks and head back the next evening to load the hay truck before dawn. *It'll be a lot of driving, but why the hell not? I got nothing better to do.* He remembered thinking. So, he threw some road snacks, a bedroll, and his prized HAMR rifle into the truck, and hit the road.

Kevin had been saving his hard-earned cash for months to make the biggest purchase of his life. Over the last couple of years, he'd taken up long-range shooting. Firstly, because hunting on the ranch required it. Elk, antelope, and deer often roam their ranch in northern Nevada but approaching them close enough to be in range for the average shooter was hopeless, causing the hunt to be unduly frustrating and a downright waste of time. But also, Kevin wanted to be a responsible hunter, one who could skillfully deliver a kill shot, without wounding and causing unnecessary pain to the animal.

Bottom line, hunting in Nevada requires proficiency in shooting long distances. And under the tutelage of the ranch's owner Kevin excelled at long-range shooting. But to achieve twenty-five hundred yards or more it required a brand new rife. After much research, Kevin set his heart and savings account on the exclusive HAMR offered by Gunwerks. It shot a .375 CheyTac round which because of its high velocity would limit wind variation, and it's mounted with Nightforce ATACR F1 7-35x56 Optics, Elite Iron bipod, fully adjustable Cadex defense tactical folding chassis, and aggressive muzzle brake to dramatically tame recoil.

It felt a bit military for Linfield, a hunter and target shooter, but it nevertheless became his dream to own this $12,000 long-range rifle. He had a tough choice to make, whether to buy a much-needed new pickup truck or a new rife. His choice reflected his priorities and the likelihood of its use. Since taking his HAMR home he'd dialed in over one hundred fifty rounds into selected targets over one mile away. And lately, he had his HAMR on his person every free waking moment, and today was no exception.

Kevin decided to wander around the various campgrounds and get to know folks, hopefully, rustle up some coffee and maybe meet a pretty girl. Something he seldom had a chance to do out on the ranch where he's lived for the last four years after dropping out of high school. As he walked about, he was amazed at the hundreds of people that were there.

Men, women, and children were strewn about the ranch headquarters and perimeter. Some were in simple campers, some slept on the ground last night and just a few wore a sidearm in an open-carry position. There were militia groups too, where many of them wielded an AR15 in a low ready position.

None of the folks Kevin met seemed angry or hostile, but just the opposite. To a person, everyone he visited was upbeat and loved their country, but more importantly, each was just excited to be there and passionate to do something about the federal government overreach. The common denominator of every family, every person he shook hands with, was the mutual frustration they had over the numerous unconstitutional actions the federal government had increasingly been perpetrating in recent years. At every camp, there was an American Flag displayed prominently somewhere nearby, on a tent, on a bumper, or mounted on a pole.

Also in many of the camps was a flag Kevin wasn't familiar with, the bright yellow "Don't Tread on Me" Gadsden Flag. This Flag was drawn up in 1775 by American Colonel and Politician, Christopher Gadsden, who during the revolutionary war hailed a flag depicting a rattlesnake on a field of yellow with the words DON'T TREAD ON ME. In modern times it has become a symbol of the discontentment of primarily rural living people in the United States, and their common overall theme. In the liberal media, it's referred to as a banner of racism and white nationalism. Just one of the thousands of mischaracterizations designed to smear the people and the political views of those who live in the fly-over or rural red states of the USA.

Kevin spent the morning in full sanguine mode, laughing loudly, enthusiastically shaking hands, and gulping cups of freshly brewed coffee from the generous hospitality of everyone there. At the last camp he visited, an attractive young blond country girl about seventeen years old caught his eye, and he had just settled in, finally gained the nerve to squat down on a nearby rock to strike up a conversation with her. She had even offered him a little grub, hot biscuits, and gravy. Just as he learned her name was Kelly, and that she was a senior at Bakersfield High School in California, her dad walked up interrupting to announce the word that was spreading across the camps.

"Kelly, Mr. Cloyden has asked us all to meet at the flagpoles at 8:30 a.m. He wants everyone to be there in attendance for his 9 a.m. joint announcement with the local Sheriff."

He spoke loud enough for everyone to hear, but was looking directly at Kevin with that skeptical dad look, that says, who are you and why are you talking to my daughter?

As her dad walked away in haste to inform the next camp, Kevin responded, "Do you want to ride with me over to the flagpoles?"

"Sure, that would be fun!" She really wanted some time away from her family, especially her little brother.

★★

Kevin stood and pointed to his truck parked by the barn, "That's my truck over there. Let's meet there as soon as you gather up your stuff. Do you need to ask your dad?"

"Nah, he'll be fine with it," Kelly responded in a spunky rebellious sort of way. "Besides I am an adult. I don't need daddy's permission."

"Ok, I'll go warm up the truck. She's a little cold-blooded," Kevin replies, pleased she accepted the invite and turns to go.

"I'll be there in a minute. I need to get my gun."

Gun! She don't need to comb her hair, put make-up on? She needs her gun? I think I'm in love.

Twenty minutes later Kevin sat in the truck still waiting. As every long-drawn-out minute went by so did another car, or truck even a motorcycle or two. Brad Paisley's song *Waiting on a Woman* came to his mind as he tried to patiently wait while his anticipation grew. Then he finally glances up and realized why it was worth the wait. As Kelly trotted with saucy assertiveness across the compound, Kevin was treated with a view that would warm a man's heart.

Kelly was dressed to the nine, swank in her Wrangler's fitted jeans, a tight tucked-in t-shirt that showcased her young figure, topped with a black cowboy hat, that perfectly offset her bright blond hair and cowboy boots. Damn is all Kevin could think. It wasn't only just the hat and boots or the fine figure she displayed; it was the .38 revolver she had openly strapped around her hips that accentuated her figure all the more. Her pistol was in a western tooled style holster, which had a big shiny silver belt buckle. It hung low on her leg with a piggin string tying it down firmly to her thigh.

Sure glad I waited. Kevin thought to himself, ironically agreeing with the Paisley song he was previously thinking about. He was so completely mesmerized at the vision of Kelly stunningly trotting toward him, he just plain forgot to jump out of the truck and courteously open the door for her, as he'd been taught by Dorthey Timmons, his "adopted" mother back on the ranch.

Kelly effortlessly climbed into the passenger seat, "Let's get a-movin'!" she says with a sense of urgency and a broad grin. The urgency was because of the fight she just had with her dad; the grin came from the noticeable attention she had received from Kevin as

★★

she trotted towards him. *That was the effect I was going for.* She thought to herself suppressing a smile. *He is one handsome boy.*

Kevin put his truck into drive and started bouncing down the old ranch road toward the highway following the procession of countless vehicles. Through the corner of his eye, he could see Kelly's family loading up their nice new crew cab and entered the lineup some five or six vehicles behind. With one big bounce, Kevin's black pelican case slid over hitting Kelly in the knee.

"What's this?" she inquired as she grabbed the case and returned it to its upright position leaning on the bench seat.

"Oh, that's my hammer," Kevin replied as a matter of fact.

"Oh, okay…" Not quite sure what he meant, not caring enough to inquire more.

"Do you know where this 'flagpole' place is?" Kevin asks inquisitively as the line of vehicles turned onto the Nevada State Highway 170.

Kelly pointing towards the large gathering of people. "Sure, it's right there."

Well, that wasn't far, we coulda walked, thought Kevin as he located a place to park. *I was hoping to get to know Kelly better, alone, spend a little more time with no interruptions.*

Sensing his disappointment Kelly intuitively said, "I want to just hang out with you today if that's okay? I need some time away from the fam, especially my annoying little brother."

"Sure, let's go see what's happenin'." Kevin threw his truck into park and climbed out, after making double sure it was locked up and his HAMR was out of sight with the bedroll covering it.

The two crossed a small gully on foot to arrive on the road joining the throngs of people. On the stage were Amos Cloyden and Sheriff Gillette behind a make-shift lectern. Lined-up across the front was what Kevin presumed to be militia.

He'd heard from several people in camp how they'd taken the job providing security for the Cloyden family and the campgrounds in general. Kelly noticed that off on a nearby hill some fifty horses and riders began to assemble, standing as sentinels over the gathering crowd.

The crowd was quite large, much larger than what they'd seen in the campground. Many were carrying signs and looked smartly dressed and clean, unlike the people he met that morning who'd slept in the dirt at the ranch headquarters. Kevin surmised they must be locals, who just came in from the surrounding towns.

"Look at the horses up on the hill!" Kelly points excitedly.

"Oh yeah, that's a bunch of cowboys." Not really sure what he should have said.

On the stage, Amos Cloyden took the microphone, and the crowd began to quiet down.

"Good morning, Patriots," Amos clearing his voice.

"Good morning," the crowd responded loudly in near unison.

"I called you all here to the stage this morning because Sheriff Gillette has an important announcement for us all. But before we hear from him, let's dedicate this day."

Gesturing his son to the lectern, Amos's oldest, Michael, takes the microphone.

"I would be honored if each of you would join me in the Pledge of Allegiance."

Removing his cowboy hat respectfully, he turned toward the American flag waving high upon the flagpole. Kevin noticed the adjoining flagpole had the State of Nevada flag tussling in the light breeze. The keen eye of the marksman in Kevin noticed both flags. *The wind is maybe two miles per hour coming from the south.*

"I pledge allegiance, to the flag…." began Michael.

Kelly noticed every single person had their hat or hand over their heart and was repeating along, except one. Kelly glanced up to the stage again noticing that Sheriff Gillette and his entourage of some ten deputies were all following Michael Cloyden's lead. Then Kelly glanced back over to the young woman who stood quietly still, hands folded in irritation, impatiently waiting for the pledge to be over.

As Michael's pledge ended, his brother Jacob stepped forward to take the mic.

"Will each of you join me as we dedicate this day to our Lord?" Hats remained off and the invocation began.

"Heavenly Father, we come before thee with humble hearts entreating thee to protect and keep us from harm as we fulfill thy divine providence in returning these United States to the Constitution, thou inspired those great men of old to pen, establishing our liberties. The government has unfortunately lost its

★★

way, and thou hast appointed We The People to restore our nation to its righteous place in serving us, not us serving the government. – Amen"

Jacob stuck his hat back on his head and returned the microphone to his dad.

Kelly took one more look at the strange lady who looked so uncomfortable before. It wasn't hard to pick her out of the crowd, as she wore almost entirely black attire and quite possibly the strangest boots she had ever seen. They reminded her of the boots that George Munster would wear in the old black and white sitcom Kelly's grandad would watch on re-runs. *What was it called? Oh, yeah, The Munster's.*

She remembered with a knowing smirk. *Munster Boots! What a strange outfit.* Kelly was now studying her, looking her up and down now, noticing the strangely dressed lady was downright snarling angrily as the prayer ended. *But why, what had Jacob said that offended her so?*

Leah Scrivener eventually noticed Kelly looking at her. So, she stared back with a look that mouthed, "Fuck you, Cowgirl." Not aware that the combination of the long plane ride, the hot drive into the desert, and the two things she hated most, the racist pledge and now, a prayer, had brought her to boiling point. She only realized it after she instinctively had both middle fingers up, while lip-syncing 'F-YOU' right at Kelly!

Kelly's flabbergasted reaction is what broke Leah out of it. She quickly dropped her hands, looked away, and composed herself. *Get it together Leah, don't reveal to these hillbillies who you are.* Kelly had looked quickly away from the stranger in shock. *God, what did I ever do to you?*

"You alright?" Kevin inquired noticing something changed her countenance.

"Yeah, just the nonsense people do." They both turned together to listen to the stage.

Amos began matter of fact. "Sheriff Gillette has come here this morning to tell us about some decision that the Government made. He wanted to tell me in private, but I told him to meet me here so he could tell us all."

He was interrupted by the crowd's grateful applause.

"Sheriff, can you give us some idea what these intruders have to say?"

"YEAH INTRUDERS!" yells someone from deep within the crowd.

Amos handed the mic over to Sheriff Gillette without hesitation.

"Well, Amos thank you for allowing me to come and address you all. And yes, there were some decisions made last night in Washington and consultation with the BLM, the US attorney, and myself… DC has decided to end the round-up operations and return your cattle to you."

The sheriff was now interrupted by the crowds' approving applause and hollers of satisfaction.

"We just need some time to close things down and remove the sensitive materials they have up there in the compound."

"NO, YOU DON'T NEED NO TIME TO OPEN A GATE" comes another voice. "No more time, no more time, no more time…" chants the crowd.

The sheriff and his entourage had completely misjudged the crowd.

In the eyes of the protesters, this was just another stall tactic to bide time and pull in more reinforcements to quash the crowd. Amos, his wife, and two sons were in the corner of the stage in an impromptu huddle, as the crowd kept loudly chanting and jeering in protest.

Finally, Amos took the microphone.

"Sheriff, here is what We the People want our duly elected Sheriff to do. You and your men go over to that compound and collect up all the weapons from that army. Then bring 'em here and pile 'em at the foot of the flag. Then tell them, usurpers, to get off 'The People's' land and go back to wherever they came from."

"We'll all wait here for one hour for you to come back and tell us they're gone. Once they're gone those cowboys up on that hill will gather up the cattle and put 'em back on the range."

Kevin noticed the Sheriff looked straight out dumbfounded. Without so much as a word, he turned and walked off the stage followed by his deputies.

For the next hour, there were spontaneous speeches about the US Constitution, property rights, and the authority of the County

Sheriff. After one hour Amos Cloyden stepped back behind the lectern again. "Folks, we haven't heard from the Sheriff and the hour is up. We've decided to give him thirty more minutes out of courtesy just in case. Then we'll head directly over to the compound."

A couple of minutes later Kelly's dad and mom emerged from the crowd.

"Kelly, we're going to head over to the compound when it's time. We want you to come with us. We came to protest as a family, and I want us to be together as a family," her dad said in earnest, entreating her.

"No, I want to hang out with Kevin…"

"KELLY" –Her mom thoughtfully interrupted. Shutting down her whiny teenager.

Kevin realizing, he hadn't met Kelly's family, pulled his hat off, and courteously introduced himself.

"Hello, I realize we haven't met. I'm Kevin Linfield from Battle Mountain, Nevada."

He stuck his hand out in a greeting to both parents. Kelly's dad firmly shook his hand. Then, her mother.

"Ma'am," with the broadest smile he had. "The last thing I want to do is get in the way of a family-planned outing. Please, "You 'all go on ahead and I'll find you there. Of course, if that's okay with you sir?" Seriously asking.

"Daddy?" Kelly appealing to her soft-touch father in her little girl voice.

Kevin quickly turned to her, "It's okay, I'll meet you there. Go with your family, we'll all have fun together." Besides, you are never gonna win this one. And, by doing this I'll earn a few points with your dad, I hope.

"Alright," frowning, realizing she had lost. "Make sure you find me." Kelly pleaded passionately as she walked by, followed by her mom.

"Be sure of it." He smiled ear to ear as he put his hat back on his head, satisfied with himself.

"Thank You," Kelly's mom whispered sympathetically as she passed Kevin.

"You're welcome." Kevin did all he could to not stare at Kelly's backside as she walked into the crowd. Kevin wandered around the crowd a bit more, until Amos came back on the microphone.

"Well folks, I just heard the Sheriff has left the area, so I guess it's time to head on over and get my cows. But I want you to all be safe. So, my two boys are gonna lead you over to the compound."

"You'll need to move out onto the highway and stop the traffic as everybody crosses, and once you're all over there you'll need to wait for the cowboys on horseback. It'll take 'em a while to get there. So, be sure to be patient, careful, polite, and courteous to everyone."

Amos paused thinking if there was anything else to say. "Okay, getter done!"

Leah Scrivener listening in the crowd writes in her notepad:

"Get yer Guns" placing firm quotes around the words,
Commands Amos Cloyden from the stage.

Amos and his wife sit down on the stage with their legs hanging over the platform. The head of the Militia security detail approaches, "Shall we bring your truck up"

"Nah, I'm goin' to wait right here in case the Sheriff returns. This is where I said I'd be, so this is where I'll wait," replied Amos.

"Okay sir, then half of us will stay with you. I'm releasing the other half to go with the crowd to keep an eye out for any crazies."

"Sounds good. Thank you," replies Cloyden.

I wonder what he means by crazies? Amos not realizing the militia had refused compound entry to a couple who made the security detail feel very uncomfortable just last night and the militia leader wasn't confident they had left the premises. So, he split his team up in hopes of avoiding an incident... *I think this is over anyway,* thought the militia leader to himself.

Chapter 7

Battle of Bunkerville

The Touquap Wash, Bunkerville, Nevada
Just three short miles north of the Bunkerville turn-off on US Hwy 15 Kristen Donahue and Patrick Daniels were excited in anticipation to be nearing their destination. After a quick stop in Mesquite, Nevada, for breakfast, they had seen many other patriots coming through the truck-stop diner. Men and women, young and old alike were milling through, fueling up, drinking coffee, and the line at the diner checkout was impressive. There was a happy tension in the air akin to a concert event, but much more meaningful, as hundreds of folks from different parts of the country and various walks of life were descending on one lonely place in the desert to make a stand for what they truly believed in.

Donahue and Daniels' anticipation was building in their hearts upon the conversation the two shared that morning over coffee, hoping maybe just maybe America was finally waking up from its long slumber.

"Do you think there will be many people?" Kristen breaks the silence after Daniels pulls onto the highway.

"By the looks of all the American flags and folks in the truck stop, I just think there may be," Patrick responds with a radiant smile from the driver's seat, wide awake now, and revived by their breakfast stop.

"Wouldn't that be exciting, if more than just the two of us saw what we're seeing in our country? Maybe more than just a few are feeling a call to action like us and are willing to do something!" continues Kristen

"But, what?

"Is it going to be more rallies, more well-meaning speeches, and empty prayers from a stage with a flag tacked up on it? Or are 'We the People' going to truly do something about the government abusing this family by showing gumption? I mean something real, something meaningful to send a message to this tyrannical government of ours!"

Patrick responded simply but with more resolve than Kristen had ever heard in his voice, saying, "It's time to do some patriot shit."

Then it went silent once again between them for what seemed like a very long time.

Daniels firmly gripping the steering wheel, intently focused only on the upcoming protest gathering, exactly like the many times he'd directed his thoughts just before entering various combat operations he'd engaged in on dozens of war zones around the world. Daniels just stared ahead quietly, oddly smirking.

"What the hell do you think is going on over there?" Kristen pointing to the northbound lanes across the large medium that separated the four lanes of north and south-bound traffic.

The procession from the Cloyden ranch had just arrived at the Touquap bridge, as it was known on the highway maps and by the locals. A nondescript desolate highway bridge in the desert of south-eastern Nevada, not far from the Arizona strip and the Utah Border. The desert wash, just fifty feet below the bridge, was dry and sandy most of the year. The line of cars led by Michael Cloyden had come to a stop, creating a blockade backing up the northbound traffic for miles in the middle of nowhere as far as you could see.

Immediately, on the south end of the bridge, there was a turnaround through the medium that would allow the line of vehicles to cross over the southbound lanes, which then led down a dusty dirt road to the compound that sprung up in the middle of the desert to round up Amos' cattle. But to Michael Cloyden's surprise, the road was already blocked off by federal agents and a checkpoint gate set up.

This caused Michael a brief moment of indecision as to what to do, so he followed his gut and stopped. So much for the feds leaving! Then quickly turned his truck to the right, settling it into an undeveloped overlook of sorts on the right side of the Northbound lanes.

"Jacob, let's make sure everyone parks here," he instructs decisively.

★★

Michael's brother Jacob quickly jumped out of the truck and began directing traffic into the overlook where his brother had just parked. It was not the original plan, but it would work. Michael joined his brother on the asphalt and quickly realized that the overlook was not large enough for all the vehicles arriving.

"If we cut down that fence, it would give us several more acres," Michael pointed out.

"There are some wire cutters in the back of the truck," said Jacob offering a quick solution to the problem at hand.

"Do it," Michael instructs without hesitation, then took over directing traffic. Jacob ran off to his task.

Just a couple of miles back in the South Bound lanes of Hwy 15 was John McConnel. He was one of many patriots who had stopped at the Mesquite Truck Stop, but only to make a pit stop to relieve himself and stock up on protein bars and hot coffee. The traffic in the southbound lanes had also begun to slow as looky-loos were caught off guard by all the going-ons in the opposing lanes.

What the hell! Why are we slowing down? McConnel was anxious to complete the long drive.

Across the medium, the Cloyden brothers were doing a great job getting all the protesters parked and the people began to congregate wondering what's next as more and more cars came in. "Fence is down... that'll be enough room for everybody... Now what?" Jacob queried his brother.

"Since they have the road blocked-off, I think I'll walk down the dirt access road into the wash and then under the bridge up to the compound. You stay here and get everybody parked; I'll lead the protesters down the hill into the wash. If I get 'em all following, it'll work just fine," says Michael assuring.

"Okay, I'll get 'em parked then I'll see you down there. Don't forget we need to wait for the horses, they're still twenty-thirty minutes away," replied Jacob.

"Got it, we'll be waiting in the wash for everybody on foot and the horses, then we'll make our march together towards the compound." Michael turns to walk towards the gathering crowd.

"See ya down there," replies Jacob.

And, just as Michael's impromptu plan had prophesied, after parking their vehicles, the occupants began following one another down the desolate dirt road on foot. There was now such a steady

★★

★★★

flow, Jacob noticed how it looked like a long winding snake of people moving off the elevated highway bed meandering down into the wash.

Miles down the northbound lanes was Leah Scrivener. She was caught in the miles of backed-up traffic caused by the protestors crossing. "Son of a bitch, I am going to miss everything!" she grumbled to no one in the car.

I promised my editor at the Washington Post that this was going to be a great story, but if I don't get there soon there'll be "NO STORY" –again posing a self-dialogue in her overinflated head.

After witnessing the highway chaos, Patrick pulled over to the side of the road just past the checkpoint and carefully parked the pick-up along the southbound lanes.

"What are we doing? asks Kristen.

"That's got to be the protest over there, but I am just not sure. Let's hoof it over there to see what is happening." Patrick sharing his hunch.

"Sure, I mean who the hell else would it be out here," Kristen agreeing and swiftly piling out the passenger side of the stopped truck.

"Let's kit up, if it's them, we want to be ready for … whatever," Patrick explains.

The two of them take the next few minutes to put all their gear on and strap in their weapons. By the time they were done, they looked like military special ops.

Daniels put on his MARPAT (desert) six-pocket pants, nylon military boots, and a cotton USMC T-Shirt which was his preference to wear under his Improved Outer Tactical Vest or IOVT which had Level IV ESAPI Kevlar body armor plates. Though he tended to leave the side plates out to increase his comfort and movement. *Besides a Marine is always facing his enemy. Still, the backplates are for those who might be cowards and quietly sneak up on you.* He remembers from a drunken conversation he had with some old Marine buddies at Camp Pendleton.

★★★

★★★

Strapped to the back of his vest was a CamelBak Classic Hydration Pack, he picked up at a local outdoor store. Wrapped around his chest was his FN SCAR 17S which fires 7.62x51mm/.308. Patrick likes it because it's so effective, lightweight, and accurate. And, though he never used its military counterpart during active duty, he always coveted one for as long as he could remember. It comes mounted with the hard-to-get Nikon M-308 SF 4-16x42mm Riflescope and a Niko plex Reticle. Good for up to 500 yards.

On his leg was a Glock 17, .9mm. He also had the smaller Glock 19 tucked in his waistband at the small of his back. This weapon he carried everywhere and felt undressed without it, even now.

On his head was a well-worn Seahawks ball cap and a Bluetooth earpiece for "COMMS" which was connected to his cell phone. He also carried 210, 7.62x51 600 rounds of ammo in 30 round magazines and another 60 rounds of 9mm in 15 round magazines for his two Glocks. He also packed a couple of protein bars *just in case*.

Kristen kitted out with much the same outerwear, but she strapped an (ArmaLite) AR-15, arguably the most vilified rifle in America. It's classified as a sporting rife, but in truth, it's the civilian version of the M16, the standard weapon of the modern US infantry. Kristen's AR shoots a 223 Remington and her first gun of this style. It's mounted with a Bushnell Trophy TRS-25 Red Dot Sight.

She also carries a Glock 17 on her leg, although she wasn't very good with a handgun. Kristen didn't like hats, so she pulled her long, lush locks into a simple ponytail as the two head toward the bridge and all the people.

John McConnel was getting somewhat frustrated. The southbound traffic north of the bridge was almost at a standstill. *You'd think you were in Los Angeles rush-hour gridlock traffic or something.*

As John looked up over to the bridge, he could see the protesters staunchly walking down the serpentine dirt road to the bottom of the wash. He also saw the Nevada Highway Patrol arriving to take control of the backlogged traffic so he concluded this must be the

★★★

place and stopped his truck just north of the bridge in the center medium near the bottom of a sloping ravine. You could barely see his truck from either side of the highway. In relative anonymity, John slid out of his truck and put on his arms and protective gear.

Similar to Donahue and Daniels, He had a utility vest, but just one plate of Kevlar and no Camo style pants, only a regular pair of Levi's button fly jeans with a casual white t-shirt, no sleeves. His customary approach came from his training to blend into the local culture. And to him, this was blending.

He also wore a trendy cowboy hat, but not what real cowboys would wear. More like something you'd buy at the Grand Ole Opry. More Hollywood than working ranch cowboy. Something no one would recognize unless you made your living in agriculture.

McConnel almost fit the part. Looking more like a dude with a vest and rifle, than a local rancher. But what McConnel lacked in rural clothing, he more than made up for in hardware and combat experience.

Strapped to his chest in low ready was a Heckler & Koch MR556A1. This weapon mimics its military brother the H&K 416. It shoots a 5.56 caliber NATO round and is deadly lethal in the right hands.

On his back, he swung a Smith and Wesson MP10 6.5 Creedmoor. The cousin to the Polish Knights Armament SR-25 .308. His Creedmoor had a folding bipod and also shoots a 5.56 NATO round.

Two different rifles for two different tasks. Both were mounted with the Vortex Optics Diamondback. McConnel had learned early on his combat tours that simplicity and interchangeability were a lifesaver, especially in long deployments with sketchy supply lines. So, John also carried 680 rounds of ammunition for his rifles and 45 .9mm rounds for the Glock 17 strapped to his leg.

John McConnel felt he was traveling lite, as he dropped his cell phone securely in his pocket after leaving his customary message on his wife's voicemail that he arrived safely and how much he loved her. Then, he headed to the Touquap wash to join the protest. John was the very first to walk out onto the Northbound Bridge, to gaze down at the many protesters who were arriving at the bottom of the road and were beginning to spill out into the wash.

At first, he was going to join the procession down into the wash but then he hesitated, deciding to stop and take a tactical view of everything. Just as he was walking out on the bridge, he noticed a cloud of dust to his west, where six or seven vehicles were charging down a dirt road into the wash. They came to an abrupt stop in a double line just under the northbound bridge, where a barricade of sorts had just been erected.

From John's perspective, the barricade looked more like a set of pipe corral panels tied between the bridge's stations. It was not a serious barricade; it was more of a tactical fence to restrain vehicles from coming up the road. Exiting the white and tan vehicles looked like a swat team immediately taking cover behind and alongside their trucks and SUVs, roughly twenty-twenty-five men and a couple of women, fully kitted out. Some with ARs and a couple with non-lethal "bean bag" weapons.

From a distance to the untrained eye, they looked more like standard grenade launchers, than a silly riot control weapon. The troop appeared to be in the thick of it trying to defend a position. What position —John couldn't guess. He was unaware that just up the Wash was the cattle compound and operations center for the round-up.

John slowly pulled his long gun up to his cheek to gaze through his scope to get a better look. Just as he did, Patrick and Kristen walked up —" Hey cowboy, you'd better not do that, you might give them feds the wrong idea," Patrick comments to McConnel. Referring to the Federal Agents below, thinking that McConnel's sighting through his scope could be considered "hostile".

"Yeah, you might be right," McConnel acknowledged dropping his gun back to the low ready on his chest. "I don't think they can see us up here," replies McConnel. *But it's best to be safe. I am not in Iraq.*

"Those yay-hoos can't see you, but THEY can!" —Daniels pointing to the top of a bluff, what looked approximately 1500 yards away to the naked eye.

McConnel grabs his small binoculars from his vest and peers up the high desert bluff, taking a few seconds before spotting the two-man team. "Overwatch," McConnel says quietly under his breath, but loud enough for both Donahue and Daniels to hear.

"Yeah, I think these fellas are far more serious than all those protesters realize. I am pretty sure I heard a drone above us too. I just couldn't get sight of it in the glaring sun," Daniels assessing the situation.

McConnel now is in full combat mode, all his senses and training have been fully engaged as he sweeps the area for additional threats. "That was a very good catch on your part," McConnel says to Daniels. "I guess I didn't know what I was walking into."

"Yeah, well, I'm an old recon Marine. We hunkered down in those bushes over there and got a real good look-see before we even walked out into the open onto this bridge. Don't be too hard on yourself. It's my combat training."

"Well I'm Army, I really should have known better." *I won't let that mistake happen again today.*

"ARMY, hell you guys just stand on a hill and call in airstrikes and artillery and shit, then you move in with all your support after us Marines do all the hard work. No wonder you didn't assess this right!" Daniels was just ribbing McConnel now.

McConnel returns the jest with a broad smile while vigilantly searching the surrounding bluffs with his binoculars. *That's actually not too far from the truth.*

After a quick scout, he notices the presence of law enforcement dramatically increasing. The Nevada Highway Patrol was fully in motion directing traffic to get both sides of the highway moving again. The Las Vegas Metro, which is officially a division of Clark County Nevada Sheriffs' Department, were arriving in force taking up tactical positions in the center turn around and between the highway lanes, effectively creating a barrier of officers and vehicles from crossing lanes or entering the dirt road that leads to the remote compound.

The original barricade that thwarted Michael and Jacob Cloyden from leading the protesters into the compound had now become a defensive line of Sheriff deputies and then another barricade of BLM and Park Service vehicles. Off into the not too far distance was a dust cloud to the due east of what, McConnel didn't have a clue.

"This is starting to get serious," McConnel exclaims rather ominously.

"There are sure a bunch of cops here," Kristen Donahue finally contributing.

"Yeah, they're pouring in," replies Daniels.

"What the hell do you think that is?" McConnel pointing over to the cloud of dust approaching the wash from behind a hill.

"It's the cowboys," comes a new voice to the conversation. Kevin Linfield had been driving his truck and just passed the three on the bridge minutes ago. He followed the long line of protesters from the stage near the Cloyden Ranch only to be one of the last to arrive, leaving no place to park.

So, he decided to cross the northbound bridge and park on the other side, once the NVHP got the highway reopened and traffic moving again. As he climbed out of his pickup, on a whim he pulled out his new rife from its case and swung it over his shoulder. In part, not to leave it in his truck and, he wanted to proudly show it off to Kelly.

"I'm sorry?" McConnel replies, barely hearing Linfield above the steady roar of commotion from vehicles noisily buzzing past them now as the traffic began to move.

"That's the horses from the protest at the stage this morning. The Cloyden brothers were leading everybody over here to get the cattle since the Feds had agreed to leave and return the cows. The protesters were going to wait for the horses to move the cows back toward the ranch."

"It sure don't look like the Feds left," replies Kristen straightforwardly.

"I never seen so many Feds."

"Or cops," interjects Patrick.

Kevin stops alongside the others to get a sense of the crowd below him. He hasn't really noticed the tactical situation. Kevin is furiously looking for Kelly and her family in the crowd directly below. Suddenly his concentration is broken by the familiar sound of a crackling loudspeaker.

"ATTENTION, ATTENTION, THIS IS THE FEDERAL GOVERNMENT. YOU ARE UNLAWFULLY ASSEMBLED ON FEDERAL LANDS. YOU ARE ORDERED TO RETURN TO YOUR VEHICLES AND DISPERSE."

Down in the Wash, Michael Cloyden is trying to organize the protesters. "You men, gather 'round here" –pointing at the same ten men who had made their way into the wash carrying long guns. Some looked like Militia types, others not, but all totted top-grade, state-of-the-art long-range rifles with military garb.

"I need you guys to stay back! - Move right under the Northbound Bridge, away from those guys," — pointing adamantly at the Federal Agents under the Southbound Bridge.

"I don't want any misinterpretation of our peaceful intent."

"Bullshit," one big guy pushes back "I came here to give these assholes a whooping," two others nodding their heads in agreement.

"Look, I understand, but you need to think about all these women and children down here. We can't have any accidents that could lead to a bloodstained armed conflict. With all these folks here, that would mean disaster... So, please move back, far back, — under the bridge."

" Okay, but if things go bad, we're gonna take some scalps!" As the loudest of the group starts to trail off away from the crowd.

Jacob Cloyden had just arrived in the wash and trotted up to his brother. "It seems everyone is parked and headed down. What's next?"

"What's going on topside?" Michael inquires.

"There are lots of cops, HP, Sheriffs' and Feds, I think we've been surrounded."

"How many?"

"Maybe 150, not really sure. What do we do now?"

"We pray," Michael responds resolutely.

"YOU HAVE BEEN GIVEN A LAWFUL ORDER TO DISPERSE. THIS IS FEDERAL LAND AND YOU ARE UNLAWFULLY ASSEMBLED. THIS IS YOUR ONLY WARNING. RETURN TO YOUR VEHICLES AND RETURN TO YOUR HOMES."

Jacob quickly gathers the protesters into a circle. Michael, at the top of his voice hollers:
"Thank you for all coming down here to help us get our cows back and to make a stand against the tyranny and overreach of the Federal Government. Just a couple hours ago we were told that the government had left the area and we could get our cows back. But now we seem to be surrounded by the government, not just by the Feds, but by the State Troopers and the very Sheriffs who told us we could get our cows. So, like Gideon and his mighty warriors, we need to ask our Heavenly Father for His help, for we are far outnumbered and without His help like lambs led to the slaughter."

With that, Michael and Jacob dropped to their knees. The remainder of the protesters also fell to their knees in the desert sand. Michael and Jacob took each other's hand, then extend their hand to the person next to them. Michael then looked into the faces of some 150 people kneeling with them in the sand holding hands in unity.

They were young and old, weathered faces and fair, men and women, all so hopeful, all so sure of what they were doing.

Jacob noticed the children, innocent and a bit unsure about what was happening, most looking up for the reassurance of their parents. It was a surreal moment of patriotism, an important moment in history.

Michael, being a man of few words began.

"Heavenly Father, we beseech thee to come to our aid in this terrible moment. Keep each of us safe from harm in this Wash but committed to purpose. Give us the strength to stand, to stand with conviction and resoluteness in the face of overwhelming odds, as we stand for what is right and just. Give us courage Father for this day. Amen."

Just as the group rose to their feet, the horses came into view over the small pass that kept them obscured from the protesters. "Hurrah the Cavalry is here!" One of the protesters yelled at the top of his lungs. The crowd went into a loud, long, and sustained cheer. The mood shifted and was much more hopeful now.

Why more hopeful? —no one was quite sure, but the addition to their numbers seemed promising, a good thing.

Michael and Jacob began to line up the protestors one by one across the wash. As the horses came down and entered the ravine, they positioned them into a secondary line of cavalry behind the protesters on foot.

"THIS IS YOUR LAST WARNING. WE HAVE BEEN AUTHORIZED TO USE NON-LETHAL FORCE. DISPERSE NOW."

As the protesters hurriedly lined up, the only reporter down in the wash, along with his cameraman began to advance forward.

"Are you really going to shoot these people?"

"STAY BACK."

"Look, I am a Journalist I want to talk to you. I am unarmed," as he and his cameraman began to move more cautiously forward with their hands in the air. The reporter pulled his shirt up and turned around to show the agents that he did not have a gun in the waistband of his pants. "I am unarmed."

"STAY BACK WE ARE AUTHORIZED TO SHOOT."

"Are you going to shoot these people, there are children here. I just want to talk to you!"

"STAY BACK OR YOU WILL BE FIRED UPON."

With that last command, the nervous journalist began to slowly retreat back into the large crowd, that was now edging forward slowly.

The men with their long rifles begrudgingly follow Michael's orders and fell back to the Northbound Bridge. There they strategically took up elevated and flanking positions to the right and left side of the gathered crowd. These positions became a necessary standpoint to have elevation over the crowd and especially over the horses and riders.

There was no direct clear line of sight to the opposing federal agents who stood terrifyingly before them. Although their positions were open and exposed to the much more elevated positions of the Federal Agents on the bluff in Overwatch as well as any reinforcements that might come from the compound that could flank the whole ordeal, still, something these men hadn't considered or were even aware of was just how many more agents there were possibly in and around the perimeter of the compound.

Back up on the bridge the four who had gathered were beginning to get tense at what they were seeing.

"Oh, shit this does not look good!" exclaims McConnel.

"I don't like it either. Those guys down there are sitting ducks for the sniper team on the bluff," replies Daniels.

"Is there any way to get word to them?" Donahue queries.

"Hell, I don't know anyone down there," McConnel replies.

"Hey kid, do you know anyone down there?" Donahue asks Linfield.

"I do, I have the cell number of a girl I just met, Kelly. I came on the bridge here to see if I could spot her…"

"Get the number out youngster, let's go," Donahue pushes. "Let's go, get a move on, let's go."

As Linfield awkwardly fumbles to get his phone out of his Wrangler pocket the conversation continues.

McConnel observes: "The Feds have put themselves in a poor tactical position. They have left themselves in a valley with nowhere to hide or retreat. From this position, we can keep their heads down and if we take out the last two vehicles with one round into the engine block the lot of them are stuck."

"And at our mercy, with our position and the guys down below laying fire at them, they'll be completely boxed in," Daniels observes.

"Got that number yet kid?" Donahue presses again.

"Just got it, I am calling now."

"FINAL WARNING. WE ARE AUTHORIZED TO USE N## (the speaker crackled loudly just at the worst moment) LETHAL FORCE. DISPERSE NOW!"

"Did they say lethal force?" Donahue feeling really anxious and worried for the people below.

"Oh, they won't shoot anybody," comes yet a fifth voice to the conversation.

All four on the bridge turn to look at Leah Scrivener who had just ditched her rental car into the shoulder and sprinted onto the bridge with cell phone in hand taking video footage while interrupting. The four silently just stared in unison at this strange-looking intruder of the conversation.

"I have been to dozens of protests like this. The cops always make big bombastic commands, but never follow through," she says confidently with a touch of arrogance. "I am a reporter."

The other four just turn away ignoring her.

That's all we need is a reporter out here. McConnel thinks to himself.

"Have you gotten your girlfriend yet?" Donahue insisting with urgency.

Linfield replies, "It's ringing, she's not my girlfriend."

"Hello?' Kelly answers.

"Kelly, it's Kevin from breakfast." Not sure if she still remembers him.

"Where ARE you? I am down here in the protest waiting for you. You better not have ditch…"

"Kelly, just listen for a moment," Kevin abruptly interrupts.

"There are guys on the hill, snipers that will shoot those other militia guys down there if we don't warn them!"

"What? Where are you?"

"I am on the bridge just above you…"

"Where? –I don't see you," Kelly looking all around.

"It doesn't matter, just go find one of those other guys down there with a rifle and tell them to look out for snipers."

"Snipers? Where?"

"Stop, listen to me it's really important…"

"Give me the phone kid," interrupts Daniels forcefully.

"Kelly, this is Sargent Daniels," using his old rank to sound very authoritative. "Now listen to me very carefully, I want you to go and find one of the other men with a rifle, dressed in camo, military looking. When you find one, call us back, and then I want you to just hand them the phone."

"Do you want me to tell them Kevin's message?"

"No, just hand them the phone, I'll give them instructions when you do."

"Which one? Who should I find? Where is he?"

"You're in the crowd with the protesters, right?"

"Yes, in front of the horses"

"They'll be right behind you, behind the horses near the bridge behind you."

"Who do I find?

"The first guys you see with a rifle, in camo. Then dial this number and hand him the phone. That's it."

"Okay, first guy, — got it," Kelly disconnects.

Geez, that was unnecessarily difficult Daniels thinks to himself as he hands the phone to Donahue. "Hand me the phone when it rings."

"Daddy, I need to make a phone call!" Kelly informs her father as she rushes off.

"Wait, what? —where are you going?"

Kelly never looks back.

Fricken boys, it's always about boys. Kelly's dad thinks to himself while he watches as the treasure of his heart disappears between the horses. *I wish I could slow her down.* Not realizing that is the last they'll see of one another.

"There she goes," McConnel exclaims as he sees this young blonde woman dashing through the horses. "That's got to be her," as he points down into the Wash.

"Yep, that's Kelly," Kevin confirms.

"Damn, youngster —she's fine," Daniels laughs.

With that, he receives an unnecessarily hard punch right in the tip of his right rotator from Donahue.

"What the hell was that for? You know I only have eyes for you," Daniels joking laughs.

"Yeah, sure you do."

Daniels was rubbing his shoulder now. That was unnecessary. It really hurt; *Kristen is no gentle little flower that's for damn sure.*

Scrivener standing nearby, Misogynist pig. "That's right– don't take that crap!" Trying to bond woman to woman with Kristen.

Whatever. Donahue rolls her eyes and looks back into the wash. I guess she doesn't know I was kidding.

Just a short couple hundred yards away, Undersheriff Roberts, who had been standing alongside his boss Sheriff Gillette on the stage earlier in the morning, is on his cell phone discussing the escalating situation with the Sheriff.

"Boss, this is getting out of hand. The BLM has not left as they promised. In fact, they are ratcheting up the situation, making it worse. They have just announced they will use lethal force on the protesters!"

"WHAT! That sounds like that moron DODGER!" Gillette replies outraged.

There's more. The FBI's HRT is here in the compound and they're kitting up to repel the protesters when they reach the compound. And the Los Angeles County Swat team is also onsite to be a counter-attacking force.

"What the hell are you talking about? Where did all these units come from? This is insane!"

The Sheriff pauses for a few moments to think:

"Here is what I want you to do. Get down there with a handful of men and tell Dodger you are taking over. He is relieved! I will get on the phone with the Sheriff in LA County and the FBI field office and tell them to stand down immediately.

Then, I want you and your men to stand in the middle between the BLM and the Protesters and deescalate the situation as best you can. Standard uniform, no long guns, no riot gear, just bodies between the parties. Command all the Feds to leave my county immediately. I am on my way back out there right now!"

Sheriff Gillette's driver overhearing the conversation was already slowing for an upcoming turnaround, lights, and siren blaring. They were a full hour drive time back to Bunkerville. Gillette was already on the phone to his counterpart in Los Angeles requesting assistance.

Roberts gathered a few of his commanders and a handful of officers in his unit and ordered the rest to follow him as he drove into the compound and then down into the wash. As they were bouncing down the dirt road past the BLM checkpoint and through the compound, he was yelling commands over the Radio.

"This is Clark County Undersheriff Roberts, — to all federal agencies operating in the Bunkerville, Mesquite area — you are ordered to stand down and rally at the compound command center."

"Who is this?" came an unidentified voice over the radio.

"This is Clark County Undersheriff Roberts, —you are commanded to stand down and return to the command center at the compound for further instructions."

"Attention all Federal Agencies, this operation is under MY command, disregard ANY commands from the Sheriff's department. They are out of their jurisdiction."

"Dodger is that you? where are you? I am on my way now" Roberts replies.

A long painful uncertain and confusing pause.

"I am under the northbound bridge with the forward unit of BLM and Park Service officers."

"I will be there in two minutes," Roberts retorts.

"We have more movement under the bridge. Looks like the sheriff's department is supporting the Feds!" McConnel declares to the group. "Wait, this is interesting – it looks pretty animated. I think they are arguing."

"LAST WARNING. YOU WILL BE FIRED UPON."

"They keep moving forward," Kevin cries out to no one in particular. Noticing the protesters are now only about 100 feet from the barricade.

Roberts finally arrives at the bridge to confront Dodger face to face, stepping out of his vehicle rapidly, he turns looking firmly into his eyes, "I am taking over here!" he says authoritatively.

"Under what authority?" Dodger argues

"Sheriff Gillette's orders."

"This is a federal operation; you have no jurisdiction on federal land.

Roberts was prepared for this. "You are on Nevada State land, under a Nevada State Highway in my county, in other words, you are not on federal land but standing in my jurisdiction. Besides this operation was ordered to cease three days ago by your boss, the US Attorney, and the Sheriff. You shouldn't even be here!"

"We were packing up to leave, but when they confronted us and threaten to overrun the command center, we were forced to engage these right-wing terrorists."

"Look at them, you dumbass! There are women and children out there!"

"And guns too," counters Dodger.

"THIS IS AN OPEN-CARRY STATE! You couldn't arrest them if they walked into a 7-Eleven like that. Besides, there are just a few folks with pistols. You need to immediately stand down before someone gets hurt."

"There is militia here too. What about them?"

"Most of those guys stayed at Cloyden Ranch with Amos. You need to stand down. Now."

"What are you talking about? Look… they have formed a skirmish line to attack, this is a well-organized planned out military operation. They put the women and children in front as human shields then they are going to charge us with the horses. But we have planned for this!" Dodger getting very agitated.

Roberts realizes that the situation is completely out of control. He now understands he is dealing with a harebrained idiotic fool who is completely misjudging the situation before him. He looks at his men signaling them to move in-between the protesters and the

Federal Agents. As the sheriff deputies start to move into position, a BLM agent makes a snide remark.

"Don't get your nicely polished shoes dirty" commenting about the standard uniform dress of his men.

The comment just hacked off Roberts. "Look you men, stand down, put your safety's on and lower your weapons, we are taking over. You need to move back and meet up at the command center. We have it from here."

The Federal Agents don't move an inch, awaiting a command from Dodger.

"Go on, NOBODY IS GOING TO SHOOT YOU!" commands Roberts.

Roberts turns to Dodger, "Order your men back. This is way out of hand. It's only going to take the smallest mistake to blow this thing up and get everybody killed!"

For a moment Roberts thought he may have reached Dodger.

Then came the first tragic report.

Then the second.

Robert's head exploded in a bloody pink mist.

The Battle of Bunkerville had begun.

★★

Chapter 8

High Ground

Paul O'Brian had been lost in thought all morning as he enjoyed the gentle warmth of the spring desert air on his southbound travel route. In an extended daydream of sorts, his mind teetered back and forth between the future and the past. He wanted to focus on the future, seeing his daughter, a new life in Las Vegas, where he might choose to work, a nice apartment with a pool or maybe even a house with a pool, where all her little friends could come over and play and swim and laugh.

I so want to be part of her life, watch her grow up become a young woman, and even find a great husband that would give her a great life and kids of her own.

Then he laughs out loud to himself, "look at me, I've already gotten her married off." Paul is beginning to dream again, something he never allowed himself to do since the divorce.

Then came the interrupting thoughts, flashbacks of the many intense deployments, the many friends he had lost, fifty-three to be exact. Men who he fought beside, got drunk with and bled on. Men he couldn't let go of. Men he still kept in a group text on his phone he titled "The Fallen," as if he could text them in heaven, hell, or the afterlife. Wherever they are.

And, where are they, exactly? Was his next thought. Again, something he would never allow himself to consider until now, on this, his first ride across the country since leaving war-torn Iraq and the combat missions where so many of his friends had fallen, never again to rise. It's just so final he thought.

He remembered from his church youth group growing up that most likely his friends ended up in hell. *But did they? Probably, they had killed so many. And, even though most deserved killing, some didn't. They were just unfortunately in the wrong place at the wrong time.*

Paul always justified the collateral damage as the wages of war, and *they shouldn't have been there* as the justification to ease his conscience when he allowed himself to think about it. However, after fifteen years of sustained combat operations, these intrusive thoughts were harder and harder to keep down.

It was like the memories he had of being a kid, trying to hold several beachballs under the water. When he started to lose his grip on one, he would overcompensate to stop it from emerging and end up losing his grip on all, resulting in their jetting to the surface erupting in a giant splash. *Yep, that was a good word picture of how I can't seem to stop these thoughts of mine.*

Especially that nightmare that just won't stop coming back, over and over, day or night, about the horrifying operation in Iraq, so long ago. How was my daughter there? Did they take her hostage? What happened? Did I kill her? If I didn't kill her, whose daughter did I kill? Is there a father out there as broken as I am over it all? I never seem to get any answers...

With that string of thoughts, Paul O'Brian is drawn back into his dream, his nightmare. It's teleportation of sorts. Even on his amazing Fat Boy at seventy-five miles per hour, he is right back in Mosul on that terrible morning where an innocent child was murdered, murdered by Paul O'Brian.

He never really knew how long his mental circuitry lapsed when it happened. Was it in minutes? Or did it play out in real-time? All Paul knew was like those beach balls, he could not stop the thoughts from crashing to the surface.

And although he felt it was incredibly real, in another sense, it wasn't. Though he would eventually awaken, meanwhile for the duration of the episode he'd be outwardly functioning, level, and still doing what he was doing in real life. Oddly, it didn't matter what he was doing, whether it was sleeping, or a conversation, or in the middle of a covert military op, or like now, riding his fat boy motorcycle down US Highway 15 in the Nevada desert, he was at the same time, zoning out in another reality. He was mentally engaged on a seal team mission in Mosul, Iraq. It was a strange truth for him, to be absorbed emotionally in another part of the world and yet completely functioning in this one.

Plus, there was an actual true passage of time, of which he was only remotely aware by the distance he may have traveled or the continuing of a conversation, or the completion of an operation in which he was engaged while "gone." It was an odd but constant routine to Paul, that over time he would gradually learn to accept and trust. That while "in Iraq" everything would be fine here in "real life" or real-time, even though he was gone.

The only trouble was the events of real-life during these lapses were lost to his memory. He could not remember the conversation he was having, the operation he was involved in, or the specific incidents that took place while gone. And the reoccurring bad dream of the covert operations on that fateful day in Iraq always ended at the same precise moment. He couldn't stop the disturbing thoughts from rising until it played out to the very end. And when it did, he was back, mid-sentence, mid-firefight, or mid-motorcycle ride. Today was no different.

Paul had been teleported yet again back to that terrible day years ago in Mosul somewhere during his desert ride to Las Vegas. When he stepped suddenly back into reality, he found himself threading the needle between cars in what appeared to be stop-and-go traffic in the middle of a highway in the desert. Immediately confusion and surprise fell upon him.

Why is the traffic stopped way out here in the middle of nowhere? And... I can't believe I am suddenly flying between slowing and stopped traffic at seventy-five miles per hour and I don't even know how I got here!

This maneuver would be dangerous enough for a very experienced and fully aware rider caught in this situation, but for Paul who didn't even know that he was there, in real-time taking such a risk, it was a jolting shock to his system. Instinctively, Paul began to slow down rapidly, squeezing the handbrake and downshifting in an automatic split-second fashion. The loud backfire from his Harley echoed off the cars on either side of him, bringing him now fully into his present situation. His adrenaline surged through his body in a burst, literally scaring him into reality.

The first sign of real combat to Earl Smoother came in a scenario that he never expected. Earl had been a loner his whole life, a recluse really. Over the years he came to find himself part of a family in the Patriot Movement as honest men and women gathered to discuss the concerns they had felt about the overreach of the federal government. They had well-attended rallies, drank a few beers, and seemed to be just good hard-working country folks. So, he initially joined one of the local militia groups in Oregon to train and eventually answered the urgent call to come and support the Cloyden's in making a stand for their property.

Earl had spent the night at the ranch and met a bunch of the nicest salt-of-the-earth type people, all saying the same thing. ENOUGH! This abuse needs to stop. He also wondered to himself, was the government abuse as widespread as some would say? Earl didn't know for sure. He suspected the truth was somewhere in the middle of all the talk, rumors, and conspiracy theories.

But Earl being a pragmatic man knew one thing today. His government was unlawfully pointing guns at its citizens and threatening to shoot them, shoot them dead. And he for one wasn't going to let that happen.

So, he decided to take an elevated position along the northbound bridge footing and laid prone with his AR15 taking aim over the heads of the protesters. Earl had only one thought as he lay there. *From here I wouldn't be able to hit much, but I can at least lay some cover fire down for the protesters if this goes bad.*

Through the corner of his eye, he saw a young girl approaching him out of the massive crowd. As she trotted towards him, he noticed just how young she was, about the age of his niece. For a moment he broke concentration from his target and looked up.

"Mister, hi! I have a phone call for you from my friends up on the bridge above us. They have something very urgent to tell you."

"What? Who? I don't know anybody up there?"

"Here -- just listen…" as she bends at the waist to hand Earl the phone.

Suddenly the young woman buckles at the knees and falls face-first into the desert sand, six inches from Earl Smoother's face. A shot rings out in the distance. Stunned, Earl began looking into Kelly's beautiful lifeless blue eyes, which were now dripping blood from her mouth.

Earl's last thoughts were in utter confusion and fear. Everything went dark as the second round delivered by the government overwatch hit its' intended target. The first two casualties of the

Battle of Bunkerville, as it will be called in the history books, lay lifeless in the desert sand.

"Target down," came the report from the spotter on the bluff.

"I would have had him on the first round if that fricken' little girl hadn't got in the way!" Responds the rifleman, in an effort to blame the girl and alleviate his guilty conscience for having shot down an innocent young teenager in the back.

"What's next," he asks coldly as the two surveil the horrific scene below them.

Within a millisecond of the first round fired, there was a full firefight occurring in the Touquap wash and the protesters were taking the brunt of it. Most had fallen to the ground to take cover. There were fallen women and children everywhere as the federal agents repeatedly fired blindly into the crowd.

Many of the horses had been shot too. Some of their riders had taken refuge behind their fallen bodies. Most of the horses had begun to flee the mayhem with or without their riders, some bucking and squealing from the burning pain of bullets hitting them in muscles and tendons if missing vital organs. Others trotting away only to succumb to their wounds a few short yards later, falling hard to the ground.

The Militia members who settled in under the furthest bridge returned fire in earnest and with surprising ability, even though it would be of minimal effect, due to the distance and range of their weapons. As the horses cleared, the feds had more time and cleaner targets in which to place their shots. Some of the men and women on the desert floor gathered themselves and returned fire with their pistols. Some from behind the bodies of the horses, and others still prone in the sand. This muster only drew attention from the overwatch who rapidly eliminated any target laying out in the open.

On the highway, O'Brian found himself tumbling painfully across the hard warm asphalt. He wasn't at all sure where he was or what was happening. He had laid his bike down as people began to slam on their breaks and in masse exit their cars. There was nothing he could maneuver around, so in desperation, he locked up his back tire and as the bike went down sliding, he was thrown off hurling over cars through the air, then instinctively in self-preservation mode, began rolling his torso as his body hit the ground's hard surface, until he came to a harsh rolling stop.

Still laying on his side, just off the road, he took his Bell helmet off and looked at his damaged bubble guards covering his elbows and knees that protected him from the hard concrete, along with his reinforced armored gloves, now scrapped and worn to a frazzle, attesting he'd escaped serious harm once again. It wasn't the first time he had survived dangers. Lifting his head to look, he couldn't see his fat boy anywhere and took it as a sign for another new beginning of some sort. But of what? – he had no clue.

As Paul painfully rose to his knees, he had just started to realize how fortunate he was to have miraculously survived, when he looked around to see there on the edge of the highway bridge a twelve-passenger van of school kids being riddled with bullets as blood visibly was seen splattering all over the interior windows. He now knew he was somehow in combat again. But was it real?

He looked in the direction of the gunfire and tried to assess what was happening. Then after dusting off the asphalt from his jeans, he did what he was trained to do. Run toward the oncoming fire.

Paul O'Brian sprinted hard through the highway medium to the northbound bridge. There, he harshly threw himself against the jersey barrier for cover. He wasn't sure what he was going to do, because he had no weapon, no plan, no opts or intel to guide him. He was simply running on instinct, training, and adrenaline. That's all he had.

At the bridge, strewn out were five others, two of which were firing out dozens and dozens of rounds into the desert. The third, a woman who was fully kitted out yet clearly in her first firefight, seldom returning fire and mostly keeping her head down. The fourth was a young man, a kid really, laying down on his back in fear with his arms wrapped around his rifle, looking scared to death. The last was a woman, holding a cell phone up over the jersey barrier in what appeared to be taking video footage, like some kind of family party or something.

Paul looked at the two men again and quickly determined that they were trained professionals and had combat experience. They must be doing some damage to the enemy below because this bridge was taking a lot of direct fire. Once Paul got his head about him and caught his breath, he carefully peered over the bridge to assess the situation further.

What he saw was disturbing carnage like he had never seen. Men, women, and horses lay strewn about the desert floor covered in blood. And, even worse were children lying dead or dying everywhere.

Who was killing them? It appeared to be some sort of law enforcement, but who? He couldn't see from the bridge.

They seemed to be focusing their fire at the three gunmen on the bridge and unknown targets under the bridge. Was it this unknown force that killed these civilians, or was it some kind of terrorist attack? He kept looking around for answers.

Then he saw some movement among the people pinned down in the wash below. A woman had jumped to her feet, out of fear to run for cover. She was middle-aged, pudgy, and slow-moving. No threat whatsoever. She was mercilessly gunned down by several rounds from the line of law enforcement. Shot in the back, she fell hard, dead before hitting the ground. That was all Paul needed to determine whose side he would rally.

Paul quickly crawled to the men on the bridge who had their hands full with the oncoming fire from below.

"Hey fellas, beautiful day isn't it!" declares Paul.

"Just fricken' peachy," replies McConnel as he fires eight more rounds down range at his target. Taking aim for another.

"What's all the ruckus about?" Paul asks.

"Hell, we were just standing up on the bridge here and them feds down below started killing all them protesters. So, we decide that wasn't okay, and we have them pinned down in that little valley below, trying to make 'em realize shooten' people is fucked-up." McConnel responded curtly between the labor of combat.

"Anything I can do to help?" Paul inquires.

"Can you shoot?"

"A little bit"

"I mostly hit what I aim for," Paul says with a sly grin.

"Well then, pick up that long gun right there and get to work," encourages McConnel.

"Have you ever shot a Creedmoor?" inquires McConnel setting his extra magazines next to Paul.

Before McConnel finishes his sentence, Paul had already fired fifteen rounds down range on target.

"Never mind," smiles McConnel

Now the four on the bridge get to work aggressively laying cover fire for the Militia below. The firefight begins to turn in their favor as the men below begin to press forward for a better advantage. The effectiveness of the quad on the bridge from an elevated position is devastating to the federal agents in the valley, which turns the focus of the Overwatch team to the bridge.

"Sniper!" cries out O'Brian at the top of his voice. —Each bolt sprinting for cover behind the barrier.

"Well, that assholes got our number!" exclaims Daniels.

"What'll we do?"

"We need to keep pressing or those fellas below are in for a shit full of hurt!"

"Where are they nested, anyone know?" asks Paul.

"They're up on the bluff," says McConnel, "we just don't have anything that can shoot that far."

Then for the first time, Paul recognizes the hardware wrapped in the youngster's arms as he takes more detailed notice of the kid again.

"Hey youngster, that's a pretty awesome long-range rife you got there. Do you know how to use it?"

"Pretty much," Linfield responds with a tremble of fear in his voice.

"You think you can point it at those men on the bluff and keep their heads down so we can end this thing?" Paul seriously inquires.

"Mister, I don't want to put my head up and lose half of it." Linfield states as a matter of fact.

"Understandable. But how about you stick your rifle barrel through that crack between the barriers and see if you can hit a target? Now, you don't need to kill anyone, just force them to keep their heads down for a few minutes. That will be enough."

"Killin' 'em would be alright with me," says Daniels with a grin.

"Don't pay any attention to this smart ass. Just see if you can keep them scared with their heads down and looking for you. They won't see you down here between the barriers and you'll have them scared to death trying to keep safe and hidden out of the fray. Trust me." Paul trying to be encouraging now.

Kevin Linfield obligingly swung around and laid out prone, scooted back some, so he could get his HAMR barrel through the crack between the barriers and still allow it to rest on its tripod legs. Taking his time, he searched the bluff until he found his target.

"I see them! They're just sitting there under a canopy at a table. It's like what I do at the range. They haven't taken cover or anything."

"Awesome, they are over-confident, thinking we have nothing that can reach them to counter-sniper," exclaims Paul.

"Shall I shoot?" Queries Linfield.

Not yet. Find something up there you can hit that will make some noise and let them know that they are being fired upon to wake them up and make them crap their pants! It can't be a real soft target because they'll never hear the report of your rife. So, it needs to make a lot of noise up there. Let me know when you find that target."

"That's easy. They have a pickup truck. I can break some glass, hit some metal."

"Excellent! Can you put a few rounds in the engine block? I wouldn't terribly mind having them walk back from up there." Paul's straight out laughing now.

"Don't shoot just yet. Let us get ready."

Turning to the other three. "Here is what we're going to do. First, load up with ammo and be ready to move. Get hydrated and eat something if you have it because we're going to need lots of energy. I want to spread out behind the barrier, enlarging the target area from where they have seen us pop up before.

Then when I give the word, the youngster will start shooting. That will give us maybe three minutes of uninterrupted time before they regroup up there and start targeting us again. During those three minutes, we will push hard with covering fire on the team in the valley, allowing the men below to press their advantage.

At the end of the three minutes, we'll drop back down behind the barrier and you two pointing at McConnel, and Daniels will rally to the north of the bridge with me for a flanking maneuver on the trucks below. Meanwhile, I want the two of you (Donahue and Linfield) to remain here on the bridge giving the impression we're all still up here." Pointing at Donahue, "that means you'll need to constantly move from position to position, firing, mimicking the four of us."

"Youngster, you just keep those ass wipes on the bluff moving positions and their heads down. If you don't, we'll all be in dead."

"What if they spot me and start shooting at my position?" Fear rising in Linfield's tone.

"Oh, you'll get fire and it'll be scary, but they will not be able to hit you. Without some sort of armor or getting up here on this bridge they'll never get you out of that position."

"What if they get up here?" presses Linfield.

"That will be her job to repel them," Paul points at Donahue.

"What if they do have armor and RPG or something?" Donahue concerned now.

"Run, like hell," Paul says clearly. "But they won't have any RPG's," smiling. "One last thing, keep your head on a swivel. There are a bunch of cops over there."

Pointing south, "if they come from anywhere, it'll be from there. If they come from the north, it'll be through us and you'll know because... well, they would have had to kill us... and we won't go easy. If the cops do surround you, just drop your weapons and surrender. Hopefully, they will just put you in jail for the rest of your life." Paul is grinning.

"Great, die here or die in prison. Not much of a choice." Linfield letting it all settle in.

"I'll die before I let them take me," says Donahue, trying to be strong.

"Okay, any questions? --- Three solid minutes of hell," Paul says as a last reminder.

"Let's go do some patriot shit!" Daniels exclaims.

Paul pauses for a moment as he thinks about Daniel's last statement.

"Okay, let's do some patriot shit! Take your positions."

Each of the five spread out along the jersey barrier, waiting for Paul's command. Paul uses his elbows to crawl over to Leah, who tried eavesdropping to hear their plans,

"Darling, I am not sure why you are up here or who you are. But all hell is going to break loose in a minute and you might want to find cover out of the fray."

★★

"I am a reporter and it's my job to be here for the public," Leah declares with childlike stubbornness.

"Okay, you have been warned, just stay out of our way," Paul says as he moves away to take his position. Mental note to self. Retrieve that phone from her dead body.

"Ready?" Paul asks of his newly formed team. Each nods their head and double grips their weapon out of the intensity of what is about to happen. With hand signals, Paul counts down.

Three.

Two.

One.

And just as promised, all hell breaks loose as Kevin Linfield hits on target the engine block of the truck on the bluff, with a thunderous explosion.

★★

GHOST PATRIOT

★★

Chapter 9

Flank the Flankers

The firefight was raging full force in the wash below, while high above sat the sharpshooters, far removed from the horrific scene in which they played such a deadly and vital role. The two men were positioned with their elbows resting on the folding table they had erected while peering through magnifying lenses in relative comfort, hidden under a shade cloth protecting them from the burning bright desert sun. It was more surreal than one could imagine, more like a video game than combat.

The spotter calling the target and the shooter taking careful aim, together in sinister harmony were orchestrating the needless deaths and destruction of people's lives. These "targets" were not some demonized enemy in a faraway land. No, they were neighbors, American citizens, everyday people, and families.

With each deadly round fired, the soul of the country separated from her constitutional underpinnings. The far-reaching consequences of the actions of these two men would result in unparalleled damage. If the country were to survive at all, it would be a miracle, because the republic will be shaken to its core and take 100 years to heal or more. But for now, 'they were just following orders.'

"Shooter, –female dressed in pink behind the brown horse," called out the spotter.

Referring to a middle-aged woman who was trapped in the open, dressed in a pink sort of Hollywood *Annie Oakley* outfit. After minutes of being in the crossfire, watching people fall all around her, she decided to pull her sidearm and shoot back. She was only to pull her trigger once before the sniper found his target.

"Tango eliminated," replies the rifleman.

"Next target."

At their feet and on the table lay dozens of ammo rounds. Most hitting and ending the lives below.

"Any activity on the bridge?"

"Na, they seemed to have found a hole or have left the area. No movement there."

Then came the silence between targets. PING… PING.

"What the hell was that?" queried the spotter, alarm setting in.

"We are being fired at!" declared the more experienced shooter.

Then as if carefully choreographed, in comes the confirmation. Crash, then two more. Crash, Crash. As the windows of their truck exploded with a booming blast, spraying broken glass through the air everywhere, they awaken in a panic.

"SNIPER FIRE!" screams the Shooter, and in one motion they instantly roll from their chairs, knocking over the table, the spotter's scope, and their supplies. The shooter rolls over into a prone position and keenly peers through his scope. *Where's it coming from, where's the sniper?* He is searching the ridgelines, the bridges, the wash.

Two more rounds come in hitting the dirt in front of him, blinding him for a second. He rolls to his left, one, two, three turns. "Shit, he's got us dialed in!" the shooter exclaims as he rolls. This causes the spotter to hit the ground again, as he was just beginning to gather himself and his equipment to go back to work. Fear settling into them both now.

Two more rounds hit the toppled table. "SHIT! Can you see him?" yells the spotter.

"No, fuck no. Every time I get my eye up to the glass, he lands a round next to me. He has us dialed in, but he must be really far off to not have hit us yet."

"After the next shot, let's move to that cover, and maybe together we can find him." The spotter pointing to the outcropping of jagged rocks in the sun, away from the vehicles and shade cloth.

Kevin Linfield was beginning to enjoy his task. He realized after the first five rounds that it would be easy to kill both those men. But playing with them was more fun.

For a moment he lifted his head from his rifle to see how the other four were doing. To his surprise there seemed to be hundreds of spent casings on the bridge as the four had stood to their feet and were laying down covering fire upon the officers in the little valley below. The four worked in military-style perfection, not saying a word, except to call out, 'MAG' to notify the others they were changing magazines.

Down below, the suppressing fire from the militia under the bridge in combination with the elevated position of the team of four above, allowed those caught out in the open to scurry to safety and be saved from the horror of the snipers on the bluff.

"KEEP FIRING KID!" Commanded O'Brian to Linfield. "The three minutes is not over."

Kevin returned to his duty as instructed, but this time he could not scope the two men on the bluff. He scanned back and forth, the massive ridgeline, the shot-up vehicles, the table… they had just vanished. "I can't find them, I've lost them." Yelled Linfield.

"Say again?" O'Brian replies, not able to hear over the noisy gunfire.

"They're gone!" Linfield says again.

"They're up there, flush 'em out, shoot the truck again, anything to stir them up from their hide," orders O'Brian.

Linfield takes aim at the truck again and begins to fire. *Shit, I messed up, I had them… I should have just killed them… I hope I don't get more people hurt down in the wash.*

The snipers had situated behind the rock outcropping and began to find targets.

"I have four active shooters standing on the bridge," reports the spotter.

"Negative, we need to find that sniper before we reveal our new hide."

"They are doing a lot of damage to our guys."

"Negative, call the drone pilot and ask for intel on the sniper."

"Our men are pinned down. We need to do something!" the spotter presses.

"Negative, find the sniper!" The shooter persisted, loud and clear.

Ping…Ping. "Oh shit, he hit the truck again." Crack, "Now the table, why is he shooting up our shit?"

"Oh… he doesn't know we moved fifty feet north! Good thing. This guy is no professional, or he wouldn't have revealed himself like that. Find him!" the Shooter again exclaims.

The two begin to search in earnest, with eagle-eyed diligence, but to no avail. A minute passes and they still can't spot Linfield.

"Okay, let's take the tango on the bridge. I'll work from right to left," commands the shooter.

"Okay, got him. Wind, three knots from the southwest, humidity…" the spotter dialing in the shot from their new strategic position.

"Wait, where did he go?" The shooter scans the bridge.

"Where did they all go?"

"They must have taken cover behind the jersey barrier, probably reloading," replies the spotter looking through his binoculars.

"Just wait and they'll pop up again."

"There they are!" exclaims Linfield. The quick reflection of sunlight, like a camera flash from the shooter's scope, was all he needed to retarget the men on the bluff. In their haste to move from shade to sunlight, the shooter forgot to shade his rife scope to compensate for the new position in the sun. Linfield has them in his sights now.

"I got 'em!" hollers Linfield to no one in particular.

"Give, 'em hell youngster!" hollers Donahue back. She is the only one left on the bridge now as the other three had moved north, flanking as planned, except for the reporter who surprisingly was in the same position as before, taking as much video as possible. *Is she dead, shot, or scared?* Donahue thought to herself.

No more playing around. It's time for them to quit killing people. Linfield takes direct aim at the men in the rocks.

O'Brian, Daniels, and McConnel had moved off the bridge and were resting and checking their ammo from a good secure position. They were still able to see the movement below them and noticed that the militia had moved forward pressing the agents hunkered down behind their trucks. "This should be over in a few," says Daniels.

"Let's just support them from here and bring this to conclusion without more bloodshed," replies O'Brian.

"I dunno, there seems to be a lot of bloodshed already," retorts Daniels as he points to the dead and dying in the wash below.

In the Touquap wash lay dozens of men, women, and horses in the desert sand. Under some of those bodies are children. It's sad to see their little limbs and bloody faces in the dust and dirt of the desert. They lay covered by the adults who attempted to protect them with their own bodies.

"There is some movement still down there," says O'Brian, as a horse not understanding what was happening is trying to respond to its instinct and flee. But it can't get up. Its' hindquarters lay limp on the desert floor.

"Hey, we have movement over here too," McConnel says in a quiet, yet serious voice.

"Whatcha got?" O'Brian inquires as the three scoot together to see what McConnel is alarmed about.

"It looks like a swat team. HRT probably," says McConnel as he views through his binoculars.

"Oh crap… these guys are the shit. They're recruited right out of every special operations unit in the military to defend civilians against terrorism," replies Daniels.

"The HRT *are* serious business," continues McConnel, "They are not like those dumb asses down there in the valley that started all this."

"HRT? Explain." Queries O'Brian as he grabs the binoculars from McConnel.

"The FBI's Hostage Rescue Team is the elite special operators of the FBI counter-terrorism unit. They are very good. They have seen real action in foreign countries like Iraq, Afghanistan, and places unmentioned, before retiring to a cushy job, killing terrorists in the United States."

"Well, they move like they are trained!" O'Brian Declares flatly. *Shit, some of these guys may have been on the TEAMS. We might have ate the same dirt.*

"Hey, why haven't you heard of the HRT?" asks Daniels.

"Yeah… I have been away for a while, living overseas. There is a bunch I don't know about the U.S. anymore. Waving his hand towards the bodies in the wash. My question is why are they here, in the middle of nowhere Nevada?" asks O'Brian pointedly.

Nice deflection. There is more to this guy than he lets on.
McConnel is thinking as he takes his Binoculars back and hands
them to Daniels.

"It looks like they are setting up to immediately flank the Militia
down below. If they do, it will be really bad," Daniels reports.

"They won't just arrest everybody?" Queries O'Brian.

"No, they'll shoot everybody, then arrest them. They are not
cops. They're counter-terrorists," Daniels says sarcastically.

"Well, we can't let that happen."

"I say let's flank the flankers," –McConnel chimes in with the
conversation.

O'Brian picks up the planning: "I am pretty sure they don't
know we're here, so surprise is on our side. We can use that surprise
to break them up. But, if they are as good as you say, that will only
be effective for a few minutes."

"Here is my recommendation. We set up an insurgency-style
attack, where one man breaks cover and fires on them as a unit
drawing all their attention to their rear and uphill, this should drive
them down the hill into the arms of the militia. When the first man
expends his magazine the next opens fire, then the third, each man
rolling down the hill pushing them down in retreat into the wash.
We'll use this strand of sagebrush to provide cover for our
movements."

"If we do this right, it will appear to them that we are a much
bigger force flanking them than they are, and they'll choose to
escape rather than fight." *I hope.* "Hopefully, Donahue and the
Militia can keep the agents in the Valley pinned down behind their
trucks to keep them from counter-attacking."

It'll work, or we will all die," McConnel says.

"Or she'll hold her ground AND we'll all die," replies Daniels.

"Let's do it!"

"I sure wish we had COMMS," says O'Brian, "I'd like to tell Donahue about the change in plans."

"We do! We have cell phones and radio comms, between us. I will let her know the plan," replies Daniels.

A few minutes later Daniels returns his attention to McConnel and O'Brian. "The cell phones are down. Probably jammed per FBI protocol. But we do have encrypted comms. Wasn't sure if she'd remember to turn it on."

"AND?" McConnel asks impatiently.

"She remembered her training and had it on. She is all set. I told her about the HRT and if all goes well, they will be dumping out into the wash like lost sheep running from wolves."

"Does she know what to do?"

"Don't kill 'em if she can help it. And let the Militia capture them," replies Daniels.

"What if the Militia kills them? Did that cross anyone's mind?" Asks McConnel.

"Na, they're Patriots, they won't just gun them down," Retorts Daniels.

"Are you sure? I really don't want a bunch of Americans – *some I may have served with* - on my conscience." Asks O'Brian

"Mostly," replies Daniels.

"Wonderful," replies McConnel.

"Good, let's take up positions!" orders O'Brian.

Up on the bridge, things are going as planned. Linfield has the Sniper team pinned down and ineffective. Donahue pops up and fires a few rounds from different positions just enough to keep the agents pinned down as the Militia Medics press forward moving the survivors out of harm's way. This phase of the mission seemed to be almost complete when a whistle came from Leah Scrivener, which instantly got both Donahue's and Linfield's attention.

"There is somebody over *there*." Scrivener pointing south and towards the medium between the north and southbound lanes.

The sniper team on the bluff had initially requested intel support from the drone pilot that circled above surveying the entire operation. The pilot reported back that there were three snipers on the bridge and most likely the position that had them pinned down. Two ambitious sheriff deputies who had been sidelined by the undersheriff's orders took it upon themselves to take a look. As soon as they were spotted, both Linfield with his side-arm and Donahue with her AR opened fire, wounding one deputy and scaring the hell out of them both. They beat a hasty retreat back to the Sheriff's command center but had the intel they needed.

As soon as the deputy's intel was received on the bluff, the government sniper team began searching the bridge in earnest. And within a few minutes, they located the muzzle flash of Linfield's HAMR.

"Got him!" declares the spotter triumphantly. There is a crack in the Jersey Barrier on the Northbound Bridge 150 feet from the south end of the barrier. See it?"

"No."

"Wait for the next flash. Wait, Wait…. THERE!"

Before the rifleman could squeeze the trigger the rocks in front of him exploded. Shrapnel of rock, and bullet fragments peppered his face and blinded him. The spotter took a bullet fragment in the face, ripping through his cheek, cutting his jaw and tongue.

Linfield not really sure what had happened to the two men he could see through his rifle scope. They both just disappeared from his view. Did I hit them? No way I got them both? For ten minutes Kevin Lindfield never broke his steady gaze at the one rocky outcropping on that desert bluff.

"I think I got them… I THINK I GOT THEM!" Linfield screamed.

Then two fist pumps into the air "Good! Get over here and help me!" replies Donahue.

The three men had silently taken their place in the brush south of the HRT team while moving cautiously and quietly into position above the Militia members below. Each of the eight team members was taken by complete surprise when O'Brian opened fire revealing himself from cover as he took careful aim to hit his target on their body armor or a non-vital target like a limb. He was an excellent shot, but nothing is guaranteed in combat. His fear – *that he knew one of these guys* – he couldn't add more trauma to his fragile PTSD. Was it guilt? Self-preservation? He didn't know what was informing every squeeze of the trigger, but it was working.

O'Brian sent eight rounds down range hitting three targets. The HRT was scrambling to return fire when Daniels opened up to a more devastating artillery fire on the men. He took no care at targeting and if he had been the first shooter that caught the team by surprise, he may have killed most of them. The intensity of his bullet blasts and placements was overwhelming and completely silenced their return fire. Now all O'Brian could hear were the cries of pain and the familiar sound of team members commanding retreat to the valley to get protection.

McConnel now began his targeting of the fleeing men wearing black with their faces covered. Two men dragging one by his body armor vest while two more covered their rear. The three men in front covered their flank at the same time blazing a path to their destination. O'Brian could see McConnel was tempering his fire as well, having several clear shots at the men dragging their friend and holding fire.

Now came O'Brian's second turn. He had stealthily moved through the brush down the hill and once again surprised the HRT with his firing from a new vantage point. He barely got three rounds off before the three men in the front of the retreat opened up their weapons in automatic, enhancing their counterattack to provide the most devastating defensive maneuver mid-retreat. O'Brian threw himself to the ground to avoid the onslaught.

Daniels took that as his cue and didn't even bother to lift his head. Opening fire blindly at the men from his new position, who now had broken into an almost panicked full run, splitting their group in half. The first three charging down the hill, the remaining five slowed by the injured man. Fortunately, Daniels shot at the sound of them running and not the men, never seeing the men left behind who would probably have been mowed down otherwise, succumbing to his lack of restraint.

McConnel concluded the operation by firing at the feet of the last five men, effectively driving them downhill and into the wash. There they rallied together to fight their next threat from the advancing Militia. It was surreal as the Feds circled up in the desert sand, they resembled the artist renderings that O'Brian had seen in school of Custer's last stand. Eight lonely men facing death, as they were surrounded by superior forces in elevated positions from the bridge above, the sagebrush on the hill over them, and the advancing militia in the wash below. The HRT was boxed in on three sides, with nowhere to go.

But death never came. The Militia members held their fire and waited. Then came a voice from under the bridge somewhere.

"Lay down your weapons."

There was no response. Then came a rife report from the bridge above.

And desert dust flew in the covered faces of the HRT.

"Lay down your weapons," comes a female voice from the bridge.

A long uncomfortable pause of indecision follows.

Then came a louder more fearsome CRACK. Linfield now letting his scoped rifle accuracy be known – that he had the commander and his team targeted and "dialed in". The bullet from Linfield's HAMR landed smack between the legs of the HRT commander.

"The next one will be in one of your heads," says the female voice of Donahue way above the wash.

There was another long disconcerting pause of silence.

Nothing but the breeze and one far-off calf calling to its mother could be heard. A reminder of what they were all there for in the first place. Cows. One man's cows. And now in the desert sand, lay the dead and injured bodies of dozens and dozens of American citizens, law enforcement agents, and horses.

Finally, what seemed like a terribly tense standoff ended, as one by one the HRT laid down their weapons and raised their hands.

"You men behind the trucks, you too. Lay down your weapons and come out," Donahue called out again.

"We're wounded," came the reply.

"Throw out your weapons and come join the others. If you can't walk, we'll give you quarter. We just want this to end!" Donahue again forcibly demands.

Slowly, each of the men and women behind the trucks in that little valley began to emerge and gather with their hands up. As they did the Militia medics ran towards the wounded officers to give aid. The other militia effectively stripped the law enforcement team of their weapons and piled them in a heap on the desert floor.

The survivors proceeded to see who, if any, were still alive among those laying in the Touquap wash. Then began the screams of horror and wailing, as the survivors found their loved ones dead, along with cries of "Medic!" from those discovering the many seriously hurt and wounded needing medical attention.

Daniels, O'Brian, and McConnel returned to the bridge to meet up with Donahue and Linfield. As they do, Linfield says, "I need to get down there and see if Kelly is okay."

As he turns to leave, "No, you can't," says O'Brian —"we need to exfil." And he grabs Linfield's shoulder.

"What?"

"We got to go. In a few minutes, there will be cops everywhere. They will be arresting everyone, and we were in the shit here. There is no time. We gotta go *now*," O'Brian says firmly.

"I don't care, I got to see if she's okay," argues Linfield.

"She's not..." says Daniels

"What do you mean? How do you know?"

"She died getting the phone to the Militia guys down there. Daniels pointing to the wash. The sniper got her."

"Oh, no..." is all Linfield could say as the devasting reality finally hits him.

Then from down in the Touquap wash came a blood curtly cry of anguish drawing away their attention for a minute. Amos and Colleen had heard about the battle at the stage and jumped into a nearby truck to arrive too late.

"NO, NO GOD, NO!" It was Amos Cloyden and his wife Colleen holding tightly to one another as they began to wade through the bodies of the dead and wounded. But their grief was not over their two sons who lay together dead in the desert floor. It was the sight of Julia, Jeffrey, Susie, and Billy's lifeless bodies lying in the Nevada dust, with the blood from their wounds crusted over from the desert sand. Next to them lay their father. Amos dropped to his knees and wept uncontrollably.

"What did I do? A whole family? What did I do?"

"You didn't do it, those tyr... Those tyrants did it," Colleen consoling her husband.

Then came a voice from behind them. "Mr. Cloyden, you are under arrest, please stand up," came the gentle but firm voice of a Sheriff's deputy.

"We gotta go! Who's got transportation?" asks O'Brian frantically.

"We do," says Daniels.

"So do I," McConnel responds.

"I have an old truck," describes Linfield.

"I do too!" Scrivener gleefully chimes in, with camera still in hand.

Everyone turns to look at the reporter in shock, surprised that she was still on the bridge with them.

"I'll need a ride with one of you!" O'Brian declares flatly.

"Let's all meet at the truck stop in Mesquite north of here. Make only one call to loved ones as soon as you can get cell service. Say absolutely nothing more than 'You are okay and that you will need to go offline for a while. Just try not to worry.' NOTHING MORE! This is *really* important; I'll explain more when we meet."

"Well, I need to call my editor and she'll need…" Scrivener interrupts, thinking about her own agenda, not the horrific scene at hand.

O'Brian took two steps forward and forcefully takes Scrivener's phone from her hand, remembering the mental note he made to himself.

"Hey, what the fuck. Give me that back!" as she charged him. O'Brian took one move using her momentum and pushed her, pulled her, and dropped her allowing her to fall hard to the ground. If you saw the move in person, you would really not know what you just saw. One second, she was on her feet, the next she was in pain on the ground and you're not sure what happened.

Then O'Brian squats down to be eye level with Leah and speaks quietly, deliberately:

"This is where we part ways. You don't know us, you never saw us, we … are … ghosts. I am surprised you lived through this day, but this is where it ends. Can I trust you?"

"Yes," Leah responds like a petulant child.

"I hope so. Because like a ghost, I have a way of coming back to haunt those who violate my trust."

"But I need my phone!" Scrivener cries as O'Brian stands tall and turns to walk away.

The five separate and head to their perspective vehicles. O'Brian decided to join young Linfield and got in his truck for the trip north to Mesquite. Along the way, they were surprised to see all the people walking north toward Mesquite, most abandoning their vehicles in the southbound lanes.

In the northbound lanes, there were some vehicles, mostly four-wheelers who turned around across the medium and headed away from the blocked bridges. Local radio stations were announcing the closure of Highway 15 North and Southbound lanes.

"Please stay clear as police and fire units are streamlining into the area," The announcer declared.

"Well hell, that didn't take long," Linfield said as a matter of fact.

"Yep, we got to keep moving," O'Brian replied.

"You're from around here, right? Got any idea where we can hide out for a while? Somewhere off the grid and without many people?"

"Sure do. I know just the place. It's the ranch where I work. It's remote, really remote. And the owners always welcome strays," Linfield happily declares.

"How far is it?"

"About five hours. It's in northern Nevada."

Humm, real remote? That might be good. A ranch means food and supplies. We might need to stay a long while.

"Do you need to make a call?" asked O'Brian.

"No, the only ones who love me are at the ranch and I'll see them soon enough. They didn't even know I went to this protest... Five hours," he says with a smile.

Now transportation. How do we get there undetected? O'Brian is making plans in his head.

"How old is this truck?"

"It's a '78."

"Any modifications, radios, tracking systems?"

"Nope?"

"Good."

"How about you? Who are you going to call?" asks Linfield.

"Nobody," replies O'Brian "There! – park over there," pointing with his finger urgently, "in case they have cameras mounted on the front of the building. Do you have an ATM card or Credit cards?"

"Just ATM cards."
"Okay, go get all the cash you can out of your accounts. Everything the machine will allow. Then, hurry off and tell Daniels and Donahue to do the same. Oh, have them leave their keys in the ignition and their credit cards on the seat in their truck, and be sure to leave the doors unlocked."

"Someone might take their truck if they do that," says Linfield

"Hopefully– meanwhile I'll find McConnel. Also, have everyone gather their weapons, ammo, and necessities and meet back here at your truck. Oh, one last thing... got any duct tape and a hammer?"

"Yep, in the truck box."

Ten minutes later everyone gathered at the Linfield truck. Each carrying duffle bags, pelican cases, and rifle covers.

"Everyone got everything they need – Money, guns, ammo, clothes? We're not coming back here or going home." Heads all shaking in the affirmative.

"Okay good, did you leave your keys in the ignition and the cards in your truck?"

"Are we leaving our trucks here? Ain't somebody going to steal them?"

"That's the plan," replies O'Brian.

"Okay, I just need your cell phones. All of them." Each dropped their phones into a plastic shopping bag O'Brian was holding along with the duct tape.

"Powered on, right?"

"This sure is weird?" Linfield asks bewildered while dropping his phone in the bag.

"I'll explain on the way. Okay –throw everything else in the truck and find a comfortable seat. We have a very long trip ahead of us."

"How long?" O'Brian looks at Linfield.

"Five hours," Linfield replies.

O'Brian abruptly turns on his heels and walks off into the sea of parked semi-trucks resting at the truck stop.

"Where is he going?" asks McConnel

"No clue," Daniels responds.

Paul searches for long-haul rigs with license plates from distant states as far away as possible. Then shimmies under four different tractors and tapes a phone securely to the frame. The fifth phone, Scriveners, he first powers off then takes a hammer to it and finely smashes it into pieces no bigger than a quarter. Then he flushes it in separate piles down the nasty toilets, just on the edge of the parking lot.

On the last phone – his phone- he uses the speed dial to call his ex. His daughter answers.

"Daddy, are you here? I can't wait any longer."

"Honey, I have been delayed. I won't be there today."

"Daddy, you promised! you promised!" beginning to whine.

"I know but something has come up and…."

His ex-wife comes on the line, "Where are you?"

"I'm not going to make it"

"What the fuck, WHY NOT?"

"I have been in an acci…." He thought better of his response. "I have been called into a situation…"

"You said you quit, you retired, you were done. FUCK YOU!"

Paul paused.

"You promised your daughter." The phone went dead in his ear.

*Crap. This is **not** how I wanted today to go.* Paul lamented wondering what he could have said different in this situation.

O'Brian taped his phone to a Canadian rig he spotted from Quebec, then trotted back to Linfield's truck and piled into the passenger side. Linfield immediately started the engine and pulled out of the Truckstop. O'Brian coincidently noticed one of the trucks carrying a phone was right in front of them, turning onto the highway in the same direction. *This is good* O'Brian thinks to himself while smirking.

Donahue was the first to speak as they settled into the drive. "Ahh, I have some questions. Where are we going? Why are we leaving our trucks and credit cards behind? Why don't we each head home and just forget this thing ever happened?"

O'Brian soberly answered: "It may not have sunk in, but we just shot and maybe killed a bunch of federal agents. The government will not take that lightly and in short order will have every resource available at their disposal hunting us down. Soon we will be the most wanted people in the world."

"Our only hope is to disappear, which frankly will be impossible. People saw us, there was most likely drone or satellite images of us, body cams, or dashcam images. I don't know, but some dead yahoo in that wash just may have taken a cell phone image of you before it all started. I honestly don't know, but it's possible."

"And somehow, they *will* figure it out. Then they will turn our world upside down. Each of us will be targeted, and they'll sweat our families, our employers, bankers, everyone we innocently opened a door at the Seven Eleven for, until we are triangulated, found, arrested, and put behind bars."

"Then there's that abrasive pesky know-it-all reporter. She'll be all over the news by 5 p.m. today making up crazy shit about us. Whatever life you had… it's now gone."

"Oh, crap," is all that Donahue replied as it sunk in.

The truck just bounced along in complete silence for what seemed like hours.

McConnel eventually breaks the silence: "Why didn't we take my truck instead of this piece of shit?" Kevin looks in his mirror disapprovingly.

"This vehicle is an electronic black hole. No computers, RFI chips, Cell Phone receivers, or Sat Nav. Same reason I took your phones. We must remain off the grid and under the radar."

"To get rid of them?" Linfield asked.

"No, to cause a diversion and buy us time to confuse our hunters, the Feds. Because once they account for everyone in the wash, they will begin to track everyone they don't have their hands on. That's us. We fall into that category."

"So, I left our phones powered on and taped them to long haul trucks. By the time they track us, it will look like we split up and headed in several different directions. Once they find each truck the phones are taped to, they'll impound them and forensically go through them, buying us some time."

"The same logic applies to the vehicles and credit cards. Hopefully, they'll end up in the hands of some dirtbags who saw the opportunity we left for them. Hopefully, the vehicles will go one way and the plastic another. Again, buying us more time."

"The last place they will know for sure we were, was in a Mesquite truck stop at roughly the same time. And, they *will* assume we were working together once they figure out who we are. And they **WILL** figure it out."

"Seems like you've done this before," McConnel says quietly with tongue in cheek.

"That reminds me. No more sharing information about or with one another. The less each of us knows about each other, the better."

"Why?" Linfield asks.

"Because if one of us gets caught, you may be persuaded to reveal intel about the others. The less you know the better we each are," replies O'Brian.

"That being said, I do need to separately interview each of you for security."

"What the hell does that mean? Why should we trust you? I just met you this morning, now I am in a truck going somewhere, nowhere, as the most wanted woman in America or the world, hell the universe! Why should I tell you anything?" Donahue raising her panic-stricken voice in fear. Then breaking down, sobs.

"I get it, this sucks. What I want to know are things like – How did you come to be on that bridge today? Who knew you'd be there? Stuff like that. I need to interview you separately from the others to silo the information between us. Then I can reasonably form a larger plan knowing what we might expect."

"I don't want, nor should I know any more than that about each of you. For all the same reasons I stated. One last thing. Together we need to come up with a believable cover story for the owner of the ranch where we are going and anyone else we meet. Something convincing, that will mitigate any questions. So, let's talk that through as we drive."

"You don't want to interview us now?" asked Daniels.

★★

"No, we'll wait till morning, once we all have had some rest and food."

"I think you should be a group of hunters who broke down along the side of the road…" Linfield floated to the group.

GHOST
PATRIOT

Chapter 10

Open Borders

Jim Johnson was in the middle of a conference call, an intense briefing with DHS regarding the Border Patrol Agents shooting incident on the southern border when Kathy interrupted.

It must be important if she is barging in like this, Johnson acknowledges.

Kathy bends down to whisper in Jim's ear.

"There has been a shooting. A mass shooting."

Not another school shooting. Johnson immediately thinks to himself horrified.

"In Bunkerville, Nevada. Many federal agents were involved, including the HRT. You better get ahead of it."

Right on cue Jim's cell phone instantly begins to ring. It's the White House. Jim abruptly stands to his feet and steps into the hall to hear the voice on the other end. Kathy looks on curiously.

As he takes the phone from his ear Kathy breaks the silence. "Well?"

"They want me in The Situation Room right away," Jim responds.

"I'll notify your detail." Kathy starts quickly moving towards her desk.

Forty minutes later Jim Johnson settles into a seat at the conference table in The Situation Room, located in the West Wing Basement, officially known as the John F. Kennedy Conference Room run by National Security. Next to him is Neil Cornwall of the Bureau of Land Management.

Crap, this is all your doing and now we got to clean up your mess! As Jim nods his head in greeting Cornwall. Also, at the table is the NSA director, Secretary of the Interior, and the Head of Homeland Security.

Then the door burst open loudly, and in came striding the Chief of Staff Theodore Smith and right behind him, President Mountebank. Everyone rose to their feet. Out of the corner of his eye, Jim noticed Cornwall was a bit slow coming to his feet.

You have a seat at the table now goofball, better make the best of it... of course, he won't. Jim smiles to himself.

Before POTUS even sat down the President starts right in.

"Anyone want to tell me what's going on in Nevada?" Interrupting the commotion of everyone taking their seat.

A stunned quiet settled over the room, as no one was quite sure how to answer or who the question was directed at.

After a moment, Jim took the lead.

"Well Ms. President, we are just getting reports in from the ground at Bunkerville. A small community in the Southern Desert about one and a half hours drive time out of Las Vegas, Nevada. Federal agents from the BLM were in the middle of impound operations regarding the trespassing of cattle on public land in the area..."

"BLM?!" the President interrupted.

The Chief of Staff began to squirm in his seat like he was about to respond.

Jim Johnson beat him to the answer.

"It's the Bureau of Land Management, part of the Department of the Interior."

"Not Black Lives Matter." Smith trying to look knowledgeable.

Jim continued. "The BLM was in the middle of impound operations when they were confronted by protestors, some of which were armed. The situation escalated and shots were fired. Apparently, many civilians have been shot and killed or gravely injured. I do not have numbers yet, because the situation is very fluid."

"Well, who the hell is in charge out there? Where is the commander on the ground? Let's get some answers!" interjects the President.

"Yes, on my way over here I arranged a cell phone uplink with a Sheriff Gillette, the local Sheriff of Clark County. Let me get him on the screen here..."

"I don't want to talk to some country bumpkin Sheriff. Don't we have one of *our* people? One of those BLM people?" interrupts the President again.

"He's mortally wounded," Jim replies a little annoyed. "The highest-ranked official on the scene there is the Sheriff, and he has taken command of the situation."

"Well, can't we get the FBI out there on the scene, I mean shit, aren't you the 'acting' head of the FBI…? Get your people on it!" The President is even more agitated now.

"It's a jurisdictional issue. There are FBI agents already on scene, but they seem to be in custody, as well as the ring leaders of the protest. It's a massive horrific crime scene and the Sheriff is pissed off and detaining everyone, until he can get to the bottom of the whole fiasco."

"WHAT THE FUCK ARE YOU SAYING TO ME?!" Screams the President at Johnson.

Gathering her composure, she leans in. "What is the FBI doing there?"

"Why are they in custody?"

"Who started this shit show?"

"What are we doing to get control of the mess?"

The media is going to have a field day with this. POTUS worries.

"I have Sheriff Gillette on the line." Interrupts the technician who works full time in The Situation Room. Everyone turns their attention to the screen at the end of the conference table.

"Hello, Sheriff Gillette … I understand you have a terrible situation there. How can we help?" begins the President.

"You can help by keeping your fucking so-called law enforcement agents out of my county," replies the Sheriff.

"Excuse me?" responds the President.

"Look, Miss… err… Mizz President, I have 182 dead here. Many more critically wounded, including that asshat Agent Dodger of yours. My undersheriff is dead along with many other deputies that I sent in to deescalate this situation. I have detained your FBI Hostage Rescue Team and some of the other BLM agents…"

"What about the Terrorists? Have you arrested any of them?" interrupts the BLM Chief Cornwall.

"Yes, we have disarmed and detained those who are carrying weapons. Though some of them had already left the scene before I arrived to take control. I have asked the Nevada Highway Patrol to set up checkpoints in a ten-mile radius. And my deputies have been dispatched to support those efforts to detain any participants in the protest. We need to look at everyone as a potential suspect or material witness. But I want to stress again you need to keep your feds out of this area."

"Why exactly, do you want us to do that? the President pressing now.

"Because my Head Deputy, Undersheriff Roberts, was killed, and your agents played a key role in this deadly screwup. As a result, my deputies are irate and the tension here is sky-high. You see, I command an agency of over fifty-eight hundred people, and we have more resources here than you could muster in time to do any good. Right now, we need to evac the survivors and secure the scene. We'll figure out who the lawbreakers are later. More disruption will not help." The Sheriff beginning to calm his demeanor.

"Sheriff, I don't know if you remember me? We met at an awards luncheon last year. I am Jim Johnson with the FBI. I understand your situation and fully respect it. Would it be alright if I fly out and liaison with you and our intel sources to capture the rabbits? Just me, no one else, no team or entourage?" asks Jim pressing.

"I remember you, Jim. Okay then, but just you – no one else. I am not going to put up with your feds and your high-pressure tactics. Got it?" replies the Sherriff sternly.

"Got it. I'll see you in the morning" – The screen went blank.

"It was disconnected from the other end," announced the technician. "Shall I get him back?"

No one answered. Everyone in the situation room sat quietly, stunned really, at the disastrous news they just heard.

The silence is broken by the Department of Homeland Security Director.

"May I suggest Ms. President that our department takes the lead here and works closely with NSA and the FBI, the Department of Interior to hunt down the perpetrators. These terrorists need to be found and brought to justice immediately. The American public will be screaming for their heads in a matter of hours. Of course, I'll loop the DOJ in to expedite the warrants for surveillance we need."

"Yes, yes. Do whatever you need to do to find these terrorists... these domestic terrorists and bring them to justice. OUR JUSTICE. Not some hick sheriff's idea of justice."

 Turning back to Johnson, "you go out there and get our agents out of this lunatics hands. Who does this 'Sheriff' think he is, holding our guys like common criminals? Make that your number one priority. If that Sherriff doesn't let them go immediately, arrest him on the spot!" *You can do that... you are the FBI can't you?*

"Let me get on the ground in Las Vegas and I'll do my best," replies Johnson.

As the President rises, everyone else rises to their feet. POTUS looks at Johnson.

"No, it needs to be better than your best. GET IT DONE! Our guys need to be on your plane when you return to DC!" The President briskly turns toward the door and departs.

Chief of Staff Smith looks at the Secretary of the Interior and says, "Stick around, we'll want to see you in the Oval Office. Oh, and bring him with you." Smith points at the BLM chief.

Johnson caught the grin of absolute glee on Cornwall's face, as he gathered his things and walked out. *I hope he doesn't pee himself!*

Dallas, Texas

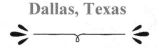

The men had arrived in their safe house in the suburb community of Plano, after their arduous two-thousand-mile-long journey, walking with a caravan from El Salvador. It was important for each of them to blend in with the nearly three thousand men, women, and children who were fleeing the economic poverty of their homeland in search of a new and better life in America. They were tired, dirty, and hungry from the covert circuitous route they had taken, splitting up and then rejoining their group to avoid any detection of their infiltration into the "Great Satan," The United States of America.

Their current stop wasn't like anything any of them had personally experienced before. It was a beautiful five-bedroom home, four full baths, and a large, fenced yard. Four thousand, two hundred square feet in total and each bedroom comfortably fit four single beds and even the office and formal dining room had beds in them. Enough beds for thirty-one men.

Their rest was broken when through the front door came their host. Jamil Roberts was a thirty-year-old American citizen who had been born and raised in Plano, Texas. His mother was an immigrant from Egypt, and he had an American father. He was born with every advantage, attending Plano East Senior High School, then went on to attend Texas Christian University (TCU) where he studied International Business.

He had lived the coveted upper-middle-class life that all those immigrants from El Salvador were fleeing to. He and his parents ironically had achieved exactly what so many desired for their own family. Freedom to live and thrive in the greatest nation in the history of mankind. Yet he and his house guests were there in an American suburb to bring it down to its knees, maybe even to its end.

For years the Muslim Brotherhood had strategically planned and infiltrated American life. They had placed men and women in significant positions throughout the American landscape. As a group, they had positioned leaders in every major city in the US. They worked quietly under the radar, yet boldly recruiting men, just like Jamil to their cause.

Individual cells had no actual knowledge of each other, yet when it came time to act, they knew their jobs and what to do to usher in the Caliphate, their utopian idea of theocracy, that was found in their holy book, the Qur'an. Oddly this was all orchestrated by one man, Mohammed Haasan, who oddly enough lives in Huntington Beach, California, just two blocks from the world-famous surf spots of Southern California. By an irony, this leader also came from Egypt.

As the leader of the Brotherhood, he quickly rose to power during the 'Arab Spring' in 2011. He had led an organized revolt of young Egyptians to overthrow the longtime dictator Hosni Mubarak. At the time Haasan found a sympathetic position with President Barack Obama, who saw the Muslim Brotherhood as an oppressed people and not the solidifying terrorist group that President Mubarak knew they were. They found the geopolitical time was right to take power in Egypt.

And then, arose the 'Arab Spring' across the entire middle east. Mubarak was eventually "encouraged" to leave power by the United States under the Obama Administration and a newly elected Muslim Brotherhood government was installed. But in the end, all the Egyptian people did was trade one oppressive government for another, and the new government was much, much worse.

The enemies of the Muslim Brotherhood, Christians, and nonbelievers were rounded up, beaten, and publicly executed in the streets. This oppression was even too much for the powerful Egyptian Military who executed a coup d'état against the Muslim Brotherhood government and eventually established a democracy of sorts. By 2014, the leadership of the Muslim Brotherhood was forced to flee the middle east countries of the 'Arab Spring'.

Many found their way to the United States under the friendly and misguided Obama administration. In just a few short years the Brotherhood had metastasized into a full-blown foreign terrorist ring throughout the United States and Canada. Now after eight years of politically conservative power in Washington, DC, the pendulum had swung the other way, ushering in a weak liberal government ruling in the halls of Washington, DC, and now was time to bring the "Great Satan" to its end.

"I have Breakfast," announced Jamil as he pushed the front door open. By design the houseguests had been arriving all night and into the very early morning, getting everyone indoors before the neighborhood began to stir and take notice.

"I have hummus, fruit, dates, tea, and some coffee," Jamil announce more loudly as he slammed the door. He was thrilled to have these men in his presence. They were heroes in his mind and martyrs in his heart. They deserved respect.

Abdula, as he was known, was the first to wander into the kitchen. He was slowly waking up. "Got any donuts?" asked Abdula.

"Donuts? I didn't think you'd want food like…" responded Jamil.

"Yeah, good American donuts, I've always wanted to eat one." Abdula was disappointed.

"I'll make a list of food for you. You go get."

"Ah, okay," replied Jamil, a bit confused. He had put so much thought into his menu selections.

In the background, he could hear Arabic. Jamil wasn't bilingual so he wasn't sure. Maybe it was Farsi.

"ENGLISH ONLY!" yelled Abdula. "We are in America now, bring no attention to yourself!"

Abdula turned to Jamil. "We will be here three nights then we be gone. Have a special guest coming, once we meet him you will never see us again."

"Really, who's coming?" Jamil inquired curiously.

"Special Guest, that all you need to know. You just get us food and clean up after us... Like a woman," Abdula said with a sly smirk.

"You got cable?" comes a voice from the living room. "What the passcode?"

"It's 1234," replies Jamil.

Within minutes Jamil hears the unmistakable slurping and moaning sounds of pornography on the television. Jamil grabs the car keys and heads out the door.

Oh wow, donuts, and porn. I thought we were to remain pure and good Muslims. As Jamil starts his car to head to the nearest Dunkin' Donuts.

John Clayton lived catty-corner from the Safe House and was juggling his coffee and other belongings as he was opening the door to his Ford F250 Super Duty pickup truck. He noticed Jamil heading out of his driveway when another man exited the front door and gave him a piece of paper. Clayton had yet to meet the young man who had just moved on to his street. He was waiting for the right opportunity to shake his hand and welcome him to the neighborhood.

He noticed that the other man looked of Arabic descent, not Mexican. And, until now the young man seemed to live alone in that big house. Clayton, never put much thought into it just assuming that his family was yet to join him. But as the other man trotted back to the house, he could swear he could see several other men milling around inside as the front door briefly opened and shut.

Oh, sure hope it's not some kind of Frat house. John thought.

John fired up his truck and eased it down the road. It had the Power Stroke Diesel in it and was a bit loud in the mornings. He didn't want to wake the neighborhood.

Three blocks away, he made his ritual stop at the local Dunkin' Donuts. *I need to quit this,* he chased himself. *But it is a Cops and Donut thing,* justifying his unhealthy choice.

As he swung himself out of the truck, firmly placing on his cream white 10x Rancher Stetson he recently picked up from the Stetson showroom factory just a few blocks down from his office, he then strapped on his "second belt," which is the standard Ranger gun belt, holstering his Sig Sauer firearm, before fastening his badge to his shirt, just above his left pocket, and headed out in his polished two hundred dollar Justin Marbled Deerlite Western Cowboy Boots.

As John entered the Donut Shop, he noticed his young neighbor at the counter picking up four big boxes of donuts. Jamil was just turning to head out when Clayton stepped directly into his path.

"I've been wanting to meet you," John begins.

"Me, really, why?" Jamil immediately sees his badge and becomes tense.

"Well, I'm your neighbor and I wanted to welcome you to the neighborhood." John sticks out his hand.

"Oh, a' Oh, nice to meet you," unsure how to reach for John's hand and hang on to the boxes of donuts.

"Here let me help you," interrupts John as he grabs two of the boxes. "I'll walk you to your car."

"No need, I got ..." It was too late. John already had the donuts and was holding the door for Jamil with a big friendly smile on his face. The two headed to Jamil's car.

"So, you're a cop?" inquires Jamil

"Nope, I'm a Texas Ranger."

"Isn't that a cop?" Jamil queries.

"No, we're better than cops. We chase the really bad guys." Clayton smugly answers.

"I guess it's good I'm not a bad guy."

"Yep, cuz I'd even bust my neighbor." Clayton realizes that this kid is nervous. "Who are all the donuts for? I noticed your family hasn't moved in yet."

Jamil stutters. "No, no, my family is moving in next month. I'm just getting the house ready."

"Oh, really how old are your kids?"

"Five and Seven, a boy and a girl." Jamil had practiced this many times.

★★★

"Oh, great my kids are the same age. They'll be happy to have playmates on the street." Clayton was lying now. His two boys were in High School.

"Oh, yeah, that'll be nice." Jamil loading the boxes into his back seat.

"Well, you sure must like donuts since you're alone."

"Just don't tell my wife, she'd kill me." Jamil thinking he was pretty smart.

"Okay, I'll see you this weekend... If you don't mind the wife has made you a welcome gift."

"Ah, no, this weekend will not be good. I'll be gone. Maybe the next weekend."

Okay, I'll see you then," finished John.

That guy is a liar. John acknowledges to himself assessing the conversation.

But why is he lying?

Thirty minutes later Captain John Clayton arrived in the Garland office of the Texas Rangers. The only thing on his mind was the thought-provoking morning encounter with his neighbor. As he came through the door, he heard the friendly voice of his assistant Charlie, "Good Morning, Chief."

"Assemble the team in the conference room. I think we have something of priority," Clayton Commands

"Yes sir."

"Oh, and good morning," Clayton says with a genuine smile.

Minutes later the senior team of the Garland field office of the Texas Rangers had assembled in their conference room. Captain Clayton got straight to the point.

"I think we might have a terror cell operating in Plano," Clayton announces dramatically for effect.

"Where?" asks the Sargent.

"Plano...It's right across the street from my house," replies Clayton.

"Holy Crap!" replies the Sergeant as the remainder of the men roll their eyes.

Clayton begins, "Here is what I know. About four weeks ago a lone male, that goes by the name of Jamil moved into a five-bedroom house across and just a bit down the street from my house. Today there are multiple combat-age males quietly residing in the

★★★

★★

house, all the curtains are closed and there is just one vehicle in the driveway. The one that suspect Jamil drives."

"In a casual 'neighborly' interview with the suspect, he was very nervous and evasive. I also caught him in at least three separate lies."

The Sergeant interrupts, "That's not much to go on, to call a guy a terrorist. I mean he could be gay and living with his boyfriends. Or they are growing pot or something. There are a lot of things that would cause this guy to be nervous and lie to a Ranger wearing a gun and badge."

"You're right of course," replied Clayton.

"But whatever it is, it ain't right and I don't want it happening on MY street. Let's dig into it."

The Lieutenant, who had been sitting there quietly spoke up. "Guys, I have worked with our Capt'n for eighteen years. If he has a hunch that there is a terrorist cell in Plano, we better take it seriously. His hunches are usually better than most intel."

Looking each man directly in the eye. "If he says dig into it, we dig deep."

Lieutenant Davis continues, "Riggs, I want you to find out everything there is to know about that house, absolutely everything! From when they grazed cows on that land up to this morning. Who owns it, who'd they buy it from... hell, who their decorator is."

"Smitty, I want you to uncover everything about this Jamil guy. Right down to his curlies. Family history, education, friends, lovers, all of it."

"Kinum, you're on the car. Same thing. Case it all down, RFI chips, sat-nav and all."

"And I want detailed records on what all of you come up with regarding financials, any banks, credit cards, and anything relating to or about your assignments."

"The rest of you set up full surveillance on that house. Track every car that comes and goes 24/7. Trace his cell phone, eves drop with parabolic mics, drones, the whole works. See how we might get eyes in there."

"On your way over there, swing into the donut shop and see if by luck he paid by credit card. Make sure you get the warrants you need first. Don't be lazy and mess this up by not crossing your t's and dotting your i's."

★★

"John, can we use your house for surveillance?"

"No, it's not in direct line of sight," replies Clayton.

"Fine, we'll use the van," referring to their surveillance van that looks like a plumber's truck.

"What about the safety of my neighbors?" John inquires. "Should we move them out?"

"No, we don't know what we have yet. Besides most of your whole street goes to work during the day. We should be fine," replies the Lieutenant.

"Let's go. I want a report in two hours."

Clayton picks up his phone to call his wife. "Honey, I would like you to gather your things and head over to your sister's…"

Two Hours Later:

Lieutenant Davis sits down in Captain Clayton's office. "Here is what we know so far. The suspect Jamil Roberts is an American Citizen, born here in Texas, Plano in fact. His Mom immigrated from Egypt in 1985 and soon thereafter married her one and only American, Joe Roberts. They met at Texas Tech and eventually settled in Plano, where their only son, Jamil was born."

"He grew up a straight American kid, went to High School then on to TCU. He works here in McKinney as a business analyst for Simpson Strong-Tie. He is NOT married, has NO kids, and has never left the country, nor even applied for a passport. He banks with Chase Bank and has about nine thousand dollars in the bank. All seems to have come from his biweekly paychecks."

"He was living with mom and dad until about four weeks ago, it appears from the debit card records when his purchases began to centralize in your area of town. This gives us a clear picture, that is when he began to reside in the house across from you."

"So, who owns the house?" asks Clayton.

"That's where it gets weird. The house was on the market about six months ago. The family who lived there were relocated for the husband's job and the house came up for sale."

"The Adams, we knew them," interrupted Clayton.

"Yes, the Adams house sat on the market for a while, then right after the Real Estate Agent's listing expired it was immediately purchased, leaving the agent out of ever meeting the buyer. We contacted the old owner, Mr. Adams and he said he never met the buyer either. The sale was all done through the escrow company in

California. In looking at the title deed it seems that a holding company in Nevada bought the house and the corporate resident agent in Nevada signed all the documents."

"Who owns the holding company?" Clayton pressed.

"Another company in Delaware, who is owned by a company in Wyoming, and so forth. Basically, it's a set of shell companies. None of the corporate resident agents live in any of these states, nor have they ever laid eyes on a real human that owns any of these shell companies."

"So, it's a dead end." – Clayton surmising.

"Not quite, the money that paid for these shell companies all came from one place. First Bank in Huntington Beach, California."

"And the account holder?" Clayton Pressed.

"We don't know yet. First Bank wants us to get a warrant. That will take a day or two."

"And the Car?" asked Captain Clayton.

Looking at his notes: "The car is registered to Jamil Roberts. He bought it off the showroom floor in Dallas. He makes his payments faithfully. Nothing very odd about it. Though it does have a GPS and we're trying to get the car's whereabouts over the last four to six weeks."

"That's pretty good work in two hours. What about the surveillance team? Anything from them?" asks the Captain.

"No, not yet. They are just setting up outside. They did find out that the suspect paid cash for the donuts. But we have got his account records now anyway," replied the LT.

"Okay, my suggestion is to pull this kid in and interview him in front of his parents. Let's see if we can flip him. It looks like he was just an average Texas kid. I'll bet he was radicalized somehow and may not realize just how deep he has gotten himself in… to whatever 'it' is. If we can get the parents in on this maybe they will help" Clayton advises.

"Radicalized? Let's be careful about 'profiling' him." Smirks the LT in sarcasm. Then he continues. "I like your approach. How should we begin?" asks the LT awaiting the next steps.

"You and one other Ranger go to the parents' house tonight and have a talk with them. Then, see if we can get the mom to demand the suspect come to the house tonight. When he does, confront him. Use the time there effectively to see what his computer browsing looks like… you better take a tech too. If he flips, wrap a wire on him immediately and send him back in. If not, cuff him and the parents up right there, on suspicion of terrorism."

"We can take them out of circulation for seventy-two hours, the weekend is coming up so we can get a couple more days out of holding them, while we investigate. Let's just keep them safe in lock-up. If they do end up in lock-up, make sure there is active listening on their phones and any visitors. We need to keep a tight lid on all this."

"If he ends up disappearing, won't that spook the others in the house?" asks the LT.

"Likely, let's have SWAT on standby in case they rabbit. We'll need to pick them all up and sort it out if they leave the house. But my hunch is they won't. They have no vehicles and if they are who I think they are, they'll stay put, waiting for orders. Surveillance needs to get a handle on how many are in there, and most importantly if they are armed, no matter what."

"Oh and get on that bank in California. That is the best lead we have. Good job." Clayton encouraging the Lieutenant.

At six p.m. at the Roberts home in East Plano came a solid rap at the door. Mrs. Roberts opened the door with a friendly smile.

"Hello, may I help you?" she asks.

"Hello ma'am, we're with the Texas Rangers." Each man removed their hats in courtesy of meeting a lady.

"May we come in?"

"Sure, is there something wrong?" she asked with concern.

"Is your husband home?" replies Davis.

"Bob, can you come into the Livingroom? The Texas Rangers are here."

"What did you say? It sounded like you said the Texas Rang…" replies Bob Roberts.

"Mr., Mrs. Roberts, I am Lieutenant Davis, this is Ranger Wilson and Technician Chang, we're with the Texas Rangers. We have come to visit with you about your son Jamil."

Mrs. Roberts gasped, "Is he okay?"

"Physically, he's fine. But he's gotten himself in trouble." Davis responds firmly.

"I was afraid he'd get himself into trouble when he converted to Islam," replies Mrs. Roberts.

"Oh, we understood you immigrated from Egypt. Are you not Muslim?" queries Davis.

"No, not at all. I converted to Christianity, that's why I fled Egypt because of the persecution I experienced because of my conversion. We're both Christians," Mrs. Roberts firmly replied.

"What does all of this have to do with Jamil?"

"Well, ma'am we believe he is involved with some Muslim Terrorists that are all living in a house not too far from here. Are you aware of any of this?"

"Is it that big house he just moved into?" inquired Bob Roberts.

"Have you been there?" asked Davis.

"I have. I helped him move his things there. We were very upset with him after he became a Muslim, he became very different."

"How do you mean?"

"He's always been a bit of a loner. Never really fit in. Never had a girlfriend or very many friends since High School. He began to spend all his extra time in his room and on his computer. He became darker and darker, his mood I mean. Then once he declared he was Muslim, we tried to talk sense into him, but he just got more petulant and disrespectful."

"I tried to appeal to him. He grew up as a Christian and I grew up in an Islamic country. I know what this is all about. This is absolutely the worse decision he could make."

Mrs. Roberts beginning to cry, now.

"So, what's he into now?" asks Bob Roberts.

"We're not real sure. We need to talk to him. You mentioned his computer. Is it still here in the house?" asked Davis.

"The desktop is still in his room, but he took his laptop," replied Mr. Roberts.

"May we look at it?"

"Sure, it's in his room down the hall."

Wilson and Chang immediately headed down the hall.

"May I sit down?" asked Davis still holding his hat.

Mrs. Roberts motioned to the open chair behind him.

Lt. Davis settled in to make his important plea to Jamil's parents.

"Mr. and Mrs. Roberts, I think we can save Jamil. But we need your help. I think if the three of us sit him down and help him understand how he can mitigate his involvement in this."

★★★

"Is he going to prison?" asked Mr. Roberts. "I don't know. We just don't know enough details. But I do know that the longer he stays involved the worse it will be for him. What I need to do is talk to him. Can you help me connect with him?"

"What do you want us to do?" asked Bob Roberts.

"I would like you to invite him over here. Tell him it's very critical that he comes tonight. Make him believe you're sick, or something. Just that he needs to come over tonight. When he gets here, we'll lay it all on the table and see if we can talk some sense into him. If we can, it might just save his life. If not, he may end up in prison for decades or even worse."

"Worse, than prison? What could be worse than prison?" blurts Mrs. Roberts, sobbing now in worry.

"Dead, he could end up dead. He is mixed up with some very bad people!" Davis sternly declares for effect. Yet, knowing it could be a lie.

Mrs. Roberts falling into her husband's arm crying inconsolably. "I'll call Jamil and get him over here," replies Jamil's dad.

Thirty minutes later, the lights of Jamil's car flashes across the front windows of his boyhood home as he pulls up the driveway. *Humm, I wonder whose SUV that is?* Wonders Jamil as he notices the Rangers vehicle in his parents' drive.

Jamil enters the front door without knocking. It's his house too after all.

"Mom, what's going on?" Jamil asks as he walks into the dining room where she, his father, and the strange man are sitting. He immediately notices she'd been crying.

"Are you sick? Dad said something about someone being…"

"Jamil, please sit down." Instructs his father, solemnly.

Jamil is concerned now. "What's wrong?" as he takes his seat.

"Jamil, I asked you here because your mom and I are very concerned… we're concerned about these men you are living with," Jamil's dad begins.

"Men, what men?" Jamil is trying to catch up playing confused.

"Please don't deny it, Lieutenant Davis here has told us all about what's going on."

"What? Who?" looking at the man at the table with them.

"I don't understand. I thought mom was sick or something…?"

LT. Davis begins. "Son, we know what's been going on. We have had you and your house under surveillance for weeks now. There is no point in denying it."

"I am sorry, who are you?" for the first time noticing the badge on Davis' shirt. "Are you some kind of cop?"

"Texas Ranger," replies Davis. "We know you are mixed up with terrorists and we, your parents and I, want to help you before it's too late."

"So, you're not sick?" Jamil asks his mom incredulously.

Then as if on cue, the other two men enter the room carrying Jamil's desktop computer.

"We have everything we need. The whole thing, messages, emails timelines," declares Wilson, in a lie. "We're going to seize this as evidence and do a complete forensic work-up on it.

The situation becomes instantly clear to Jamil Roberts. The cops are investigating him, and they have duped his parents into helping them.

"No dude, you're lying. There is nothing on that computer except for some old computer games I used to play in high school," Jamil smugly replies.

But Chang was ready for the denial. "That's true. But your MAC Tower here and all your Apple hardware are synchronized to your laptop and your phone. So, if I have one device, I can see all your devices. Their history, calls, and well... everything," Chang was doubling down on Wilson's ruse.

"You're busted kid!" Wilson drives home the point.

As the two turn to head to the SUV with the computer, they close by saying – "you better take the deal."

Jamil takes a long reflective moment to think.

He turns to his parents. "How could you do this, betray me like this?"

Then Davis takes control of the conversation. The next two hours become a verbal cat and mouse game of interrogation.

Davis began by asking some basic questions of Jamil. Things the investigation already determined.

"When did you move into the house?"

"Just the one car in the driveway?"

"Where Jamil worked."

This was to develop a baseline in the interrogation. With each question Davis would watch particularly to see if Jamil's eyes moved right, activating his memory center in his brain. Or left, which is a sign that he was using the creative center of his brain and in fact, making something up. This continued for about fifteen minutes. Often repeating the same questions in a slightly different manner.

Then Davis started asking more detailed questions.

"Who are the men in the house?

"When did they move in?"

"How many are there?

"What are their plans?"

Each question building upon the previous one and with each answer is revealed just a bit more about the crimes.

Then Davis moves quickly to his confrontation of Jamil's role. He lays out what he presumably knows Jamil has done. That Jamil will be in prison for the rest of his life and there is no hope for his future. This portion was extremely difficult for his parents.

The more Davis spelled out Jamil's bleak future the more inconsolable his mom would become. This was particularly effective on Jamil. He was torn between the loyalty he pledged in his newfound religion and the pain he was inflicting on his parents.

Jamil was feeling trapped. He was fidgety, licking his lips and often dropping his head into the palms of his hands in frustration. Davis had seen this before; it was textbook Reid Interrogation Technique behavior that he learned in training. Then came the words Davis had been waiting for.

"It wasn't like that…" Jamil whispered under his breath.

Suddenly there was a change in tone from LT. Davis.

"I know son, this isn't completely your fault. You have been brainwashed by these guys. They have you believing a lie about the Muslim Religion. It's actually a religion of peace. They have you duped into believing this fundamentalist stuff. You don't realize it but it's all mind control."

Davis goes on developing his made-up theme in order to develop some hope in Jamil's' heart. It was working on his parents too. Davis extends his hand and puts it on Jamil's shoulder as a sign of empathy and understanding. All the while making a mental note

★★

that Jamil is making no denials to Davis' largely made-up allegations.

Jamil is becoming unsure of himself now and is beginning to lose his resolve. He begins to ask questions about this idea of mind control and the religion of peace. He begins to harken back to the time in his life when things were not so tumultuous. Trying desperately to reconcile it all.

Davis now begins to present alternatives to Jamil and his family. He offers ways to escape their terror and shame. Jamil quickly takes the exit in front of him and begs the question. "What should I do?"

Davis' expert training kicked in and suppresses his desire to present his ultimate goal, wrapping a wire around Jamil to get the evidence they need. Instead, he methodically reveals his plan. Each request is a bit more intense than the last.

Then Jamil hesitates, "Maybe I should just wait and…"

Davis quickly interrupts him. He knows if the word lawyer comes up, all his progress in the last two hours will be lost, and the interrogation must legally end.

"Jamil, I have a way out for you. Just listen for a second. I need you to help us and in exchange, I'll help you."

"Listen to the man," pleads Jamil's mom in desperation.

LT. Davis places his cell phone on the table and only now begins to record the conversation.

"What I need you to do is help me nail these guys who have brainwashed you," Davis continues with the plan to give them the information they need. It involves dead drops at Dunkin Donuts, willing wiretaps, and micro cameras in the house. And of course, his testimony in the trial. He'll want hard evidence of movements, weapons, names, and network.

Then comes the final ask. Davis presents it very casually. "Of course, you'll be wired for your safety."

"Wait… what? If they catch me with a wire, they'll kill me?"

"No, the wire is for your safety. We'll be right outside at all times. If anything goes wrong, we'll be crashing in the front door!" Davis knowingly exaggerates.

"How will you know if I'm in danger?"

"We'll give you a safe word, a code word, that if at any time you use it, we'll be there."

★★

Jamil's mom is thinking now. "Maybe we should talk to somebody a lawyer or something," fearing for Jamil's safety.

Davis heads that idea off again. "Jamil this is your only chance. If you don't take it then I'll have no other choice but to take you and your parents into custody right now. You will all be going to prison."

Davis looks at Wilson and Chang in the other room. The two rise to their feet and walk in with handcuffs in hand.

"No, it's cool. I'll do it." Jamil replies in a defeated tone.

Chapter 11

The Second Shift

After a long bumpy ride with perceptive life-changing conversations, and pondering soul searching, the journey presses on, to an obscure and desolate lonely ranch in the far northern plains of Nevada, just miles from the small country town of Battle Mountain. Leah Scrivener quietly peeked out from underneath the tarp covering her at Mt. Tobin.

Where the hell are we? Hell… I guess. It had been a long cold night in the back of the truck in which she was a stowaway, and to make matters worse, they were still moving.

The last couple of hours on the journey, after they'd turned off the pavement was even more painful, as she bounced and slid hard from side to side on the bumpy ditch-filled dirt roads. The sun was just coming up over the mountain range as she glanced at her watch and realized it was 5:47 a.m. *Shit, no sleep at all. I wonder where we could be?*

Suddenly, the truck took a hard pull to the right and immediately thundered the beats of the wooden planks, as the tires went over them one by one, till they crossed the cattle guard. Then gently they came to a stop. The truck was greeted by what seemed like a dozen dogs, sounding the alarm to their owners that strangers had arrived on the premises. As the truck doors opened and the occupants began to stretch and disembark their "chariot", Linfield gave a quick warning.

"Stay in the truck a minute. I need to properly greet the security team," mentions Linfield.

Leah realized the dogs had stopped barking. It was silent, except for Linfield's movement as he swung his legs straight out from the truck. Then the low growling came from under the truck, first one, then two, then more.

"It's all right guys. It's me. That'll do," came a quiet, calming voice from Linfield.

Linfield had only walked ten feet when the rambunctious dogs emerged from under the truck. A couple were hesitant at first, most greeted him with wagging tails. Soon they all joined in and surrounded Linfield in the joyous greetings that only dogs can give to a long-lost friend.

"It's okay now!" Hollered Linfield to the occupants of the truck, having greeted the security team.

"That's a hell of a welcoming party," chuckles O'Brian, as he stretches and wipes his eyes, being the next out of the truck.

Linfield is now completely on his knees being lovingly mauled by the pack of ranch dogs. About ten in all, McNab's, Queensland's, an Australian Shepherd, and a couple of Border Collies, who were circling the pack trying to keep them together out of their intense instinct.

"WHO's OUT THERE?" comes an old strong voice from the opening door of the house about ten yards away.

"It's me Pop!" hollers back Linfield. "I brought some friends."

"Well, you'd better get 'em all in here, we just started breakfast," comes back as the front door slams loudly, behind the voice.

As the four men and one woman emerge from the truck, each stretch and try to understand exactly where they are.

O'Brian had begun to head to the front door. "No-- this way," instructs Linfield pointing, "we'll go through the Ranch Hand's entrance. It's around back."

O'Brian changes direction and the remainder follow Linfield to the rear of the house. The whole pack of dogs follows, just happy to have the attention of new friends.

As they circled to the rear of the house, they came across a big wooden porch and several horses saddled and tied to the grain feed trough just at the entrance to the steps leading up onto the porch and the main door entering the house. Inside came soft sounds of several people stirring and laughing. The familiar clanging of dishes and general comments like "who wants more ham?" and "fresh pot of coffee ready".

It was like an old western movie or something out of times long past. Maybe a touch of nostalgia flickered in the air as the soft glow

★★★

of interior light streamed out onto the porch interrupted by the shadows of bodies moving inside.

"Follow me," says Linfield, as he skips with familiarity every other step bounding up and onto the porch.

"Hungry? You are in for a treat."

Linfield opens the Ranch Hand's door and peels his cowboy hat off all at once, wipes his feet thoroughly, and greets the men inside. Around the big table are five men of differing ages. The oldest sits at the head of the table. Whisking in from the kitchen is an older woman, in her mid-sixties, moving at an unfettered pace serving and clearing away dirty dishes all in one fell swoop.

"Morn'n," greets Linfield.

"Where the hell were you all night?" answers one man at the table.

"LANGUAGE!" comes sternly from the woman in the kitchen.

"Looks like he got him too much to drink or maybe a little filly" came another.

"Cowboys…" scolds the old man at the head of the table. "I am sure Kevin has an explanation. Sit down and eat some breakfast."

"Pop, I brought some friends with me. Can I introduce them?" replies Linfield.

Pop respectfully stands to his feet and greets the other four. "Welcome, welcome. You're all welcome here. com'on in."

The remaining four enter through the door and follow Kevin's courteous manners in wiping their feet and removing their hats.

"Hungry? I bet you are. These fellas were just leavin' and we'll have room at the table."

As if on cue, the four men rose to their feet and scuffled to the doorway. A couple still stuffing food into their mouth.

"Momma! The second shift just arrived," yells Pop into the kitchen.

"I HEARD, I heard," replies the strong female voice.

"Kevin, you get your guests some hot coffee and clear that table for my food," she instructs Linfield from the kitchen.

"Have a seat." Pop invites the guests to sit down.

Outside they can hear the galloping hoofbeats of the other men on their horses riding off for the days-work, as the sun begins full light to the ranch. The dogs yipping in glee as they follow the cowboys. Soon it got quiet outside once again.

★★★

"Pop, momma, let me introduce you to my friends," says Kevin Linfield.

Momma steps into the kitchen doorway as Kevin is pouring coffee.

"This here is Kristen Donahue, and her boyfriend Patrick Daniels, they are from Idaho."

"This one is John McConnel, also from Idaho. And last but not least, Paul O'Brian from ….?"

"Las Vegas," replies Paul.

"Idaho? I chased cows up in Challis, Idaho when I was a kid," Pop replies matter of fact, trying to find a connection between them.

"Well, I am from Challis. Never Cowboy'd though," replies McConnel. "I know a few."

"This is Chuck and Dorthey Timmons. They own this whole ranch," Linfield continues. "Most of us call them Pop and Momma if you live and work here."

"It's nice to meet you all," replies Dorthey, "this is our home, and everyone is welcome."

"Till they ain't," mutters Chuck underneath his breath.

"It's nice to have another woman here," looking at Kristen, Dorthey continues ignoring her husband.

"What's your line of work up in Challis?" asks Pop of McConnel.

"I am retired Military. Me and my wife just wanted a quiet place to live after all the 'World Travels' I did, serving."

"How about you two?" Looking to Donahue and Daniels, "What's your story?"

"We're from Hayden, I am a retired Marine. Kristen here is a mom and a Patriot." Kristen smiled. She liked the reference.

"And you Mr. O'Brian, you seem to be the quiet one."

O'Brian looked up from the plate that was just put in front of him. His mouth was full of the best ham he ever tasted. "I'm just a dad from Las Vegas. Unemployed right now." A little food noticeably lingering in the corner of his mouth.

"So how did you all meet?" came the question that O'Brian dreaded.

Kevin Linfield fielded that one. He spent the next twenty minutes telling Chuck and then eventually Dorthey Timmons as she joined the group at the table, the entire "cover" story of the eventful never-to-be-forgotten red-letter day before. Leaving out some of the more terrible details for the sake of Momma's conscience.

The two older hosts listened intently and asked a few clarifying questions along the way. Kristen noticed there wasn't an ounce of judgment in their questions. They just wanted to understand what transpired. But, as Kevin's recollection progressed, Dorthey's countenance began to fall, and worry came over her face.

O'Brian noticed it too. "Ma'am, we don't need to stay here long. We just need a place to rest then we'll move along. We don't want to put you to any trouble."

"No, you staying here is not my concern. It's all the tragedy. The death and pain of so many. That's what grieves me. You're Welc…"

Pop interrupts. "Let us seek the Lord on the best course of action. We'll tell you at supper what He says."

"I'm sorry who?" McConnel obviously confused.

"They are going to pray about it," Kevin chimes in.

"Oh, I see," McConnel replies under his breath, hesitantly. *Who does that anymore?*

"I bet you're tired. Let's find you a place to bunk down." Pop slowly rising to his feet.

"Kristen, of course, you'll stay in the house with us. The crew bunkhouse is no place for a lady," redirects Dorthey.

As the men walked out into the morning air of spring, the "house dogs" broke the still morning yet again.

"Now who? We got more visitors today than in a month!" exclaims Pop."

That's probably very true. Kevin reflects on the last time they had anyone come to visit their very remote ranch.

As the group walked around to the front of the house, they noticed the dogs circling Kevin's old truck. They're sounding the alarm. There is something amiss.

"Them dogs seem to think we're still in the truck," states Patrick Daniels observing.

"Somebody is, my dogs don't bark at cows, dear, antelope, or any other creature than strangers," replies Pop.

Before Pop had even finished his sentence, O'Brian had pulled his Glock from his concealed holster in the middle of his waistband at his back and had it trained on the truck. He slowly circled to his

★★★

right, away from the group to the corner panel of the truck at about fifteen feet. The dogs sensing the tension from the men increase their cries, barks, and yips.

Pop, stepping onto the front porch seemed to be retreating.

Good, I'd hate for the old man to get hurt. Thought McConnel. A split-second later Pop was holding a 12-gauge pump-action Mossberg 590 with a pistol grip.

Well dam, Where the hell was he hiding that? McConnel replies to himself impressed.

Pop racks a round in the chamber. It's an intimidating loud sound for sure. If you know it.

"Whoever is there -- you better come out slowly. We have guns on you, and I don't like trespassers!" Pop hollers.

It was still quiet, no response. Pop was starting to wonder if his dogs got it wrong.

"I'm going to send my dogs into that truck. They'll bite you. They'll bite you good!"

Still nothing... not even a stir.

"Susie, Johnny, away to me," commanded Pop. The two Queensland's sprung straight from the ground and onto the truck bedsides. Each caught their front feet over the edge of the bedside then used their hind feet to propel themselves over the top, leaving scratch marks in the old truck's paint from their hind claws. It was an impressive feat to see two blue merle, stocky muscular dogs spring flat-footed four or five feet into the air on command like that, especially without a running start.

Daniels noticed to himself that this old truck had many similar scratches on her, all around the exterior of the truck bed. *The dogs must do this often.* He thought to himself.

As soon as the two dogs cleared the top, they were in the bed growling and snapping their massive jaws. Tearing ferociously at the tarpaulin that was covering Leah. It sounded like a terrible feeding frenzy, screams of fear and pain coming from within the truck bed and the aggressiveness of the dogs, growling and snapping.

Then frantically came, "Get them off, get them off!" screamed the female voice from the truck bed.

★★★

"Susie, Johnny, that'll do!" Once again commanded Pop. The two dogs instantly stopped and laid down in place in the truck, eyes fixed on Leah, waiting for their next command.

"I give up. Make them stop!" Leah was crying in earnest now.

"Come on out. You have guns pointed at you and both dogs are not done with you," instructs Pop.

Leah Scrivener slowly untangles herself from the tattered Tarpaulin and says while sobbing. "I can't get up -- they're lying on the tarp," referring to the two forty-pound dogs laying in position. "They're too heavy."

"Susie, come," commands Pop.

Out flies the female Queensland from the truck and trots to Pop's feet, assuming a heel position.

"Now come on out," commands Pop once again sternly to Leah.

Slowly Leah's head emerges from the truck bed. She is disheveled and red-eyed from crying and fear.

"Move slow," once again Pop instructs.

"You sic'd your dogs on me!" whining now. "How could you?"

At that moment O'Brian recognized her. "Oh, shit!" and drops his weapon barrel and assumes a ready position.

"Do you know this woman? Friend of yours?" asks Pop.

"We know her, we thought we were rid of her," replies Linfield. "She's no danger Pop. You can drop your shotgun."

"I need an ambulance. Those dogs attacked me," Leah being self-righteous.

"Oh, you don't have a scratch on you," replies Pop as he casually turns away toward the porch.

"Johnny, Come!" The male Queensland that had remained in the truck sprang to his feet and seemed to fly right out of the truck and to Pop's side in a heel position along with Susie. It shook up Leah once again. She let out another whimper.

"I need to go to the hospital right now!" Leah demanded like a petulant child.

"Oh, stop, –you don't have a mark on you," replied Pop even more sternly. This time no longer holding the Mossberg. There was no need.

Where did the shotgun go? Wonders McConnel still amazed at what just happened.

★★

"Check yourself out. If you find one scratch on you from my dogs, I'll personally take you to the hospital and pay for it." Pop now getting annoyed with the demanding attitude of this young woman.

Daniels was wildly curious as he watched Leah stand next to the truck and examine herself for bite wounds. *Odd, I don't see a scratch on her. Just as the old man said. Humph. But it sounded like she was being eaten alive.*

Leah was finally satisfied that physically she was okay but decided to carry on playing the victim card she always used.

"Well, I don't seem to be too hurt. But I should be taken to the hospital anyway just to be checked out for sure."

"The Hospital is fifty miles down that road. Get to walking," replies Linfield as he begins to remove his belongings from the truck. Daniels and McConnel join him.

Leah just indecisively stands near the truck and contemplates her next move. *Walk, stay, or make more demands.*

O'Brian sees what she is thinking and approaches her while holstering his Glock. "I told you if you ever were to see me again, you would regret it."

"You took my phone… I want it back," whimpers Leah, very scared.

"Regret is all you will get. Regret is all you deserve," replies O'Brian to the frightened reporter as he begins to walk toward the truck and help the other men unload.

Out comes Dorthey and Kristen through the front, in response to the talking they heard from the guest bedroom window that was to be Kristen's accommodations.

"Oh, shit!" declares Kristen loudly.

"Language," counters Momma.

"Sorry, it's just that we thought we were rid of this crazy bitc..."

"Language," counters Momma again with a courteous smile.

"Looks like we have another house guest," mentions Pop as he walks past the two women passing one another. "Missy, grab your things and I'll show you where you're going to bed down in the house."

"Com'on Cowboys, I'll take you to your luxury suite," laughs Pop as he walks off to a cluster of buildings about a hundred yards away from the house. The four men follow.

★★

Daniels cautiously looks back and hollers to his girlfriend. "Keep an eye on her. No phone, internet, or carrier Pidgeon's," referring to Scrivener.

"Good call," states O'Brian as they continue following Pop. "She could literally be the death of us."

Pop, not being as deaf as Dorthey thinks, overhears the comments about the young woman.

What have they gotten themselves into with this young lady? He ponders.

Chapter 12

They're Just a Myth

Sunny Saturday in June – Portland, Oregon

A*Oh, my, she is beautiful!* Mike Simpson admired his stunning daughter as she emerged from the dressing room on the day of her wedding. He had waited, planned his whole life for this moment. *This is what it's all about.*

He and his wife Susie had spent their entire modest life working in the hope to get to these moments. *These moments are what make life worth living.* He thought to himself.

Mike's daughter smiled a broad smile as she looked at her daddy, a man of sixty-seven, strong and confident. A good man, a daddy who loved his two little girls and absolutely adored his wife of forty-one years. She could tell he was so very proud of her as he quietly choked back the tears of joy.

Get it together dad, you need to be there for her. This day is about her, not you. Mike admonished himself.

"You look radiant!" Mike declared sincerely as he looked into his daughter's face.

All at once, her lifetime of growing up flashed through his mind's eye. Her birth, losing her first tooth, riding her bike without training wheels, soccer games, and waiting up late into the night for her to come home from, who knows where, when she was in High School. And now, another milestone.

"Are you sure this is the guy?"

"Oh, Daddy, of course, he is. I held him to the highest standard and he eventually met that standard," was her confident reply as they began that traditional walk down the center aisle of the old Presbyterian Church in downtown Portland.

"Oh, what standard was that?"

"It was *you* daddy; I wanted a husband just like you. I want a marriage just like yours and mommas. I wanted the fairytale, just like you have," she was whispering now as their friends and family rose to their feet.

The organ plays, *Here Comes the Bride*. That was it, he lost it, breaking down and the tears started flowing. He bit his lower lip so hard he could taste a little blood.

"Great– I was trying to hold it together," Mike mutters under his breath.

"It's my job."

"What's that?" as he looks at his daughter.

"Making grown men cry in public." She pulled her daddy tighter this time with both hands.

In the front row, on the bride's side was Susie Simpson standing proud and strong as she relished the scene unfolding in front of her very eyes. Her oldest daughter was making the most important decision of her life. To promise herself to one man for the remainder of their lives. A promise she would not take lightly, that Susie was sure of.

She took a quick glance over her left shoulder to be sure their youngest daughter was allowing this moment to be seared into her psyche. And she was, smiling in adoration of her older sister's graceful poise as she walked down the aisle in chic elegance. Then looking back to her right again, she noticed Mike, *oh god, he is sobbing again. He is such a wuss when it comes to those girls of his.* She thought. *I do love that man.*

Mike took his place next to Susie.

"Here, you big baby," Susie hands him a white handkerchief from her pocket.

"Had it all ready, didn't you?" Mike says sarcastically. Susie just smiled back.

"Who gives this woman to this man?" comes the question from the Pastor.

"We do," answers Mike and Susie in unison. With that response the responsibility God had given them to raise their daughter ended. They looked at each other knowing, it was a job well done.

Later that evening Mike and Susie were at their hotel reflecting on the day's events.

"What a beautiful, fantastic day this was!" Susie being very sanguine as she was putting her make-up on. "Everything was just, just perfect. And the flowers…"

Mike cuts her off, "Are you about ready? We do have reservations at 8 p.m."

"Just about. Where are you taking me?"

"I'm not telling, and you aren't going to trick me that easily. I've not been tricked by the best of them," referring to the inmates where he once worked.

Mike was a retired Captain at the Oregon State Prison outside of his home in Eastern Oregon. It was not a job he ever thought he would take, let alone spend his lifetime doing. But when he was young, he needed to feed his family, so he applied. To his surprise they actually hired him. Then just like that, twenty years went by, and they gave him a pension, and the next season of his life began.

He and Susie had an austere life. Mike putting in his eight hours every day and Susie being home to raise the girls. She loved the "farm life" as she put it. Though they didn't actually have a farm, just one acre where they raised chickens, a big garden, and lots of dogs and cats.

A pony for each girl when they were young, and horses later came along. The horses were sold off when each girl discovered boys, then college bound. Now Mike and Susie were empty nesters, traveling much of their time in their Class A Motorhome seeing the United States one city at a time. They were very satisfied with their retirement lifestyle and were more in love every day.

They often giggled at how their love continued to grow deeper, more mature. Not stale, as some saw maturity, but more meaningful, wiser somehow. Mike never referred to Susie as his wife but as his bride. The very girl he married. Sure, their bodies showed age, but that was not the girl Mike saw.

Every day he awoke and brought Susie her first cup of piping hot coffee and then would bend down and kiss her neck, slowly, lovingly, passionately. As if to say thank you for making love last night. Even though they might not have. No, it was his deliberate way of saying thank you for loving me yesterday and all the days before and the ones to come. They were bonded like so few married couples are these days.

"Ok, I'm ready," Susie made her entrance into the living area of the suite they reserved for the wedding weekend.

Mike wanted this to be a honeymoon for the two of them too. A special weekend of family, romance, and spoiling his bride. He set his phone on his lap and looked up.

"Damn. You still take my breath away." Mike exhaled.

"Was I worth the wait?" With that comment Mike rose to his feet and pulled Susie into her arms, laying a passionate kiss on her. She braced at first, then slowly succumb to her husband's passion and melted into his arms.

"Maybe we should just eat in?" Mike slyly smiled.

"Oh no you don't mister, you got me to get all dressed up for a night out on the town. I didn't do all this so it would end up all thrown about the hotel room." As she pushed him back flirting and took a swirl around showing herself off.

"But baby, I can show you a good time... I promise." Mike pressed.

"Yeah, I heard that one before. It may have been true once, but now you need thirty minutes advanced warning of the 'good time.' Get your wallet, you are taking me out."

"That was cold," Mike not surprised by the deflection of his advance and feigning hurt all at the same time.

"Cowboy up big guy, maybe there will be a little reward for you when we get back to the hotel tonight," Susie says with a grin.

Mike trots back into the bedroom and grabs his wallet and jacket. As a matter of just rote practice, he picks up his Sig Saur .45 P220, and the extra magazine. Places them in his concealed holster and tucks it all in the waistline in the small of his back, puts his jacket on, and takes one final last look in the mirror. *I am getting old, but I am staying in shape and healthy.*

Mike took a training class nearly twenty-six years ago to receive his concealed weapons permit. His then Sergeant at the prison recommended it to all of the fairly new Correctional Officers (CO's) for the safety of his family. "You never know when, not if, you'll run into one of these dirtbags on the streets. At some point, they all get out."

"The only one that will be serving his entire sentence will be you!" Referring to how many years most CO's work compared to the revolving door for inmates. "The odds are, you'll eventually meet up with someone who hates your guts and will want to harm you or your family," the Sergeant admonished.

From then on Mike carried his Sig and an extra Magazine, even though that long-retired Sargent's prophecy had never come to pass. Mike never once ran into an ex-inmate on the streets and never was required to pull out his weapon. Now that he had been retired for a few years, he wondered if it was even necessary anymore. Nonetheless, he carried out of habit more than anything else, although he enjoyed going to the shooting range a couple times a year just to keep proficient.

"Where are you taking me?" Susie asks again as they get into their 2012 Toyota Camry. This time she is almost squealing giddy with excitement.

"You'll see."

Mike had heard about the famous steakhouse, Sayer's Old Country Kitchen in downtown Portland that had a bone-in Cowboy cut steak that was to die for. And, which after eating one, might actually come to pass. They called it the "Flintstone" because it was so big, it looked like some slab of meat a caveman would have eaten from a dinosaur. And, if you ate it in one sitting, it could kill you!

They also had a selection of Whiskey from around the world, which he would love, and a small jazz band, which Susie would love. He figured they would take their time and enjoy the evening together, go back to the hotel, see if the "reward" offer from Susie might still be good. Then have breakfast courtesy of room service in bed to top off a great second honeymoon.

"This sure has been a great day, it was great to meet our new mother-in-law, Joannie McConnel. I do wish her husband could have made it… His name is John, right?"

"I think so, yes, John. He is a retired Army Ranger you know," sounding clever.

"Is **this** the place we're going? Oh, steak!" Susie was just talking a mile a minute nonstop in excitement as they pulled up to the valet. Mike and Susie were greeted by a valet at each door and as they were opened for them.

"Oh, nice," Susie, loving all of the attention. "I feel like Cinderella."

"Geez, girl, I got to get you out more," Mike says with a smile as he held the door for his bride and the two entered the restaurant.

✭✭✭

It was all Mike had hoped. Music, whiskey, and the best five-star meal they ever had. But they declined trying to eat all their "Flintstone," instead they decided on doggie bags, even though their last family dog died last year.

They stood for just a quick minute before the valet brought their car around. It was a different young man than before. Mike noticed the prominent tattoo on his neck, and dreadlocks tucked up under his uniform cap.

"Hey, can you give me directions back to the Regency? I am a bit turned around," asking the Valet.

"Sure, it's easy. When you pull out of here, take the first right. Then go six blocks, turn right again and that will take you right to your hotel."

"Are you sure that seems further than the route we took to get here?"

"Yeah, that's the way you want to go. There are some road closures back that way."

"Oh, okay… Thanks."

As the valet closes Mike's door he smiles and mutters "racist" under his breath with contempt.

Mike was grateful for the tip. "Ready baby?" Mike asked.

"Are you ready?" Susie retorted. "This is your thirty-minute warning." Susie smiling, wondering if Mike got the hint.

He got it but the drive back shouldn't take thirty minutes and besides, he left his prescription glasses back at the hotel, which he was sure Susie was aware of. First right, here we are. Now six blocks and another right.

"Where are we going now? Is there more to come in this evening?" Susie asks expectantly.

"No, no, the valet gave me some directions to avoid some road closures."

"Then back to the hotel?"

"Yep, back to the hotel, we're going."

"Oh, okay." Susie feeling a bit let down thinking there might be yet another surprise that night.

Okay, here is the sixth block, right turn here.

Immediately the traffic slowed and then came to a near stop.

"What's going on?" Susie trying to understand why the sudden stop.

✭✭✭

"It seems to be some kind of demonstration, or march or something," Mike answered.

"This late at night?"

"I don't know. I'm going to back up. Crap! I can't. There are way too many people behind us and lots of cars in front of us."

"Why is everyone all dressed in black… They're all wearing masks… I don't like this!" Susie is quickly getting scared.

"I'm not sure what to do. I can't move the car. Make sure your door is locked." Susie hits the auto-lock button and secures all the doors.

Mike takes an earnest look at the crowd for the first time. ANTIFA. "Antifa!"

"What's an Antifa?" Susie getting even more worried now.

At that moment Mike sees a break in the crowd behind them and points the rear end of the car towards the opening and slowly moves the car backward. This movement brings them unwanted attention. The crowd around them forcefully presses around the car. Mike keeps rolling slowly. Now the crowd is savagely hitting the car, beating on it mostly, as they can see the occupants are scared.

This fear tactic only emboldens the others. More press in and many start loudly chanting "Racist, racist, racist…" Now they are viciously pounding on Mike and Susie's car with fists and poles… flag poles.

"Get me out of here!" Susie cries out in fear now. She's beginning to sob.

Mike presses down on the pedal and the car begins to pick up speed and the crowd begins to part. *Alright, we're making progress now.* Mike thinks as he sees hope for escape.

But all the commotion only attracts more aggressive crowd members, and they swarm the car once again bringing it to a full stop.

"They're like a pack of animals!" screams Susie. "Go, go, go… get me outta here!"

"I can't —not without killing anyone." Mike's truly torn at what to do.

"Get me out, now, out, now!" Susie is hysterical now and tears are streaming down her face.

Mike had come to his decision, he shifted to the car into drive and was about to push the pedal to the ground letting the chips fall where they may.

CRASH came the familiar sound of glass breaking. Mike looked to his right at the precise moment to see the ball pein hammer being withdrawn from the passenger window frame. Susie was stunned, covered in glass, as hands started reaching into the car. She started fighting the hands frantically, slapping and biting as fiercely as she knew how. Susie had an inner strength that made her a strong fighter, but nothing had prepared her for this.

Mike tried to open his door and get out to stop the assault on his wife. As soon as he pulled the door handle, he realized his mistake. All the door locks immediately popped open and, in half a second, Susie's door was open, and another hand came in, this time with a knife, cut her seat belt and she was gone. Dragged from the car in split seconds.

Mike was in full fight mode now, the only thing on his mind was to rescue Susie at any cost. He tried again to push his door open to no avail, the crowd pressing in were too formidable to push the door open. He released his seat belt to scramble out the passenger door, his window shattered simultaneously as Susie's did.

But this time Mike grabbed the hammer and jerked it from the unsuspecting aggressor. Mike spun the hammer in his hand and returned the aggression, reaching out the window cracking one, then two kneecaps with all his strength. That cleared the angry crowd back from his side of the car. Now he was able to scurry out of the car and push the crowd back swinging the hammer wildly. Even the two men with broken kneecaps crawled away from this enraged madman.

Once Mike pushed these animals back, he turns his attention to Susie's side of the car. One man had her by the neck in a chokehold, Susie was terrified, grasping her attackers' forearm with both hands desperately trying to get her breath. Mike had to get to her. He quickly stepped on the door frame to climb over the hood to rescue her.

When out of nowhere he heard a surreal pinging sound, as an aluminum flagpole hit him across the right side of his head from behind. The blow knocked him off the door jam and against the open door of the Camry. As Mike slowly regained his senses, he heard the crowd in unison, holler "Whoa…" with great approval.

Mike looked for the hammer in his hand, it was gone falling and taking a bounce into the crowd. To the crowd, Mike looked incapacitated, and like a pack of wolves moved in for the kill. But Mike had a bigger motivation, it was to save his bride. With his right hand, he reached to the small of his back and pulled free his Sig. At the same moment, he saw another attacker coming at him with a brick.

From behind his back, without even turning, he let the first round loose. It found its target, point-blank range, hitting him center mass, sending the assailant back four feet into the crowd dead. This didn't seem to cure their blood lust as Mike sent four more rounds striking into the chest of three more attackers. This got a brief pause from his side of the car, but not Susie's.

Susie was now visibly limp from her attacker's chokehold, but he wouldn't let her fall to the ground, instead, he danced some sort of crazed dance. Mike swung his weapon across the top of his car, took a moment to aim precisely, and fire one round into the right eye of her attacker. Susie's limp body fell with his. This only enraged the faceless wolves all the more.

Two began to wildly kick Susie's lifeless body, then two more. It had turned into an orgy of violence. Mike sent four more deadly .45 rounds into the bodies of Susie's brutal assailants.

Mike went to fire again and realized his slide was locked back. As he reached for his second magazine, his eyesight went black. Someone from behind had crushed his skull with a brick. He woke briefly on the ground. He had been kicked by the crowd nearly all the way under his car.

He looked one more time for his bride. His last memory was seeing her lifeless body on the ground just opposite of him, under the car, her eyes-wide-open looking for her husband to save her. He tried one more time to reach for her, it was just too far to reach.

He never broke his eye contact, locked on her face as faceless feet danced in celebration for the fascist lives they had taken that night. But it came at a cost to these young senseless Antifa. The next day the headlines in the New York Times read:

23 PEACEFUL PROTESTERS DEAD AT THE HAND OF WHITE SUPREMACISTS

… apparently, Mike spent his second magazine before succumbing and at such close range, many of his rounds went clean through their bodies, claiming a second and even third life. Emergency services would not enter the area on the order of the Portland Mayor. Those who may have survived bled out at the scene. Including Mike Simpson.

Chapter 13

The White Supremacist Did It!

The Investigation

Jim Johnson has made a modest home at the Eureka Casino Resort in Mesquite Nevada, a small rural town in Southern Nevada just a few miles from the site of the "Battle of Bunkerville" as the media now calls it. The Federal government has basically taken over a majority portion of the convention space and most of the hotel rooms in this small hotel property and truck stop. Jim likes to concentrate, so he cleared out much of his hotel suite to organize and form a makeshift office of a sort. Of course, his secretary Kathy has come to Nevada to join her boss at his "West Coast Office" she had in joking called it, though it doesn't feel much like a coast in the middle of the Mohave Desert.

I cannot believe I have lived here for two months, and we have gotten NOWHERE in figuring out how all this started. Johnson thinks to himself slightly miffed as he pours through another report and analysis from one of the intel agencies of the federal government. *We have drone footage, downloads of video or pictures of every phone we could find, which took too dam long!*

Apple would not easily allow the FBI to get into at least two-thirds of the missing phones. It took a court order and a call from the White House Chief of Staff to convince Tim Cook of its importance. *We have accounted for every human in a ten-mile radius that was in possession of a phone.* The NSA did a metadata dump on every number of every phone, then the FBI agents painstakingly interviewed every single person, man, woman, and child.

We know who every one of these people is except for these six signals heading north to this truck stop. Then they all scatter, within an hour of each other heading to who knows where. The CRT cameras in and around the truck stop that day give us no clue, because hell we don't know who we are looking for.

Then there is this motorcycle? Perplexed, Jim holds up a picture of the totaled Fat Boy, strewn about the highway. *It's registered to a Joshua Lee Cooper, who is in the Navy.*

He seems to have been deployed when this went down, but no one will let our guys talk to him. He is just 'unavailable.' What ships don't have communications gear, telephones, or Skype? Of course, they do, but this sailor is unavailable?!

The magic key must be these six phone pings, it's got to be. We even tried to look at financial records of gas charges or store purchases made the day of the protest, the shooting, the round-up. I'm not even sure what this is... I need a break.

Kathy poked her head into his room. "The President is on the phone."

"Oh, great... Put her through." spoken in sarcasm, as he was **not** looking forward to this.

"Please hold for the president," says the White House operator.

"Hello Johnson, this is the President"

"Hello mam..." Johnson is abruptly cut off.

"Have you seen the New York Times?"

"Ah, well no, I am in Neva..." He's cut off a second time.

"They have attacked us again?"

"Who?"

"The White Supremacists! They are attacking our nation at every turn and you're not doing anything about it!"

"I am sorry, who?" Johnson is completely unaware of what happened in Portland the night before.

"The WHITE SUPREMACISTS! they murdered twenty-five, maybe thirty innocent protesters in Portland, Oregon, my very own hometown. They were murdered in cold blood. I might have known some of them!"

"Well Ms. President, I haven't heard anything about it. But I'll check into it as soon as I am off the phone."

"How the Fuck do you not know anything about this? What am I paying you for? You are the head of the most powerful law enforcement agency in the world, and YOU DON'T KNOW! How the fuck does that happen?"

Jim was losing patience now, "Well two months ago you ordered me to Nevada, to personally take charge of this Bunkerville matter. And I am still here."

"Have you caught them?"

"Who?"

"The perpetrators in Nevada?"

"No, we're not even sure who shot first."

"What does that matter?"

"Well, because that will help us determine what transpired"

"Let me help you, the WHITE SUPREMACISTS did it. Probably the same ones you can't catch and who murdered my friends in Oregon!" The phone went dead.

I hate this job right now...

The phone rings again.

"It's the White House," Kathy yells loudly through the door.

"Please stand by for the Chief of Staff."

"Johnson? It's Theodore Smith. Are our men out of Jail yet?"

"Our men sir?"

"Yes, yes, the FBI Swat guys. Did that crazy Sheriff let them go?"

"No sir, they have been charged with manslaughter and are being held in the Clark County Detention Center. All of the Federal agents are..."

"That is unacceptable! UNACCEPTABLE!" now Smith was yelling at him too.

"You go down there and get them out right now! Take the Army with you if your need but get them out today!" The phone line went dead in silence once again.

"Kathy, would you get me the Attorney General please?"

A few moments later. "The AG is on the line" Kathy declares.

"Glenn, it's Jim. I need your help again. I got Smith and the President screaming at me to take the Army to Las Vegas and do a jailbreak for the HRT... Nope, I am serious. Can you try to explain it to them again?"

"No, the Sheriff is not remotely budging. He's madder than they are. Besides they have all been charged and a Nevada Court Judge has ordered them held without bail... manslaughter..."

"I know, yes, I know, but it's in Nevada Jurisdiction now and it would take an Army at the very least. No, we are supporting the

★★★

Sheriff's investigation, I'm certainly not in charge. They're not telling us much and we are receiving information in pieces, just requesting resources and investigation footwork."

"No, I don't blame them either. They lost good men that day… okay thank you for your help. Thank you, bye."

Jim hung up the phone, worn out. "Kathy, I am going in my room to rest for a while. You can take the Jet back to DC if you want, I know your son has a ball game tomorrow."

"That would be wonderful." Kathy poking her head back through the door smiling. "If you don't mind, I'll go now."

"I don't mind at all, have a good rest of the weekend, I'll see you back here on Tuesday. Oh, when you're on the plane, would you have someone get me a report on the shootings last night in Portland Oregon? Maybe the field office there. Just have them email it."

"Will do." And with that Kathy was gone.

"Thanks," Jim replies to no one.

Jim stood to head into the bedroom section of his suite to lie down. In a split second, everything went black, and he fell to the floor hard, real hard.

Jim woke up a few hours later at Mesa View Regional Hospital in Mesquite. "Mr. Johnson, hi, I'm a nurse. You're in the hospital."

"What happened?" Jim mumbled somewhat incoherent.

"We don't know for sure; we were hoping you could tell us?"

In walked the emergency room doctor. "Hi Mr. Johnson, I guess you were found on the floor in your hotel room by the maid when she came in to bring you towels. Do you remember that?"

"No, I don't."

"What do you remember?"

"Saying goodbye to my assistant and thinking I was going to lay down for a nap, then I was here."

"Okay, well you just rest now, and we'll get you admitted."

"Do I have to stay? I have a lot to do, and I am with the FB…" he was gone unconscious again.

The next morning, a new Doctor came to Jim's room. "Hello, Mr. Johnson, I am Dr. Sanjay. I am a visiting Neurosurgeon at the Hospital. How are you feeling this morning?"

"I feel rested, and ready to get out of here."

★★★

"Do you know your name?"

"Ahh, Jim Johnson."

"Do you know what state you are in?"

"Confused, no Just kidding. I am in Nevada."

"Do you know who the President is?"

"Yeah, she's a bitch."

"I am sorry?"

"Never mind, what's with all the questions?"

"Well Mr. Johnson, after you blacked out again last night the emergency room ran an MRI and then a CT scan on your entire body to see if we could figure out what may be the problem."

"Well, what did you find?"

Dr. Sanjay paused for a minute, which seemed like ages, swallowed, then continued.

"It appears you have two lesions in your brain, and they are pressing on your frontal lobe. That's likely what caused you to blackout."

"You keep saying blacked out, did I faint or something?"

"No, you were wide awake, you just were gone, checked out, missing for a few hours. Then you came back. Then you were gone again. That is what concerned the ER doctor, so he called me out from Las Vegas."

"So, what are these lesions, you mentioned?"

"Well, we're not sure, but most likely a primary brain cancer."

"Wait, what. I have brain cancer?"

"Well, we won't know for sure until we remove the lesions and have them biopsied."

"Then how do you know it's cancer? Maybe it's something else, like a cyst or something, my friend had one of those after he came back from serving overseas."

"Well maybe, but it's not likely because cysts don't present in pairs like this. It's likely primary brain cancer."

"What does that mean, 'Primary Brain Cancer'?"

"It means it only presents in the brain, like a Glioblastoma Multiforme or GBM for short."

"Wait, are you saying I could have cancer in other places in my body?"

"No not likely, the CT scan would have shown other lesions and you seem to only have the two in your brain. That's why it's called

★★

Primary Cancer. It means it didn't metathesize from another part of the body to the brain."

"That sounds better then, at least I don't have cancer all over."

"Actually, no. Primary Brain Cancers are the most serious kinds. There is very little we can do and the cancer itself is very, very aggressive. Meaning it grows really fast."

"Shit doctor, what are you telling me here. I'm going to die?"

"Your life expectancy is on average twelve to fourteen months with treatment."

"So, you're telling me I have fourteen months to live and there isn't much you can do about it? Man Doc, you really know how to lay it on a guy."

"We can do a lot of things to help you live as long as possible. It's that treatment that gives you the twelve to fourteen months."

"What are we talking about? The treatment I mean."

"It starts with surgery to debulk the mass and remove it from your head, then radiation and chemo treatments to kill any residual cancer. That takes about three months, then we wait six weeks to see where we are."

"And if it doesn't kill the cancer?"

"To be clear, it won't kill the cancer, it just buys you time."

"Then when the cancer returns, we what, do it again?"

"Pretty much."

"How many times are you going to cut my brain open, then radiate it and shove poison into my body — three maybe four times? Then what happens?"

"When your body can't tolerate the treatments anymore, then at some point, the family decides to discontinue the treatments."

"Then what?"

"The cancer will eventually come back with a vengeance, and you'll go into Hospice care."

"I'll die in a hospital somewhere with tubes sticking out of me."

"Well, no in this state you can go home on hospice care."

"I'll die at home with tubes sticking out of me. GREAT! No to either option. What happens if I refuse the treatment?"

The doctor looked at the MRI again. "A GBM this advanced can double in size very quickly, –every couple of weeks to be exact. I'd say you'd have six to twelve weeks. But during the last four weeks, you will have lost all function."

"Back to that hospice thing again…"

"I am afraid so."

"Shit."

"But you're not sure if it this Glioblast . . ."

"Just call it a GBM."

"You're not sure I have a GBM, right?"

"Pretty sure."

"How sure?"

"90%"

"How will we know for sure?"

"We'll need to open your skull and do a biopsy."

"Sounds like we're back to surgery."

"It is major surgery, that's why we usually remove the tumors while we are in there."

Jim noticed the Doctor was calling it a tumor now. *I don't think he wants to scare me with the word tumor at first… he waited until I let it sink in some.*

"So, my head gets cut open either way, and if we do that I might as well get the entire round of treatments."

"That is what most patients choose to do."

"Well, this sucks."

"I am sorry. What would you like me to do, I can schedule a surgery suite in the next few days…?"

"Well, whatever I decide to do, it won't be here. I live in Virginia, and work in D.C.…." Jim didn't want to reveal who he was.

"Anyway, whatever happens, it will happen there. And I will get another opinion, no offense Doc."

"None taken. Please get a second opinion, I just encourage you to not wait too long. The cancer is likely advancing rapidly."

"Doc, right now I feel fine. Can I get discharged? —Hey doc… how will the end be? Will I feel a lot of pain? Tell it to me straight, don't hold back."

Doctor Sanjay looked one last time at the MRI. "Where these are located, you shouldn't have much if any pain. Maybe a bad headache worst case. You'll just want to sleep more and more, then you won't wake up."

"That doesn't sound too awful." Jim is letting the news sink in.

"I will talk to the Hospitalist about seeing you discharged. But when you do, I want you to go straight home and see a Neurosurgeon out there, don't waste time. Please consider this an urgent matter."

"Got it Doc. Head straight home, thanks… I guess."

"Hey doc, this conversation is just between us, right?"

"Correct, by law I cannot discuss your case with anyone without your written consent."

"Good."

Dr. Sanjay smiled a professional straight-thin smile and left Jim's room. Jim was left alone mulling over his thoughts:

I guess I am going to die.

What the hell is a Hospitalist?

Later that afternoon, he was wheeled to the front door of the Hospital and Jim jumped into the cab he had called.

"Please take me to the Eureka," Jim said, all business. "Oh, is there somewhere I can get a cheap cell phone?"

"You can get one at the Truck Stop, right where you're staying," replied the driver.

"Great, drop me there and I'll just walk to my room afterward."

"Yes sir."

Jim dialed out on his FBI cell phone. "Hi, Kathy, enjoying the game? Oh, good. Can I ask a favor, please send the jet back for me immediately. No everything is fine; I just have a couple of important things to do in Virginia. Thanks, I'll just be a day or two, then we'll ride back to Nevada together. Thanks, I appreciate you. Yes, that means you have a little more time off."

I am sure glad she wasn't here when I … fell out, blacked out, or whatever. I want as few people to know about my business as possible, including Kathy.

In the convivence store at the truck stop, Jim was surprised to discover he could purchase a new "burner phone" from a vending machine. How strange. But first, he had to get cash from the ATM, because the cell phone vending machine didn't take credit cards. Even weirder.

Once Jim returned to his hotel room, phone in hand, he wrestled opening the packaging and trying to activate his new phone.

What a pain in the butt this sealed plastic packaging is to extricate the purchase from. After five minutes of fighting it, he gave up, got a knife out, and cut the packaging to bits getting inside.

Shit, I guess you can only buy it, using it is another question...

After five more minutes of reading the instructions about how to activate the phone, finally, the lights came on and he was in business.

...And, activating it is yet another question.

He had just one call to make on this phone. And it began to ring.

"Hello?" came a familiar voice.

"Doc, Doc it's Jim Johnson."

"Oh, shit I was wondering if you'd ever call? I guess it's time to call in my marker?"

"I told you I would only ever call you when I need to call in that favor. Today is the day." Jim being very serious, very covert sounding.

"Ok, what do you need?" asked the voice.

"I will be there tomorrow morning and we'll discuss it. Say 10 a.m.?"

"That'll be fine, I'll see you then. Do you remember how to get here?"

"You're in the same place?" Jim confirming.

"Yeah, I haven't moved, where would I go..." The phone went dead.

Shit, why does everyone hang up on me?

Jim threw the new phone on the bed and headed for a much-needed shower.

I have some work to catch up on before the plane picks me up.

After a shower, he sat down, opened his laptop, scrolled down until he found the report from Saturday night's shooting in Portland and ... *Wait what's this?*

The initial analyst on the six missing cell phones. And a weird report from the Texas Rangers, Garland office. That's odd, I rarely hear from them. Let's look at that first.

Jim starts skimming the report.

So, the Texas Rangers have stumbled on a terror cell? Hmm... eighteen Military age males gathered in a large house in Plano. Objective unknown.

Confirmed informant agreed to provide intel.

Believe it's tied to the Muslim Brotherhood, still confirming.

*Oh, good it's **not** more 'White Supremist' – I guess. For the Presidents obsession anyway.*

They believe it's building up to a major operation.

FBI field office in Dallas, lending investigative support. *That's good.*

Jim Types a reply:

Lt. Kinum, Texas Rangers

CC: Dallas Field office, FBI.

Dear Lt. Kinum,

Amazing work on this.

Federal jurisdiction does not apply unless the criminal operation extends out of Texas. The FBI will remain supportive to you in any way possible. Please keep us apprised on the investigative progression and reach out if you need assistance.

Jim Johnson,

Director Counterintelligence, Federal Bureau of Investigation

PS: Are you related to the President's Secretary by any chance?

Jim's cell phone is vibrating. "Hello, Jim Johnson, –Okay I'll be ready. See you then."

Cool, my ride is on its way. I need to be at the airport at 9 p.m. Maybe I can finally sleep on the plane.

Jim slowly rose to his feet and finished dressing, tidying up his room a little bit while packing before returning to his computer. He knew once he settles in and started working, he'd lose track of time. Before he did, he called his security detail to be ready to go to the airport at 8:30 p.m.

"Yes, sir we'll be ready. We'll have everything ready in DC too."

"Thanks, sorry for the short notice," Jim replied.

"No problem, sir. Did you have a good rest?" asked the voice of the phone.

"Ah, rest?" Jim not sure now.

"Yes, sir you just crashed out last night and this is the first we have heard from you since yesterday."

"Oh, yeah... well once Kathy left, I just worked, crashed out as you say, then woke up and worked all day. It's been very productive." Jim stumbling through it.

"Well great, see you at 8:30 p.m."

"Right, –bye now."

Ha, they didn't even know I went to the hospital last night. Well shit, my own security detail didn't see a big red ambulance come and take me away last night, lights and siren and all. I am not sure if that was providential or incompetence. I'll go with providential ... for now. It seems the only one who knows what happened is me and Dr. Sanjay. This just might work.

Now, let's take a look at what they found out about the missing cell phones and who they belong to. Jim opens the document with great curiosity. *Well not much here. It seems the only phone they found so far was taped to a Semi Truck tracked all the way to Minnesota.*

Apparently, it was so hard to track, because this particular truck was a long-haul rig and it just kept moving. It seems as soon as they had a lead on its location and were able to react, the truck was on the move again. Finally, it was located in an industrial truck mechanic's shop as it stopped for maintenance.

Geez.

If it hadn't stopped, we might never have found him.

But wait, we DIDN'T find him? Just his phone. The investigating agents figure he must have gotten off at one of the truck's other stops and accidentally left his phone.

The truck driver said he never gave anyone a ride,

hmm. And, the driver never even saw the phone. Well, where did they find the phone then?

Jim kept reading.

The Mechanic turned over the phone.

Why did he have it? It doesn't look like they asked him. Well, who owned the phone, did we find that out? Here it is:

> **Kevin Linfield**
> **The Timmons' Ranch**
> **Battle Mountain, Nevada...**

Oh shit.

Chapter 14

Just One Word: "Lawyer"

Afghanistan
Sleeper returned from a long stressful three-night operation on the top of an abandoned building in some town he can't remember the name of and doesn't even remotely care anymore. He drops his gear carelessly on the floor and his body on his rack in the airconditioned box that was delegated to the SEALS. His eyes began to close from exhaustion, and his mind began to dream of mountains, rivers, and flyfishing...

"SLEEPER YOU'RE WANTED IN OPS.... SLEEPER"

"SHUT THE FUCK UP!" came another loud voice from the other end of the box. One of Sleeper's teammates.

"Sorry, I was ordered to get Sleeper... Sleeper, com'on they want you in ops."

"Wake up man, I got orders to get you, sorry you gotta wake up."

Just like that Sleeper was on his feet and moving for the door. It happened so quickly that the young private who was ordered to get him was scared shitless. After all, the Teams guys are revered by the regular troops and feared by most of the squad.

They pretty much did whatever they wanted when on base, not bullies really, but Command let them get away with things no one else could, simply turning their heads the other way. They didn't follow much of anything they didn't want to unless it was an important mission, then everything was tight and shipshape, to use a Navy term. As a team, they were all business and were the guys you reliably listened to when you were in trouble and the shit hit the fan.

Privates like the one tasked with such orders almost looked at all the special operations teams as pretty much Superheroes, like the ones in the Marvel Movies they grew up watching. The Team guys knew different because they all too often carry their teammates home in body bags. They die, just as easily as everyone else, and unfortunately far too frequently.

"Come on kid, take me to your leader," Sleeper smiles at the young kid, all of maybe nineteen.

"Sorry sir, I hated to wake you, but I had orders."

"SHUT. THE. FUCK.UP!" comes a booming voice from another of Sleeper's Teammates.

"Let's go kid before we get a double tap in the forehead by one of these assholes." For a brief second, the kid looked extremely worried, then he saw Sleeper's joking smile.

Sleeper let the door slam loudly on the way out just to be an ass.

"Where we going kid, CENTCOM?"

"No, admin... the base commander wants to see you."

"Really?" Sleeper is running through his head what he might have done to warrant this kind of attention.

"I overheard you have some sort of special phone call from the DOD."

"Hmm..." Sleeper is really puzzled now.

"Of course, you didn't hear that from me."

"Hey kid, may I give you a tip that will serve you well in this man's Navy... err. Army?" Sleeper took a quick look at what branch he served.

"Yes, please I am looking for guidance..."

A little too eager kid.

"YOU don't get to call me Sleeper," he paused for effect, then: "If you gotta say 'you didn't hear it from me,' you shouldn't have said it." With that wisdom, Sleeper left the kid standing embarrassed outside the Commander's Office.

"Go right in Sergeant," the commander's clerk instructed.

As he walked into the sterile office, he stood at attention in front of the One Star General's desk. "Sergeant Cooper reporting," Sleeper announces.

"Sit down Cooper," the commander orders. "Good job on last night's mission, I was just looking at the after-action report."

"Thank you, sir." Sleeper more comfortable now.

"You must be tired, so I won't keep you long. I will get right to it. Son, are you in trouble?"

"Excuse me, sir?"

"You got the FBI looking for you and they are being very persistent."

"For me sir, I... I can't imagine why." Sleeper was no longer comfortable but visibly concerned.

"Well, they have been on the DOD's case for weeks now to be in touch with you and, well, the DOD just stonewalled them because of the sensitive nature of your operational posture. But I heard from the Joint Chiefs office that I need to arrange a phone call with you. So, somebody is pulling some pretty big strings to make this happen."

"Well sir, I have no idea what this could be about. What do you want me to do?"

"Sergeant, just to be clear... I am on your side. I am always on my men's side. If there is anything you need to tell me, it's now. Because if I am lied to, I won't be on your side anymore. Now's the chance to keep me watching your six."

"Honestly, sir I have no idea what the FBI wants. I will talk to them if you order it."

"GOOD. It's not my orders, I am following them... I want you to go shave, shower, and put on some clean BDU's, no ribbons, no Tridents, be as plain Navy as possible, and report to my clerk and he'll get you on the line with them. I don't need to tell you, give no indication whatsoever to these guys where you are or your mission. It's strictly 'need to know' and those fuckers don't need to know."

"Okay sir, I'll be back in thirty minutes. I want to grab some chow too; in case this takes long."

"Good idea. Oh, and remember, with them, you are only a civilian and you are not required to answer any question you don't think is in your interest or comprises your current mission. These bastards are sly, smooth, and tricky. If at any time you feel you need a lawyer for representation, stop the conversation and I'll get you a Jag officer." *That would piss them off and stall them for a while.*

"Do you think it'll come to that?" Sleeper now more than a little scared.

"Hell, I don't know. In my twenty years, I have never had the Joint Chiefs office call me for anything. This is completely new ground for me too. It just feels ... I don't know... off."

"Okay sir, I'll be back in thirty minutes."

★★

Thirty minutes later Sleeper is ushered into a small, plain, secured room, for teleconference calls. It's 100% soundproof and impenetrable to outside eavesdropping.

"Okay Sergeant, sit right here and in a couple of minutes I will connect you to Washington."

"Wait, I thought I was going to talk to the FBI?" Sleeper just wants to be sure he's on the right call.

"Yes, Sergeant, the Hoover Building is in Washington, DC."

I guess I am talking to the top guys, not some small-fry lackey field agent.

"Just watch the screen."

A few brief moments later the screen flickered on. Two agents were sitting in what appeared to be a conference room with a glass wall behind them. He could see a much bigger office behind them, with lots of people in suits hustling around. To sleeper, it looked like a stockbroker's office in New York or somewhere.

In the conference room sat one man and one woman, "Hello, let me introduce ourselves." spoke the man authoritatively. "I am Agent Hernandez, and this is Agent Titus. We are with the Counterintelligence division of the Federal Bureau of Investigation."

"What can I do for you?" replies Cooper.

"Well, for the record, you are Joshua Lee Cooper, who resides at the Kingsbay Naval Submarine Base, in St. Marys, Georgia, social security number 546-31-7412?"

"Sometimes," Cooper answers evasively.

Agent Titus interrupts, "Which part is sometimes? Your Name, your social, or your residence?"

"Sorry, that's Classified."

"Okay, let's start with … where are you now? We don't know because the Navy won't tell us," continues Agent Hernandez pressing for more information.

"Sorry, Classified," *this is kind of fun… and necessary for now.*

"Look we'll be here all day if you want to play this way," Agent Titus is already impatient.

So far, all the questions were without question classified, and he wasn't legally required to tell anyone his name SS#, or address unless they had the clearance.

★★

"Look, you are not in trouble. We just want to talk to you about your motorcycle. Are you the Joshua Lee Cooper who owns a 2014 Harley Fat Boy, jet black with Virginia License No.– S L E E P E R 1? I mean did the Navy get us the wrong Joshua Cooper?" presses Hernandez.

My motorcycle, what the hell does my bike have to do with this? Cooper decides to answer, mostly out of curiosity. "That sounds like my bike."

"So, we do have the right guy, now we are getting somewhere," replies Agent Titus. "Can you tell us if you were riding your bike last April in Nevada?"

"No," Cooper interrupts abruptly.

"Oh, were you on deployment at the time?" continues Agent Hernandez.

"Sorry, my whereabouts are classified," stonewalls Cooper.

"Are you telling us you cannot tell us how your motorcycle was strewn all over the highway in Nevada?" presses Titus.

"No," replies Cooper.

"Who the fuck do you think you are? –some kind of secret agent, or something? It says here you are a Sergeant on a submarine, and that's why it's so hard to reach you."

"I mean, if you were on duty somewhere or anywhere in the world for that matter, then you couldn't have been riding your frigging motorcycle down the highway in Nevada, RIGHT? So just tell us if you were on duty and the Navy can account for your whereabouts and that will be the end of that. But if it was you, we will dig into your life like nothing you have ever seen, and eventually, you'll be sitting alone in a prison cell. So just answer the question!" Agent Titus exasperated now.

"Well, the hard way or the easy way – you choose?" Hernandez concluding.

Chance, what the fuck have you gotten yourself into? I guess they don't have any idea who or where you are, so fuck these guys. I'm not helping them. Let's let them dig into me and I'll let the DOD keep them busy. If Chance wants to show his face in whatever the hell they want him for, that's his decision, not mine. He has saved my life way too many times for me to give him up, with or without a fight. Let them dig...

"Well, what's your answer. Were you on the bike or not?" Agent Hernandez asks more gently, hoping his partner didn't overplay her hand.

Cooper had just one short answer for the pair of agents, "Lawyer."

With that one-word answer, the screen went blank, the transmission cut from the Afghanistan side. Cut off by the clerk on the General's orders. While Cooper was getting cleaned up, the General gave his clerk two orders. The first order: Record and transcribe the transmission, the General wanted to know if Cooper had lied to him. The second order: If Cooper says the word Lawyer, the conversation ends. The clerk followed his orders to the tee.

Cooper emerged from the teleconference room. "I guess we got cut off."

"Huh?" was the only reply of the Clerk.

Cooper was relieved he didn't attempt to get them back.

The General emerged expectantly from his office. "What did they want?"

"They want to know about my motorcycle."

"What did they want to know?" the General was seemingly curious.

"They wanted to know if I was riding it back in April."

"What did you tell them?"

"I told them, no."

"Well of course you weren't. You were here, chewing on sand for your country. You didn't tell them that did you?"

"No sir, that's classified."

"Good. So glad it was just that."

"Me too," replies Cooper.

"You're dismissed. Go get some sleep."

"Thank you, sir." Cooper heads out the door.

"Well, is he telling the truth?" the General looking at the clerk.

"Hard to say."

"Really, why?"

"Well sir, he didn't say… anything. By the time Sergeant Cooper was done with those two, they weren't even sure they had the right Joshua Cooper. The Agents were convinced he was some squid in a submarine somewhere. Cooper was so remarkably evasive you'd think the Taliban was interrogating him."

★★

"Hmm… you better get me the transcript." *What is this young man up to?*

"I will have it to you within the hour," replies the Clerk smartly. "One more thing Sir. Cooper did ask for a Lawyer… 'er well, he actually just said the word, Lawyer. Do you want me to get a Jag officer out here?"

"No, not until he requests one." *What a cool customer Cooper is. There is something deeper here and I need to be proactive. But what?*

"On second thought, set up a call with the Jag Corp Commander. I want some counsel." *I don't want the FBI digging around in my command.*

"Yes sir, as soon as I can get it on your schedule."

Hoover Building

Agent Titus breaks the uncomfortable silence. "Well, did you get them back?" asking the FBI tech whose sole job is to coordinate teleconference calls.

"No, there is no one to connect to, it's like they disappeared from the face of the earth, with NO TRACE at all."

"Well, maybe the sub submerged or something," Agent Titus wondered out loud.

"Naw… he's an operator. I would bet a SEAL," replied the more experience, Hernandez.

"What gives you that idea?" Titus puzzled now.

"It just adds up, the DOD running interference, making us believe he is a Squid, Cooper's demeanor, his expert training in avoiding interrogation. I mean if he was some dude in a sub, he would have been all concerned about where his motorcycle is and why we're claiming it's all over the highway in Nevada."

"Unless he already knew it was all over the highway in Nevada," Titus countered.

"Well, there is that. He could just be an exceptional liar and doesn't want us to know he was on the bridge in Bunkerville. Either way —we're going to find out." Hernandez reiterates with conviction, "My bet is he's an operator."

"It doesn't matter we'll get him. We are the FBI after all." Titus states proudly.

She doesn't realize how the DOD protects their own. If he's a Squid, it will be hard. If he's a SEAL, it'll be almost impossible, thinks Hernandez, while nodding in hopeful agreement.

Battle Mountain, Nevada

The old phone in the living room is ringing its bells off. Dorthey Timmons finally makes it from the kitchen to the living room to answer the phone. "Hello! Timmons Ranch."

"Momma, it's Jimmy," answers the caller.

Dorthey immediately begins to tear up, "JIMMY! How are you? It's sooo good to hear your voice. I thought you forgot about us with all your fame and success back east. When are you coming to see us?"

"Momma, I miss you too and it has been too long." Jim Johnson choking up himself on the brink of tears when hearing Momma's voice. I just don't know when I'll ever get back out there" — *Especially before I die.*

"Hey, do you ever get to see Mark? You guys live in the same neck of the woods."

"No. Mark is super busy like me, our paths don't seem to cross." Jim being embarrassed to admit. They had been best friends so many years ago.

"Well, you should, he's one of my 'lost boys,' just like you. You need to make staying in touch a priority, you're FAMILY after all!"

"I know, I know, and of course you're right. But I am calling for another reason."

"Oh, what can I do ya for?" answers Dorthey, all business now.

"Do you have a new 'Lost Boy' by the name of Kevin Linfield?" Jim is being very serious now.

"Well, sure. Kevin is a fine young man and shaping up to be a fine Buckaroo. Why? How do you know him?" inquires Momma.

"I don't really know him, but his name and address came up in an investigation. Has he been there long?"

★★★

"A couple of years, I guess. Why all the questions about Kevin?" Momma is letting worry overcome her.

"Oh, it's probably nothing. Tell me, Momma, does he have any new friends of late?"

"Well, I guess you could call them that, in April he brought some strays to the ranch that needed a place to stay. So, you know us… we took 'em in. Just like we did you."

"So, they are kids like I was?"

"Oh, no their full-grown, two young women and three men, all ex-military… the men I mean. The young girls are opposites, one's real nice, helpful too, while the other is a spoiled city girl… I think she hates it here. But we love on everybody, you know that. No matter where they're from." Momma finished with a sincere sigh.

Shit, how did this happen? The two people I love the most have the most wanted people in America staying hiding out with them. What a mess.

"Momma, I don't suppose Pop is around, is he?" *He's always had a clearer head about these things than Momma is.*

"Oh, no he's run into town to get some things, he'll be back tonight though."

"He doesn't have a cell phone on him, does he?"

"Who, Pop? HA! He wouldn't know what to do with one, even if he did. He always says if humans were meant to be leashed, they'd be a dog. Ha, Ha…"

"Okay, I want you to have him call me as soon he gets in, okay? It's really important."

"Well sure Jimmy, I have your number here I'll have him call you, soon as he gets in."

"Wait Momma, I don't want you to use that number, that's my work number –call this one, write this down."

"Well okay Jimmy, I need to get a pencil and paper…" *It's sure good to hear Momma's voice. Jim thought to himself.*

"Okay, I'm ready… go ahead."

"Here is my number: 702-555-7272, got that?"

"Are you in Nevada now?! Your new number is in Southern Nevada."

"No Momma, it's just a temporary phone. Be sure to have Pop call me at this number, and only this number when he gets home. You got that right?"

★★★

"Yes, Jimmy, I'll have him call. Now you be sure to get a hold of Mark, okay?"

"I will Momma, I promise."

"You better, I don't want to take a switch to you like I used to."

"I remember Momma, I got to go now... Hey Momma, I love you."

"You had better! Bye now."

"Bye, Momma." *I wonder if I'll ever see her again. Her heart will be so broken...*

Calling Mark is a good idea. Jim Johnson quickly looked up Mark Fenton's number in his cell phone but dialed it in the new burner phone he had been using ... a lot more than he expected. In seconds it started to ring.

"Hello?"

"You don't sound one bit different." Jim started the conversation.

"JIMMY! –you old horse turd. How are you?" Mark Fenton immediately recognized his old best friend's voice.

"How'd you know it was me?"

"Well, I didn't for sure, I didn't recognize the number. But as soon as I heard your voice, well com'on, you're my best friend, you're like a brother. It's so good to hear from you!"

"Well Mark, we have a problem and I'm really going to need your help."

"My help? You're the director of the FBI, what do you possibly need me for."

"It's about Momma and Pop, they're in trouble and they don't even know it."

"Oh, I am all ears. You've got my attention."

Jim spent the next thirty minutes bringing Fenton quickly up to speed about the Timmons' guests. Then, together they hatched a plan on how to protect these two precious people and resolve their threat.

"If DHS or the White House finds out about this, they'll rain hellfire down on that ranch."

Mark interrupted. "We got to get them out of there."

"Yeah, the guests. Not Momma and Pop," Jim responded. "If they disappear, they'll be chased to the ends of the earth, demonized by the media to no end, and they'll lose their beloved ranch! Besides, we both know Pop would never leave that ranch."

"Well, I think I have a place to put them, and we can keep an eye on them while you finish your investigation. Either clearing them or arresting them," Tom interjects.

"We just need a private plane big enough for six with a range of 2000 miles and off the radar."

"ACE!" They both said in unison.

Ace Baker was another brother, another of Momma's "lost boys" who lived on the Timmons Ranch. He was about seven years their senior and was still around when Jimmy and Mark lived In the Bunk House. He was always like a big brother to them both.

And after leaving the ranch Ace found himself in a very rewarding aviation career. He loved to fly and would fly anything and everything he could, eventually settling down in Newport Beach, California, with a very successful plane restoration business. Ace was his given name and had nothing to do with his Aviation Career, though he'd be the very first to admit it was a great fit for his career.

"I'll call Ace and see if we can get a flight arranged. You call our brother in Texas." Jim directed. "If this goes smooth, with any luck, we can have them relocated as soon as tomorrow."

Later that night, Jim's burner phone started to ring with the call he'd been expecting all day at about 7:10 p.m. *Just enough time to feed the animal and feed the crew, settle down in his big chair and call me. Yep, it's from the 775 area code. It's Pop.*

"Hey Pop, thanks for calling me back."

"Well, hello son, how have ya been? It's been a while," Pop said sternly, as a matter of fact.

"I know, I am sorry I haven't called, I just don't have a good excuse. Sorry."

"Don't apologize to me, It's Momma who hurts when her boys don't call. Hell, I don't even notice."

Bullcrap Pop, you're just as hurt as Momma, if not more when any of us don't stay in touch.

"Pop, you have a big problem, if you aren't aware." Abruptly changing the subject. "Kevin and his friends are the targets of a nationwide federal manhunt. So far no one has been able to figure out who they are, but it won't be very long now. We need to get them out of there as soon as possible, like tomorrow."

Jim spent the next forty-five minutes explaining to Pop in detail what they were suspected of. Pop listened carefully and deeply. Then when Jim finished, Pop only had one comment and one commitment.

"Sounds like they're Patriots. I'll talk to them right away about your plan and see if I can convince them, it's their best move."

"Thank you, Pop, I'll call you first thing in the morning to see if they agree."

"Sounds good, bye."

The phone went dead.

Geez, Pop. You are so full of conversation. I hope he's convinced. Otherwise, he'll never convince them. Not by a longshot.

Pop had already made up his mind that this suggested plan was the best thing for these patriots. Now that Pop knew they were patriots, he also knew God had bigger plans for them, something meaningful, nation-changing or, nation saving. Pop meandered out heavy-hearted to the bunkhouse to make a short announcement to the patriots.

As he pushed through the door, he saw them all laughing and playing cards. A real comradery had been built between them all. Even Leah was begrudgingly fitting in, trying to anyway, or making the best of it.

Pop, opens with, "Where's Kevin?"

"Kevin rode out two days ago to check the mother cows out in pasture 53" replied Leah.

"Oh, that's right." *He'll be gone ten days at least. That's a complication.* "Well, tomorrow morning rather you all scattering to do your chores, after breakfast, I would like you to stay and have a conversation with me and Momma. I want to tell you about Jesus, our founding fathers, and the purpose of life."

"Oh, all the simple topics," O'Brian chimed in. Pop Just smiled.

"See ya'll in the morning."

It's past my bedtime.

Chapter 15

Calling In a Promise

White House Lawn
The White House Press Corps gather in full force on the White House South Lawn with high hopes of catching some off-the-cuff remarks or even B-roll footage from President Mountebank before the Commander in Chief heads to Marine One and departs on the primary agenda for the day.

"Ms. President, MS. PRESIDENT!" hollers the 'gaggle' as they are often called, squeaking in unison.

"What is the Federal Governments' response to the shooting at your hometown in Portland, Oregon?"

With that one question, President Mountebank broke stride, spun on those expensive designer heels, and strode straight to the cluster of reporters. POTUS almost looked mad. Bordering on pissed off. The truth be told, the President was mad, but presented the concerns with sincere earnestness.

"The terrible massacre in downtown Portland of peaceful protesters cannot and will not be tolerated. We will bring every resource to bear against these cowardly terrorists."

"Are you saying there were more than just the two White Supremacists that killed at the scene? They weren't lone gunman!?" Interjects the reporter from *Rolling Stone*.

"It's clear that the incident in Bunkerville and Portland are closely related. And we are working with our local partners in EVERY jurisdiction to bring these horrible fascists to justice."

This is the very first time in two months that the President had addressed directly the "Battle of Bunkerville" in part because the President was embarrassed that the HRT and so many Federal Agents languished in Nevada Jail. But also, the staff dissuaded comment by the President until they got to the bottom of it. But now, the President was no longer going to wait; it was time to let the public know that Administration was going to act.

"Ms. President, Ms. President, –isn't it true that the agents involved in the incident in Bunkerville, have been arrested and are being held without bail in a Nevada jail?" asked a National *Fox News* Reporter.

"Yes John, that is true, I have dispatched the acting head of the FBI to Nevada to secure their immediate release. Our agent is in Nevada as we speak."

But *Fox* had a quick follow-up. "How is Jim Johnson going to accomplish that? Does he have the jurisdiction?"

Mountebank tactfully ignored that question and promptly took the next one.

"Ms. President, how are the two incidents connected?"

"It obvious, isn't it?" President Mountebank then continues. "It's a clear act of racism in plain sight. These White Supremacists are organized and conspiring together to overthrow this duly elected government. But this administration will stop them."

"How are you going to do that? What's your plan?" comes the follow-up from the *Washington Post* reporter.

"We are going to do what EVERY other administration FAILED to do. First, we are going to end this violence with extreme prejudice by identifying the leaders of the coup d'état and bring each and every one to justice. Then…"

"But how are you going to do that? I mean law enforcement hasn't even been able to catch the killers that were on the bridge in Bunkerville?" quips the report from *OAN*.

The President pauses. *How does she know the detail of the manhunt that is underway? Somebody has been leaking. Disturbing to say the least.*

Out of utter frustration, the President responds. "It's true we are tracking six people that have not been accounted for from the 'Battle in Bunkerville'." POTUS has now adopted the medias' label.

"But they will be captured very soon and when they are, it will be clear that the hick sheriff out in Nevada is the crazy one and our valiant men and women in federal law enforcement are the true heroes, repelling the insurrection by these fascists."

"So, there is more than one?" comes the obvious follow-up from *OAN*.

That question was also ignored. But the gaggle took immediate note.

"Look! As Governor of Oregon, I fought these racists groups every day. I know firsthand their anarchist tendencies, how well organized they are, and their stand of the 'browning of America.' They are serious business and now the Southern Poverty Law Center says these groups are growing exponentially, the biggest threat there is to the peace and tranquility of the United States. They have been a bunch of ghosts, silently lingering, but no longer. This needs to end; they need to end! NOW!"

"One last question … *CNN,* go ahead."

"You had mentioned another action step. Besides rounding up the fascists, what else do you intend to do?

"I think Governor Northfork in Virginia has the right idea. It's time to disarm these crazies. In modern America, there is no need to have an armed populace. That is why the government exists, to protect its citizenry. I will follow Northfork's lead and pass comprehensive legislation to stop all manufacturing, sales, and possession of anti-personnel weapons."

"But an Assault Weapons ban has been tried before?" The FOX reporter quickly interjected facing being talking over during the press conference. "It was proven that it didn't work."

"That's true because it didn't go far enough. What I am proposing - no strike that - what we will pass is a ban on any weapon that can kill another human being." With that, POTUS turned gingerly on those expensive designer heels and smartly walked away.

The gaggle stood there stunned for a moment in shock. Then circled up to coordinate their narrative of what the President just said.

Andrew Airforce Base

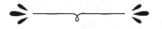

Jim Johnson had been watching the entire shocking press conference on his phone on final approach into DC. He felt refreshed and rested as he was able to sleep the entire flight from Nevada.

"Oh shit," Jim says under his breath.

This woman has lost her mind. In one ill-conceived press conference, she undermined his investigation in Nevada, pissed off Sheriff Gillette, handcuffed the Portland investigation to white supremacists, and enraged seventy-five million Americans against their government. God, does she want a civil war? I think she just declared one.

I better settle on my plan today. I am afraid she's going to make my decision for me.

Jim picks up his burner phone. "We are still on for 10 a.m? Good, I'll be there on time."

Jim Johnson's security detail dropped him in front of the Hoover building. Jim walked directly to the lobby restroom and changed into casual clothes wearing a Washington National's red, white, and blue ball cap, sunglasses, then gently folded up his three-piece charcoal pin-striped suit neatly tucking it into his carry-on bag. Strolling right back out without anyone noticing, he caught a cab and headed to his destination, Autumn Funeral Homes.

As he walked through the door, he was greeted by John Jackson. "Hey Doc, it's good to see you."

"I'm not sure I can say the same. Let's go into my office."

Fifteen years ago, Jim Johnson busted Dr. John Jackson for prescribing Opioids to undeserving patients with little or no medical need. After Jim's thorough investigation, it was revealed that Jackson's only motivation was to pay for his wife's cancer treatment, which was truly exorbitant. Jim decided to have mercy on Dr. Jackson and talked him into pleading to a misdemeanor and agreeing to give up his Physician's license.

Jackson readily agreed so he would not be locked up while his wife was dying, so he could be there for her to the end. Jackson was so grateful, he promised that he would repay the favor anytime he asked without question, and Jim was finally there to take Jackson up on that promise.

Jackson, "So I guess you're here to call in my promise."

"I am. I have a problem and I think you can help me," Jim replies. "Before I begin, I need your word, an absolute promise that no one, not a soul will find out what I am about to say or do. Can you please promise me that?"

"I owe you the most precious months of my life. You allowed me to be with Sara when she needed me most. You saved me... from me. You have my utmost sincere word whatever you say or do from this point on, I will take to my grave, and no one will ever know."

Jim opens straightforwardly with, "I am dying."

"I am sorry to hear that."

"I have brain cancer and I want to die quietly, with no fanfare, no relatives. Just me and God."

"Have you been diagnosed?"

"They are pretty sure it's a... GBM." Jim chokes up for the first time.

"Oh, I am sorry, that's what Sara had," Jackson said gravely.

"I didn't remember that. I guess I have come to the right place."

"What do you want from me?" Jackson pressed gently. "I can't help you, I'm not a doctor anymore and besides this particular cancer is a specialty..." Jackson probing and curious as to why Johnson was there.

"No, no that's not what I am looking for. What I need is a secure place to live out my last few weeks. Someone who will keep me comfortable, wipe my ass and feed me... a nurse," Jim realizing what he was asking.

"Jim, you can get a hospice nurse to care for you at home..."

"I know, but there would be a paper trail, death certificates. I don't want that."

"Oh. I see. May I ask why?"

"No," Jim stared blankly into his eyes.

"Well okay, no questions asked. If I was to do this, I need to keep up my government appearances and work schedule. You'll need constant care towards the end." Jackson was thoughtfully thinking this through now.

"I have an office in the back that I can make you comfortable in. I'll just sleep here at night."

"Oh, I can't ask you to do that," Jim pushed back.

"If you want this to be completely quiet, we need to avoid any appearance of a change in life and my business. What you are asking me to do is highly illegal, and I don't want to get caught."

"It is?" Jim hadn't thought of that.

"Sure, you need a nursing license at the bare minimum and a facility, if we're not going to do this at your home... right?"

"Right," responds Jim, very uncertain at this point. *This is more complicated than I realized. I can't do this at home because when I am missing that will be the first place they'll look.*

Jackson continues, "Then there is the disposal of the remains. Your only option is cremation if you want it kept completely quiet."

"I do," Jim nods, kind of numb now and in shock.

"No death certificate I suppose?"

"No death certificate."

"Well okay, I made a promise. I'll do it. I take it you're not opting for any treatments if you don't want anyone to know you're dying?"

"No treatments," Jim had decided instantly at that moment.

"Well, I better start getting things ready. This time will come faster than you think," Jackson speaking as a Physician and a husband of a cancer patient."

"What do I need to do?" Jim feeling somewhat relieved now.

"Nothing, I'll take care of everything. Besides, you don't want to be seen shopping for hospital beds or any other needed details. You just go about doing what you are going to do, and I will do my part." Jackson is meticulously making plans in his head.

"Wait one second."

Jackson briefly heads into another room and comes back tossing Jim a big prescription bottle of Dexamethasone.

"What's this?" Jim reading the bottle.

"Steroids."

"Why do I need these?"

"Your brain is going to swell as the tumor gets bigger. It will cause you to lose function pretty fast. These little pills will keep that swelling down."

"Tumors, I have two tumors." Jim was correcting and expressing his undeniable fear all at once."

"Oh, thanks for telling me." *His time is shorter than he realizes.*

"Don't they have long-term side effects?"

"Yes." Jackson looks at Jim in disbelief like 'stupid question.'

"Oh, yeah I guess there is no 'long term' for me. Hey, they're expired and in Sara Jackson's name."

"They are leftovers from Sara's treatment. They'll work fine. Just take three a day for now." Jackson stood up ready to leave the room.

"Now you want a ride back to the Hoover building?"

"No, how about to my house? I need to get a few things. John, how will I know it's time for me to come here to stay permanently?"

"Oh, that's a good question. How about you call me every day at 6 a.m. and again at 6 p.m. That way if you can't physically come to me, I can come and get you." Jackson thinking that should work.

"How will I know it's time?"

"Oh, you'll know, or you will be unconscious. Which means I come get you. It's not perfect, but it's all we got. By the way, you shouldn't leave town, this can happen quickly."

"Sounds like a plan. John, you will hear things about me when I come to stay with you... don't believe them."

You believed the best in me; I'll return the favor. Jackson thought to himself. "I won't, now let's go. My car is parked around back. I noticed you are calling me John now?"

"I guess we're friends now," Jim replies discreetly.

"I guess so."

After stopping at his apartment, taking a quick hot shower, and putting a new standard designer pin-striped three-piece suit and tie on, he ordered a cab and headed back to the Hoover building. When he arrived, he strode right on in, as if he owned the place. He figured no one would notice... he was wrong. Immediately his head of security approached him at the elevators.

"Where'd you just come from?"

"My house, I needed to get cleaned up."

"Sir, you can't leave here without giving me notice. I am responsible for your safe..."

"I'll come and go when I please. You serve at my pleasure, not the other way around."

With that, Jim entered the open elevator and pressed the button. His head of security began to follow.

"You'd better find another ride; this one is full," Jim recommended annoyed. Johnson's security chief stood there, dumbfounded, slack-jawed, and watched the elevator door close.

As Jim entered the office, Kathy greeted him with her usual coffee and set of reports.

"Good afternoon, Mr. Johnson."

Jim paused and briefly looked at his watch. *It is just now noon.* "Good afternoon, Kathy. How on earth did you know I was coming into the office and not heading straight back to Nevada?"

"It's my job to be where you are, to do that, I need to know where you are," she quipped with a knowing grin. "I am packed for our flight back when you are ready to go."

"We're not going back?" Jim thought about the best answer to give ... "Not right away, I need to do some things here first."

"Well, I just don't want you to get in trouble, I mean did you hear what the President told the press?" Kathy expressing her earnest concern about the political pressure coming his way.

"It'll be a couple of days is all."

"A couple of days? — it needs to be a couple of hours!" Kathy pressed intently.

"I will leave when I am damn good and ready. What is it with all the people that work for me acting like I work for them?!" Jim shutting down the inquiry harshly and uncharacteristically.

Something is wrong, he's feeling the pressure from the Oval Office or something. Kathy returned to her desk and worked quietly.

Jim began to be more productive than ever before. *It's funny how efficient a man gets when he is limited on time.* Jim thought as he began pouring over the reports before him.

Let's see, –how do I draw attention away from the Timmons ranch and keep the White House focused on a false flag? Oh, nothing better than a leak to the press. But what? Who?

As Jim kept reading, he thought of all the "Lost Boys" that have come through that ranch. Some he knew well, others he'd only heard of by name, and many came after him. Almost all had made something of themselves.

The Timmons had the most effective Christian Ministry he had ever seen. Their kindness, patience, and love had impacted so many lives, hell, generations. It would be a shame to see them come under the eagle-eye scrutiny of the US government. Especially, when that kindness is what brought this last bit of trouble on them in this way.

I need a new threat, something digestible to connect all of this together, that will keep the media and all of the various agencies focused on, for the foreseeable future. Something so mouthwatering, luscious, and delightfully tempting that everybody will chase it. I got it! —Where is that number of Julie Smith at the New York Times.

"Julie Smith," comes the annoying sounding voice on the other end of the phone.

"Julie, Jim Johnson."

"Well hello Director Johnson, how's your investigation going? Where is it – Bunkerville, Nevada?"

"Errr... fine." Jim was caught off guard by Julie's awareness of where he is... or supposed to be doing.

"Are you working on chasing down the President's comments from this morning?" Jim asked.

"The patriot ghost angle, who isn't? I think every reporter in the press corps is. Why?"

Oh, good they have a name for my fictitious group already.

"I thought that maybe I could help you get a little flesh on the bone of these... Ghost Patriots." Jim had stumbled and got the name wrong. But Julie didn't miss it for a single beat being in reporter mode.

"Whatcha got for me?"

"It depends if this will be off the record?"

"If you want it to be and I use it. It just depends on how good your information pans out." Julie is being obnoxiously smug now.

"Well, I could just call the *Washington Post,* I am sure they would like to hear this information straight from the Director of the FBI..."

"Jim I am a Pulitzer Prize winner; I must protect my reputation and can't muddy it with anonymous sources."

Oh, she is playing hardball now. Jim continues. "Okay, nice talking to you..."

"Okay, okay, how about I call you a highly place source at the FBI."

"Nope."

"How about, a highly placed source with knowledge of the investigation," Julie is reluctantly giving in now.

"Okay, that's the way it better read. It's against the law to lie to a Federal Agent." Jim smirking to himself.

"How can you help me with my investigation of these Ghost Patriots?"

Jim starts to spin his web. "The President was correct that there is a new threat of domestic terrorists that we are tracking across the entire Western USA. They have planned coordinated attacks in

★★★

various locations across the country and we have them under surveillance as we speak."

"So, there is not just the six that the President mentioned?"

"No, It's a full network."

"Oh, shit this is serious." Julie exhales in excitement.

"It's as serious as it gets," Jim confirms with a lie.

"How many of them are there?"

"Unknown."

"Was the Battle of Bunkerville one of the coordinated attacks?"

Jim pauses for a moment to determine his fabricated answer. "Likely SOME of the participants are connected to this network."

"Bingo. The six the President mentioned?"

"Undetermined."

"I'll take that as a yes."

"What about the shooting in Portland? Is that connected as well?"

"Undetermined. The investigation is just beginning."

So that's ALSO a yes. Julie rivetingly adds that to her notes.

"What can we expect next from Law enforcement?" Julie running out of questions now.

"We are pulling FISA warrants to surveil the suspects to bring their plans to an end." Jim is lying, sort of, he plans to apply for the specific warrants as soon as this article hits the papers. A little dirty trick he learned under the previous leadership of the FBI. *I am going to use this article as the predicate to justify and apply for the Warrant. I'll be dead before they figure it out.*

"FISA Warrants, that is serious business!" Julie exclaimed.

"Alright Julie, you get to work, and we'll be in touch." Jim bringing the conversation to an end.

"Can I call you if I have more questions?"

"NO," Jim says firmly without any recourse. Jim doesn't want to give his burner phone number and absolutely doesn't want calls on the FBI equipment.

"Okay, thanks for this. I must admit I am surprised though."

"Oh, why is that?" Jim wondering.

"Well, you have always been Mr. Boy Scout, always coming down on leaks from your department. Why now?"

Jim thought this question might come up. "The President spoke out of turn this morning, out of her passion to get these guys. I just

★★★

wanted to get the story straight for the American people before some other journalist creates some Fake News and scares everyone."

"Well thank you for trusting me."

"You're the only one who I thought of to get this right." Oh, the irony, Jim thought.

Jim began to hang up the phone.

"Director Johnson... Director..."

"Yes, Julie I am still here," replies Jim.

"Is there a leader of this Ghost Patriot Group?"

Jim paused deliberately while considering his answer. Then in that moment, he was inspired.

"Yes, yes there is."

"Oh, can you tell me his name?"

"No, I'll do one better than that, I'll get you an interview."

"Oh, shit really! When?"

"I'll be in touch." The phone went dead.

I see another Pulitzer in the Horizon! Julie Smith smiled a broad smile to herself.

GHOST PATRIOT

Chapter 16

Principled Men Must Stand

The stillness of the predawn hour was no stranger to the Timmons Ranch. For forty years Pop had woken well before the sun rose and prepared his day with Prayer and Bible reading. This morning though, he had trouble entering in because his mind was concerned, his spirit troubled.

The cover story that Kevin Linfield recounted of the five guests on the ranch was riddled with half-truths. Pop didn't really know who or what kind of real trouble they were in. The recent call from Jimmy gave him great cause for concern as Pop had great trust in Jimmy.

But God brought these strangers to him and Momma, that he was confident in. Now he needed to have the discernment of God to determine what to do or say next. He returned his racing mind to the Word of God. Speak to me Lord, *speak to me. I need you more than ever.*

Outside on the porch sat Leah. She often woke early to ponder, write, and pen notes of the odyssey she was on. *This will make a great book.* She began to energetically write:

As it reads in her diary:

> In two months, I have made quite a remarkable transformation. The first few weeks I was angry and argumentative, with well, almost everybody. I hated this hillbilly ranch with a passion. I hated the food, the tedious chores, the people, the pungent smells –pretty much everything.
>
> At one point I actually stole the keys to one of the trucks and snuck quietly tiptoeing into the night to run away, only to be held back by those wretched guard dogs. They just stood their ground in front of the driver's door and snarled. After about ten minutes of trying to negotiate with the unreasonable

animals, I finally gave up and quietly returned to my bed defeated.

The next morning, Momma leaned down to serve me a plate of eggs and whispered into my ear. "We love having you, but no one is making you stay." Somehow, I began to believe her.

In time my mind began to clear, albeit slowly and I shed most of the unresolved anger. Everybody was expected to earn their keep, so I was assigned some basic chores. All the small animals requiring minimal effort were my job. The daily feeding and caring for the chickens, the dogs, the turkeys, the quail, and rabbits.

At first, I was honestly scared of the clucking high-strung chickens, as they would race about. I never seemed to trust them. Now, to my surprise, I like them the most. I just see them as stupid and funny all at the same time.

I also like that they come when I call them, and it became even fun to collect their eggs. The quail and rabbit hutches smelled horrible at first and were a pain in the butt to clean. Both animals were afraid of me, well, all humans, and I couldn't seem to bond with either of them. The quail from time to time would storm the door of the pen when it was opened, and if I wasn't fast enough, I would spend much of the remainder of the day trying to catch the escapees. This brought great joy to the others as they watched me run about trying to lay hands on the little birds.

At times the men would sit on the front porch drinking cold beer and place wagers on the birds or me. Donahue didn't like the attention I garnered from the men, but I did. Even though I would act pissed, inwardly I liked it very much. I would affectionally pet and hug the dogs while they ate, but they would just trot off after their bowls were clean completely aloof to my affection.

Sometimes I wondered who owned the ranch, the Timmons, or their dogs. The turkeys were just weird hands down. Besides feeding them daily, and raking up their stinking pen, I had the responsibility to herd them into the garden and back to their pen each day. It was much like herding slow-moving feathery pieces of furniture twice a day.

All of that consisted of my "chores." But there were two things I love to do every day. Bottle feeding the three orphaned calves the Timmons had. It was amazing and eye-opening how aggressive those "little suckers" got the minute I would enter their pen. They would do a complete 180 turning into sweet babies once they got the rubber nipple in their mouth. It is so much fun!

And, I LOVE working in the garden with Momma. Momma took the time with me to explain agricultural processes like transpiration and Photosynthesis, and the rationale behind why Momma likes organic gardening, and the reason to rotate plantings and crops. Something is rewarding about putting a seed in the ground, watching it germinate, and reaching for the sun. I learned about good bugs, bad bugs, pollinators, and the practice of growing soil, not plants. I find it so intellectually stimulating and something very wholesome.

Momma, from time to time, would tell me fascinating Bible stories about gardening, sowers, seeds, pruning, field workers, and other things. But I just thought it a bit weird and politely listened out of courtesy to Momma. Which as I think about it, why on earth do I even care about Momma's feeling enough to be courteous? Then, I recalled the events over the past few months, how Momma was patient with me as I helped in the kitchen. I had always thought she was a good cook.

But once I was in the kitchen with Donahue and Momma, I realized I was worse than a half-skilled rookie. Momma would bake a pie from scratch, never looking at a recipe and seldom used the microwave! Once Momma slaughtered one of those feathery pieces of furniture, plucked it, cleaned it, and effortlessly had it on the dinner table the same day. I was told that I wasn't required to help slaughter the turkey, but I was required to watch. When Momma, hung the turkey upside down in the barn and slit its throat I almost fainted!

What's wrong with me? Just two months ago I watch people being shot and killed all around me. Later that day when we put the turkey in Momma's, huge country oven, I apologized. "I am sorry I got all woozy today when you killed the turkey."

Momma didn't even bother to look up, "If you didn't feel a little something I would be concerned for you. Taking a life, any life is not a natural behavior. We were originally designed to live in harmony with all of God's creation." That made sense to me and for the first time this God stuff connected with how I was feeling.

As Leah sat on the porch writing, she heard the Bunkhouse beginning to stir. *It's funny how men make such different noises than women, burps, farting, coughing, moaning, hacking, and spitting.* She smiled secretly to herself as she had learned and even come to adore those men in the bunkhouse.

Over the last few months, they had laughed and sweated a lot together. Together they bounced in noisy trucks on country roads, dug fence posts, and ate hearty meals. But it was playing poker together Leah just loved.

She discovered she was much better at poker than the lot of them. Which meant she was just a smarter player. Except for Pop, he didn't play poker. So, she challenged him to a game of chess and after losing ten games in a row, she decided there was much more to him than she thought. As an accomplished Chess player, she had never had anyone beat her so badly before.

She had never really met a man, any man for that matter that she liked, until the men on the Timmons ranch. Even the Buckaroo crew had their unique charms, though they weren't around a whole lot. There was one Buckaroo she secretly wished she saw a bit more of and that was Kevin.

For a man younger than her, he was the sweetest, most sincere man she had ever been around. When she would lose the quail from their pen, it was Kevin who swiftly pulled her aside and told her, "Quit chasing them around, cause you'll never catch them. Just leave them overnight and you'll find them under the pen in the morning waiting to be put back in."

"Really?" Leah exclaimed.

"Well, that's if nothin' eats them overnight," Kevin replied as he walked away.

"But who will entertain everybody?" Referring to the wagers from the porch, in a cutesy sort of way.

"Don't be their cheap entertainment. Just be the woman God created you to be," replies Kevin firmly, as he swung his leg on his horse. "Tomorrow, I'll show you how to catch a chicken without making a fool out of yourself." With that, Kevin rode off to the barn with a big grin.

But who did God create me to be? Leah was confused by the transformation even she saw. *I have never had a man talk to me like that. I don't think I like... well... maybe, yeah coming from him I like it.* Leah decided and genuinely smiled back.

She never really liked men or at least the metrosexual men she knew. She just thought of them as another version of women with the right tool. And, tools they were. Leah had never really had a meaningful relationship in her life. But now that she was away from all that city life, she was sprouting feelings of enthusiasm, hope, appreciation, and her soul was stirring back to life if it ever had been alive.

She liked the interaction, the attention, and certainly the respect she was gaining. It was interesting, she had always thought that respect was something you demanded, and strength was what you forced on others. But now had discovered that she had earned respect from these, these patriots without any demands. And strength, oh, she learned real female strength from Momma without a doubt in her mind.

Momma never wanted or tried to have the physical strength of men. She was just quietly smarter, earning immeasurable respect from all these men around her. The idea of misogyny wasn't in her vocabulary.

Momma told Leah when she asked about women's liberation, "I am IN control. Don't you know that the man is the head, but the woman is the neck!"

"Is that from the Bible?" Leah wondered somewhat confused.

"Nope, the movie *My Big Fat Greek Wedding,*" laughed Momma.

Oh, I get, –she's in control. Leah smiled back.

Leah had changed so much she was even feeling more comfortable in the non-designer clothes she was wearing. At first, she thought of them as "hick clothes," much like the people she saw down in the Touquap wash in what seemed like a lifetime ago. But now she had come to realize they are not really about fashion, but utilitarian for life on the ranch.

★★★

Sure, there were some nuances to them, like what Kevin and the Buckaroo Crew wore. Kevin tried to .explain the history and tradition of the Buckaroo to Leah, but she wasn't that interested in listening and frankly, would just zone out. She just remembers the big wide brim hat he gave her that Sunday afternoon while on a picnic.

"It fits perfectly!" she exclaimed almost giddy.

"The transformation is complete," Kevin replied, as she put it on.

That idea hadn't sunk in until this morning. What she had come to realize is the clothes she was wearing were comfortable, practical, and she found ways to show off her attributes as a woman. Which was a different way of thinking all in itself for her. Since when, did she care about her physical image? In fact, she had mostly hated being a woman over the years, and she told the world by the way she dressed.

I guess the transformation is complete.

Bunkhouse

The strong smell of men, sweat, manure, and body odor never seemed to be disruptive to the men bedding down in the bunkhouse. Once they were down for the night, nothing really disrupted their sleep in the bunkhouse, except the occasional "pee call" that seemed to come more often as a guy aged.

O'Brian was up early again as he once again awoke to the sweats from his reoccurring, dream, or vision, whatever the hell it was. He instinctively reached for his friend Jack. *Crap! That's right this is a dry ranch.*

That was the only thing Paul didn't like about the Timmons Ranch. Otherwise, it was a pretty cool place to hang out or hideout as it were. His little Emma had been on his mind, quite a lot. He was worried she'd never believe him again. *Her mom won't help with that, I am afraid.*

The men in the Bunkhouse were beginning to stir, he could hear their breathing change. Paul loved that this group of men and women had become a cohesive team in the two months they'd been living

★★★

together. He kept drilling them daily in different exercises of door-busting, advancing, and retreating, evacuating the wounded, and of course marksmanship.

It's not like he required it, but between the chores Pop had them doing and the insistence of mostly Donahue, it was a great way to redeem the time. Even, silly Leah would try to join in the evacuating drills, plus she was trying to learn some wound treatments. Sort of a Medic in the making?

All Paul knew is he was never going to be downrange from Leah Scrivener while she had a weapon in her hand. He didn't trust her that much. *A leopard doesn't change her spots.*

Plus, he had an uneasy gut feeling this thing is long from over. Not that he really knew, out in Battle Mountain there was very little contact with the outside world. One small television, no cable, or dial-up internet and the radio. That was it. And, without cell phones, they were running deaf and blind.

Pop really didn't know how 'wanted' they were but respected their request that their presence be kept quiet. *Hell, the old man barely spoke anyway.* The rest of the bunkhouse was awake and stirring now.

It was time for Paul to rise to his feet and be the first one to the bathroom because he wanted to get the warm water before the rest of the guys. Then, into the main house early for breakfast. He just had a feeling something was going to change today.

Breakfast at the Ranch House was pretty typical, although quieter than usual because the Buckaroo crew including Kevin Linfield, was still out in the "back forty (thousand)" as Pop liked to say. *I think that's a play on words of some sort.* Paul thought to himself wondering, but he really didn't understand it. *I'd Google it if I could.*

After breakfast Pop called everyone into the Livingroom for as he put it, "A little Pow-Wow."

"Grab yourselves another cup of hot coffee if you want. This will take a few minutes."

Momma happily poured more coffee for anyone holding up their cup. Once she was done serving, she retired into the kitchen. Leah tried to follow her to help with the clean-up, but Momma shewed her back into the meeting. "You need to listen to this," admonishing Leah.

Pop cleared his throat as he wound up preparing to say his peace, which would be more words than he was used to speaking all at one time. It was something he had been deeply thinking and praying about all night.

"Momma and me, we're a little disappointed in you all." He paused and looked around the room to be sure they understood the gravity of his words. Then he continued.

"You 'all haven't been totally honest on yer purpose for being here. It has come to my attention that what happened down in southern Nevada you had a whole lot to do with. And I guess the feds are looking for you real hard."

Did he turn us in? Thought O'Brian instantly concerned. *If he did, we don't have a chance to get out of here, the HRT is probably surrounding us now.*

A quick look around the room made O'Brian realize Daniels and McConnel had the same thoughts. Both were immediately on edge. Donahue picked up on the heightened alert of the men but was not sure why. Scrivener was just childishly concerned that somebody else would tell her story if she was arrested, she wasn't ready for it to be over.

Pop continued, "just relax everybody, I said we were disappointed, not angry with you. I understand why you told us half-truths, a ruse as they'd say. I wanted to see if we can put our heads together and see if we can find a solution." The tension slowly eased in the room.

"I do think we need to get you out of here, the feds will come-a-lookin' sooner rather than later, so I have made some arrangements. But first I want to tell you some things, I believe God told me."

They all looked up, *"Oh where is this going?"* Daniels thought to himself. *Not more of this religious crap.*

Pop was solemn now, "At the onset of this country, God himself set apart a handful of men to begin anew a nation that was unlike any other, before or since. These men took the greatest risk imaginable to their lives, their family, their wealth, and their sacred honor. It's hard to understand why anyone would risk so much, except that God called them to it and their soul demanded it."

"The circumstances were dire, and their chances were nil. But they proceeded ahead against the most powerful nation on earth. It wasn't a calculated risk; it was a suicidal risk. One that most likely, very likely would end them and their families."

"But they proceeded forward because they believed in what was right and righteous. And principled men MUST stand against tyranny. Some were trained and knew the horrors of war, others were naïve, but each proceeded forward not knowing the future of their actions." Pop paused to look directly at those around him, letting eye contact identify each individual.

"Momma and I knew from the moment you all piled out of Kevin's truck that there was a special mantle on you, each of you as individuals, and also as a united team. A team that God himself put together. In these months, God has used this time to pull you together and give you a trust and cohesiveness that would only come in a place like this. A place that was set apart as well."

"You see for forty years Momma and I have taken in boys, Momma dubbed them 'Lost Boys' after the orphans in the story of Peter Pan. But they were also literally lost, both spiritually and in life. God had each of them live and work on this ranch until they became Born Again, and their lives were set on God's path. They have all become, men of principle, men of integrity, and men of God. Warriors for Christ."

"Not all are warriors like you, but each has a specific role. Some are in law enforcement, some are politicians, some are welders, but all are warriors that you can count on. The funny part is that Momma and I have always thought there would be a bigger purpose to our ministry way out here in the middle of, nowhere."

"Not to say this ministry hasn't been noble, it has. But God told us many years ago that it would literally be world changing. I think that time has come." Pop stopped to slowly take a drink of his coffee; it was getting cold now. Then he continued.

"I am convinced that this group… this team of Patriots will be used by the very hand of God to realign our country back to the way He created it. But you won't be alone. God will use the Lost Boys to begin a movement, bring resources, and provide a powerful far-reaching network. But this will only be the beginning, others will join too, just like in the revolutionary war many joined for various reasons, some for money, some for position, and others out of compulsion. But came they did."

"You will see others join as the word spreads and God moves upon the hearts of men. What I am saying is hard. Just like the first American Patriots, this will be hard, costly, and seem futile. But in time you'll see His hand in your life and your purpose. It. Is. What. God. Has. Called. You. To. Do!"

Pop paused. He can't remember for the life of him when he had ever said so much. He looked up to see Momma, standing in the kitchen doorway smiling ear to ear, with tears rolling down her face.

The room stood still in stunned silence. They knew in their heart the truth of what was being said to them. But each wanted to fight all of what it meant. Their lives were now changed forever, their plans, hopes, and in some cases dreams of settling down far away from war. The truth be told, each had hoped that their actions on the bridge, would someday be understood, forgiven and they would be able to eventually return home.

But with Pop's revelation, it finally sunk in that they will never be able to return to the life they wanted. God had other plans. After a few long minutes, Donahue broke the stunned silence over the room.

"What do we do now? I mean if your God has plans for us, we can't set up here in Battle Mountain forever."

O'Brian chimed in, "We need to bug out. The feds will be closing in and we can't be here when they come."

That sad truth filtered through the group, gripping each of them.

"I have already made arrangements to get you out of here," responded Pop.

"Oh really– what do you have in mind?" came Daniels.

"One of the Lost Boys will be here to pick you up tonight," answered Pop.

"Where are we going?" asked Leah.

"I don't want to say for security reasons. Besides I don't even know the details," Pop answered.

"Wait just a second, who are the Lost Boys again?" Realizing his life was about to be placed in the hands of strangers.

Momma chimed in defensively: "These are MY children. You can trust each of them as you can trust me. You don't have to take their word, you can take my word for one simple fact, if they say they are one of Momma's Lost Boys, I vouch for them 100%. END OF STORY."

★★

"Well, that's good enough for me," laughed McConnel. "If Momma says it, that settles it."

Momma really is in charge! Admired Leah.

Pop expands on the Lost Boys – "These men, we raised like our own children."

"They are our children!" pressed Momma.

"The funny part is they don't all know each other. Some have heard of the others, but in most cases, they were like the older brother who grew up and moved away, before the younger brother came into his own. They only know about the older boy by the stories we told them and the chain of relationships."

"How many are there?" Leah asked now completely fascinated.

Fifty-Three, thought Momma as she was about to answer, when Pop got there sooner.

"I don't want to say," cutting her off.

"You have your own cell of Terror... er... Patriots. That's amazing! It will be very hard for them to be traced," laughed McConnel again.

"The only key to this network is you two," O'Brian interjected. "You should bug out too."

Pop surprised, "No son. We'll be staying here. This is our mission and calling. We can't leave until God relieves us."

"But if you're captured, they'll make you talk and give up your so-called 'Lost Boys'," O'Brian pressed harder.

"We'll just choose to trust the Lord to give us the words before our captures if it comes to that," Pop said with a confident smile.

Somehow, O'Brian knew it was true.

All of a sudden, Leah realizes that Kevin wasn't mentioned at all. "Is Kevin going with us?"

"It was part of the plan, but we'll never collect him in time for tonight," Momma answered, knowing her affection for Kevin.

"Will he be able to catch up with us?"

"That's the plan. They are looking for him too, the sooner we can get him outta here the better," Pop said with earnest.

Leah's countenance fell immediately, and Momma saw it.

"Well, you all better get out of here and do your chores and get ready to get going tonight. I bet I have a bunch of laundry to do today," Momma, taking charge.

"Let's all gather here at 6 p.m., and we'll head down the road," Pop commanded.

The remainder of the day was melancholy for the whole ranch. The last set of chores were done, much-needed laundry was washed and dried. Leah kept looking in silence back to the ridgeline with the hopes Kevin would be heading in on his horse.

"He's not coming," Momma mentioned in a whisper as she walked by with a load of laundry.

"I know," Leah responded under her breath.

Precisely at 6 p.m., they all gathered at the front porch. Pop walked steady and composed out the front door and tossed a set of keys to everyone standing in the semicircle. It was keys to every vehicle on the ranch, Pop's truck, all three ranch trucks, the hunting jeep, the ranch tractor, even Momma's SUV. Everyone was confused.

"What are we driving there?" asked Daniels sarcastically.

"No," Pop said as matter of fact.

"Everybody, toss your gear in my truck then grab your vehicle and follow me."

Once all the gear was in Pop's truck, he took off down the main ranch road, but before they left the ranch proper, Pop made a hard sharp left along a freshly cut alpha field. As they traveled along this decent farm road, pop turned his headlights on, as the sun began to set, and darkness slowly fell over the ranch. No one knew where Pop was headed except of course Momma.

Then as abruptly as they started, Pop stopped in the middle of the road. They all pulled up behind him.

"Now what?" Donahue came out of one of the ranch trucks. Lastly, the tractor arrived with Daniels aboard.

"We're going to make a runway! Spread out every 100 feet, then turn your vehicle toward the field with your lights on high beams. Then hustle back here for your gear. Light it up!" exclaims Pop loudly.

After a few minutes the whole group reassembled at Pops truck, and as if on cue landing lights appear in the air above their innovative makeshift airstrip. As the landing lights grow brighter in the distance, the distinct sounds of jet engines are heard in the distance.

"How are you going to get all these vehicles back?" asked Leah.

★★★

"Oh, Momma will ferry me back and forth till I get 'em all put away," replies Pop.

By now the jet sound is getting louder and louder as the plane makes a bumpy landing, coming to a complete stop right in front of the group.

Oh, shit, a Cessna Citation! Says O'Brian to himself. *I wonder where and how far we are going? At least it'll be comfortable.*

Momma affectionately hugs and says goodbye to the team members, while Pop firmly shakes the hand of each of the men, with a broad country smile. "May God go before you," are Pop's final words to each.

The pilot has climbed down and loaded all the gear in the belly of the plane, making sure the weight was distributed properly for the short take-off he has planned. He especially was glad that all the bags went in the belly as he realized how many weapons he was transporting.

I am sure glad we are going from private airfield to private airfield. The DEA and FAA would not like this.

O'Brian was extremely anxious to get in the air. It was his training, the longer you sit on the ground unprotected the more dangerous it is for his team. He was watching out the window and watched the pilot greet and love on the Timmons. It was familiar, affectionate, and loving –especially from Momma.

"Oh yeah, he's a Lost Boy," O'Brian said under his breath.

GHOST
PATRIOT

★★★

Chapter 17

The Insurrection

Colin Johnson, an intelligible twenty-nine-year-old unemployed coal miner originally from Richmond, Virginia, was forced to move back home with his parents because of the policies of the Mountebank Administration. The country had struggled for generations to gain energy independence and just when the oil and gas industries were on the brink of producing the energy that the USA needed Mountebank adopted new policies that took the country back to the 1970s. And Colin was one of the many victims, as he was permanently laid off from his good, –no –great paying job as a coal miner, as was his father.

Colin's great-great-grandfather was born into slavery. His grandfather a sharecropper, became a prominent landowner and farmer. Colin's uncle still farms the same land, but his dad knew the farm would not support another family and hired on in the mines as a young man, a boy really.

Colin was the first to go to college in his family and received his bachelor's in education, with a teaching credential, planning to become a teacher in a rural community. Mountebank's economic policy drove consumer confidence to the very brink of recession and just as Colin hit the job market, there were no teaching jobs available. Not for a new untested teacher anyway.

Thankfully his dad pulled a few strings and was able to help him get a job as a miner. Colin wasn't averse to hard physical work. He was a rugged well-built outdoorsman, hunter, and fisherman. So, getting dirty was okay with him, but his true passion was to help other kids advance in their lives. Especially poor rural kids who didn't see much of a bright future for themselves, except for a trade, welfare— or manufacturing meth.

★★★

Colin knew without question education was the answer. He always thought it ironic that all his altruistic plans still ended him back in the mines. And unfortunately, now he'd lost that job too. The truth be told, he was normally an optimistic upbeat guy but, in his heart, he was getting more and more discouraged. And this last bit of political news was not only attacking his constitutional rights but his life's passion, even his identity as a skilled hunter and outdoorsman.

"Dad, did you see that crazy announcement by our so-called President?" Colin asks at the breakfast table.

"No, can't say that I did," replies his father.

"DAD, you got to pay more attention to the world around you! It's gone crazy! Mountebank wants to send the whole country down the same path our dumbass governor is taking us. They want to ban ALL guns across the country. How do you not know about this?"

"It's easy, I have a job that takes me underground four days a week. I need this job to put food on the table for me and your mom… and now you. In a few years, I will be retiring and then I'll have the TIME to be an activist. But for now, I am a coal miner," replies Colin's dad, not looking up from the breakfast table.

"But it's clear now that these Liberals want to start a civil war. It's the only conclusion that one could come up with. First, they make us all poor and dependent on the dole, then once they have pushed the principled, the backbone of this country beyond all unimaginable limits, including the first amendment, THEN they think the time is right to take the one right we have to protect ourselves from an overreaching and tyrannical government. I can tell you that it will be too far, and something is going to break."

"Son, this isn't 1776. A group of musketeers is not going to take on this technologically superior army of ours. It is the strongest army in the history of the world. Your AR-15 is just no match for a modern tank or, worse yet, a drone strike."

"Oh Dad, don't you see, this will not be the Red Coats and Blue Coats lining up on the battlefield and shooting at each other at close range. It won't be a battle of modern mechanized armor. This will be an insurgency war to bring the tyrants to heal and force them to relinquish power to the sensible servants of the people, —to Patriots."

"But Son, that's what elections are for."

"Dad, wake up! The elections are rigged, the media and the tech monopolies have the public in their... their mind control. At least half the population lives on the coasts and in the cities. THEY HAVE NO CHOICE but to comply with their governmental overlords. Just as the Loyalists did during the Revolutionary War. They will pick the side they project will be the victor and the side that will keep them in their comfort and security. They are the dependent ones, dependent on infrastructure, mass transportation, law enforcement for personal protection, and the food and fuel industries. But take that all away, and in ninety-six hours, anarchy reigns. Just look at New York when the power goes off, or what happened to New Orleans after Hurricane Katrina. It was chaos all within ninety-six hours!"

"Let's just hope that doesn't happen," Colin's Dad responds scoffingly.

"I agree, but the Liberals are pushing and pushing, if someone doesn't intercede, our country is going to go into a 'very dark winter,' as President Mountebank likes to say."

"An insurgency you say?" Colin's Dad is pensively considering the thought.

"Yep, an insurgency and don't forget that we have thousands of repopulated veterans who just spent the last fifteen years fighting against insurgencies in Iraq and Afghanistan. Those veterans are literal experts at insurgency. They love their country, and they gave it their oath to protect her from her enemies, foreign and DOMESTIC."

Although Colin had never served in the military, he had been spending a lot of time over this last week at the Virginia General Assembly in Richmond, the oldest legislative body in the United States. He had been demonstrating with what he loosely called 'The 2A Supporters'. It was an armed unorganized mix of the Patriot movement groups, including various anonymous gun rights factions along with just ordinary unaffiliated Americans who supported the Constitution. They were gathering in peaceful protest against the legislative action of the Commonwealth of Virginia legislature, to effectively end gun ownership in the State of Virginia.

Over decades Virginia had become increasingly more and more liberal, as it became a bedroom community for Washington, DC. As a result, the voting block became more liberal and influential turning a red state, blue in the Assembly. Over the last year, Governor Northfork had been pushing for "sensible gun regulation" which was a flat-out bold lie. It was a gun grab, that defined an assault weapon as any weapon that could end a person's life. This idea was catching momentum quickly across the liberal states, as all eyes were watching Virginia's lead.

Now the President has hitched her legislative policy to a like-minded Virginian's. It was during these past five days of protests at Virginia's capital that Colins' worldview was changing or evolving as he would later say. The Republicans were putting up a brave fight trying to stop the "sensible" bill from passing. But it was a losing fight. They just didn't have the votes.

Today was the final day of debate after which an immediate vote was to be taken. Governor Northfork promised to sign the bill before the day was over. It seemed likely to be a futile last-ditch effort for both the republicans and the demonstrators. But neither group wanted to go down quietly. The Republican minority leader had one final do-or-die procedural "Hail Mary" to stall the vote.

In the Virginia house, it would take a quorum to advance a bill to the vote. So, he asked – demanded – that the Republicans just not show up to work. Just a few of the republicans gathered that morning early on the statehouse steps for the announcement to the protestors and the media. The Governor, not to have his plans thwarted, held his own Press Conference in the stately decorated 18th century office of the Executive Mansion.

"If the Republicans attempt this violation of house rules and the will of the Virginia people, I will order the State Police to track down every one of these traitors to their oath and have them brought back by force if necessary. We will have a quorum and get this needed legislation passed!"

Meanwhile, at the Republican press conference on the Capitol steps, a reporter passed on the Governor's message to the rebellious minority.

"Did he actually say that?" responds the Minority Leader.

"He did —just moments ago. What is your reaction?" replied the local reporter hoping to incite a newsworthy statement.

The Minority leader was a bit stunned, not knowing really what to say. In his state of confusion, he then pushed forward one of the other republicans who was there to represent his district. Tal Jordan was well-known as the highly vocal and sometimes argumentative representative from Mecklenburg County. He was a sixth-generation Virginian and served his country as an Army Ranger in Desert Storm. Infuriated, he stepped to the lone microphone.

"What's my reaction? I am going home back to Mecklenburg County. If the Governor wants to follow through with his threat, he better send young troopers who have no families at home. Because I will not be returning here to the Statehouse under any circumstances. And I will not be threatened."

"How will you stop the governor from having all of you brought back?" asked another reporter. There was an uncomfortable pause on how to respond. Then Colin just simply stepped to the microphone, uninvited.

"These men, our representatives, are making a hard stand against this unconstitutional gun grab. There are SIX THOUSAND of us here today and we will STAND WITH THEM!"

The crowd went crazy in thundering applause and cheers.

"USA! USA! USA!"

Colin was emboldened and empowered all the more.

He looked directly over his shoulder at the Minority Leader, "Sir, we will guarantee your safe passage to wherever you need to go, under our protection. Additionally, we will secure this Capital for the People, WE DECLARE THIS GENERAL ASSEMBLY CLOSED UNTIL FURTHER NOTICE! No more work today, Liberals go home."

NO MORE WORK TODAY! NO MORE WORK TODAY! chanted the demonstrators in unison.

Almost on cue, the Virginia Lightfoot Militia emerged from the crowd and approached the Minority Leader. "Sir, we would be honored to escort you and your folks out of state and out of the Jurisdiction of the State Troopers," came the Lightfoot Militia Leader.

"Ah, ah okay, I guess." He didn't really foresee the press conference going this way.

"Let's get you out of here before the Troopers can figure out how to stop you," says Representative Tal Jordan.

"May I suggest we head to West Virginia; I am confident you'll find quarter there," says the Militia Leader. The twelve-man team formed a military escort around the eight representatives and pushed

★★★

their way through the crowd with two in the lead, one of which was the leader, and two at their "six" –five on each side. All with their weapons in the low ready.

No Trooper is going to try an arrest with this group. Tal Jordan thought to himself. *This is like the professional security detail I saw in Iraq.*

Tal looks to Colin, "Now what are you going to do?

"Me?" Colin said exasperated.

"Yeah you, you're calling the shots."

"I don't know, I am just a schoolteacher."

"Well, schoolteacher –get your students organized and do it quickly," says Tal with a knowing smile.

Colin back on the microphone now, "May I get each leader from the various groups represented here today, up to the microphone?"

Within a few minutes, there were roughly forty-five men standing on the steps looking to Colin for direction.

Colin spins around, privately mutters to Tal, "Now what do I say to them?"

"Secure the building and have the building evacuated. By now everyone inside will want to get out and go home to safety."

"What about the Troopers inside the building?"

"I'll talk to their Captain with you. He knows me," directed Tal.

Colin turns to the leaders.

"We need to secure all the entrances to this building. Then we need to set a perimeter, so they think twice at trying to make us move out of here."

"The three percenters will secure the entrances," cries one voice from the crowd.

"Great!" replies Colin.

"The Oath Keepers will organize the perimeter with the help of the other leaders here."

"Okay, the rest of you on him," commands Colin.

"We ain't taking any orders from a nigger!" protests a man from the crowd. In unison, the other men gave a mad dog stare at the racist protestor.

Tal took the microphone so everyone could hear, "Look, any individual that is not up for this HARD STAND should just leave now. This is gonna get worse before it gets better, and you might just think it's in your best interest to go home." He immediately hands the mic back to Colin.

"WHO'S WITH US!" Colin shouts out.

"OORAH!" Came the answer back in concert from all forty-three leaders.

"Any questions?"

"What about COMMS?"

Tal took this one. "Leaders turn your radios to Channel 2, that will be for leadership coordination. Use your standard channels for your own respective unit's coordination. If you don't have COMMS in your units, well, I guess you're shit out of luck, you should have brought some. I promise you in a matter of hours they will have the cell towers in the area shut off. Send up smoke signals or something," Tal said with a smile and a slight smirk.

"Also, before law enforcement can react, each unit needs to send out scroungers to locate provisions. We may be here for several days, and soon they'll have this part of the city shut down."

"What about the libs inside the Capital and the Troopers?"

"We are NOT holding hostages; they are going to be allowed to leave in an orderly peaceful manner. This needs to remain a peaceful protest."

"It'll be peaceful until it isn't," replied one man interrupting.

Colin ignored that comment and continued, "Representative Jordan and I will address this situation personally and see what we can work out. Now let's get to work, we don't have much time." The men scattered at full tilt.

Colin and Tal headed into the entrance of the Virginia Statehouse massive halls. To their surprise, the State Troopers who were commissioned to protect the officeholders and building had built a contemporary makeshift barricade just inside the main doors.

"Oh, oh, these guys have taken this real serious," Colin exclaims to Tal.

"Capt'n, Captain Brewer can you hear me?" Hollers Tal. "It's Tal Jordan."

"What do you want Jordan?" comes an apprehensive reply.

"Capt'n is that you, we want to talk," presses Jordan.

"You're not taking this building!" Captain Brewer yells back straight away.

"Captain, just take it easy, we've known each other a lot of years, there is no need for all of this, this aggression."

"You've sided with these insurrectionists, you're no friend of mine anymore. Now I am ordering you to leave the building and have your insurrectionists disperse and leave state property. We have called for back-up, and you'll be surrounded soon by every law enforcement agency in the state," demanded the Captain.

Colin replies, "Now look Brewer, these men and women out here have decided that they are not going to let this unconstitutional bill pass, they have order..., er ASKED, that the remaining Legislators in the building go home. We're here to help facilitate their safe departure."

"We'll stay put until help arrives," confirms Brewer.

Tal responds "Now, Capt'n, it may take days to negotiate a peaceful end to this, in the meantime your... your hostages will want to eat, see their loved ones, go home. Let's let them."

"No sir, they'll stay right here where I know they are safe."

"Well okay then, but they are YOUR hostages, not ours. Just send word when you want to arrange something," answered Tal.

Both men turned and left the building.

"Now what?" Colin asks.

"Oh, those cowards inside will pressure Brewer to work something out, just wait and see. Besides, any attacking force that may come will think long and hard about their safety. I just wanted it on the record that we were not the ones holding them against their will."

"He'll lie about it later," Colin retorted.

"I have it all recorded," and having said that, Tal held up his cell phone triumphantly.

The Hoover Building, Washington, DC

"The White House is on the line," Kathy announces over the interior intercom.

"Oh Goodie," replies Jim Johnson to himself as he picks up the handset.

"Mr. Johnson, I have the President's office for you. Please hold the line," says the flat monotone voice on the other end.

"Johnson?" comes the voice of Chief of Staff Smith.

"Yes, this in Jim Johnson."

"The President would like you back to Washington immediately," demands Smith.

"But we are beginning to make some progress in Nevada."

"I don't give a shit, get back here NOW! We have something major brewing in Richmond." The phone line abruptly went dead.

Well, now I won't need to explain why I'm already back in DC.

"Kathy, get the field office in Richmond, Virginia on the line, please?" Jim asked over the intercom.

After ten minutes of briefing over the phone by the Special Agent in charge in Virginia, "Okay, I want you to allow the locals to deal with this. The last thing we need to have is the HRT involved in another shootout," ordered Johnson with authority. *A shootout which it just may become.*

"Kathy, get me everything we know on Colin Johnson and Tal Jordon from Richmond, Virginia." *I have a feeling the President is going to thrust us right in the middle of this.*

Undisclosed Location, West Texas

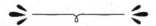

The flight had gone reasonably quick in the Citation. Everybody tried to get some rest in the small chairs of Cessna design.

At least there's plenty of legroom. McConnel thought as he slightly dozed off only to be awakened as the plane again made a bumpy landing.

"Where the fuck are we?" Donahue asks.

"I have no idea, but it's flat and dry…"

"I bet we're somewhere in the Great Plains," replies Daniels.

Over the speaker comes the announcement as if on cue: "Welcome to Texas."

Scrivener staring out the tiny little window. *This is Texas? What a shithole.* She wasn't in a very good mood. She didn't like being out of her comfort zone and lately that had been happening a lot more often than she wanted.

The plane landed roughly on the bumpy open prairie plain and quickly stopped to a standstill, in the middle of nowhere. The loud noisy engines shut down and out emerged Ace Baker.

"Morning everybody. I hoped you enjoyed the flight. I tried to make it as smooth as I could, except for the takeoff and landing. Sorry about that. It was necessary."

"Hi, I am …" started Donahue.

"No names please," Ace rebuked in haste.

"The less we know of each other the better. I do need some help getting the baggage out. You might as well all get out and stretch your legs. It may be a while before your ride gets here."

After a few minutes of unloading and stretching, Ace climbs back into the plane and talks on the radio for a couple of minutes. Then leans out of the doorway. "I have to go. They're starting to wonder why my transponder is off. I got to get back in the air. Nice to be of service, praying for you all."

With that, the plane door slammed shut and locked. The engines fired up and the plane taxied away. The five watched as their ride made a hard right turn and picked up speed across the field. Each had extremely serious doubts about their situation as the plane lifted off, leaving them all standing there in the middle of nowhere, possibly stranded. No one spoke a word until the plane was out of sight.

It was Leah first, "Here we are in shithole nowhere Texas. What do we do now?"

"We wait," says O'Brian.

"Wait for what," says Donahue.

"A ride," as O'Brian makes a bed of sorts in the dirt and lays down.

Daniels, not so quick to accept the situation takes an intense search scouting around with his binoculars.

"What are you looking for?" smiles McConnel.

"A shower," says Daniels.

For the first time his girlfriend, Donahue, takes a good look at Daniels. "You are filthy. How did you get like that?"

"I was behind all of you in the tractor back in Nevada. It was dusty back there!"

They all started busting up at the revelation of Daniels bumping along on the tractor in the dark behind all the other vehicles' dust.

About an hour later a dust cloud arose on the horizon, within twenty minutes or so a dirty four-door Ford pick-up stopped at the group. Daniels cautiously, reached under his bag and gripped his Glock not sure of who this could be. The driver's side door slowly opened and out came a handsome cowboy.

"Hello, folks" announces the driver. "My name is Glenn Kinum, Momma sent me to give you a ride." Daniels released his grip on his gun and jumped to his feet. *That was the correct password.* Daniels joked inwardly to himself.

Each of the group introduced themselves and of course, Kinum, removed his hat when meeting the ladies, as was his custom.

"Toss your gear in the back and I'll get you to the ranch house. I bet you're hungry?" instructs Ranger Kinum to the travelers.

"What took you so long?" Scrivener demanded, lightly for her. Donahue smiled to herself. *She's baaack.*

"I do beg your pardon for the wait. I only got the word you were coming last night, and I was in Dallas. It's quite a drive to get here. I did the best I could."

"Is that where we are, near Dallas?" Scrivener followed, back in reporter mode.

"No, not hardly," is all Kinum said.

They drove for about another two hours before they came to the main ranch house. It was beautiful, an oasis really, in the middle of the Great Plains. It was green, with trees, a beautiful lawn, and a swimming pool.

As they pulled up in front, Daniels exclaimed, "Is *this* where we are staying?"

"Yep, this is my family's hunting lodge. We have brought guests here for generations to hunt and relax. It's off-season, so nobody is here."

"I guess this will do," Daniels says with an approving grin.

"Couldn't we have landed a bit closer than this– that was a long drive?" Scrivener complaining once again.

"Well, Ac… er, …your pilot felt it would be better to set down in direct flight path to Love Field so no one would make the connection here. *Love Field is Southeast of here.* O'Brian silently noted to himself.

★★

★★★

"Is there any livestock or animals?" Questions Leah hopefully.

"No, we only bring horses out when we have guests," Kinum continued. "You're out here all alone in the middle of a million acres of a prime hunting ranch, in hunting season, of course."

Glenn Kinum bounded up the stairs of the main house, crossed the porch, and unlocked the front door. "Make yourself at home. The bedrooms are up the stairs on the second floor. The kitchen is through there and the gym is here."

As he opened the door, "down this long hall is a study down there with books and games. The laundry is at the back of the kitchen. If you want to clean your weapons or reload cartridges, we have a gunsmith shop straight out back. There are also some fun toys in there you might find entertaining too. There's not much in the refrigerator right now, but plenty of food in the root cellar and the pantry. I will bring out fresh supplies tomorrow."

As each Patriot entered the magnificent grand entrance of the lodge, they were stunned by the grandeur of the place. The main living room sprawled out at approximately four thousand square feet. In the middle of the room graced a massive and stunning natural stone fireplace standing as the centerpiece of the lodge. And to the right, an elegant floating wooden stairway leading to the second floor with eight bedrooms each with their own posh private baths, with another extravagant sitting room and TV room.

"Oh, you're not staying here with us?" O'Brian asked.

"No, I have a job in Dallas, so I'll be back tomorrow night. In fact, if there is nothing else, I'll be heading out." Glenn waited briefly for an answer.

All five of the Patriots were stunned at the dazzling exquisiteness of it all, especially after the modesty of the Timmons Ranch.

Finally, McConnel answers for the group, "I think we'll be just fine here, Thank you."

"Alright, make yourself at home, I'll see you tomorrow," Ranger Kinum retreated out the way he came.

Leah and Donahue headed up the wooden stairs to pick out bedrooms. McConnel headed to the kitchen and Daniels followed Donahue with the bags. He was looking for a much-needed shower. O'Brian grabbed the gun bag and headed out to check the gunsmith shop.

★★★

He expected a simple gun shack, maybe a Tuff Shed. What he found was mind-blowing. The gunsmith shop was actually a soundproof extension of the house, a custom garage of sorts with a portico out back overlooking an outdoor shooting range.

Inside it had everything O'Brian could imagine in his wildest dreams. An indoor pistol range, reloading benches, a self-serve stocked liquor bar, a cigar humidor, and a wall of sporting rifles and pistols, the finest he had ever seen. O'Brian smiled to himself, *Oh, I could get used to this!* Then immediately, opened the bag and started to clean the team weapons.

Chapter 18

That Went Better Than Hoped For

Hoover Building, Washington, DC
"I have Agents Hernandez, and Titus on the phone. They want to give you the update you requested" says Kathy echoing over the intercom.

"Director Johnson," Jim picks up.

"Sir, I think we have found them," says Agent Titus setting an eager opening.

"Well, that sounds promising. Fill me in," responds Johnson.

"Well maybe we have a location, counters Martinez," more cautiously.

"Just fill me in," Johnson repeats himself.

"We have been able to track five of the six phones from the Mesquite Truckstop with some help from the NSA and a bunch of extensive groundwork. The first phone was located a couple of days ago, which as you know belongs to Kevin Linfield of Battle Mountain, Nevada. The other four phones were tracked to different locations… well, all over the country."

"Apparently, some smart-ass taped them each to different trucks that originated in Mesquite, but then those trucks traveled all over in their normal trucking duties. Each truck was a long-haul truck, so they just kept moving not knowing about their taped cargo and never being on a routine delivery route of any kind made it impossible to track. It was hard as hell to catch up to them because they never stay in one place very long."

"It was a bitch!" interrupted Titus.

"Finally, we got one in New Hampshire, one in New Mexico, one in Ohio, and the last one in California."

"And the sixth one?" asks Director Johnson.

Oh, he is paying attention.

"The last one seemed to go dead in Mesquite on the day of the conflict," replied Martinez.

"So, it was a giant wild goose chase?" pressed Johnson.

"No, no, we were able to find the owners of all but two of the phones," counters Titus.

"We know where they are then?"

"We have addresses for the phones, but their personal locations are a bit more difficult," Martinez this time, trying not to overstate the present condition of the investigation.

"We ran each person's bank and credit card use and well, their cards have been used all over the freaking place, sometimes in two different states within hours of each charge. And apparently, two of the suspects purchased gas in Las Vegas and San Francisco," Titus responded.

"What about purchases on the day of the incident?" asked Johnson pressing on.

"That's what's funny. They all withdrew cash from the ATM at the truck stop, then didn't use their cards again for a day or two. One even went a whole week," replied Titus again.

Director Jim Johnson sat and thought seriously about this for a minute. "Oh, these guys bugged out, they got cash and then all took off in different directions. You need to get agents on those cards and find each one of them and those trucks. Let's find each of them," falsely directing his agents.

"What about going directly to their homes, I mean maybe they just went home?" asks Titus.

"We know all the phone owners except two. Shouldn't we just find out if they are there?"

"Wait, one of the phones went dead, and the other you don't have a home address on?" presses Johnson.

"Yeah, that one comes back with a DOD mask on it. And they are not being helpful to us in identifying its user or owner," as usual, continues Martinez with disdain.

So, no name or address on two of the phones, thinks Johnson, *this can be useful.*

"What about the motorcycle?" Johnson asks.

"We spoke to the sailor who owns it over a video call. He's a submariner who didn't seem to know it was missing," quickly replies Martinez.

"Have you verified that it wasn't him riding it?"

"Not yet, he was pretty evasive."

"Lots of 'it's classified' responses," chimes in Titus. *I wonder why Martinez didn't spill his suspicion about the SEAL connection.*

"We have more work to do there," continued Martinez trying to stay on point. Hoping Titus didn't share his concerns until he was ready.

"So, you're okay to have us go to the residence of each of these suspects and see what we can see?" asked Martinez awaiting confirmation.

Jim Johnson thought for a minute.

"You two go to each address and make your inquiries. Have the cyber team follow the leads on the bank and credit card charges, coordinating with local field offices to make arrests as needed. Those are your hot leads, I am sure."

"Then why are we doing the traveling to the suspect's houses?" asked Titus, a little confused.

"Because I want this handled with great care. It's so politicalized and media charged, I don't want it getting out to the public that we have suspects. If it does, they'll go deeper underground than they already have and we'll…er… you'll have a media circus."

And you'll have the President up your ass, thought Martinez.

"I want you to go carefully, slowly, and thoroughly on this. Only report to me. No one else. Got that? Me only."

"Yes sir," both answered. And the line went dead.

That ought to keep them busy for a while until I plan my next move. Johnson picked up his burner phone and called Julie Smith.

"Julie, I have a bit more for you on our investigation," Jim opens with caution.

"Hello, Director Johnson. I am not in a great place to talk…"

"This won't take long," presses Johnson. "We have now focused on just one suspect. It turns out that his phone was traced to the Truckstop in Mesquite the day of the Standoff."

Oh, I like that 'STANDOFF'. That works. Thinks Julie.

"This one phone went dead, and the suspect jumped a long-haul truck and has been giving us the slip as he jumps from truck to truck."

"Oh, wow… where have you tracked him to?" Julie intently listening and scribbling notes while sitting on the toilet.

"He has been tracked first to New Hampshire, then New Mexico, back to Ohio, and now we are focused on California. Each time we think we have him, he just evaporates." Johnson is playing with her now.

"Just like a ghost…"

Julie has been playing with the name of Ghost Terrorists or maybe Ghost Supremacist. But it was hard to define with a group of people, but now only one person seems to be the target of this manhunt. It was almost disappointing.

"That's pretty clever to use the long-haul truckers, isn't it? Julie trying to buy time to come up with a follow-up question.

"That's it for now," replies Johnson.

"Wait Director, one more question…" at that precise moment Julie slips and drops the little pad she was actively scribbling on. In her hastened effort to save the pad, she let go of her grip on her iPhone, and right between her legs, it slid with the familiar kerplunk sound, as it fell into the dirty brown water of the toilet. "SHIT!"

Julie missed the irony of her words.

Back in Washington: "Julie, Julie…" I guess I lost her. Johnson hung up the phone then turned his attention to determine precisely what his next move needed to be.

Plano, Texas

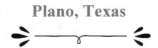

Abdula seemed to be extra nervous, Jamil immediately noticed. He was pacing, randomly looking out the window a lot, and checking the phone continuously. Something was about to change, happen... Jamil didn't know what for sure.

Jamil had been persuaded to wear a wire by the Texas Rangers. For weeks now he routinely gave daily reports to his contact LT Davis and exchanged the flash drive that held each recording. Although everything got picked up by the surveillance truck outside their house, this provided a duplicate record of everything. Davis used the flash drive pick-up as an opportunity to get a feel on how his informant was holding up under pressure.

Jamil had begun to hate Abdul and most of the men he was "serving." They were not the true committed Muslims he believed they should be. Sure, they would put down the television remote control to pray, eat, go to the bathroom, or do other activities, but otherwise, they just sat on their asses and ordered Jamil around. They treated him rudely like a slave and called him "Nawar" which he came to understand to be a derogatory term meaning Gypsy. All Jamil knew is that when they first started calling him that, they would all laugh.

At first, Jamil let it roll off his back. But now his name was seldom used, and he was getting sick of it. The morning donut run was getting old, but this was where he would meet with Davis for a few minutes.

"I think something is about to happen," said Jamil Roberts reporting as he sat down.

"Oh, why?" Replied LT Davis.

"Abdula is worried or anxious… I'm not sure. I think they're about to get a visitor."

"Oh, why do you say that?"

"Because Abdula keeps making everyone clean up after themselves and he's nervous, looking at his phone all of the time, stuff like that."

Davis thinks thoughtfully for a bit, "We are not seeing any intel that anyone might be coming. Are you sure he's not just tired of being cooped up in the house all the time? They haven't left even once in all of these weeks."

"Well maybe, but I am telling you something is going to happen," Jamil insisted as he handed Davis the flash drive.

"I got to get going, Abdula likes the donuts warm." Jamil rushed off heading to the counter to pick up his order waiting for him.

Davis picked up his cell phone and called Sergeant Glenn Kinum, "Sarge, have you gotten any further on finding the rightful owner of the house?" He listens for a bit and then replies. "Okay, press those assholes at the Attorney General's office to get off their backside and get us the cooperation we need in California, to get those bank records. This is taking way, way too long." He disconnects and sips his hot coffee.

*This just does not feel right, California is usually very
cooperative when it comes to government intrusion into people's
privacy. Why are they dragging their heels now?*

Jamil just got back to the house with the donuts, and it was in
utter calamity. Abdula was marching around the house yelling and
screaming in Arabic. The men were picking up their mess and
cleaning up the house almost in fear. One man had the television in
his arms and was headed outside running towards the trash can in
the garage.

"What's going on?" Jamil asks Abdula.

"GET RID OF THAT!"

"What?" replies Jamil in confusion.

"THAT, POISON, THAT PIG FAT!" Abdula pointing at the
donuts Jamil had just carried in.

"NO TRUE BELIEVER WOULD EAT THAT... THAT
POISON! GET IT OUT, OUT!"

Jamil swept up the boxes of donuts into his arms and followed
the man with the T.V. *What the fuck has gotten into this guy, he
sends me down to get donuts every morning and now, they're
poison?* When Jamil finally enters back into the house, Abdula
abrasively thrusts a piece of paper into his hands.

"GO, GET!"

Jamil looks down apprehensively at the paper in his hands. It's
a grocery list, a long list. Most of the things on it are the items he
bought the first day they arrived.

"We have a special guest tonight," Abdula confirms. "GO,
GET."

Jamil turns on his heels and heads straight to his car. As he sits
down in the driver's seat, Jamil begins to talk to himself. "I don't
know what the fuck is going on but it's something big. The boss man
is running around the house screaming orders and he seems very
scared. I have been sent to go buy groceries. I guess we have a
houseguest coming tonight."

The men in the surveillance van heard every word and were
immediately in action. The first call was to Davis. The second call
was to Capt. Clayton. "Sir, we have a special guest coming tonight,
the house is all in a twitter. I thought you'd like to be updated."

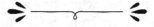
Garland Office of the Texas Rangers

"Kinum, get in here!" cries Captain Clayton.

"Yes sir."

"Somebody is coming to visit our unwanted guests tonight."

"Who?"

"That's what you're going to find out for me. I want you to check the airlines, charter flights, trains, car rental companies, anything that moves and looks like it is heading into the immediate area. I want to know if there is any and I mean ANY unsavory character coming to the Metroplex. Start with today, then move back the timeline day by day, until you find something... er... someone that would fit our profile."

"Got it," replies Kinum.

"I have been working on the California Bank to find out who owns the house. Where does that prioritize?"

Clayton pauses, "Both are a high priority, and you need to give them equal attention... 100% on both!"

"Sir?" responds Sergeant Kinum.

"That's why you're a **Texas Ranger** and not some 'Federallie'," smiled Clayton.

"Sir, YES SIR!" Kinum turned and walked out of the office.

"KINUM! Check with our Federal Partners too. Just in case they stumbled on something they don't understand. You can connect the dots for them."

Three hours later...

"I got it! I got it!" Kinum exclaimed. "It's Mohammed Haasan! That's who will be arriving at DFW from Orange County, John Wayne Airport. He lands in just... twenty minutes.

He is also the guy who made the money transfer to buy that house in Plano! HE IS RUNNING THIS OPERATION!"

"Way to go Ranger!" affirms Captain Clayton. "Now we need to figure out what they are all up to. Notify TSA of his arrival and get a tail on him. I don't want to lose him for two seconds. Notify the shift in the surveillance truck to be on their toes, they will be having a visitor in under two hours. Also, give a heads up to Plano PD. Just in case we need their assistance."

★★

"What about the FBI, shall I notify them?" asks Kinum.

"Not yet, we need to see what they are up to first, I only want their help if this goes national," replies Clayton. *The FBI has wanted this guy for years. It sure would be fantastic if the Texas Rangers busted him.*

"Get moving!" The entire Rangers office was charged and full of commotion now.

Plano, Texas – One hour forty-three minutes later

"Line-up, smile, Praise Allah! We are about to meet one of the greatest men in our lifetime," says Abdula in Arabic to the group of men assembled in the great room of the house in suburban Plano Texas. Of course, Jamil was having a difficult time understanding all that was happening. The Arabic translator in the surveillance van could only get a handful of most of the words.

It was hard to pick up all the conversation fully as the microphones planted had only a limited range. Additionally, the dialect that Abdula used was extremely informal, full of slang. The translator was familiar with a more formal, traditionally educated Arabic. Up until today, the Ranger would use the transcripts to review the actual conversations. But now, real-time translation was more important than ever.

Just at that moment, a black sedan pulled up in front of the house, in a quiet attempt to draw zero attention. A personal security man jumped from the front passenger seat and quickly opened the back door. Out emerged a nicely dressed man of about fifty, though, with his grooming and impeccable appearance, he looked easy forty-five years old. Smartly the two walked to the front door of the house and right through as it was opened for them.

Inside there was giddy excitement almost in celebration as each man met their hero, shaking hands and a sort of respectful bowing of the head. Soon, the group settled in on the floor sitting cross-legged, with the exception of Haasan, who was given a large comfortable chair and his security stood at his side. Together they made powerful figures, which was exactly what they had hoped to achieve.

Jamil was sent to the kitchen to prepare the food and drink, never being introduced to Haasan. *I really am just a Nawar, a no-good Gypsy to these guys. If it wasn't for me, they would not have had a place to hide and the supplies to prepare for… whatever they are planning to do.* Jamil complains to himself as he reluctantly prepares some dishes.

"Shit, we can't hear much of anything!" says LT Davis in the truck. "Roberts needs to get closer," not understanding that Jamil Roberts had been banished from the meeting. He would bring in dishes and trays of drinks, serving their guest first then immediately sent right back out.

The meeting took the shape of a mixture of teaching from the Quran and giving courage, then praise to the men sitting on the floor. There was a lot of head nodding and seriousness. What Jamil could tell for sure was that they were going to break up into groups and go on a mission very soon. Where – it was not clear and at this point, he was out of the loop.

Haasan had handed out crude maps to the seated men, but Jamil couldn't get a context where these locations were in the US and unfortunately all the notes were in Arabic. Davis' frustration was growing even worse. They could only get parts of the conversation at best. The details needed for an investigation like this were really lacking, to say the least.

They picked up some keywords:

"Five days."

"No return."

"Killed or Kill (lost in translation) Great Satan."

"Electricity."

Otherwise, it was a lot of praising and honor given from Haasan to the men. After about two hours the meeting ended as fast as it started, and Jamil had missed it all. He stood in the kitchen isolated while Haasan said his goodbyes and "Allahu Akbars," then was gone as quickly as he had arrived.

As soon as Haasan was away, Abdula came into the kitchen and said, "You go home now."

"Wait what?" said Jamil.

"You all done; you leave now," Abdula put a hand on Jamil's back and abruptly escorted him to the front door.

"But I need to clean up." Jamil protested.

"You go. Come back in five days and clean up."

The front door closed behind him.

"Shit, now what? I am heading to the donut shop," Jamil says for the benefit of the surveillance truck.

"We've got less than five days to figure this out, what –I don't know," says Davis to Clayton over the phone.

"I don't know either, but it's mega important."

"Should we pick up Haasan?" Davis listens for a bit. "Okay, we'll tail him to DFW and watch to be sure he's back on the plane.

Hoover Building, Washington, DC

Kathy reaches out through to the intercom, "I have a Captain Clayton from the Texas Rangers on the line.

"Put him through," says Johnson.

"Hello Captain– how's your investigation going?"

Clayton responds a little concerned. "We have something serious going on here. We just are not sure what. We do know that Mohammed Haasan is involved, probably leading this cell."

Clayton pauses for effect, then continues. "Something, big, very big is about to happen in five days. There will most likely be several coordinated attacks across the United States. What the targets are, is unclear —but we're going to need your help."

"Okay, what do you need from the FBI?" calmly asks Johnson.

"First, we would like you to pick up Haasan in California and interrogate him with our help. Then we'll need the HRT to help us close this operation down."

Johnson thoughtfully thinks about the request for a few seconds.

"It's not ripe yet. You need to get these guys in action. So far all they have done is sit in a house in Texas and have a meeting with a suspected terrorist. I mean we could have INS round them all up for being here illegally but that will only delay the inevitable and it certainly won't bring Haasan to justice."

Clayton sees his point. "Can you snag Haasan for us?"

"No, this guy has been tortured by the Egyptian army, he won't tell us anything. An FBI interrogation will be a joke to him. But I will wiretap his home, office, car and keep a close eye on his whereabouts. Let's see what we get on 'signals' from him. If he doesn't know we are onto him, he may give us some clues as to what they are up to, so we can head this thing off. If we still don't know on the morning of the fifth day, we'll raid his house and ask him," smiles Johnson knowingly.

Clayton acquiesces to Johnson's wisdom, "I see your points here. I think that is a good plan. We'll work this hard over the next four days and if we can't settle in, we'll sweep the house the morning of the fifth day in a coordinated fashion and bring them all in and put them on the grill."

"Let's keep our teams in communication," replies Johnson.

"Five days then," and the phone line went dead.

Precisely at 6:00 pm, his burner phone started to ring. Johnson needed to locate it in his briefcase which took a little digging.

"Hello. Hey Jackson, no, I feel fine. Okay, okay. I will talk to you in the morning. Oh, did you get that package I sent you? Oh, good. Just open it and follow the instructions the moment I come into your care. Yep, when I start to lose it. Alright, I'll talk to you tomorrow."

Johnson turns off his burner phone completely and starts to reread the several reports he has been mulling over.

I'll bet you the shooting at the border a few months ago was the guys the Rangers are surveilling. So, we may be able to pin the murder of the Border Patrol Agents on them.

Then there is this closing down of the Virginia Capitol. It sounds like the 2A people have had enough and are making a statement to the world... and that wacko governor. I hope nobody gets trigger happy, that will turn into another blood bath. Maybe, my little surprise will help keep that from happening.

This poor couple in Portland were just in the wrong place at the wrong time. These Antifa people need to be ended. If I was the Portland Chief of Police, I would have put a stop to the mayhem they have created. Now they are metastasizing into a real national threat.

Bunkerville investigation is winding down and it seems everybody is either dead or in jail awaiting trial, including the HRT members. Sherriff Gillette is still pissed and ignoring any federal involvement for support. I guess he doesn't trust us, I don't really blame him.

I see they have Amos Cloyden in jail, charged with conspiracy. Everyone is accounted for but the six rabbits. Humm, I see that Martinez and Titus made their first stop at the Timmons ranch. Kevin Lindfield wasn't there and there is no mention of the other five. Johnson flipped to the 302 report.

Reporting Agents (RO's) approached the Timmons ranch at approx. 6 a.m. to inquire into the whereabouts of Mr. Kevin Linfield. They were greeted by the ranch owner Charles (Chuck) Timmons. Regarding the location of their employee Kevin Linfield, Mr. Timmons indicated that Kevin hadn't been there for some time and that they were more than welcome to look around. RO's carefully searched the Buckaroo bunkhouse as Mr. Timmons stood by and watched. Mr. Timmons declined the RO's request to inspect the other employees' property who shared the bunkhouse. "I just want to respect their privacy" was his stated reason. RO's also noticed an adjacent bunkhouse and requested to search it. Timmons readily agreed and allowed the second search. It was vacant and seemed to have been recently cleaned. When RO Titus inquired why no one was using it, Mr. Timmons replied. "It's a seasonal hand (employees) bunkhouse and Mrs. Timmons recently did some spring cleaning for new hands they were considering to hire." Both RO's asked to search the main house and were denied. Mr. Timmons indicated that subject Linfield, did not live in the house and it would be improper to allow the FBI to search a house that was his alone, and was restating the fourth amendment to us. After some attempts to persuade Mr. Timmons to the search, RO Titus said she would go and get a warrant for the search. Mr. Timmons politely said: "Well, bring back the warrant and I'll make lunch for ya," with a broad smile. Both RO's were satisfied the subject Linfield was not present on the ranch and returned to the airport to travel to Idaho.

Johnson closed the folder feeling kind of tired. *Well, that went better than I had hoped.*

He stuffed the file into his briefcase and headed to Kathy's desk.

"Kathy I am going to go home and review these further, I need to get some rest."

"Okay, I will call your detail."

"Don't forget you have a 9:00 a.m. briefing with the President in the morning."

"Oh, no I can't forget that," Johnson replied. "I have everything I need to be ready right here." He patted his briefcase.

"Have a restful night," smiled Kathy as he headed out the exterior door. *This job is really taking a toll on him. He looks real tired.*

GHOST
PATRIOT

★★★

Chapter 19

NY Times Headline Story

Jim Johnson diligently waded through the stack of mail he had yet to open upon his return from Nevada. At the bottom of the pile, the newspaper caught his eye. The headline read:

GHOST PATRIOT TERRORIZES AMERICA

The caption was in eighteen-point type, the exact headline he had hoped for. *Julie Smith went for it hook line and sinker. You can always count on the New York Times to get it wrong.* Jim smiled knowingly as he thought to himself.

Jim set aside the stack of mail and found his big chair and plopped down in it. He opened the paper and began to read.

A domestic terrorist cell operating in several states has its grip on the throat of America says a highly positioned source, who was not authorized to speak publicly on the matter.

Jim skips to the next paragraph.

This one group has taken credit for the STANDOFF and massacre in Bunkerville, Nevada, the violent attack on peaceful protesters in Portland, Oregon, and the INSURRECTION that has actively taken over the Capital Building in Virginia.

Oh, shit I never said that… this will send POTUS into orbit.

★★★

Third paragraph:

Federal Agencies promise to respond in an unprecedented fashion to protect the Citizens of the United States.

They do? Geez, woman –you are going to stir up a real riot with this BS. You took this way too far.

Jim read on, but the balance of the article was just backgrounding the details of the previously mentioned incidents.

Surprisingly Julie Smith actually got them pretty factually correct.

Jim's initial response was to immediately pick up the phone, call Ms. Smith, and give her a piece of his mind about how completely irresponsible she was. But after a moment, he thought better of it and just decided to ponder a bit more on how this may or may not work for his overall high-level conspiracy and misdirection plan.

After a few minutes, Jim's eyes began to close. *I guess I am tired.*

Early morning came much sooner than he thought, and John Jackson grabbed his cell and made his obligatory call to Director Johnson's burner phone just a couple minutes before 6:00 a.m., then patiently waited for the connection… it rang so many times the phone system disconnected automatically.

"Oh, no something must have happened," Dr. Jackson said to himself. John now began to move around his house deliberately and swiftly. He was completely prepared for this.

He grabbed his "Go Bag" which was full of everything he would need to be away from home for an extended period of time. He also retrieved his old medical bag filled with the supplies he anticipated he might need to care for Johnson between Jim's apartment and Jackson's funeral home. He double-checked to make sure the coffee pot was off and headed out the door, locking up behind him.

Once in the funeral van, he called Johnson again. Still no answer. An attempt he made several more times in the short twenty-minute drive to Johnson's apartment, while also pausing to snap on a pair of rubber medical gloves at one of the many stoplights.

★★

Once he arrived, Jackson was careful to back in quietly and to take notice that there were no government-looking vehicles on the street. Something Johnson adamantly admonished him to do, as often his security detail arrived early and waited for Jim to get ready. Seems clear. Jackson thought to himself as he put the van in park.

Jackson leaped from the van, then got ahold of himself, not wanting the neighbors to notice as it was now approaching 6:30 a.m. Jackson used the front door key he was given and slowly opened the door. He emerged into a fairly dark living room with just one dim light on.

Immediately he spotted Jim unconscious on the floor. He had passed out and slid from the big chair to the ground with a newspaper wrapped under and spread out all around him. His arms and legs were contracted into the fetal position and his hands balled up into a tight fist. Jim had his eyes opened but they were locked fully over to the right. Jackson looked him up and down to see if Johnson had any injuries. He had only peed himself, which ironically the New York Times took the brunt of.

"Jim, this is John –I am here… I am here. You have had a seizure. Just try to remain calm, okay buddy? I am here for you."

Dr. Jackson stumbled searching through his medical bag and found an IV needle and a long rubber tube that goes with it. "I am first going to get you started on an IV to help you maintain body function." Jackson pokes the needle into Jim's vein in the left arm.

"Now I am going to give you some medicine to help with the seizure." Jackson now draws 60 cc's of Levetiracetam, commonly known as Keppra.

"This will take a while to kick in and help. In the meantime, I will take you to my office." Jackson was briefly considering giving Jim a sedative too but had second thoughts of not being able to get him in the gurney considering the overall deadweight of Jim's body after a sedative injection.

Once Jackson felt he could leave him safely, he rushed to the van and retrieved the gurney from the back. Jim took one quick minute to look around to see if anyone was watching. The coast seemed to be clear. He then wheeled the gurney into the apartment.

★★

It took a few minutes to jockey Jim onto the gurney and securely buckle him in. John pushed the gurney to the front door then stopped and looked back. *Oh, the newspaper. And Jim's phone…*

Without further hesitation, John gathered up all the pee-soaked newspapers and searched for Jim's phone. He finally located two phones in Jim's briefcase sitting on the kitchen table. *Which one is the burner? It must be this cheaper looking one.* With that speedy on-the-fly decision, he threw the FBI phone on the table and took the entire briefcase without thinking.

He placed everything in an organized fashion on the gurney, Jim's briefcase, his medical bag, and the soiled newspaper, and casually headed out the door, covering Jim, head, and body with a sheet. He only paused to lock the door. Once Jim was loaded up and the gurney was strapped down, John climbed into the driver's seat and slowly pulled out.

He wasn't three blocks down the street when a big black Chevy Suburban with blackened-out windows came speeding past them.

"There's your security," John tells Jim who was pretty much in the same physical state, strapped down in the gurney. John glances at his watch, 7:04 a.m. *They're early. That was a close one.*

1600 Pennsylvania Avenue, 9:00 a.m.

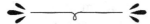

"Where the hell is this guy? I wanted some answers today and he doesn't show up?" declares POTUS venting.

"We have been trying to locate Director Johnson for hours now and he's just disappeared," responds Chief of Staff Smith to the full security briefing, comprising the heads of the DHS, DOJ, CIA, NSA, DOD, ATF, FBI, and oddly Neal Cornwall Director of the BLM was also invited. All were present but Jim Johnson the acting director of the FBI.

Across Town at Jim Johnson's Apartment

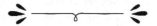

Johnson's security detail had arrived early. At his apartment, they waited until 8 a.m., sipping coffee and reading the latest NYT article about the Domestic Terrorist threat facing the United States. Overnight it was the lead story in every media source around the world and the spin had taken off recklessly, rashly, and faster than anyone thought possible.

At 8 a.m. Johnson's security detail began to call Jim Johnson's cell phone as it was unlike him to not be on time. His home phone repeatedly gave no response, as it just rolled into his voice mail. Then they called Kathy, to confirm they were in the right place to make sure something hadn't changed overnight schedule-wise.

" He was pretty tired last night. If he hasn't come out by now you better go get him. The President will be waiting, impatiently I might add," responded Kathy from her desk at the Hoover building.

Kathy quickly dialed the direct line to the Oval Office.

"Susan Kinum," comes the voice on the line.

"Susie, it's Kathy. Director Johnson is running late," then she paused, waiting for the next question (Where is he?) that never came.

"Okay, I'll let him know," responds Susan Kinum the personal secretary of the POTUS.

Kathy assumed she meant Theodore Smith, the Chief of Staff.

At that point, the Director's security detail swiftly broke a front window and unlatched it. One agent slid quietly through the window and opened the front door for the other two. All the while he was pointing his Glock downrange into the apartment to fend off any threats that might emerge from one of the other rooms.

Once they all had access, they began a thorough sweep of Johnson's apartment, weapons drawn, one by one declaring CLEAR, CLEAR, and then a third loud CLEAR. Signaling to the others that the apartment was clear of any threats.

"Where the fuck is he?" demands the security chief. Immediately, they search the apartment for foul play.

"The bed does not look like it was slept in," declares one agent.

"No meals made recently," says the second from the spotless kitchen.

"No sign of a struggle," says the Chief.

"Wait, here's his phone on the floor in the kitchen," declares the second agent identifying a possible red flag.

The phone had been set to vibrate and the agents had called it so many times in the last thirty minutes that it vibrated off the table where Jackson left it and onto the floor.

"Oh, shit –that does not look good. He is NEVER without his phone, and he sure wouldn't have left the phone on the floor," says the Chief.

Then he picks up his own phone and calls the FBI dispatch. "We need a forensic team straightaway to Director Johnson's apartment ASAP. Notify the DC HRT to be on standby. I also want security to seal his office, no one goes in or out, shut down all communication in and out of that office. We may have a possible hostage situation."

Within a couple of minutes, FBI security burst through the door of Director Johnson's office and began their sweep, guns drawn, all the while Kathy was protesting… LOUDLY. Kathy was immediately escorted away from her desk, phone, and computer to sit in the conference room. Then they began their rigorous search for anything that would lead them to Director Johnson's whereabouts.

The White House Oval Office, 9:20 a.m.

Susie Kinum enters the oval office and bends down to POTUS quietly whispering into her ear, "Director Johnson has been held up."

"NO SHIT!" replies the President.

"Johnson is running late, let's begin the meeting," POTUS goes on.

"So, I read the article last night in the *New York Times*. Tell me how *they* seem to know more about this domestic terror threat than I do?"

There was a long uncomfortable pause, as each person waited for the other to respond. Finally, the newly minted DHS director responded. Director Helle had just passed Senate approval as the new DHS Director, and this was his first official meeting at the White House. Every director in the room had their eyes fixed on Helle, knowing the controversy surrounding his appointment.

There had been a highly contested public debate as to his qualifications and appropriate temperament for the position. His inappropriate social media content seemed to be problematic for the conservatives. Statements he made –like:

★★

"–If you don't pass a background check when buying a gun, you should immediately be arrested. You're obviously a criminal and you need to be put away before you commit a more heinous crime."

"–Rights afforded in the Constitution are not necessarily permanent rights."

"–Sensible gun legislation means the ban of all guns that can harm another human being. All life is precious," echoing the direct public statements of POTUS.

"–The insurrection in Virginia MUST be quashed immediately and with absolute vigor. Otherwise, we'll have these 'protests 'in every capital in the United States, including in DC!"

"–Burning down of police departments and certain cities is simply America refreshing liberty at its roots for the new leadership."

These original controversial social media posts were just a handful of the thousands that were deleted prior to his nomination to the DHS. Of course, the conservatives wanted to know what he might have said that was more radical. Those protests fell upon deaf ears of the liberals and his nomination was approved down party lines.

"I think the problem here is that this answer belongs to the FBI and well… they are not represented here." Helle, stating the obvious and rubbing POTUS 'nose in it.

"Well can any of you give me a progress report?" demands President Mountebank.

Helle seized the opportunity to impress her. "I have studied the reports in detail and can shed some light on what we now know. The FBI has focused its investigation on the six rabbits from the STANDOFF in Nevada. They have begun extensive interviews of the six phone owners that seem to be the people we are looking for."

"Progress? Any fricking progress? Have we arrested them?" demands POTUS again exasperated.

"No, the FBI has taken a more passive approach to this investigation. Through a probing method, not sure that these are the people we want or if they are, we don't want to drive them further underground," Helle continued.

"What do you think?" POTUS once again barked.

★★

"What I think is not relevant. It's not DHS 'investigation,'" Helle demurs, side-stepping.

"What has the FBI done with the white supremacist in Portland?" POTUS changing the subject.

Helle thumbs through the file brief in front of him. "Nothing. They are leaving that up to the locals and their murder investigation. They don't seem to think there is a federal crime here."

"What do you think?" POTUS getting angrier.

"What I think is not relevant. It's not DHS 'investigation.'" Helle demurs once again.

"And the insurrection in Virginia?" POTUS starting to fume.

This time the ATF director responds, taking the heat off Helle. "There is not much we can do but wait it out."

"How can that be? We are the most powerful country in the world, and we can't bring a handful of racists to heel. A drone strike comes to mind," presses POTUS.

"Six thousand is not a handful," mutters the ATF director.

Now DOD chimes in: "We cannot use the US Military within the borders of the US, especially against citizens."

"What the fuck are you talking about? We do it all the time. Hell, we have the National Guard right outside, twenty-thousand of them to protect me... and the capital of course."

POTUS had stood and opened the curtain in the Oval Office windows and adamantly pointed at the fences surrounding the White House and Capitol building.

"Let's send them these troops and some tanks into Virginia and end this thing once and for all. If the protesters don't disperse, run them over like the Chinese did in Tiananmen Square."

The entire room sat in stunned silence.

Now she has the right idea! Helle silently agrees - trying not to crack an approving smile.

"We would be better off waiting them out in Virginia. It would be a terrible idea to get into a publicized firefight of any kind with six thousand citizens, especially after the massacre in Nevada. Besides, I am sorry, mam, but the Posse Comitatus Act does not allow..." begins the DOD director before being abruptly cut off.

"What about this stray motorcycle that nobody seems to claim. That must have something to do with these White Supremacists in Nevada?" POTUS changing the subject without pause.

★★

Helle, replies again, "We have contacted the owner of the motorcycle who is an on-duty submariner with an alibi of being at sea in April and has no idea how his bike got clear across the country. The FBI also recovered a cell phone, one of the six we tracked from Nevada. It seems to have a DOD mask on it, so the FBI assumes it belongs to him."

Most of what Helle presented to the President was a half-truth. Neither Jim Johnson, Agents Martinez, nor Titus made those same conclusions.

"What the hell is a DOD mask?" interjects Theodore Smith.

DOD replies, "Certain highly classified positions in the military's contact information is completely masked from inquiries, including their address, cell phone, etc. Only other high-level government agencies recognize what the mask is, or even know of its existence. The masking protocol is HIGHLY Classified."

"Does that include someone assigned duty on a Submarine?" pressed POTUS, actually appearing interested.

"It could, I don't know the details, but our submarine fleet is one of the most closely guarded secrets. We certainly would not want to have a foreign country like China triangulating one of our sub's locations," said the DOD director speaking with real uncertainty.

"What about our men languishing in prison in that hell hole Nevada?" POTUS now ranting about the HRT and BLM Rangers in the Clark County Jail. "They better be free and home with their families soon," POTUS changing the subject again.

This time Neal Cornwall interjects without invitation or common sense. "Well Ms. President, the FBI, and the DOJ have failed us...er... I mean you... in securing the release of our political prisoners from the clutches of Sherriff Gillette in Nevada. They are as you say, languishing in subhuman conditions." Cornwall is very pleased with himself to have the courage to be involved with this very important meeting.

Kiss ass. Thinks Helle, *but a useful kiss ass. That is why I made sure he was present here today.*

"Hmm," clearing his throat is the experienced Attorney General who had been listening and observing quietly. He was hoping to get out of the politically charged meeting unscathed until that idiot Cornwall spoke. Now he needs to clear the blatant accusation.

"Ms. President, under our Federalist system we have no legal authority to intervene in the criminal charges made by a state and upheld for a trial by a state judge even on federal employees. Furthermore…" now he was rudely cut off.

"I DON'T GIVE A SHIT!" Yelled President Mountebank. "ALL YOU PEOPLE DO IS GIVE ME EXCUSES! I ordered that lazy ass Johnson to get them out months ago. And they are still there. It looks bad, really bad on this administration. And it gives these White Supremacists, more resolve when we can't even protect our own troops. No wonder they are so emboldened when we are so impotent!"

President Mountebank sat for a long period, allowing everyone in the room to get defensive. POTUS just stewed for several minutes then began to speak.

"Apparently, these domestic terrorist, these white supremacist organizations, are trying to overthrow our country. I have dealt with them before as Governor of Oregon and they are really serious business. And, according to a savvy reporter at the *New York Times,* they are planning something really big. Bigger than these other attacks, something I cannot even fathom. The FBI seems to be MIA, literally MIA." She points directly at the empty chair assigned to Johnson.

"And no one here is leading our defense from these horrible people. What I need from all of you is to coordinate your intelligence together and get to the core of this threat and present to me in our next meeting the coordinated defense. It shouldn't be hard. From my experience, these people are just plain fat and stupid. I want no more excuses, no more department boundaries, no more legal mumbo jumbo. Get it done … Now!"

Susie bursts through the door and announces: "President Mountebank, the press is waiting to come in. They have been waiting for some time."

"Oh, yes that's right," says Theodore Smith, "I thought it would be a good time to comfort the country with a response from the leader of the free world to the Times article."

"Oh, that is a GOOD IDEA!" exclaims POTUS, pleased for the first time all day.

"Susan, please show them in."

"Gentlemen, look manly here next to me. But I'll do all the talking." POTUS instructs the Directors.

That was weird. They all think at the same moment. But not Susie, she gets it.

Susie ushers in many of the White House Press. The Oval Office was too small of a room for the entire Press Corps, so they drew straws for this meeting. Somehow all the legacy media won the draw.

The Press Secretary opens the meeting. "The President has just finished a domestic security meeting with all of the department heads and would like to update you on their response to the coordinated attack against our democracy by these White Supremacists. First question please."

All their hands went up as cameras started flashing and videoing. Then came the rumbled clamor from the gaggle of reporters.

Press Secretary:" Yes, CNN?"

CNN Reporter:" Ms. President, the Nation is in fear of further attacks on our democracy. Can you tell the CNN viewers how you are protecting us?"

Perfect, just like I coached him. Press Secretary thinks.

POTUS:" My team here is way out ahead of the threat. It wasn't news to us, the NYT's story, and we have these evil racists under our surveillance. It's just a matter of time for them."

Press Secretary:" Next, CBS. . ."

CBS:" What is the timeline in bringing this insurrection in Virginia to an end?"

Right off the list, I gave them. Press Secretary smiles.

POTUS:" A timeline I cannot share with you because that would be tipping our hand. Rest assured we are working directly with Governor Northfork and the local law enforcement to bring this insurgency to a quick and enviable end."

CBS:" CBS has a follow-up."

I said no follow-up. Press Secretary remembers wondering where this is headed.

CBS:" How will this insurrection hinder your legislative agenda regarding sensible gun control?"

Oh, that was a perfect Tee-up. Press Secretary. *Why didn't I think of that?*

★★★

POTUS:" Hinder it?" POTUS scoffingly answers. "It'll fly through the House and Senate now. These criminals are playing right into my hands and demonstrating to the American people why this legislation is crucial. Don't be fooled by the Second Amendment Argument, it's a false argument. This is not about taking guns away; our legislation is about keeping guns out of the hands of violent criminals. Criminals, like those who are encircling the Virginia Capital. The world sees it for what it is. A CRIMINAL INSURRECTION!"

The cadence of the presser paused because the President was yelling. Something she seemed to do uncontrollably, something in which the press secretary tried to coach her on.

Press Secretary:" ABC is next."

ABC:" Have you determined whether these horrible attacks are all connected?"

POTUS:" Well that's a stupid question."

ABC: *Your Press Secretary put it on the list of approved questions.*

POTUS: Continued with a smile as if she was joking, "Of course, they are connected, anyone could see that –hell, Ray Charles could see that."

ABC: Reporter a bit defensive now. *That was bigoted.* "Please explain for the American People." *Give her a way to recover from such an asinine response.*

POTUS:" They're all white supremacists. I have dealt with them before as Governor of Oregon. The attackers of the innocent Agents in Nevada…

"WHITE SUPREMACISTS!"

"The attackers of the innocent protestors in Portland, my hometown…"

"WHITE SUPREMACISTS!"

"The Insurrectionists in Virginia…WHITE SUPREMACISTS! … Obviously."

Press Secretary:" MSNBC, Your question?"

MSMBC:" What are you doing about the Federal Officers locked up in Nevada?"

Shit that wasn't on the list. Press Secretary dismayed.

"WHITE SUPREMACISTS!" answers Cornwall in his bubbling excitement.

★★★

"Excuse me?" replies POTUS in shock.

"I only meant to say that the Sherriff in Las Vegas was a WHITE SUPREMACIST!" he yells inappropriately like POTUS.

"The Sherriff, Sheriff Gillette, must be a White Supremacist if he holds our men. Right? He must be in on it." Cornwall wasn't sure what his point was.

My 'Excuse me question 'was asking why you are talking at all, not asking for an explanation. As POTUS stared an evil death stare at Cornwall. *Who is this fucker anyway... who invited him? How did he get into my office?*

The press secretary sensing the presser was about to go off the rails: "THANK YOU EVERYBODY. LET'S GO NOW," as she begins to herd the reporters swiftly out of the room.

"Ms. President, where is Director Johnson?" comes an uninvited, unscripted question from *OANN* who had accidentally won the straw drawing.

"He hasn't been feeling well," replies POTUS conspicuously lying.

A *FOX* reporter asks another unwanted question as he is pushed to the Oval Office doorway: "Who is leading this coordinated response then?"

"Director Helle is the lead on this investigation as DHS is supposed to be in times of crises according to the Patriot Act," replies POTUS smugly and without consideration of the truthfulness of her decision.

"So, it IS A CRISES?... If they are all white supremacist, then how do you reconcile that the apparent leader in Virginia is a BLACK MAN?" yells the *FOX* reporter incensed as he is shoved out the door.

No one answered those questions.

"It will get worse before it gets better," Helle mutters under his breath.

Chapter 20

A Black Man Leads a White Supremacist Movement

The tension of the dramatic situation over the last twenty-four hours in Virginia had been terribly tangible. The men and women who had bravely taken the stand and seized the Capital grounds were organized extremely well. They had formed an elite intel group, established a command-and-control center, a provisions depot, and even a triage center. There seemed to be developing amongst them a comradery of mutually respectful cooperation, even enthusiasm.

Colin, who had never been in such a controversial situation found it weird that so many looked to him as the leader. He was in way over his head, and he knew it. Providentially placed by his side, was "THE" man for this time, this place, and for this ever-changing situation. Tal Jordon was an experienced savvy military leader and politician, who deeply loved his country, especially Virginia.

As the hours went by, Colin became more and more frightened that his actions may have led all these well-meaning people into real, life and death harm. When he stood at the mic in front of an anxious crowd, he never dreamed it would come to what was clearly a military stand. This was nothing like what had ever been seen in the history of the United States.

This was not a bunch of hippies from the '60s or '70s having a "sit-in" or the Black Panthers facing off with local police. It wasn't "Occupy Wall Street" or the short-lived "Chaz Zone" in Seattle. It certainly wasn't the angry and violent anarchist Antifa, who were just violent communists, using a fake moniker to effectively fool the powers in government regarding their true intentions. Even the STANDOFF in Bunkerville, Nevada was not clearly understood as a defined principled response to the overreach of the Federal Government. The clarity of the Cloyden's stand was lost in the media's self-serving narrative.

This was a group of men and women from all walks of life from all over the country who had come to the point of feeling powerless. They understood what the U.S. Constitution promised, and they also knew that those promises had been violated, stolen, bit by bit, over the course of their lives. They had been patient, willing to make corrections with each election, hoping to see change in the direction the country needed. But the last national election was so fraught with fraud allegations, media intervention, and fake news, clearly going against all logic and common sense so that now the people felt forced to make a stand.

As Colin heard in a radio broadcast, provoked by all the fraud accusations, was one simple statement from an outraged radio host:

"This woman could not have gathered more votes than the most popular President ever, who ran the best-funded and most effective election of all time. The election itself had such a copious turnout that more people showed up to vote than we had registered voters! And she did it all without ever actually getting out of her basement and on the campaign trail! This flies in the face of common sense and we all know it!"

As for the protesters who surrounded the Virginia statehouse, they had lost all hope that their vote had ever counted. They decided to make a clear and principled stand at the Second Amendment, the only amendment that was placed by the founding fathers for a moment in time just like this. The Second Amendment was established as part of the "Bill of Rights," to protect all the other Amendments. And that is exactly what they intended to do.

But it was not going to be easy by any means. Within a few short minutes, law enforcement had cordoned off the five-block area in every direction. Then, within an hour they effectively evacuated every business and home. It was literally a no man's land.

Next, the cell towers went down, followed by a power outage. The media quickly went to work spinning their lies of insurrection, hostage-taking, and a pending overthrow of the Virginia government. Typical pro-big-government fake news.

★★★

Next came the media spin-off the fear that all the capitals in every state would be overrun by white supremacists, forcing the state governments to evacuate and close down until further notice. President Mountebank actually started talking martial law – nationwide, but that idea lost momentum as the governors aggressively pushed back at the assessment of the situation. They could not see the justification for it.

The insurgence seemed to be localized only in Virginia, though the media were effective in convincing the public that the country was at the brink of a coup de tat, egged on by the current administration. The odd thing was, neither Tal, Colin, nor anyone else had been contacted by law enforcement. There was only an eerie lingering silence from the other side.

"We seem to be fairly ready, well, as ready as we can be," says Tal as he approached Colin just outside their command tent.

"From now on you'll need to restrict your movement to these areas," continues Tal, as he points to a highlighted area on the map.

"What the fuck, why?" Colin started.

Tal points up at all the high-rise buildings surrounding them. "All of those buildings have a sniper team, some several, and you my friend are their main target."

"Are you kidding me? They'll shoot me! What threat am I?" Colin being in denial.

"You are the leader; the face of this little dance party and they'll be targeting all of the leaders, including you," Tal presses.

"Wait a minute, I didn't sign-up for this, I didn't sign these guys up for this. I want these good people to go home to their families when this is over," protests Colin.

"I'm just a schoolteacher for God's sake."

"Ha, not anymore… you are now the number one domestic terrorist in the country!" Tal responds articulately throwing a dose of metaphorical cold water in Colin's face.

"If I could get you inside the Capitol building, I could keep you much safer," Tal retorts.

"I'll keep that in mind," says Colin resolutely.

"Should we just throw out the Assemblymen?" Colin thinking of his own personal safety.

"No, that would be too messy, and the Troopers would put up a fight. Nobody wants that, too many causalities on both sides and it would certainly cause a violent reaction from those guys." Tal pointing out where the gathering law enforcement is stationed.

"We really don't want that. The way we are set up, too many people will die, and I don't want that to happen to even one of them if I can help it. Many of these men have seen combat in the Middle East, but I estimate about half haven't. We don't want to pop their combat cherry in a full-blown assault and defense in the same action from two different sides. Let's just be patient and let this play out. Maybe we can make our point and get out of here with our lives."

"Maybe we should just surrender now?" Colin asks sincerely.

Tal took a look at Colin in a 'did you just say that?' sort of way.

"These men are not going to give up that easy. All they needed was a leader and you raised your hand. But the minute you show even a hint of cowardice, they will toss you out, kick you to the curb and find somebody else. Someone they can depend on, but with fewer brains."

"You're the one God chose for this hour, don't ever doubt that. He will give you what you need to courageously lead these men… and women. Besides you don't want to surrender either," Tal ending with encouragement.

"No, I don't. I guess I am scared," Colin sheepishly answers.

"Me too schoolteacher, me too," Tal smiles genuinely at Colin.

1600 Pennsylvania Avenue

POTUS has moved herself to the situation room to call Governor Northfork.

"What do you need from me? Anything –and I'll make a way," she opens up the conversation.

"Well Ms. President, right now we are still assessing the situation and the best response."

"Just say the word and I'll send in the Army, a couple of tanks and some drones, whatever you need," pushes POTUS demanding further action.

Northfork pulls the receiver away from his head and looks at it in disbelief. *What the fuck? –these are Virginians, not Russians!*

"Ma'am, I think we're ok for now. If I need to, I can call up the National Guard. But for now, we just need to contain the situation and see if we can end this peacefully."

"Just don't let them negotiate you out of your gun legislation. You are leading the country with this, and we can't falter now! These, these... criminals are just proving that we need sensible gun control," drives the President like she was at a campaign rally pushing her agenda.

"I totally agree, and I refuse to lose momentum on its passing. But this will need to be dealt with before we can pick up headway again," Northfork replies, in typical politician doublespeak.

"Okay, well anything you need to end this quickly and I mean quickly!" POTUS hangs up the phone.

"Thank you, Ms. Presi.." –*She's gone, I hate it when she does that.*

POTUS puts a call in to the Head of the Joint Chiefs.

"General, this is the Commander in Chief, I just got off the phone with Governor Northfork of Virginia. I told him he has access to whatever he needs. Troops, tanks, drones, anything... Of course, whatever is within the boundaries of the law. I am just making it clear to pave the way," POTUS listens quietly for a couple more minutes.

"What does it matter that there are three thousand of them. You are the head of the most powerful fighting force in the world, are you not? So how can you be afraid of a bunch of fat, dumb weekend warriors?" She listens in silence for a while longer.

"Then surround them and send in those SEAL TEAM SIX guys and cut the head off the snake, you know a little 'Shock and Awe.' Just get it done, I want you to pave the way. Pave the way..."

POTUS hangs up the phone again. *I never thought those Joint Chiefs would be such cowards. I need to appoint a woman General to give them some balls. Maybe a black woman, who won't take their shit! Yeah, I'll make her the boss of those cowards...*

Across Town, Washington, DC

Doctor Jackson had gotten Jim Johnson settled comfortably into his bed. After twenty-four hours he finally got the seizures to stop. Jackson had taken one of his back offices and fixed it up as a nice bedroom, complete with a flat screen TV, sitting furniture, and some decorations he purchased at Bed, Bath and Beyond.

John didn't really care that much for Johnson, but he did deeply respect life and wanted to make this deathbed time as comfortable as he could for truly anyone. Over the last week, he had gotten his old medical books out and refreshed himself on what to expect these next few days or weeks. Jackson had Johnson lightly sedated now and didn't expect him to become more conscience going forward. *But maybe he'll awake from time to time, GBM's can be weird.*

For now, he kept Jim clean and comfortable. He played relaxing music for him and gave him around-the-clock care, all while operating his business as usual. Jim wasn't eating, which was the first sign that made Jackson realize it was a matter of days not weeks.

Jackson was actually surprised how much work it all was, laundry, medication prep and administration, changing his diapers and bedding multiple times a day. He always had a staff of nurses and CNAs to do these busy tasks when he was a doctor practicing in a hospital. But now he was acting full-time hospice, in deep undercover, and he had his own business to attend to as well.

Then he added the restriction that none of his employees were allowed in the back area, where Jim's room was located by the crematorium. He made up a fictitious new city regulation as an excuse to preclude anyone accidently finding Jim, hidden, and tucked away.

This is much more work than I anticipated. Jackson thought to himself as he changed Jim's diaper for the third time that day. *Especially for a guy I don't care for much. But a promise is a promise, and I never go back on my word.*

★★

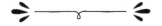

Battle Mountain, Nevada

Kevin Linfield woke at precisely 3 a.m. He sat up inside his Sheridan Tent, a canvas tent made especially for cowboys who work on the range and find themselves in need of dependable shelter. He reached for his feet and gave his back a long and sustained stretch. A behavior he watched older Buckaroo's do over the years. *It seems like a good practice* thought Kevin as he successfully reached for his toes, even though he wasn't of the age to experience the benefits of the back pain relief it gave some of the older men.

Kevin was heading out early before sunrise. He would be days ahead of the rest of the Buckaroo crew who gave him a good ribbing about his desire to get back and see Leah. *No living this down, they'll be a real cocklebur under my saddle from here on.* They were right, the entire camp. His mind was on Leah and not really on checking the cows, as every one of the crew picked up on.

He was now getting ready to break camp and leave hours before daylight to try to make the three-day ride in two. Starting well before daylight and making camp each day after sunset to make up the time. He was traveling light too, leaving most of his gear in the ranch truck and only taking his slick folk saddle, bridle, and a light bedroll. Of course, he'll take the HAMR too.

He just didn't trust his co-workers –that they wouldn't take a few shots with it, mess with the sites and waste a bunch of money on shells, which they wouldn't be able to replace until the next trip to town and a special order. Besides, Kevin had come to truly enjoy that gun and especially his proficiency with it. The HAMR was unfortunately still too long of a rifle to slide into a traditional saddle scabbard.

Kevin skillfully rolled his bedroll around it and tied it down across the back of the cantle of his saddle. It was still pretty broad as it stuck out a foot or better on both sides of his horse. *Good thing I cowboy in Nevada, not in the Rockies or somewhere there's a lot of trees. I'd be tangled all the time.*

Kevin quietly carried his extra gear to the truck by the glowing embers of the fire from the night before and laid them in without a sound. He took one final look around to be sure he didn't miss

★★★

anything when he felt something soft rub up against his leg. It was Gunner, one of the Queensland Heeler working dogs that they had taken with them.

"Hi Gunner, did I wake you? Or did you come to see me off?" Kevin whispered caringly as he knelt down to give the dog a hard scratch between his ears.

"I'll see you at the bunkhouse, okay? You enjoy the ride back down in a few days."

The four dogs always rode in the truck, unless they were working. It saved the dogs for what they were there for.

"Saving you and your horse from the extra miles of circling up strays," Pop would always say.

Once Kevin was satisfied that he had fully loaded all his stuff into the truck, he gave a tug on the cinch to tighten his saddle down onto the back of Rosie. Then he stepped into the left stirrup and swung his right leg over without a sound. Rosie, being a finished bridle horse had just shifted her weight in the slightest to counterbalance the downward pull of the left stirrup as Kevin stepped up. Then almost imperceptibly shifted again left to meet her rider as he placed himself in her center of gravity.

Rosie was nine years old and had the miles and experience for her work, but more importantly, she was properly trained and nicely finished as a working cow horse. Every Buckaroo within a hundred miles had heard of Rosie, and truly felt it was an honor to see her work cows. She was a prized gift to Kevin when she was just two years old and Kevin ten, and he had become the hand he was because of his horse Rosie. It was a true partnership.

Kevin picked up the tightly braided rawhide reins in his left hand, holding them like an ice cream cone, taking the romal (the remainder of the reigns) in his right, being careful not to bump Rosie's mouth, then in the slightest bend at the hip, Kevin leaned forward and all so slightly placed pressure in the right stirrup, gently squeezing with the left leg at the thigh and Rosie knew precisely what Kevin wanted. She bridled her head, by tipping her nose in, to balance the spade bit on the bars of her mouth (the space in a horse's mouth where the incisors end and the molars begin), rocked back gently on her hindquarters, and stepped her left front across the right front, repeating, again and again, pivoting to the right until Kevin took the pressure off the right stirrup at precisely 180 degrees, then

★★★

she quietly walked forward and into the darkness. Gunner started to follow.

"Gunner, –STAY," commanded Kevin. Gunner stopped in his tracks and just stared at the departing horse and rider, just in case Kevin changed his mind.

"See ya at the headquarters," came a voice from one of the tents. *I guess I wasn't quiet enough.* Kevin frowned.

Oval Office, 1600 Pennsylvania Avenue, Washington, DC

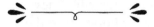

DHS Secretary Helle and POTUS Mountebank have both just taken their first sips of steaming hot Kona Hawaiian coffee brewed fresh in the white house kitchens French-press, as they settled in for their planning meeting with the steward closing the door behind himself. Jim Johnson had been missing for more than twenty-four hours and so, the necessary decision to place DHS in charge of the coordinated investigation against the "White Supremacists" has become fortuitous. Imperative in POTUS' mind.

The President begins: "Jim Johnson is out. If he ever shows up, he is out as Director of the FBI and OUT as the lead in this investigation," POTUS announces wholeheartedly.

"So, what do you need to bring these bastards to 'Justice'?"

"Well Ma'am, I have been looking at this investigation from the thirty-thousand-foot level and I do NOT see it making any real traction. It's puttering, slowly, in the same old cop on the beat methodology that gets us ten years of investigations and no convictions."

"Go on," POTUS nodding to what he said so far.

"We have the premier intelligence agencies in the world. We can anticipate what kind of sandwich you'll have this afternoon before you order it. And we are not using these resources in this or any other investigation against domestic terrorists. If you are on foreign soil, we'll target you in a minute and send a cruise missile through your bedroom window, take you and your progeny out to end the line of future terrorists. But here in the US, we doddle, we tinker, we plan, we obtain warrants, and are too concerned with citizens' rights. All the while, these animals kill innocent civilians and terrorize common everyday citizens. It's ridiculous, just ridiculous."

"Well, we agree, but what do we do about it? The Attorney General tells me time and time again that it's all completely necessary. He drones on about the Fourth, Fifth and Sixth Amendments. Then my favorite, the First Amendment, as if it is some kind of poison pill to keep us from stopping them. I keep telling him repeatedly the Constitution was not written for modern times."

"It is an antiquated document, like the Bible. The Constitution was for farmers and Davey Crocket. I mean just look at the Second Amendment, it was for Musketeers, who took five minutes to load each bullet. The Framers of our Constitution could never have imagined the current threats we face from modern weapons of war on the streets today, weapons that can shoot .50 caliber bullets at 100 rounds a second, killing thousands of black men alone." That was an exact line from a speech she gave on the campaign trail.

"It's crazy and these White Supremacists are all behind it! They want their guns so they can overthrow this government and move into the White House or burn it down. Then kill everyone of color," POTUS paused and took a long breath, then continued.

"So, I don't know what to do." That was the opening Helle was waiting for.

"I do," then he paused, waiting for the next question.

"Okay, tell me your plan," POTUS pressed impatiently.

"In order to keep the 'Constitutionalists' happy and off your back, we set up a counter, or better titled 'Action Force' that can be mobilized behind the traditional investigations of the FBI, ATF, DEA, etc. Where they get bogged down, we use other means to speed up the investigation."

"Speed up how?" the President intensely curious now.

"Well, the exact details are better left unspecified, as you should not have too much awareness of ..."

"Right. Plausible deniability," POTUS shakes her head affirming.

"Correct. Let's just say, we'll use proven field methods of surveillance, interrogation, and evidence gathering to bring these criminals to justice swiftly and end the threats to the United States," continued Helle.

★★★

"But how? You can't have the CIA running around 'disappearing' people and torturing them," states POTUS.

"No, what I am proposing is a clandestine group, pulling from every federal resource, while operating autonomously under the DHS authority and my direction. Then, once we have the perpetrators, the confessions, and the evidence, we'll turn them back over to one of the more traditional law enforcement agencies to prosecute and take credit for."

POTUS paused and thought about this interesting idea for a full three minutes. Helle started to get uncomfortable that he might have gone too far too fast with the President. Then POTUS broke the silence.

"Well HELL, that sounds good. But whatever you do, –you better bring results, or I'll pull the plug," POTUS taking authority.

"Anything you need from me to get started?"

This was just the question Helle was looking for. "Just your authorization." As Helle reaches into his brown leather satchel and hands her a piece of paper with one simple paragraph.

The President of The United States hereby authorizes and gives full autonomy to DHS Secretary Helle to form an Action Team to use and coordinate all the resources of the United States Government in the apprehension of Domestic Terrorists and aid federal law enforcement in bringing them to justice.
This Day… Signed President Mountebank.

The President took a moment and read it over and signed the vague document. It was government-speak that gave absolutely no accountability to either party. She had seen it many times before, more than she could count.

Helle took it and placed it back in his satchel hidden from sight. *Good, –I have my get out of jail free card.* Then began to stand.

"If there is nothing else?" he inquired of the President.

"Just *results* Mr. Secretary, just *results*," POTUS said with earnest.

Chapter 21

It's All PSYOPS

God and Country

Ranger Kinum had just turned into the main gate of his family hunting ranch. Every time he did, he thought to himself gratefully: *I can't believe I almost lost all of this because of drugs and foolish thinking.*

Kinum was born into a prominent, wealthy, and powerful family in Texas but when he hit his teens, he made some serious life mistakes that almost completely ruined his life. Out of all the entitlement he was so sure of, at age fourteen, he ran away, got mixed up with drugs and stupid peers who were doing the same. He became homeless, with his mind spun out from the drugs, he agreed to be the getaway driver in a bank robbery. *What the hell was I thinking?*

As he and his so-called friends loaded up in Kinum's truck and headed to the bank, he made a rolling stop and was promptly stopped by the Dallas PD. Unbeknownst to him, there was an AMBER Alert put out on him by his parents as a missing child and his license and truck tags had been tagged on every Texas law enforcement computer in the state. "If located contact Lt. Clayton, of the Texas Rangers."

So, the minute he was stopped for that traffic violation, the patrol officer called Clayton and held Kinum and the others in the vehicle until one of the Rangers could arrive to pick him up.

Once Kinum was gone, the Patrol Officer ejected the other occupants and only then found the stolen guns, discovering what they were up to. Kinum had avoided the jail time with just this one condition, threat... or promise. "Go and live on the Timmons Ranch in Nevada until you are eighteen or go to jail until you are eighteen.

★★

Life is full of choices… and consequences," said Lt. Clayton of the Texas Rangers.

Clayton was only a Lieutenant at the time and played golf with Kinum's father. He knew how broken-hearted Glenn Kinum's parents were and took a special interest in finding the boy before he made a complete mess of his life. He presented the tough choice to him without his parents' consent but was gambling on their agreement once they heard their son was involved in a potential robbery attempt.

"Can't I just go home?" whined Glenn.

"No, you have messed up that option. Don't get me wrong, your parents want you home. They're the ones who asked me to find you. But you have made some criminally bad choices that won't allow that now. Running away, using drugs, and a bank robbery!"

"Those are serious choices with felony implications and serious consequences. Besides, it's completely out of your parent's hands now. It's in me and Judge Stewart's hands, so you have a glimmer of hope here. The Judge was the one initially to suggest the ranch in Nevada. He told me to tell you that you have the one option and if you didn't choose Nevada, for me to file charges and he'll be sure you get jail time."

The jail time part, Judge Stewart didn't say. Clayton lied to pressure Kinum. Glenn was cornered.

"I'll go to Nevada…"

Clayton and Judge Stewart afterward convinced Glenn's parents to sign off on the Timmons Ranch plan. It was really the only way to 'save' me. And save him it did.

Both physically and spiritually as Ranger Glenn Kinum went on to become a fine man of character that followed in the footsteps of the man who became his mentor Captain Clayton of the Texas Rangers. Thank God I did. Glenn thought to himself thankfully as he shut off the ignition of his truck in front of the main house. *Who knows what would have become of me?*

Glenn bursts through the front door with a big smile on his face. "I bought all kinds of goodies for you Patriots! Come and get 'em!"

Ranger Kinum had a blast shopping for the Patriots as they had become known through the media in a derogatory way. Kinum of course thought of it in a more positive way, the traditional meaning.

★★

O'Brian and McConnel answered the call to unload the truck and came trotting down the stairs. After several trips in and out with arms full of supplies, everyone gathered in the kitchen excited to dig through the many boxes. This was Kinum's second trip from town with supplies.

The first was just the basics, this one was from the Patriot's shopping list. Kinum was happy to do it. *I have been blessed and want to be a blessing. It's good sometimes to be born into a wealthy family.*

"Once we have got this all put away, I would like to have an intel meeting in the living room. There have been some new developments," announced Kinum.

Then he picked up a special box he had set aside and wandered into the dining room and opened the contents.

About fifteen minutes later, everyone was relaxed, sitting in the living room, laughing, and munching on chips and dip, cookies, and beverages. Kinum walked in and tossed encrypted satellite phones to each member. The only one that didn't receive one was Leah.

Patrick Daniels was the first to comment. "SAT Phones! In the words of my father –BITCHIN!"

Kinum began his briefing as each person opened their box and began to play with them.

"These phones are the latest military grade encrypted SAT phones. No one and I mean no one should be able to hack into your communications, identify you, or triangulate you." I hope. "Especially on open, unmonitored lines."

"The phones work through a private satellite that covers North America and Mexico, the Middle East and Europe, and most of North Africa. Outside of the team, no one will have your numbers, besides me and one other Lost Boys, who will give the call sign 'WantabeBuckaroo'."

"What the fuck kind of call sign is that?" asks Donahue.

"It's a call sign that a non-military, non-LEO will remember," continues Kinum.

"You need to remember that we must keep the connection points to a minimum between the Lost Boy Network and you guys. The only reason we have a redundant contact for you is in case something happens to me. Which is highly unlikely."

"What about Kevin?" asked Leah, "will there be a way to contact him?" Leah asks hopefully.

"We are developing a plan to have Kevin join you here soon, he'll have his own SAT phone. Which leads me to my second and more concerning bit of information." Glenn, paused for a moment to distract everyone's attention away from their new phones. All eyes were intently on him now.

"The FBI has shown up at the Timmons Ranch looking for Kevin. They did not indicate that they were looking for any of you, but it is clear they are on the trail of each of you in response to the Bunkerville Standoff. So, it is just a matter of time before they visit each of your respective homes."

Again, Glenn paused to let everybody think about it and let it sink in.

"You might think about warning them."

Joannie won't say anything. McConnel thinks to himself. *She doesn't know anything. Even if she did, know something.*

Oh shit, Jennifer is going to go ballistic. I'll never get to see Emma, ever again. O'Brian worried.

My address is Patrick's address, and my kids are with their father. None of them have anything to tell, crosses Kristen Donahue's mind. *I'm good.*

I got no one but Kristen, and I have never been sure about how long that will last. Daniels thinks briefly. *Investigate away, I got no one to warn.* As he brings his attention back to his new phone.

I hope they find me. Are they even looking for me? I wonder if my editor even remembers me saying I was going to the Cloyden ranch? She is such a bitch. Oh, they probably couldn't care less about me anyway. Worries flood Leah's thoughts. *I only have Kevin,* smiles Leah. *I think.* Then comes the familiar deep frown wrinkle on her brow line as she contemplates her future.

Kinum went on, "So, we have decided that if there is a concern that your family members are a liability, you can bring them here for safekeeping. It may be a long stay though, with no end in sight. Which will be the case for each of you too, I'm afraid."

"Oh, bummer," chimes in Daniels with an ear-to-ear country grin. "We gotta stay here in this lap of luxury."

"What we are trying to do is keep you out of the way of the FBI and any other federal agency, until things calm down and you're not on the top of the list for the government's concern," continues Kinum.

"How are we going to do that?" asks O'Brian. "That may take years, and I hate to sit here on my ass waiting on a bunch of people I don't know, hoping they figure something out. You're asking for a lot of trust." O'Brian pushing back now.

"First, we have someone placed very high up in Federal Law Enforcement, who is giving us very good intel about all of you. Secondly, all hell is breaking loose in our country. We have had a shooting in Portland, Oregon, which was blamed on you. And now the Virginia Statehouse has been taken over by a disorganized group of Second Amendment supporters who the President says is affiliated with the 'White Supremacists' that killed hundreds in Bunkerville.

"What the fuck!" exclaims Daniels. "I am no White Supremacist." None of us are. How did all of this get pinned on us?

"PSYOPS," declares McConnel knowingly. "It's the art of winning the hearts and minds of the people you are trying to control. PSYOPS is a planned and coordinated Intelligence Operation designed to target people's vulnerabilities to influence them. They target their enemy's will to fight, will to obey, or will to support, in order to manipulate and control them."

"PSYOPS detachments typically have graphic design, media, and photography skills to support their Intelligence Analysts. Here in the US the media willingly plays that role. PSYOPS sometimes supports humanitarian activities, maintains, or restores civil order, and surely portrays friendly intent and actions correctly. But more importantly, it counters enemy propaganda, misinformation, disinformation; and denies the enemy the ability to polarize public opinion against the US Government."

"How do you know all of that?" asks Leah worried she might have been used throughout her entire journalism career.

"I lived it, breathed it, and implemented it against our enemies all across the world. At the basest level, that is the main mission of an Army Ranger."

"We get friendlies to fight our enemies," replies McConnel resolutely.

"Wait, I don't understand how that applies here? Are we the enemy, are they trying to win us over? I am confused," Kristen paused as she tried to gather her questions.

"Are we the friendlies or the enemies?"

"That's the mystery of the whole PSYOPS thing. It's a Psychological Operation. The only ones that understand the end game is the one implementing the operation. Remember back in Operation Desert Storm, against Saddam Hussain, in Iraq?"

"We had bombed the hell out of the Iraqi army, we cut off their supply lines and destroyed their communications. Hell, the Republican Guard was using carrier pigeons to try to get messages to their command and control. They were slowly running out of ammunition and were starving for basic supplies, like food and water."

"Then the US Army PSYOPS dropped flyers on the battlefield. Hundreds and thousands of flyers with images of Iraqi prisoners eating bananas, resting on cots, with plenty to drink. It broke their will to fight any longer. As a result, the fourth largest army in the world surrendered in masse."

"You still didn't answer Kristen's question," Leah still confused.

McConnel continued, "The government is using the US media to manipulate the American people into believing a lie that they have a common enemy. These… 'White Supremacists,' whoever they are. They need to demonize a group, make them a faceless terrorist threat to the security of the citizenry of the US."

"Then they will pile every group of people or individual who stands in the way of their goal as an enemy, and label them as a 'White Supremacists,' even black people or Hispanic people. Groups that are counterintuitive to the label of 'White Supremacists,' will all be heaped into the enemy pile if they oppose the one primary goal."

"They will declare a grand conspiracy, a threat against the sovereignty of the United States of America. They will use familiar scary terms like Constitutional Crises, Rule of Law, Equity, Systemic Racism, Existential Threat, but they don't mean them in the traditional sense, not in the Oxford dictionary sense. No, these words will have no meaning except for what is expeditious and on their immediate agenda. Purposely they are trying to confuse people and get them to obey and not give support to their enemy."

"The Communists still do it, the Nazis did it. They lulled the citizenry into passively surrendering their power over to the government, with the promise the government knows best how to protect them. And it cost the world millions and millions of innocent lives. The threat is now repeating itself, right here on American soil in the freest country in the history of the world."

Leah is now completely frustrated, lost, and scared. "You haven't answered Kristen's question! What the fuck, how are we... er... you the enemy of the people? These four or five people cannot overthrow the United States Government and cancel out 240 years of history."

"No that's true. You are right. We... us five, don't hold the power. Our representative government doesn't even hold the power. Right?" McConnel asks Leah for confirmation.

"Well sure they do; the government has all the power." Leah pushes back defensively.

"Do they? Can they appoint themselves sovereign, in charge over all the citizens in America? What if they do?" McConnel making his point.

"Well, they would just be voted out. And a new representative will be voted in that isn't crazy." Leah being a bit annoyed with the absurdity of the question.

"Well, if that is true, who actually holds the power?" McConnel sensing 'the penny was about to drop' in Leah's understanding.

"The people obviously," Leah is becoming more frustrated. "You still haven't answered the question..."

"If the people hold the power, and the government wants it. Who is the enemy?" McConnel smiling now as he hears the sound of the penny about to fall.

"Oh shit, the people, the FUCKING PEOPLE are the enemy!" Leah finally wakes up to the reality of what is happening.

Leah Scrivener has just been "Red Pilled." O'Brian smiles to himself. Referring to the movie *The Matrix* and the idea of truth being revealed to someone that was deceived.

Kristen now has a clarifying question, "But why us, why are we the ones who are supposedly leading this rebellion, when we don't have anything to do with all these other happenings? We've been hiding out in Nevada and now here. Wherever the fuck here is."

Daniels answers this one, "We were simply an opportunity of convenience for their plan. We all never laid eyes on one another until we met on the bridge in Bunkerville. Then out of necessity, circumstances forced us together. Now we are a team hiding together. But the powers that be, don't know that."

"That's right and they don't care. We just accidentally fit into their PSYOPS," McConnel replies.

O'Brian had been thoughtfully sitting there listening and thinking intently about all that was said. He was extremely pissed off. He was pissed off that his plans to live his life with Emma had been completely derailed. He was pissed off that it might be years before his plans could be put back of track. But he was mostly pissed off that his country was being dismantled by a bunch of self-serving, power-hungry… communists.

"I for one will not stand for this. I took an oath when I entered the Navy."

He let that slip. Says Daniels to himself. *He's a SEAL!*

"I pledged my allegiance to the UNITED STATES of America and saw many of my closest friends give their lives for that Pledge and to that Oath. I will be dammed if I sit here on my ass waiting for someone to fix this country and clear my name. This country trained me with a specific set of skills to use to protect her. I thought I did my part, but God has other plans."

"So, I for one am NOT going to sit this fight out. The most important fight this country has faced… since the civil war. Besides, the sooner we become part of the solution straightening this out, the sooner I can start my life with my daughter."

There was a long pause. Then Kinum broke the silence, "Then what do we do?"

Now, it was McConnel's turn. "My expertise is in country warfare. It includes PSYOPS, but it also includes Counter PSYOPS, of which I am an expert. If you are all in, then I am in. I will also lend my particular expertise to the cause of the country I love."

"Oh shit, you guys will need a Jarhead to do the dangerous stuff, count me in," replies Daniels.

"I go where he goes," replies Donahue in agreement. "But I think I could use more training," in an apprehensive tone.

★★★

"Can I just go home?" asks Leah. They all looked at her with a blank stare. "I didn't think so … so I'll be your medic!" Leah says with an acquiescent jesting smile.

They all started laughing...

"You need to inform your Network, that they have an active combat team at their disposal. We'll sharpen our edges and will need some support and lots of intel. Plus, we'll need our sniper back," instructs O'Brian to Kinum.

Kinum shakes his head in agreement.

"KEVIN?!" asks Leah like a love-struck teenager.

"Yes, Kevin," replies O'Brian in an annoyed father sort of way.

Washington, DC, Autumn Mortuary

Dr. John Jackson watches as Jim Johnson labored in breathing. It won't be long now. "Jim, you're going to be with the Lord Jesus soon. Just let go when you're ready." I need to get things set up in the crematorium.

"Jim, I will be back in just a moment."

As John took a quick walk down the hall, he was thinking about heaven and the afterlife like never before.

It's funny, I am a Dr. and a Mortician, but I have always just ignored the idea of the afterlife. Oddly, Jim Johnson was a believer in Heaven and was quite confident that is where he was headed. Over the years, Jackson had noticed a difference in the peace of the Christians he treated as they approached death.

They were such a contrast to the others, the non-Christians. Their end always was fraught with fear or at the very least anxiousness, trying to cling to every moment of life they could. As a mortician, he saw the complete desperation in the loved ones left behind, as they awkwardly stumbled with assuaging fear, with terms like; "He's in a better place now," or, "He's with the Angels." Not one person ever said, "Well he's feeling the heat now." But the Christian families celebrated! *It is a strange contrast.*

Jim Johnson was no different than anyone else. In one of his last waking moments, as he sat in the office that John converted to a hospital bedroom, Jim told Jackson of his source of confidence.

★★★

★★

"I accepted God's sacrifice for my sins when I was a boy. At that moment I was Born Again and sealed with the promise by the Holy Spirit. It wasn't something I did; it was something someone else did. It was something Jesus did for us all. We just need to receive it."

Those words had settled in John's heart for days, swirling around in his understanding. *It was something done for me… not something I could do for myself. I had never heard Christianity put that way.* It made sense to him because there he sat caring for a man that he wasn't even sure he liked. But this man, Jim Johnson did something for him, he didn't deserve. And, because of it, he felt it necessary to serve him in his dying wish. *Is that what this loving God thing is all about?*

It consumed his thoughts, buried deep in his heart when he fired up the crematorium and watched the flames, and felt the intense heat. *Is this the other option, a crematorium for all of eternity? Or Being Willing to love God because of how he sacrificed his Son for me to avoid that!* The heat burning his face now, waking him to the present realization of turning down the furnace to low.

The decision is NOT about avoiding Hell, it's about loving and serving the God who rescued me from hell by allowing his own Son to pay the price that I owed. I think I get it now. Who would do that? Give his own Son for me?

Jackson was back with Jim as his breath became increasingly shallow and less rapid.

"Hey Jim, your job here is done. I get it now. It's about God's love, not about His anger. I get it. I think I really do." At that precise moment, right at the end of Jim's earthly life, John Jackson experiences his new spiritual birth. Jim Johnson was going to be in the arms of his Savior.

"Well Jesus, here he comes," sighed John Jackson with a smile.

★★

Chapter 22

My Escorts Are Here

The covert assault team had arrived at approximately 2 a.m. by what appeared to be a non-descript private jet. Once they disembarked and unloaded their equipment, they promptly kitted up and were driven for a two-hour trek into the stark sagebrush-covered mountains of Nevada in a black twelve-passenger Ford van with black tinted windows. Throughout the plane ride, and now in the van, there was little to no conversation.

The six men were professional military operators who had been recruited from the US Army DELTA Force for this specific mission. This particular group of men had served in most every continent in the world on similar dangerous missions. DELTA has always been known to be a closed group of fighters who had free reign to just "get the job done." This mission was no different. Except they were on US soil with a different set of rules of engagement.

On this mission, their orders were to capture and transport a young male (age nineteen) to Guantanamo Bay, Cuba, for interrogation. The collateral damage was to be minimal, just get in and out on the QT, without notice. Bring "NO ATTENTION TO YOURSELVES," was the direct command of their new civilian leader, Director Helle.

"We're about ten mikes out," declared the driver, who had been flown in two days earlier to secure private transportation and gather intel for the mission. The driver found his role to be relatively easy. He was on US soil after all and had a full understanding of the customs and logistics of his home country. Thankfully, his job was smooth going thus far and he was able to find a good approach to the target location.

Though he readily admitted he had not been able to confirm the actual target — this "Kevin Linfield" guy who was wanted for terrorism. There was little if any commotion on the ranch where they were ordered to carry out the extraction plan. There were just the simple ranch owners, an older couple going about the daily chores. But Director Helle was convinced that Linfield was there, somewhere, in hiding, and wanted his new "Action Team" to apprehend him immediately.

"We're on foot from here," says the driver as he shuts the engine down and turns off the headlights.

"I'll take you in from here."

The seven men took one last equipment check then headed out in stack formation behind the driver in the lead. They arrived at the Timmons ranch headquarters at precisely 5:30 a.m.

"Overwatch in place," chirps the COMMS.

"Okay, let's do this by the numbers," commands the team leader as they begin their stealth approach.

The driver finds cover and watches the whole operation through a set of night vision binoculars. His job was to listen for any local emergency radio traffic that might indicate their presence. The five men move in precision through the rocks and trees just outside the main entry road to the ranch.

Once they arrived at the first set of buildings, they formed back into a stack formation and headed swiftly and quietly towards the bunkhouse. All at once, they froze as a light came on in the main house. Through the windows, they could clearly see an older man moving about. They waited five seconds and then proceeded once they realized they had not been seen.

The fourth man in line peeled off and took position in the adjacent barn as planned. This position gave him a clear open vantage point over the egress points accessible to each residential building. He was there to cover any potential "squirters," who might try to escape. As the remainder of the team silently approached the only door to the first bunkhouse, they immediately breached through the entrance.

"Clear, no one inside," came the voice of the team leader over the COMMS.

Next, they approached the Buckaroo's bunkhouse. Again, they breached it immediately. This time they took a little more care in searching for Linfield. The FBI report mentioned that this bunkhouse would likely be where they would find Linfield and expect the occupants to be armed. But yet again, it was empty.

"Clear," came the team leader's voice over the COMMS.

"Proceeding to the main house," communicates the team leader.

Breaching the main house was the last resort part of the operational plan. Linfield was expected to be in one of the bunkhouses, but they'd search the main house if they couldn't locate him there. The main house was a bit trickier. They would need to split the remaining four men in two and breach the main door through the front and the rear door, off the kitchen (the ranch hand entrance).

They planned on the element of surprise, but they now knew that at least one of the occupants was up and out of bed. They would need to move very swiftly and breach the entrances at precisely the same moment. Each team of two split up and paused just outside the light-fall of the house. They were waiting for the man in the house to move out of the kitchen, where he would likely see their approach.

"WAIT ONE!" commands the team leader.

That was all it took, his voice, a strange voice outside was enough for Susie's furry head to pop up from her comfortable spot near the heater, then her ears went forward to listen one, two, three seconds. Then without hesitation, she sprinted across the kitchen floor trying hard to get traction, her paws clicking on the slick linoleum, straight through the doggie door to investigate the strange noise she heard. This of course alarmed all the other house dogs and they followed in a full sprint immediately after Susie.

As soon as Susie cleared the back porch, she spotted the strangers waiting in the dark with her canine eyes. She stopped and let off the alarm. BOWARK! BOWARK! It was a different kind of bark, one she used for real danger. Pop understood it and so did the other dogs.

Susie now had a laser focus on the team leader and his partner who were crouched in the dark hiding just outside the back porch. The other dogs spread out, some going right and some going left. Working dogs, especially heelers, by instinct never head straight in. Instead, they intuitively circle behind their target to their heels and drive their subject to their master.

"Oh shit, dogs," says the team leader over the COMMS.

"Got 'em," says Overwatch. With a flash of his barrel through his silencer. SHEWOK came the sound of the round, hitting Susie smack in her girth as she stood just in the light. She fell dead with a yelp.

Of course, this commotion drew the front porch dogs to full attention as they scanned the front area for intruders, humans, they were sure from Susie's bark.

From that point on, it was silent. Not a bark or a growl.

"Where are the other dogs?" asks the team leader.

Overwatch answers. "I got nothing. They must have run off."

"Who's out there?!" Hollers an old male voice from inside the house.

The commotion of the dogs had gained Pop's attention as he picked up his Mossberg racking a round as he began to head to the back door. *It must be human for this kind of commotion.*

But when Pop walked through the door, he spotted Susie's body lying in a pool of blood with half her insides hanging out. *It's people. It's people with guns!*

He deliberately let off a shot into the air with his shotgun to warn off the would-be intruders. Then quickly retreated back into the house, turned off the kitchen lights, and knelt down out of sight just inside the door behind the exterior wall.

"WHAT'S YOUR BUSINESS HERE?" yells Pop at the top of his lungs.

In response, silence. "I'll send my dogs after you if you don't state your business," yells Pop once again.

Momma came to the interior kitchen door frame with a Winchester 30-30 in her hands. "What's going on Pop?" she whispers with concern.

"I don't know. There is somebody out there, but I don't know who. They're being really cool. You watch the front door like we practiced."

Momma and Pop had lived out in this remote country for a long time. Both were experts with many weapons. Knowing it could be several hours before any help might arrive, they had practiced together on what they would do in various dangerous scenarios.

Momma picked up the phone and called 911 just like they practiced. "911 please state your emergency." After a couple of minutes explaining the dire situation the operator stated, "We have Sherriff Deputies on the way."

"All right, we have called the Sheriff's and they are on the way. You better be gone before they get here," announced Pop wanting to avoid a fight if possible.

Still silence was the answer.

Next, over COMMS was Overwatch, "The sun is starting to rise. We better get to doing what we came here to do."

"Okay, well, now that surprise is out of the question, we need to breach in force. Let's gather up and enter through the front door. That will leave the old man watching out the rear."

The driver switched to his inferred binoculars. *There are at least two people in the house. One in the back and one sitting as cool as a cucumber in the front room.* Then at the same instance, came a local radio dispatching of the Lander County Sheriffs to the Timmons Ranch.

Once they came together, the four lined up and began to cross over the large gravel turn-around in the front of the house in stack formation, completely unaware of the dogs still standing guard on the front porch. The house dogs on the front porch instantly spotted their movement in the dark and let off the alarm. This signaled the other dogs who were watching and waiting for a command to reposition.

"Oh, shit, more dogs," Overwatch says to himself. With two pulls of the trigger, he once again silenced the barking dogs. But this time both bullets went through the dogs, rendering them dead upon impact, and hit the front exterior of the house with a loud thump.

In response, Momma pulled the trigger of the 30-30, levered in another round, and let another bullet fly. Both rounds striking within an inch of each other in the center of the door. This stopped the advancing men in their tracks.

"Fall back," commands the team leader. *What the hell was that? Apparently, our intel sucks. This isn't going to be a quick easy snatch and grab. Dammit.*

Over the COMMS: "There are at least two, I repeat two tangos in the house," announces the driver.

"No shit," came the reply from the team leader.

"Additionally, radio traffic reports that the Sheriffs are on their way. ETA one hour fifteen," the driver again.

"Copy," replies the team leader.

"We are going to need to do a hard breach through the front door," announces the team leader.

"You had better do it right now, the sun is coming up fast," replies Overwatch. "You will be in the open crossing the driveway turn-around."

With that, one man, the breacher, moved quietly across the turn-around and slowly and silently went up the steps onto the porch and to the front door. There he went about his business setting a breaching charge on the front door. Momma sat focused, silently listening, and waiting. But her old ears just didn't hear the man on the porch.

"Breach set," whispered the man over the COMMS. That Momma heard.

"Pop, there is someone on the porch," whispered Momma as quietly as possible.

"Move out!" Commands the team leader. The three men are up and moving in stack formation across the gravel turn-around.

"JOHNNY, RICKY, AWAY TO ME!" commands Pop at the top of his voice.

In a flash, dogs came from nowhere and everywhere, growling and yapping while trying to herd the three men towards the house. Johnny, a Queensland Heeler, the leader and most aggressive of the pack was the first to bite down on the heel of the last man in line. Johnny gave a good hard tug and down to the ground, the man fell. Not really sure how he found himself on the ground.

"Shit, more dogs," Overwatch said to himself in disbelief. He was trying to target them, but the dogs were moving so fast, in and out, yapping and nipping at the team members, that he was having trouble getting a clear shot.

"Son of a Bitch!" yells the second man in pain as he is viciously pulled to the ground by Ricky, a stout Red Merle Australian Shepard. Ricky had latched onto the butt of this man and pulled him right down. Ricky's canine teeth had sunk deep into the meaty area and jabbed his sciatic nerve. It was very painful and for a moment he thought he was shot with blood pouring out of his body.

The team leader was completely surprised by the attack. The dogs came in so fast and so quietly, it caught him off guard. He spun

180 degrees and started to take aim at the dogs, any dog at this point. Then he fell prey too, to Johnny.

Just as the team leader pulled the trigger to execute one of the other dogs, Johnny latched his teeth deep into his calf above the boot. It was not a nip as Queensland's are prone to do, it was a full-on bite deep into the muscle. Johnny was excited and had forgotten his defensive training. Or he sensed the danger to his masters and was using all of his canine instinct to protect the Alpha of his pack, Pop.

Johnny had pulled the team leader to the ground and locked his jaws. He twisted and shook his head as if he caught a rabbit hunting and was trying to end its life. As the team leader fell, his shot went wild and ricocheted off a nearby rock. Then came the Blam, Blam, Blam of the team leader's sidearm, his Sig Sauer, ending Johnny's life and the assault on the team leader's leg.

The "firefight" of sorts startled the breacher, and he flinched, dropping the pliers he was holding onto the wood flooring of the porch, making a "per-clunk" sound. That was all Momma needed to get a noise target on the man and to open fire. She let three rounds fly in rapid succession straight through the wall.

The large bore round easily went through the wall and found its target. Two rounds hit the back of his body armor, spinning him instantly, while the third round hit his left biceps sailing straight through the armhole in his armor, and continuing into his torso. That bullet had lost velocity causing it to ricochet back and forth in his body cavity, bringing his death before he ever hit the deck of the porch with a heavy thud.

When he landed, he fell on the trigger of the breaching placement, and it exploded in grand fashion. The front door blew off its hinges into the middle of the living room. Wood and metal splintered and flew in every direction like the ordinance of a grenade.

Pop jumped to his feet and came sprinting into the living room, leaped over the door on the floor, and stood in the gaping hole where the front door once was. With his shotgun, he first took aim at the immediate threat, the body directly in front of him. In a split second, he determined that threat was neutralized and then took aim at the men on the turn-around. Three rounds flew from his pump-action

Mossberg. They laid down a big pattern, kicking up dust and peppering all three men and two dogs with buckshot.

The men scrambled to their feet the best they could and ran for cover. That gave the opportunity Pop needed. He had never taken a man's life before, but that didn't even cross his mind. Pop like a thousand other times when skeet shooting, took aim at the last man slowly limping across the driveway.

He brought the shotgun to his shoulder, scoped down the barrel, exhaled, *gently squeeze, don't pull the trigger,* he reminded himself. Just like he taught every young boy who ever came to his ranch. Then Pop squeezed. BOOM! The shotgun reported its unique resounding sound as it sent the devastating group of tiny pellets downrange.

Pop's aim was perfect, as the mass hit the team leader smack between the shoulder blades, throwing the man forward with such force that even though he hit his body armor, it actually broke his neck. The team leader fell to the dust of the turn-around, his life ended by a gentle rancher who genuinely loved everyone he ever met.

This all happened in just a few seconds. Overwatch had been trying to eliminate the threat of the dogs, two of which he did. But the explosion and the shots from the house happened so quickly he was slow to catch up. He aimed at Pop and squeezed the trigger, but Pop disappeared back into the house before the bullet could find its target.

Pop was so concerned with Momma; he didn't even notice the silent intruder of the Overwatch round that hit the sofa. Momma still sat in her favorite recliner where she was standing guard. The explosion had scattered chards of wood and metal everywhere and a large twelve-inch stick had lodged into Momma's chest.

"Momma?!" Chuck Timmons has only now realized the trouble his wife was in. "Oh shit, you're hurt bad."

"Language," Dorthey replied with a smile.

"You hang tight –I'll call an ambulance."

"There's no time, Lover. Jesus has already been calling me, but I wanted to wait to say goodbye to you."

"No, no... you hang in there. I don't want to run this place… without you … hang on," Chuck pleads with tears running down his old, leathered face.

★★★

★★

"It's been a good life, my love, we have served our Lord with all of our mind, with all of our heart, and with all of our soul. But Jesus is calling me to Himself. I can hear Him. My strength is draining, and I am ready."

"Oh, Dorthey," Chuck was sobbing now. "I don't want you to go."

"I know, but you'll be with me in Glory soon. We won't be apart long. Would you just pray for me?" whispers Dorthey Timmons with one of her very last breaths.

"Oh... I don't have any words." After a second thought, Pop steeled himself and then in the midst of the chaotic situation found just the right words for his wife.

"Father, you have given me this precious gift, my partner, my lover, my friend. Your Son is calling her now, so I present her to you. The Bible says you are the giver and taker of life. So, if it's her time to be with you in Heaven I release her yet again to you. Come now, Lord Jesus."

Chuck was sobbing again now. He looked down at his bride and saw a confident smile on her face.

"Look, Chuck, do you see them? The Lord has sent me two glorious Angels to escort me to Heaven. Do you see them!?" Dorthey exclaimed as she pointed to the middle of the living room.

Chuck looked over his right shoulder and caught a glimpse of a blinding white flash of light. He rubbed the tears from his eyes and saw... nothing. Then he looked back to Dorthey's body lying in a slump on her recliner. "Oh, Dorthey how will I do this without you..." Chuck threw his face into the breast of her still-warm body and wept.

Time passed until his grief was interrupted by the yelp of a dog being targeted and shot by the snipper on the little hill directly above the ranch house. Pop opened his eyes wide to the sunlight now streaming over his face as it rose through the east-facing window. He wiped the remaining tears with his forearm and sat up.

Those bastards are still out there. He told himself. Then suddenly he was filled with a terrible resolve. He picked up Momma's 30-30 and found the box of shells she laid on the floor. Filled its magazine and then did the exact same with his Mossberg from his pocket.

★★

★★★

He crawled to the front door opening and took a quick look. *No one.* Then he pulled the unhinged door over to the opening and set it up to hide behind. *It's of solid oak. It'll provide some protection* he told himself. *Now let's just see where you three are.*

By now Pop had determined that only two men had run for cover and there was one on the hill sniping his dogs. *That's manageable.* Pop was deadly with a 30-30 Winchester. He had used one his entire life and if he could see his target, he could hit it. So, scan for targets he did.

"There's one," Pop said to himself. The target's head was just poking, barely visible above a rock at about fifty yards out from his front porch. Pop could see him clearly now as the sun was rising fast in the sky. Then, without taking his eyes off the man, Pop brought the long gun to his shoulder, took notice of the wind, gazed down the barrel, exhaled, and squeezed the trigger.

The report of the 30-30 was impressive. All Pop saw was a showering mist of blood where the man's head once was. *Two to go.* Then Pop fell back behind the wall inside his house.

Overwatch quickly scanned several target points, starting with the doorway. Nothing. *This thing is not over.*

"Has anyone seen this Linfield guy?" squawks Overwatch on the COMMS.

"Negative," comes the reply from the driver.

"Well, the sun is up, and I don't like sitting out here exposed ––and with only a third of our team," announces Overwatch.

Before he was able to finish the sentence, the log which he'd concealed himself behind exploded, as the incoming report from the house hit its target once again … "SHIT! He has me dialed in," complained the sniper.

Pop saw a slight movement on the hill and took the shot. Though he didn't actually see a target. *That ought to stir up some commotion.*

"Target the front of the house, all guns," commands Overwatch. "Three, two, one, –fire!"

Pop had never experienced anything like it in his life. It seemed like the whole house was exploding, a piece at a time. Everything seemed to move in slow motion, pictures were falling from walls, glass was breaking, shattering everywhere, the stuffing from the couch was drifting about like snow. Then he felt it. A hot burning

★★★

pain first in his right leg, and then again in the small of his back, in the kidneys. *I've been hit.*

"Well, I'd better not just sit here and get shot up. I'd better do something," Pop said to himself. Pop rolled over onto his chest and combat crawled to the front entrance again. This time he could see the third man who came out from cover and was spraying his house with automatic fire.

Pop poked the barrel of his rife through the little gap between what used to be the door frame and the tilted door, took aim, and squeezed his trigger just once. It's a devastating thing to see a man shot center mass with a 30-30 round. It knocked him clean off his feet and straight back against a large boulder. Then he slowly slid down the rock in a trail of blood with a surprised look on his face.

"Didn't see that coming, did you?" said Pop to himself. "Well, this will end you," Pop let loose another round into his forehead. The last thing Pop saw was his military helmet spinning in the air end over end like a football, before rolling onto his back and into cover. But the bullets still riddled the house.

"There must be more guys than I thought," Pop grunted. Pop could feel his back being soaked with blood. *I can't reach it to apply pressure. My clock may just be running out.*

Pop was just lying there helplessly now watching his ranch home explode all around him, then his focus fell on the wedding picture of him and Dorthey. *We were so young.* Pop began to tear up with gladness.

"Ceasefire and reload," came the command from Overwatch. "They may have had enough." Not knowing that Dorthey was dead.

"By my estimate, the Sherriff's will be here in ten mikes. We should think about bugging out," replies the driver.

"Fuck that— we're going to finish this!" demands Overwatch.

"We're gonna be shooting at friendlies then..." protests the driver on dull ears.

"Open fire!" commands Overwatch again. The house begins to take rounds again. But this time Pop hears automatic gunfire from the hill just east of him. *There's more men than I thought.*

They can't take much more than this... was the last thought Overwatch ever had, as the 375 Cheytac round entered his right ear and exited with most of his brain in tow.

Kevin Linfield had heard the report of rapid-fire weapons two miles after he broke camp and was making the last stretch home. He loped his horse forward, then as he became more concerned, he went to a canter, then a full gallop.

As he reached the ridge one and a half miles away from the ranch headquarters, he dismounted Rosie and unpacked the HAMR. He laid out on an adjacent rock and peered through the scope. He could not believe his eyes. The Timmons ranch was under a full-on assault by military assailants.

At first, he didn't know what to do, so, for the longest time, he just stared through the scope in shock. Then he saw one man fall and shot again through the head. The shot came from the house, and it was then Kevin knew that Pop and Momma were fighting back. That's when he decided to take the life of every assailant he could, to defend the only real parents he ever had.

From his position, the easiest target was the sniper. But that proved to be harder than expected. The first shot was high. Kevin dialed in his scope. The second, hasty shot didn't account for the humidity. The third round found his target perfectly.

Ironically, his target was shooting at the house with such rapidity, he never heard the report of the first two rounds. Of course, he didn't hear the third either, because the sniper was dead before the sound caught up with the bullet. Kevin continued to scan the ranch complex looking for another target.

Oh, shit something's wrong. Overwatch has gone silent.

"Overwatch checks in," comes the command over the COMMS. Silence was the answer.

"Overwatch check-in," still no answer.

"We gotta get moving. The Sheriffs will be here any moment," proclaims the driver with concern.

He could now hear the distant sirens of the two sheriff's vehicles approaching.

"Moving out!" says the last man who was firing on the Timmons. It was the Action Team member who was concealed at the barn to eliminate any "squirters." He broke his cover and started to dash across the driveway turn-around, completely unconcerned with the hidden danger he was in.

Kevin immediately saw the movement and took aim. *Squeeze don't pull* is what Kevin thought as he took the most difficult shot of his life. A moving target from one and a half miles away. He aimed at center mass, between his shoulder blades. His inexperience in combat didn't take into account his elevated position and the bullet landed at the base of his neck, nearly severing his head from his body.

The driver watched his fellow teammate fall to the earth as his neck exploded. Only then, five seconds later, did he hear the report of Kevin's weapon far off in the mountains above him.

Sniper. Oh shit!

The ranch headquarters filled with the approaching sound of sirens from the two sheriff's deputy units as they roared across the wood bridge and sped into the ranch compound.

Nothing else to do here. Time to bug out says the driver to himself. He gathers his belongings and slithers through the cover of sagebrush back to the van. Then immediately heads off to the airport and the waiting plane.

The deputies soon ascertain that they arrived too late to help Chuck and Dorthey Timmons. They called in the massacre and ordered an ambulance for Pop who was barely holding on, the only survivor. About ten minutes later, Kevin came loping into the headquarters.

"I am sorry," Kevin hears from one of the Deputies meeting him at his horse as he dismounts, "but Momma is gone."

"Oh. No! What about Pop?" whimpers Kevin.

"He's inside, it doesn't look good. He's been shot in the leg and back, there's... there's a lot of blood."

Kevin sprinted off with his jingle-bobs on his spurs ringing like a Christmas bell. As he entered the front room, it takes him a full five seconds to find Pop in the mess that was once the house he grew up in.

"Over here," says the other deputy who was knelt down with Pop gently reassuring him. Kevin stumbles over the old oak door and makes his way to Pop's side.

"Pop, how ya doing?" Kevin asks.

"Doing pretty good, just resting here, it's been a long day," smiles Pop still staring at his wedding picture lying broken on the floor next to him.

"Momma told me I'd be with her in Heaven real soon. I guess I didn't think it would be the same day," Pop smirks.

★★

Oh, good he knows about Momma. "You hang in there— we'll get you to the hospital and get you fixed up" Kevin says as confidently as he can.

"Na, my escorts are here. They have come to take me to Jesus and be with Dorthey. They're waiting." This time Pop can see the massive angels standing in the living room amongst the rubble.

"They want me to go now. But before I go, I have one request of you Kevin Linfield."

"Sure Pop, anything," Kevin replies with tears running down his face.

"I want you to keep studying your Bible, get to know the Lord more deeply than you'd ever think possible and … continue the ministry," Pop says closing his eyes for the last time.

"Okay Pop, –I promise!" Kevin resolutely declares.

In a flash of light, Pop was in the presence of his Lord. Waiting next to Him, was the love of his life Dorthey, looking perfectly and exactly as she did the day he married her.

Just like their picture he was staring at moments before.

Chapter 23

An Interview with Ghost Patriot

The pile of mail in Julie's inbox at the *New York Times* was stacked so high that it kept sliding off onto the floor. *I wish she'd just go through it,* thought the mail clerk who was just too old to still be working as he again stooped down to pick up what fell, feeling the strain to his back, all the while trying to add today's mail to the stack.

"What's this?" he grunted, as he reached for a small manilla envelope that had fallen into the crevice between Julie's desk and her cubicle wall. His old legs pushed up with uneven force to get his wobbly body erect while clutching the unopened envelope.

Then once again, he stacked the new mail on top and set the slightly dirty envelope precariously at the crown of the stack. *It'll all be on the floor tomorrow.* Then he moved on pushing his mail cart forward to the adjoining cubicle delivering mail to the next employee.

At about 10 a.m. Julie came in and plopped herself down in her chair while talking on her cell phone. She carried an oversized computer bag with an even bigger purse hanging over her right shoulder while clutching a steaming hot Starbucks Cinnamon Dolce Latte topped with whipped cream in her right hand. As she laid her bags onto the already busy desk, along with her hot latte treat, it jiggled just enough to cause the lost envelope to be serendipitously found, as it slides off the top of her inbox between her arms to land right in front of her face.

"Ugh, what the fuck is this?" she says to herself.

"No, no, I wasn't talking to you," Julie replies into the phone.

Julie glanced at the envelope just as she was about to toss it in the trash, then something instinctively told her to open it.

"Uh-huh, that's right," she continued the conversation as she studied the envelope. *Hum, no return address and it's postmarked two weeks ago?*

"Fucking mailroom," she says aloud.

"NO… I'm not talking to you," she sarcastically responds to the person on the other end of the phone, as she takes a sip of her cooling latte, then using her finger swipes some whipped cream into her mouth. *This is incredible!* she sighs in delight.

Inside the envelope is a flash drive and a short note.

Everything you need to know, everything I promised. – Jim

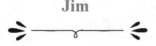

Jim, who is Jim?

"Honey, I got to go. Something has come up. Baby, no, really, I need to go. You can yell at me when I get home. I won't borrow your shoes again, I promise… I got to go. Okay, Love you too. Bye… bye. Okay bye. See you tonight."

She finally presses the disconnect button on her cell phone. — *Boy, she can be bitchy at times!*

Julie fumbles through her computer bag and drags the 17-inch DELL laptop across her desk, pulls it open, and presses the on button. Then she waits for it to log on and load the programs into the memory. Being an MS operating system, this takes way longer than it should and far more protracted than Julie has patience for. Not that she is in a particular rush this morning, she just doesn't like to wait for much of anything.

"Com'on, you piece of crap," she says to her computer.

After a good three minutes the familiar desktop, full of every program on her computer, reveals itself. She inserts and pushes in the flash drive, then clicks on the one file in the drive.

It's a video file. Once it loads up it immediately begins to play.

"Oh, fuck –it's that Jim! … Jim Johnson the director of the FBI," Julie says to herself, curious and surprised.

Jim had made a video specifically for Julie to reveal to her what and who was behind the Patriot movement. It was in the envelope that he had entrusted to John Jackson four weeks ago. He had filmed the video in his FBI Director's office, with the American flag in the background as he spoke, saying:

"Hello, my name is Jim Johnson. I am currently the acting director of the FBI and I officially hold the position of Director of Counterintelligence. In those positions, I hold the highest levels of clearance and have access to every piece of intelligence that comes into the United States government from every intel agency we have. I am the one who briefs the President and her administration on the daily threats our country faces. I am also a Patriot, in fact, some in the media have called me the Ghost Patriot. After this video, some may call me a traitor. But rest assured, I deeply love my country.

It's out of this love that I have taken action. It's become clear to me from the intel I have seen that the United States Government, under the leadership and direct knowledge of the President of the United States, has been working to divide our country in an effort to usher in Marxism under the new brand of Democratic Socialism. But don't be fooled, it is the same old Marxism that has put nearly one hundred fifty million innocent people in their graves.

The truth is you can no longer trust the department heads of the federal government, especially those with Law Enforcement powers. This attempted dismantling of our constitutional system begins by creating a false crisis that is rooted in division. Let me give you just a few details of what I am referring to.

- The STANDOFF as the media has called it in Nevada, was a desperate overreach of power-hungry Politicians, specifically Senator Red, to grab land from a Ranching family that had a 'right to use in order to line his pockets with monies from the renewable energy sector –specifically China. What they didn't count on, is the American people standing up for their rights and pushing back. They pushed back, first by exercising their First Amendment rights, then standing their ground with their Second Amendment rights. A confrontation occurred and someone pulled a trigger that led to a shootout. Just like the Battle of Bunker Hill of 1775, it became a bloody incident that has sparked a resolve in the American Citizenry and a sobering reminder of who "We the

People" of the United States are in the present day. The Battle of Bunkerville will one day be seen as the spark that lit the flame of the new revolution of the Republic.

- My next example is the shooting in Portland, Oregon, just months later. The government and the media called it an act of White Supremacy to murder innocent peaceful protesters. This narrative is in fact, a devious, misleading, deliberate misdirection tactic because the intelligence and just plain common sense has revealed that the shooting of 'innocent protesters' in Portland was quite the opposite. The specific intel shows this older couple were attacked by Antifa for being white and in the wrong area of town. They simply got lost and had taken a wrong turn into a riot. Not a protest, A RIOT! These riots have been going on nightly for the past eighteen months and the local police can't seem to stop them. And the local governing officials have no desire to end them. Why? Because they adhere to the same Marxist ideology as Antifa. They even took the extraordinary step of canceling all mutual aid agreements with local adjacent Law Enforcement agencies, placing their own Police Department without help or back-up from other Law Enforcement Agencies. In other words, they cannot marshal enough officers and equipment to stop these terrorists. Don't be fooled, Antifa are simply the 'Brown Shirts' of the leftists, the Marxists of today. They have destroyed the beautiful city of Portland and are coming soon to a city near you. Let me be clear, this couple was brutally attacked and pulled from their car, beaten and killed by the Antifa mob. The husband who was retired law enforcement attempted to protect himself and his wife from the brutal attack with a legally possessed firearm. He failed and eventually they were overcome by the mob and were viciously murdered. There was NO RACISM INVLOVED. It was a white couple, murdered by white rioters for recreation.

- And lastly, the 'Insurrection' at the State Capital in Virginia is also not an act of racism or White Supremacy. The leader of the whole protest is a black man for God's sake! The three thousand loosely associated protesters were forced to take a hard stand when the Governor of Virginia decided to circumvent the State and Federal Constitution and take the sovereignty from the people of Virginia and bestow it upon himself. Let's be clear, –he intended to arrest those who disagreed with him and place them bound and gagged in the statehouse to have a mock legislative session. The protesters would not stand for it. This unconstitutional action by the State Governor galvanized them, and as a result, they closed the State Capital. The media continues to report that they are holding hostages. That is also not true. Some of the state representatives have refused to leave. The protesters have merely offered them safe passage, the same as they provided to the Republican representatives. But the Virginia Democratic State Representatives refused, preferring to be martyrs in the subversive media circus surrounding it all.

Citizens of the United States don't be fooled by the Marxists making a power play for our country. They are trying to divide us with a fake double-dealing narrative that America is a racist country. And, that the existential threat to our Republic is the 'White Supremacists.' It's just a label they have put on their enemies to dehumanize them and gather support and allegiance to their ideology. No different than the labeling of the Jews, or gypsies, or homosexuals in the 1930s in Germany.

In those days their enemies were either a 'Jew or a Jew lover' – both were as equally despised. They are simply appealing for identity or a faction for you to choose. We cannot fall for their deception. What they want is for us to turn on one another and hate one another so they can seize power and property from us all.

It's happening right now, and the media is helping them. Neither choose to tell the truth and they both refuse the actual facts. The media have become the propaganda arm of the Marxists, no different than Joseph Goebbels and like Goebbels, they are pushing us to "Total War."

It's not too late to stop them. We must rise up! Which is what I am personally going to do. I have left my post with the FBI and will take my experience and training underground in support of the

★★

people of the United States! Will you join me? Get active and get organized. And of course, pray.

Saving our Republic will be difficult, as great darkness has fallen upon us. But the darkest hour always comes just before the dawn."

Julie just sat there stunned.

"What the… holy, shit," *I have another Pulitzer coming my way.*

The first thing she did was call her editor. Then after spending the day with him, the New York Times legal department, public relations department, and the electronics guru, to determine the legal publishing issues, it was verified by compliance that the person on the video was in fact Director Jim Johnson of the FBI, so, she began to write.

Be professional, not too verbose, and tell the story. She told herself as she placed her fingers on the DELL keyboard.

GHOST PATRIOT REVEALS HIMSELF, reads the headline.

Perfect! She smiles to herself.

1600 Pennsylvania Avenue

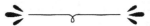

Later that day in an emergency meeting Director Helle, the Attorney General, and the Press Secretary meet with POTUS and the Chief of Staff.

"I knew it, I knew it. He's a **FUCKING TRAITOR!** I told you guys from day one he was no good. I told you. He was working for the enemy all along right under our noses!" Fumed the President.

They all shook their heads.

"Is there any way we can stop the Times from going to print?" asks POTUS of the Press Secretary.

"No, no way. The story is out on the web already and will be in the evening edition tonight. Tomorrow it will be the lead story. They have already booked every opinion and talk show for the next two weeks. This is big and they know it."

★★

"Can't we knock this off the news cycle with something better? Something less damaging?" presses the Chief of Staff.

"Well, maybe a nuclear war," replies the Press Secretary.

"Humm," replies Helle under his breath.

"I WAS JOKING!" the Press Secretary exclaims, clarifying her statement, knowing that all Oval Office conversations are now recorded, for the first time since Richard Nixon.

"My point was in journalism –this is BIG! It is a story of a generation. Nothing but a world-shattering event could get them off this news cycle for the next umpteen weeks."

"Sure, and my point is with any 'luck' maybe something else will come along that will be more important for the media," arrogantly replies the Homeland Security Director.

"Something, –sort of like a nuclear attack."

The President takes back the meeting. "All I know is we're fucked. The media will be digging into this like a dog with a bone. There'll be no letting go, and with no other story, we will be found out."

"Unless we send them chasing another tale," replies Helle.

"What do you mean?" asks the Chief of Staff.

"Let's officially throw Jim Johnson and the entire FBI under the bus. Run the narrative that they are all corrupt and that we are moving to dismantle the entire department. I mean, we don't have to do it. Well, at least not right away. But send the narrative that DHS has known about this problem for years and has been diligently taking action behind the scenes to DEFUND them. Have the DOJ, announce indictments…"

"Whoa, wait a minute. We don't have any indictments pending against the FBI," replies the Attorney General.

"You'd better do it first thing tomorrow, starting with Jim Johnson," Helle says sternly.

"If you want to save this administration, that is."

Then he turns back to the President. "We just need to get ahead of this and give the media a misdirection to slow this down."

"Will they go for it?" asks POTUS of the Press Secretary.

"No… well, maybe … if we can come up with something that will genuinely take their attention to change the news cycle. Otherwise, it will be seen for what it is, an ass-covering."

"Okay, well, you'd better call a press conference ASAP, and let's see if we can get ahead of this," instructs POTUS.

"If any of you have any questions, please check in with me," announces the Chief of Staff as he dismisses the meeting.

"Director Helle, please stay back for a brief conversation with the President," everyone left the two of them alone.

"Please give me a quick update regarding your investigations into these White Supremacists?" asks POTUS.

"We have redirected our attention to Jim Johnson and all of our resources are now on him. He can cause real major damage to you and your efforts. I am convinced he is the head of this thing," replied Helle, in a bald-faced lie.

He didn't want to tell the President about the massacre of his newly formed Action Team in Nevada. With this new information he had just been informed of forty minutes earlier, it seemed like the perfect red herring to redirect to. Besides, the President needed plausible deniability.

"Oh, that sounds good. I am glad you are ahead of it," POTUS replied in feigned relief, suspecting he was lying.

"Madam President, how far into the FBI do you want me to dig?"

"As deep as it goes Director Helle, as deep as it goes," replies POTUS.

"We need to find out how deep these traitors have infiltrated our government. Start with Johnson and uncover every stone, not leaving any unturned," sternly directs the President.

"Okay, but this will disrupt the investigation of Bunkerville, Portland, and Virginia. I mean, the … er, … it's the FBI who is… was investigating those incidents, and now I will be investigating those investigators. This will be very disruptive." At this point, Helle is just making it up offhand, ad-libbing as he goes.

"Mr. Helle, it is clear to me that the nexus of this White Supremacists threat is Jim Johnson. I am certain if you dig there, dig into the FBI, you'll find the nest of vermin that were behind these events. So, you will not be abandoning the investigation into those terrorist acts, you'll be revealing the true perpetrators of them."

"Great, then we are on the same page!" exclaims Helle as he begins to rise from his chair, relieved he had succeeded in redirecting the President away from his disastrous first attempt at "modified evidence gathering" and failure in his new role.

Whitehouse Press Room, 4:00 p.m.

"Thank you all for coming today on such short notice," opens the Press Secretary. Then she continues.

"Today the Department of Justice, based on the investigation of the Department of Homeland Security has issued an arrest warrant for James (Jim) Johnson, the former Director of the FBI. The charging documents allege acts of treason, conspiracy, and terrorism, along with a dozen other felonies."

There was an audible gasp throughout the room from the reporters.

"Which you can view in detail from the formal indictment which should be officially released tomorrow. The Department of Homeland Security has had Mr. Johnson under review after discovering several improprieties in his career which led to the charges he is now facing. I am told that this investigation has been underway for nearly a year now and that the media accounts and the video that are circulating around today are just an attempt by Johnson to deflect his inevitable prosecution. Based on that video, the Department of Justice has determined that Former Director Johnson has fled justice and is hiding incognito in another country to avoid arrest. The Department of Homeland Security is following up on several leads as we speak, as to Mr. Johnson's exact whereabouts and they are confident he will be in custody very soon." The Press Secretary took a deep breath before asking the question of the gaggle, the question she does not want to ask.

"That concludes my official statement. *I hate this part.* Any questions?"

Every hand flew up in the room and some just started barking out their questions. The questions came firing fast and so did the answers. The Press Secretary allowed no follow-ups.

CBS: "Is Director Johnson the Ghost Patriot?"

Press Secretary: "We're not sure, but he does seem to say he is in the video." *I should have been more conclusive with my answer.*

CNN: "Is Mr. Johnson a Traitor to his country?"

Press Secretary: "Yes." *That's better.*

FOX News: "That is the most serious of charges. A conviction could lead to the death penalty. What evidence do you have that he is a traitor?"

Press Secretary: "When the court releases the evidence, you will come to the same conclusion this administration has come to. Yes, Former Director Johnson is a traitor. He deceitfully used his position to spy on and then subvert the sovereignty of the United States of America for the purpose of terrorism. For the enemies of our country, and the racists that continue to destabilize our way of life, it should be a serious charge, because these are serious crimes. Next question."

Washington Post: "The Times is reporting that several of the incidences that you have mentioned in recent months, Bunkerville Nevada, Portland Oregon, and even the Virginia Capital have been misdirection as to the real motive of this administration. How do you respond?"

Press Secretary: The Times source is a traitor. Bottom line. Nothing and I mean nothing, he says… Mr. Johnson has said, has any viable credibility. AND you are a failure to journalism to repeat his nonsense!"

"She's doing a good job knocking down the questions and the narrative," says Theodore Smith while watching the television in the residence with the President.

"Yep, she has a pair of balls on her I'll tell you. Of course, it helps that we have the truth on our side," President Mountebank calmly replies with a glib smile.

The Hoover Building, 4:55 p.m.

"Director's office," answers Kathy for the last time. She was just informed she was relieved of her job.

"Hi, Kathy, it's Captain Clayton, of the Texas Rangers again. I'm still trying to get a hold of Jim. Is he around by any chance?"

"No," Kathy's not really sure what to say and begins to tear up.

"I know you have called several times trying to reach him. But he has been relieved of duty. So …" Kathy was choking up now out loud, out of concern for her friend and boss.

"So, honestly I don't know what to tell you."

"Well hell, –that explains a lot. I couldn't reach him on his cell and today when I called the line was out of service. So, who's in charge now? I have some important Law Enforcement stuff to discuss with someone … anyone in charge," Clayton follows up.

"I don't know. This whole place is in disarray. Try calling Homeland Security," Kathy regrettably answers.

"Homeland? no –this is an FBI matter. Who's in charge at the FBI?" Clayton real curious now.

"Well Mr. Clayton, the FBI seems to have been 'defunded' and well … no one is in charge as far as I can tell. I have been told to go home immediately, not come back, and not leave the country. The entire Hoover Building has been told to go home for that matter. At this point, only the field offices remain open. I think." Kathy starting to cry now.

"So, I can't help you. And neither can the FBI in DC. Try calling the Dallas field office or Director Helle's office at Homeland. I am sorry I cannot do more."

"Oh Kathy, I am so sorry. I can hear it in your voice that you are under a lot of stress. You go on home and lick your wounds, God's got this. I'll call the field office in Dallas. May God be with you," replies Clayton with real sincere empathy.

"Thank you, Captain Clayton, if you hear of anyone looking for a good assistant, I'll be looking for a new job…I guess," replies Kathy.

"I'll keep that in mind, truly. Bye now."

"Bye, Captain."

Texas Ranger's Office, Garland, Texas

"Kinum, turn the TV on and find the national news!" hollers Clayton loudly out the door of his office.

As Clayton steps out of his office, he stops at his secretary's desk. "I have a new task for you. Every thirty minutes call the Agent-in-Charge at the Dallas FBI field office. Then thirty minutes later, call Director Helle's office at Homeland Security in Washington DC. Keep doing it until you reach one of them and then patch it

★★★

through to me anytime day or night." He walked away before he even heard her reply and stopped in front of the television.

Some of the Rangers had gathered there. They were all stunned in silence, listening to the News Anchor trying to handle the shocking story. Clayton reads the reader board headlines.

DIRECTOR OF FBI WANTED FOR TREASON... FBI HOOVER BUILDING CLOSED... FORMER FBI DIRECTOR ADMITS BEING THE GHOST PATRIOT – TERRORIST.

Then the bottom reader board cycled back around to the beginning.

"Holy shit!" exclaims Clayton.

"I want everybody in the conference room in thirty minutes! Recall everybody from the field. Have them all here in thirty minutes!"

"Kinum, come join me in my office please," Clayton calmly orders.

"Yes sir," Kinum answers without hesitation.

"Shut the door. We need to pray," Clayton says in a still, contemplative, humble voice.

★★

Chapter 24

The Stakes of a Nation

The Insurrection

The men and women anxiously standing their ground around the Virginia Capitol were abuzz with conversations about the news of Jim Johnson and the defunding of the FBI. It was news that wouldn't directly affect most Americans as much as it would the three thousand patriots around the Virginia Statehouse who were acutely aware of their precarious situation, they found themselves corralled in. Granted the nights thankfully had been relatively quiet. They had regular security patrols on a tight schedule and no real meaningful contact with the law enforcement that cordoned off the area.

Just as Tal Jordan had predicted, about half of the so-called "hostages" decided they had enough of their conditions inside the Statehouse and requested to leave much to the objections of the State Troopers. First, it was just a couple occupants here and there, then a handful at a time, until only half of the original group remained, with, of course, all the State Troopers. To the chagrin of Governor Northfork, the media only interviewed those who left the Statehouse.

Each gave a glowing report about the helpfulness of the protesters in assisting their safe departure, and how at no time were they ever held hostage. Instead, they were just following the Commander of the State Troopers' direct orders to shelter in place. Oddly, those interviews received only minimal local coverage in the media.

What the protesters didn't know was the complete chaos law enforcement was actually experiencing surrounding the perimeter. Originally, the local Richmond PD was just told to simply hold the perimeter of the area and wait patiently for the FBI to take command. But the FBI never came and with the latest news, it was highly unlikely they ever would. The Governor strongly flirted with the idea of calling up the National Guard but became concerned with the political consequences of such an aggressive move, especially with the antagonistic way the President was suggesting approaching the whole situation nationwide.

The Chief of the Richmond Police just told Northfork the naked truth. "We are outnumbered, plain and simple. Without significant resources, they can come and go as they please. The best option is to wait them out. Especially now the 'hostages' turn out **not** to have been 'hostages' held against their will."

Now there is a counterprotest beginning to build. Their presence began to test the perimeter, many of which are Antifa who seem to want to challenge the police more than they want to make an ideological stand against the protesters. The tension was slowly building on the streets and Law Enforcement was losing the initiative in protecting the city.

Kinum Family Hunting Lodge, Texas

O'Brian decided to take some time away for himself and watch a little television. Glenn Kinum recently had the satellite television restored at the lodge for the entertainment of his guests. Paul poured himself an ice-cold beer from the tap into a frosted mug. He discreetly added a couple shots of Jack Daniels and then threw back a shot for good measure.

After settling in with a big plate of nachos, he began flipping through the endless guide of 600 channels that had just been restored. It took some time to wade through the channels while munching on nachos, a job at times that took both hands. In all the flipping through the unfamiliar channels, he inadvertently stopped at the news.

"Holy SHIT!" came a loud holler from the upstairs den.

"You guys, you guys, you need to come see this!" came the directive from Paul to no one and to everyone. First to arrive was Donahue. She just came in and stood silently and stared unwavering at the report. Then, came McConnel and Daniels. They had been downstairs playing an enthusiastic game of pool.

Daniels was finally the first to make a comment. "Oh, this can't be true. It's some PSYOPS or something. I mean who would believe that the director of the FBI is an undercover agent for the…er… us? That doesn't make sense."

"It's mind-boggling," answers O'Brian. "But there he is on the news, this Jim Johnson guy, presumably the guy we're running from, now on national television saying he orchestrated not just the 'Battle of Bunkerville', as they are calling it, but all these other 'attacks' that have been taking over the news lately."

"Did he say that?" quickly replies McConnel. "That's not what I just heard and saw. What I watched was a set of precisely edited videos of this Jim Johnson guy saying a couple of things to support the narrative that the media framed for us, their viewers. He never claimed, in what we just saw... he never claimed to be the Ghost Patriot, nor did he take responsibility for anything. It was the voice-over and the headlines that told that story. I mean I don't know this guy; I don't know him from Adam, but I have an eye for propaganda, and they are trying to dissuade us from the real story here, the truth."

"Oh, there you guys are!" Leah exclaims happily as she bounds into the room. She has been in a good mood ever since she heard that Kevin was coming to Texas soon.

"What are you guys doing up here? Inside? It's such a nice day."

"We are being manipulated by *your* friends," answers Donahue, exasperated at Leah's mood swings. Kristen gets up and abruptly walks out of the room.

O'Brian takes another contemplative long swallow of his beer. *I hate this shit.*

Daniels thinks *this is the crazy stuff the CIA always tried to figure out. I prefer to be a door kicker, a knuckle dragger.*

"I need to think about this. Somehow this may be to our advantage," says McConnel thoughtfully as he heads to the door. *I just need more intel.*

Leah and Daniels remain as O'Brian begins to passively flip through the channels.

"Wait. Go back," grunts Daniels. "Red Dawn... Patrick Swayze, yeah! That's a good one from my Father's Day. F'n commies." The two settle on watching it.

Leah decides she doesn't want to watch more war and jumps to her feet, "I'm hungry," not having a clue of the slight Donahue had thrown at her earlier.

Texas Rangers Office, Garland, Texas

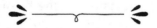

Captain Clayton begins the meeting with a sobering statement. "I think we must presume we have lost the support of the FBI in this operation."

He waits for a visual response from his team. They all silently shake their heads in agreement. "Which means we have a multistate terrorist operation on our hands and much of it may be out of our jurisdiction."

"That's why we are Texas Rangers and not just cops," replies Kinum. Let's protect the American people and worry about where it happens later."

That statement was met with vigorous agreement and low mumbling within the room.

"This is what we think we know. There are seven electrical power switching stations throughout the US. If they are taken out – destroyed - the lights, go out for most of North America. That includes Northern Mexico and almost all of Canada. We think that is their target or targets," Clayton begins his briefing with a matter-of-fact tone.

"We have all heard about EMP's attacks, –Electromagnetic Pulse threats from a foreign enemy, well, this is the cheap man's version of the same threat with more long-term impact. We're not talking about frying the circuits like an EMP, we are talking about the destruction of the physical plant. That's what we think these guys in Plano are up to. But this threat has never actually been seriously considered because it would take a pretty serious force, I mean a small army to take them all at one time, in various states... it would also be a one-way trip."

"A suicide mission, I presume," responds one of the men.

"Yeah, and that would mean someone, one of the attackers would most likely be caught, interrogated and the sponsoring government would be identified. The national response to an event like that could likely mean the total nuclear destruction of that entire country. It just didn't seem feasible. But what we have in Plano is a group of terrorists who have no allegiance to a country, just to Allah. They are economically poor recruits with nothing to live for here on earth, only their paradise in heaven."

"Plus, the money their family will get for being a martyr," says another, with a smirk.

Clayton continues, "I have spoken to the Governor, and he has given us the authorization to muster every Ranger in the state to protect the station here in Texas. But we cannot travel and protect the other six stations, even if we had the manpower. Which we don't... hell, we barely have the manpower to protect this one! He did promise to contact each Governor of the other states and give them a heads up to promptly tackle the situation and threats they are facing."

"So, we are thinking there are other cells positioned in the other states, right?" asks Kinum.

"That's what Jim Johnson and I were working on before he... disappeared... or whatever you want to call it," referring to the video of Johnson. Clayton shaking his head.

"It only makes sense. Each attack will take a team of about twenty or so operators, which is exactly what we have in Plano," answers Clayton.

"Let's just gaff one of those guys up and interrogate them, or hell, all of them," suggested another Ranger.

"That was discussed. But there is too much risk. If one gets away, or the others are warned, even one man's disappearance will give rise to an alarm throughout the other cells. That was our concern. The plan was for the FBI, in a coordinated effort with the various state agencies to act in concert. But that plan was dismantled by the 'defunding of the FBI.' We are now on our own and we have to move quickly," Clayton continues.

"So, what are our critical needs?" asks Sergeant Kinum.

"Trained Men," replies Clayton soberly. Even with every Ranger we can spare in Texas, this is a significant station to protect

★★★

and defend. Plus let's face it, we're cops, investigators, not a team of special operators who have the high-level training to do this."

"Why not get the National Guard in?" asks Kinum pressing again.

"They move too slow, and their presence will again tip off the terrorists," replies Clayton. "This threat is imminent. It will happen in the next twenty-four to forty-eight hours."

"What about the other switching stations?" asks Kinum again, realizing the wide impact this will have if they fail.

"Each State is on its own. We don't have the mechanisms in place to coordinate with them, just to provide the intel we have. The only advantage we have is that we are ahead of the game here and know what these bastards are up to. We also have a supportive governor, who has given us his full authority," replies Clayton.

"What if one or all of the other stations are taken out?" asks another Ranger.

Clayton has been concerned about this and expressed this to Jim Johnson. "The experts are not sure; it's never happened before in the history of our country. They are afraid of a total collapse of the power grid in North America."

"So, if we successfully protect the station in Texas, Texans may still lose their power anyway?" Kinum asks in a follow up.

"We don't think so. Because Texas is a lone Republic, our engineers were required by state law to make everything autonomous, meaning, we have an independent and stand-alone power system separate from the other states. All of our infrastructures are Texan, and we alone control the 'light switches,'" Clayton laughing now.

"There has always been the underlying belief that we may need to go it alone… even after we joined the Union."

"So here is our plan…" Clayton continues his serious briefing of the Rangers.

Next Day: Texas Rangers Office, Garland, Texas

The Rangers office had been working all day and through the night to determine their operational plan in stopping the attack on

★★★

the electrical grid of the United States. Over the last twenty hours, it had become clear regarding two things Lieutenant Davis concluded.

1. The Muslim Terrorists were likely to attack tonight.
2. The Rangers were undermanned to protect the Texas Station and cannot respond to any other attacks across the country.

Captain Clayton was convinced that they must be surveilled around the clock, no matter where they went, even if they traveled out of the state. With that directive, LT. Davis was in charge of the overall national operation and to get the local state troopers to marshal the resources needed to secure the other transformers. It was without question a big job, and it was moving way too slow.

The other states' trooper offices were undermanned, trying to fervently protect their statehouses from an unknown and unidentified threat that the President and their Governors had declared. Davis was finding it hard to be taken seriously in the other six states while they were busy putting up fences and assigning around-the-clock protection to their statehouse to deter an insurrection like the Commonwealth of Virginia.

Sergeant Glenn Kinum was tasked with the protection of the Texas station. He too was finding it operationally challenging as he didn't have enough manpower to adequately defend the large complex. He just didn't have the manpower, equipment, or expertise to cover multiple entry points and vulnerable areas of the station.

I really have no idea how to do this properly Kinum thought to himself as he stared at the schematics of the sprawling electrical station. So, he commandeered an expert from the Texas Public Utility Commission to come to Garland and brief him on the unseen vulnerabilities of the station. But even with a direct chartered flight from Austin, Kinum wasn't sure if the expert would get there on time.

The terrorists are setting the timeline here, we sure aren't.

After some long thought, and a short silent prayer, Sergeant Glenn Kinum made an abrupt decision that may just end his career. He grabbed his cell phone and headed directly to the exterior exit of the building.

"I am going to grab some fresh air and clear my head," Kinum told Davis as he headed for the exit.

LT. Davis barely acknowledged him or looked up while arguing on the phone with some bureaucrat in another state.

Once outside, he made two well-considered calls.

First, from memory, Kinum dialed Paul O'Brian's SAT phone as soon as he was absolutely sure he was out of immediate earshot of anyone coming or going from the building.

"Ah, hello?" comes the answer from O'Brian from the other end, completely unsure if his phone was actually ringing. It was the first call he had ever received.

"O'Brian, it's Kinum. I am going to need your help," began Kinum.

"Well sure Glenn, whatcha need?" responds Paul in a jovial and friendly way. "You've done so much for us I am happy…"

"No, it's not that kind of help," interrupts Kinum. "I need your operational expertise in the operational planning and protection of the electrical station." Glenn realizing, he had a resource just a phone call away in O'Brian.

"Okay, shoot," replies O'Brian, serious now.

"I am directly in charge of protecting a large facility, with too few men. We know that an undetermined number of assailants will be attacking it in the next twenty-four hours. Our protection force is a bunch of cops, who are dedicated, but very inexperienced and not remotely equipped for this type of operation," Glenn begins his briefing grimly.

"How fortified is your facility?" interjects O'Brian.

"Wide open, it's a civilian target... a power station," replies Kinum.

"Let them have it," replies O'Brian. "It's not worth letting some of those men get killed over infrastructure that can be rerouted… worked around, just let them take it without a shot, then surround them and take it back in due time, when you can muster the support of other troops. Put them on the defense, which is the less desirable position."

"Not possible. This station is the only switching station for all the central US. If it's shut down, there will be no power for months in much of the US, Canada, and Mexico," Kinum replies not expecting that reply from O'Brian.

I thought this guy was badass. Kinum bewildered doesn't say it aloud.

"Well, that's a horse of a different color," counters O'Brian thinking of a scene from *The Wizard of Oz*, Emma's favorite movie.

"You need a counterstrike team. Your assailants will be focused on their efforts to attack and destroy all the defenders and the facilities. They will likely be depending on surprise and will keep their rear lightly defended if at all. The beauty of a counterstrike is that the surprise will be on your initiative, it will divide their force and if stealthily executed, it may prevent their effort to take the facility."

"How many men does it take for this counterstrike team?" Kinum asks concerned thinking of the manpower he has.

"At a minimum four, six preferably with Overwatch. But you need an experienced cohesive team who have practiced together this type of counterattack. However, you don't have enough time to pull together a bunch of cops, even if they were all operators in another life in the military," counters O'Brian.

After a long pause of careful consideration, Sergeant Glenn Kinum, asks the obvious question he had called to ask, "Can the Patriots do it?"

"Who?" asks O'Brian not realizing 'the Patriots' is the moniker that is now attached to them.

"You guys, you, McConnel, Daniels, Donahue. That's four right, you're a team?" presses Kinum.

Oh, this guy walked me right into this, thinks O'Brian before responding. "It would be better if we had Linfield with us."

"There is really no time, nor have we gotten his phone to him to give him a heads up. It's just the four of you," Kinum keeps pushing.

"And Leah," O'Brian mutters almost under his breath.

"Who?" Kinum not quite hearing.

"Leah Scrivener, she has been training with us as a medic."

"Oh, Lord," Kinum replies in obvious dismay.

"I know, I know," O'Brian replies about Scrivener resolutely.

"I will have a helicopter on your front lawn at 0600. Be prepared to be on mission for three nights," sternly commands Kinum.

"I will need maps, a plan, and troop placements," presses O'Brian.

"I am sending them in an encrypted email to you now. Let me know if you have any questions."

"The whole thing is questionable," respond O'Brian as he disconnects. *–What have I gotten myself into?*

"I am sorry, what?" Not realizing the phone was dead. *Should I call him back? No, I'll let him call with his questions,* thinks Kinum.

Kinum makes his next call to Ace. "We need a HELO at the ranch at 18:00 Central time. Five passengers and gear. It needs a range of 500 miles." Kinum paused to listen to Ace's complaints about the short notice.

"Stopping for a ground refuel should be fine," he paused reflectively again, then replied again.

"Pick-up may be necessary, in twenty-four to seventy-two. I will advise," Kinum listened to more complaining.

"Ok. Thanks, I'll try to do better, thanks. I knew you'd come through. I appreciate your effort."

Then Kinum hung up the phone. *–Geez, that guy is a whiner.*

Kinum Family Hunting Ranch, 18:00 hours Central Time

I am a freaking miracle worker, declares Ace to himself as he sets down the borrowed AgustaWestland AW139 helicopter on the lawn of the ranch at precisely 18:00 hours. This was no easy task, securing a civilian helicopter with the range, speed, and load capabilities for this mission. In fact, it was very difficult and almost downright impossible.

Ace had to consider not only the odd number of passengers but their equipment, which was heavy. This was a rare aircraft to find, but with some urgent networking from the Lost Boys, they thankfully found a friend of a friend to loan the helicopter. It was hangered at Love Field in Dallas, and Ace was required to fly his jet to Dallas from California, then literally walk across the long tarmac and board the freshly fueled helicopter. He made his deadline with almost no time to spare.

While in flight from California, he received the latitude and longitude coordinates of the drop-off point from O'Brian, as he was in charge of determining the ideal insertion point to sneak in behind the attacking force of terrorists. His team would be there several hours before their targets. As soon as the retractable landing gear touched the ground, the Patriot team jogged to the HELO, burdened with bags of gear. Each was fully dressed in night camo and looked like the professional soldiers, that at least three of them were anyway.

"Hello, Ace!" O'Brian greets appreciatively, as he opens the sliding door on the helicopter. "You're right on time."

"Of Course, I am," replies Ace in his not so understated way.

"No changes on our destination tonight?"

"No. Just keep her low and fast as we discussed," replies O'Brian.

"This bird will do 190 miles per hour. I'll have you there in no time," declares Ace, as each of his passengers climbs into the swanky corporate helicopter.

"Damn, this is the fanciest HELO I have ever been in!" exclaims McConnel.

"My only one," replies Donahue. "Are they all like this?"

"Ah, NO!" laughs her boyfriend as the last one to embark.

Leah just sat in the very back seat with much of the gear, very pensive. She was deeply frightened about this mission and trying not to show it.

Plano Texas, 18:00 hours Central Time

"They are on the move!" declares the Texas Ranger duty officer in the surveillance van over the radio to headquarters in Garland, TX. A couple of twelve passenger vans had just pulled up quickly to the suburban home as the Muslim men briskly and efficiently filed out one by one through the garage into the vans. It took them all of sixty seconds to clear out of the house for the last time.

"The bird has been deployed and we will follow at a three-mile distance as planned," referring to the Matrice 210 version 2, a long-range UAV or drone, carrying a DJI Zenmuse XT2 R 640 camera on a gimble that gives infrared and high definition 4K imaging.

Fly, baby fly. The duty officer presently thinks to himself as the drone follows the vans at 400 feet above watching them merge onto

Sam Johnson Highway (US 75) headed south toward the LBJ Freeway (I-635 Dallas Loop).

"Have they given any indication if they are going to split up and head to different targets?" inquires Captain Clayton in response to the report from the surveillance van.

"No, they are moving in the same direction," came the answer.

"Okay, you may want to close up on them. If they split up, the van can follow one group, the UAV can follow the other," commands Clayton. *–This is not optimal, but we have no other choice without more Rangers.*

"10-4," responds the duty officer.

"Kinum, it's time to execute your plan and get your assets to the substation," directs Clayton over the radio.

"Roger that, I have three HELOs touching down in two minutes. Executing, 'Operation Patriot Defense,' at your command."

"Operation Patriot Defense? Who came up with that?" replies Clayton.

"I did. I figured it was perfect with all the talk of the Ghost Patriot and stuff in the news." Responds Kinum, wryly over the COMMS as the sound of choppers began to drown out his transmission.

Smartass kid.

"Execute, Execute. All teams execute!" commands Clayton.

Chapter 25

Counter Strike

Darkness
The bright red sun was beginning to disappear behind the vast horizon of the Great Plains as the corporate helicopter made its gentle landing on the hard unforgiving Texas landscape. Daniels was the first to disembark, then Donahue, each taking a bended knee on the opposing side of the chopper in the ready position while meticulously scanning the horizon, looking for any undetected threats. The other three carefully unloaded the gear while the blades of the HELO remained in motion for just ninety seconds and then began to distinctively power up as Paul slammed the door and gave it two open palm raps. The customary signal the machine was clear to take off.

Ace, glanced over his right shoulder and gave Paul a quick smile and salute as the bird began to lift off. Ten feet into the air she rotated ninety degrees and accelerated quickly, again staying very low to the ground.

One of the best chopper pilots I have ever seen, hell, the best fixed-wing pilot I have ever seen. And Paul O'Brian had flown with the very best in the world. Paul watched as if mesmerized for thirty more seconds, just long enough to see Ace disappear while remaining low and fast. *He doesn't seem to be much more than twenty-five feet off the ground,* which was part of the covert operational plan, O'Brian and Kinum had strategically worked out.

Kinum and his team were to approach from the same general direction, and he didn't want Ace to be seen on radar by his pilots. So according to plan, Ace flew the chopper as low as possible, putting at least 100 miles to "his rotor" as Ace put it, then, popped up behind a mountain and took a normal flight altitude for the sake of any other aircraft in the area.

Once the dust, noise, and commotion cleared, O'Brian went to work.

"Ok, you guys, –kit up and strap on your gear. We have a little walk to take," commands O'Brian.

"Walk? Where are we going?" asked Leah in a surprised tone.

"About ten miles that way," O'Brian pointing with an open palm north by east.

"Shit, –ten miles, why? Why didn't we just fly the extra miles and land where we're going?" Leah is frustrated now.

"You don't pay attention to anything said to you, do you?" barked Donahue. "We had a two-hour briefing, and this was all covered. We are walking in because we do not have any idea how many, nor where the placement of enemy hostiles will be. So, we're going to try to get there first and scope out the situation."

Scrivener, lashed back at Donahue in full bitch-mode that she had seething deep down in her gut for quite some time. "Fuck you, Donahue. I am as new to this as you are. Maybe I missed part of the briefing, or maybe you were so busy running your mouth I didn't hear all the plan, but I am here now, and I will walk the fucking ten miles right along with your fat droopy ass, you can be sure of that!"

Donahue started aggressively moving toward Scrivener at the same moment reaching for the KA-BAR Commando Knife on her hip. "How about I just cut your throat right here and save the fucking terrorists the trouble?"

McConnel reactively stepped in before it went too far. "Put it away and save the adrenaline for the Hajjis. Besides if you kill her here who will carry her gear?" McConnel whispered directly to Donahue with a sly smile. Donahue remained chest to chest with McConnel quietly fuming for about forty-five seconds, still very pissed off.

"Okay, but that little whore is not coming back from this operation I promise you!" she declared loud enough so Scrivener could hear.

"Yeah, well FUCK YOU and the horse you rode in on. I am ready for you anytime." Scrivener yells in a shrill.

O'Brian had had enough of the squabbling. "Shut the fuck up and gear up, we leave in two mikes."

Precisely sixty seconds later O'Brian checked his compass and set the heading from memory and began walking with Donahue on

★★

his heels, then McConnel, six feet behind, while Scrivener is awkwardly scrambling to catch up, and lastly, it's Daniels covering the rear.

Daniels took the six and promptly fell back into his years of marine recon training, constantly scanning the small ridgelines, walking backward from time to time to see if there was anyone following. He kept a good smart twenty-five feet between him and the others as a combat buffer, just in case.

O'Brian took point and pulled ahead a good fifty feet, also to have a combat buffer and in case he stepped on any IEDs. The buffer distance would possibly save the others. Both men already wished they had left the two squabbling women behind.

Scrivener and Donahue were scared, and fear makes you forget your training. When you forget your training, somebody dies, even trained professionals.

One hour and twenty minutes into their exhausting march, and that's what it was, a march, O'Brian, and McConnel were moving so fast that Donahue had to slowly jog at times just to keep up, which she clearly was not in shape for. Scrivener was a little fitter, but her small build was being worn down by the heavy gear she was carrying. She couldn't even attempt to run even if she was able.

Suddenly, O'Brian stopped and held up his left arm bent at the elbow, his hand in a fist. The sign to hold and remain quiet. The remaining four went to a knee and their weapons went up to combat ready, two pointing left, two pointing right, just as they had trained.

Then O'Brian went to his knee. They sat still in absolute silence for a full five minutes just listening and watching. Once O'Brian was unquestionably confident that they were the only ones there, he showed them four fingers and signaled they rally to him. They all moved in unison, staying low in a crouching position.

"Spread out, we rest here for fifteen minutes, eat something, and hydrate. This may be your only meal tonight. Oh, and hold the noise down, you two act like you're hiking down the trail to Yosemite Falls or something. I could hear you half a mile away," whispers O'Brian, looking at the two women with a look that says – *What's wrong with you two?*

"Before you spread out, let's have a COMMS check," O'Brian presses his transmit button on his headset.

"Check, check."

"Five by five," responds Daniels.

"Five by five," responds McConnel.

"Five by five," says Donahue into her headset.

One, two, three, four, five, six, seven, eight, nine .... long seconds later. "Yep, I hear you," replies Scrivener after scrambling to find her transmit button.

"Spread out. From here on keep your COMMS on," commands O'Brian.

Exactly fifteen minutes later, O'Brian declares one command over the communications:

"Let's move out."

Each emerges from their resting place and assembles in the same spot, except Scrivener.

Daniels was the first to notice as he was in the rear. "Scrivener, where are you?" queries Daniels over the COMMS.

"I'm coming," she replies frustrated.

"What's the hold-up?" queries Daniels again.

"I am packing my stuff. I couldn't find my Cliff Bars..." They could hear the frantic tone in her shrill voice. Thirty seconds later, she finally joined the group dragging her backpack.

"Why was your food in your pack?" whispers Daniels as she passes him to get into position.

"What?" replies Scrivener over the COMMS system. Which caused everyone to turn in unison and look at her trying to wrestle her pack on.

Daniels comes up behind her, lifts the pack, allowing her to get both arms in the straps, and then lets it drop.

"Never mind," he says in a frustrated voice. The weight of the pack hitting her shoulders almost toppled her to the ground. But Scrivener was able to reposition, stay on her feet, hoisted her weighted pack up, and fastened the waist belt, which brought balance to her and the over-heavy pack. Then, she bent down at the waist and picked up her AR-15 from the dusty dirt where she dropped it and fastened it to the sling on her chest.

"Maybe I should have let you cut her throat," McConnel says to Donahue, feigning seriousness.

"Move out!" commands O'Brian, slightly pissed, and deeply concerned about the whole scene.

As he began to hit his stride a mischievous smile came over his face once again as he reflected on his shrewd deviousness in equipping and training Scrivener on the AR-15. In her other life, she had written several derogatory and unresearched news stories for the liberal media about this particular weapon. *Now it's her constant companion and best friend, laughing under his breath. Even if she drops it in the dirt, before the night is over, she just may need it.*

Two hours later, as they climb a crest of a small berm, the exterior lights of the substation illuminate the Texas sagebrush in every direction the eye could see for a mile or so radius.

"It looks like a spaceship," Scrivener says in amazement under her breath. She wasn't too far from the truth either.

It was a sprawling facility; the size of a good two Dallas city blocks long and equally just as wide. Every inch of it was lit up with that low-density incandescent light which gave it a sunset kind of illumination.

"There she is," says O'Brian.

"It's time to check-in," O'Brian picks up his SAT phone and dials Kinum's number.

"We're here. About 1.5 klicks to your northwest. Any intel to report?" O'Brian listens for a while then responds.

"That's good. Any updates on the Hajjis ETA? Are we still at the force count of twenty?" O'Brian listens again for a few brief seconds.

"That's good —we will deploy as planned. Maybe we can discourage them right as they pull up, send them all home to Allah. And you Rangers can go home to your families."

More conversation and then O'Brian concludes the call. "Alright, I'll give you a ring when it's over."

Turning to the team, "Okay, here is what we know and can confirm. We have twenty trained military-age men arriving within the hour presumably right down there." O'Brian confirms the plan on the map showing the dirt road with entrance access just below them.

"We stick to the plan. I will nest up here in Overwatch and Scrivener will act as my spotter. McConnel and Daniels, you will set up an ambush on either side of the road and Donahue will shut the door behind them. As they cross this point, I will take out each driver, hopefully crashing each van into the far side of this curve

★ ★

where you'll be waiting. Once the vans come to a stop, light 'em up. Don't let one man get out of the van. Once you see no movement in the van, frag both vans and immediately rally up here. That will keep law enforcement forensics busy for years as they scratch their heads and try to figure out what happened. If we have any squirters, either Donahue or I will eliminate them. We'll exfil tomorrow night at the LZ, 19:00 hours. Any questions?"

"Police our brass?" asks Donahue, naively.

"Impossible in this terrain and the dark. Besides we reloaded every one of these rounds, they're absolutely untraceable. All the investigators will know is that somebody ambushed them, which is kinda obvious."

"Are we firm on the ETA?" asks McConnel.

"Affirmative. The Rangers have a flying drone with infrared over them as we speak."

"What about potential party crashers?" Daniels asks.

"They have been tracking only twenty men. As far as the intel goes that is all there will be. And the Rangers have a surveillance van following the target at one klick. They will remain on station at this intersection and keep an eye out for us. If anyone comes in behind the Plano group, we should have a heads up if they join the caravan. This is the only way in, so we'll see them and hear about it," affirms O'Brian.

"What do we do if more men arrive than what we expect?" asks Donahue concerned.

"Shoot more bullets," replies O'Brian.

"Just try not to let anyone get out of those vans and fight. There are only four of us…"

"Five," says Scrivener.

"… Five of us, and we *cannot* get into a firefight. It will not end well with a numerically superior force. All we have is 'surprise' on our side, and once we lose that initiative, retreat here and let the Rangers fight it out."

"Got it," says Donahue.

"Just stay out of the light fall of the facility and keep concealed at all times. Those Rangers will also execute an Overwatch, and I don't want any of you falling prey to friendly fire. Only Kinum knows we're out here. If there are no other questions, let's move out —and be careful!"

★ ★

McConnel, Donahue, and Daniels pick up their gear and steadily head down the hill to their ambush location. O'Brian and Scrivener worked out a secure Overwatch position in the rock outcropping that would conceal them without danger of a ricochet from a counter-sniper.

Once they settle in a prone position, O'Brian dialed in his Leupold 10x scope on his RAD M91A2 Sniper Rifle, while Scrivener used the night vision binoculars to spot the rest of the team.

"Looks like everyone is in place," reports Scrivener.

"Good. I need you to keep a strict eye on those approaching vans for anyone exiting, then call them out on the COMMS, just like we practiced. You should be the only one calling out targets," reaffirms O'Brian.

"Got it," replies Scrivener, like a little sister to her big brother, which is how she had begun to see O'Brian.

I wonder if she has let it sink in that the 'Targets' are actual human beings. He thinks to himself as he reconfirms the location of his team. *This young lady has come a long way since the day I threatened her on the bridge back in Nevada. I almost like who she is becoming, though it's clear Donahue doesn't.*

"We have company," reports Donahue concisely over the COMMS.

"Shit, Kinum was supposed to call when they turned off the highway," O'Brian says aloud.

"Okay, execute the plan," O'Brian orders.

"Two vans just passed me at a high rate of speed. They will be at the curve in five, four, three, two…." Donahue reports.

O'Brian targets the first van driver perfectly and expertly squeezes the trigger on his long gun, sending a 7.62mmx51mm reloaded round into the chest of the driver in the first van. The driver lurched back into the driver's seat instantly losing the grip of the steering wheel. The van veered straight, just as expected, and lodged nose-first into the four-foot berm along the left side of the road. The van hit hard which threw the driver first against the steering wheel and then slamming into the windshield, cracking his head open like a melon.

None of the passengers in the first van were even wearing seatbelts, so, the hard impact not only threw the driver forward but also every other passenger found themselves violently strewn about the cabin of the twelve-passenger van, injured and bleeding.

O'Brian had only two quick seconds to target the following van and kill that driver too. The second van had the same exact fate, but this time it didn't plow into the berm, but the rear quarter panel of the crashed first van. The impact was so hard and so sudden, the second van dramatically flipped up on its nose in a sort of slow-motion, then toppled over to the side, slamming hard into the dirt.

The passengers had no chance to survive what was to come next. Both vans were completely in disarray and all passengers were either wounded or dead. Not one of them could muster a defense before McConnel and Daniels opened fire with their M249 light machine guns, better known as SAWs, or Squad Automatic Weapons, as shown in the standard ambush V with overlapping fields of fire tactics manual. It took only ninety seconds of rapid and sustained fire to riddle over 600 rounds into both vehicles. Then, it was eerily quiet as both men left their hide and cautiously walked within forty yards of the vans.

"Frag out!" Hollers Daniels first.

Then came McConnel, "Frag ..." but his voice wasn't heard as the deafening sound of the detonating grenade was followed immediately by the igniting fuel tank explosion from the first van.

Neither of Donahue's "heads-up" alarms was heard as the second van exploded too.

"...two more, two more..." came the warning of Donahue over the COMMS.

"Say again!" replies O'Brian.

"...two more, two more vans." Donahue's warning was clear.

"Oh, shit!" exclaims O'Brian surprised as two more vans appear rounding the curve in the light of the burning vehicles.

The two new vans had come with such speed and surprise, O'Brian missed the first opportunity to shoot the first driver, but not the second, and a repeat of the first two vehicles was played out in front of the Patriot team, but this time the fourth van piled into the large burning mass of metal and smoke.

By now everyone was out of place and McConnel and Daniels were a good fifty yards from their SAWs and just beyond that was the third van stopped in the road with ten armed hostiles disembarking the vehicle.

"Rally on Donahue, Rally on Donahue," commands O'Brian.

And with that Daniels and McConnel sprint down the road toward Donahue's last position almost unnoticed. Two of the Hajjis spotted Daniels and took a few shots before O'Brian ended both their lives, as a more accurate round found its target.

Donahue, seeing her boyfriend and McConnel sprinting away from the ambush broke cover and signaled her position. In all the commotion, she never heard the fifth or sixth vans speeding up the road. She was instantly hit by the fifth van like a deer popping out of the bushes in front of a car on the highway, sending her body twirling into the Great Plains desert.

Both vans came to a hard stop in the middle of the road sensing the ambush that took half their team, separating McConnel and Daniels from Donahue. Both men had no choice but to retreat, hide and evade, being separated from their SAWs with only their sidearms and a couple of frag grenades, not to mention being dangerously outnumbered with twenty men to their southwest and ten men to their immediate north.

"SITREP?" inquires O'Brian.

"McConnel and I are in fighting condition and evading a superior force," replies Daniels, in a whisper.

"We are separated from our weapons and only have our sidearms," continues Daniels between breaths.

"Donahue, SITREP?" inquires O'Brian. No response over the COMMS.

"Donahue, report!" Still no response.

"Daniels, any knowledge of your girlfriend's whereabouts?" asks O'Brian, sarcastically.

"Negative."

"Can you get to her last known location?"

"Negative," answers Daniels resolutely.

"Okay, sit tight, let me see if I can get eyes on her," replies O'Brian.

"Leah, get your eyes down there and see if you can locate Donahue... Leah?" With no answer, O'Brian, glanced briefly over his right shoulder to see why Scrivener wasn't answering.

"Crap. Where the hell did you go?" O'Brian says to himself and returns to his rifle scope and begins to scan the terrain. *There you are.*

He spots Scrivener, quietly and smoothly moving through the rugged terrain in the direction of Donahue's last known position. Leah was the only one to have seen Donahue being struck by the fifth van. Without thinking or reporting in, she grabbed her medic bag, her AR-15, and headed straight for Donahue.

Of course, she didn't remember to turn her COMMS up, nor heard O'Brian's recall orders. She had just one thing on her mind. Save Donahue and not get caught.

While cursing and swearing O'Brian felt the vibration of his SAT Phone.

"Yeah," answers O'Brian.

"O'Brian, it's Kinum, the two vans just turned onto the dirt road heading to the substation complex."

"Two more vans on the way? Oh shit! —MORE Vans?!" demands O'Brian.

There is a pause as Kinum is trying to catch up. "What's the SITREP?" requests Kinum.

"We have encountered a total of six vans so far, with an estimate of sixty combatants in play. We did our best to thwart their efforts and believe we eliminated half of them. But that still leaves thirty headed your way. If two more vans are coming, you'll need to add twenty to that number," clearing his throat, O'Brian continues dismally.

"Currently, this team is combat ineffective. We have two MIA, leaving just three of us in the rear. But as soon as we rally and can come to your aid, we'll advise. For now, I can give some limited intel, this Overwatch currently remains undetected," reports O'Brian in a sort of disjointed way.

"Understood. If you need to bug out your wounded, let me know. I will give Ace a call. We'll take it from here. —Kinum, out." The phone went dead.

The Hajjis were patrolling the road on foot to secure the perimeter, while they rescued three of the twenty that were in van four from their wreckage. Those three seemed to be ambulatory and able to fight. There was still some movement in the van, but not for long as the remaining rescuers fled from the wreckage just before the Rocket Propelled Grenade (RPG) struck the fourth van and destroyed it completely in a loud blast with the wounded still inside.

Shit, –no honor among zealots, I guess. O'Brian observes as he watches the scene below. *I still don't see vans seven and eight that Kinum promised. Where are they, I wonder? Did the Rangers get that wrong too?*

Once van four was fully engulfed, the remaining men, loaded up in the three remaining vans and sped away.

"All clear, repeat, all clear. All teams meet at the rally point!" orders O'Brian.

"Rodger that," reports Daniels.

Still no response from Donahue or Scrivener.

Texas Substation, 250 miles Northwest of Dallas Metroplex

In position to defend the substation were twenty-six Texas Rangers and Sergeant Kinum. They were broken up into five teams of five to protect the seven crucial areas of the station. Leaving Kinum and one sharpshooter to give intel and eliminate the threats at a distance.

This is an impossible defense for thirty hostiles with RPGs, horrible if there are fifty. Kinum thinks to himself.

"What are the rules of engagement for me, LT?"

"If it moves –kill it," responds Kinum without a second thought as he peers through his binoculars next to Ranger Alverez who flew up from the Houston office.

"From here, I can get nearly a mile out in the light fall from the facility. I will have a hard time identifying friend or foe though. I used to do this in the Marine Corps, you know?" replies Alverez.

"I read that in your .PDF resume file, that's why I asked for you," Kinum smirks.

"If it's moving out there, consider it an enemy and kill it."

"Roger that."

"I've got three vans coming down the road straight toward us. What do you want me to do?"

"Can you stop them and put them on foot?" asks Kinum.

"I can try," replies Alvarez.

★★

With that, Alvarez pulls the bolt back on his .338 caliber FN Ballista and chambers his first round of the night. Takes direct aim on the grill of the first van, fires, and immediately chambers another round and lets another .338 bullet find its mark in the engine block of the first van. His target sputtered and lugged as the engine died and came to a stop at the right side of the dirt road.

Then, he repeated the procedure with vans two and three till all vehicles were dead or immobile. But as soon as they stopped, the doors of the vans instantly flew open and out piled combatants.

Each had an AK-47, and a reloadable shoulder-fired missile launcher, with three rocket propelled grenades, known as RPGs. They immediately began to spread out. All but those from van three. Those men seemed to be hesitant to leave the protective cover of their van.

As the first two jumped out, they had fallen prey to O'Brian's marksmanship stationed directly behind them. Then came the report from nearly one and a half miles away to Alverez.

"I think there is somebody out there shooting my targets!" exclaimed Alverez to Kinum.

"Well, whoever is out there, don't let them do all the work. Shoot some of the bastards yourself!" commanded Kinum.

Both snipers were now working their field of fire. Since O'Brian seemed to be clearing the third van, Alverez started killing the men disembarking the second van. But it wasn't enough and a couple of dozen melted into the cover of darkness and terrain. Soon both snipers grew quiet, except for a single shot echoing here and there as they scanned the darkness for the assault that was unquestionably sure to come.

"So, who is this guy shooting my targets?" asks Alverez, bewildered.

"I don't know. Maybe the FBI showed up after all," replies Kinum in an obvious lie.

Rally Point, 1.5 miles from the Substation

Daniels and McConnel emerge from the brush just as O'Brian finished packing up his gear.

★★

"We're on the move!" O'Brian declares.

"What about Donahue?" Daniels asks.

"Where's Scrivener?" McConnel asks, noticing she was not present.

"Donahue is MIA and Scrivener was last seen heading toward her last known position to render aid. We'll need to circle back for them later. Right now, we need to form a fire team and help defend that station. Every one of the Hajjis has an RPG and those Rangers have no viable defense to what is coming their way," reports O'Brian.

"What is the known force size?" McConnel asks.

"Twenty-five to thirty, but we are expecting maybe twenty more fresh fighters," replies O'Brian with a serious tone they had never before heard.

"Hell, they are just going to set out in the dark and launch rockets at the station until they destroy it. Those cops don't stand a chance," McConnel says resolutely.

"That's why we have got to get moving," O'Brian states as he promptly stands to his feet and slings his gear on.

"We'll just need to trust Scrivener to find Donahue and do her medic thing. Besides, they would just slow us down."

"The station is a good two klicks from here, how are we going to get there?" asks Daniels.

"We're going to run," smiles O'Brian.

"Shit, I was afraid you were going to say that," Daniels replies as he begins to follow O'Brian, with McConnel to his rear scrambling down from the sniper nest to the long dirt road.

From there both men spread out to collect their SAWs and extra ammunition. Having strapped them on they tried to catch up with O'Brian, who surprisingly didn't wait for them.

"What the fuck, this guy runs like an antelope," says Daniels between quick heavy breaths. McConnel didn't respond as his body was feeling the weight of his gear and fatigue from the march in and then, of course, the combat.

All three men were deeply concerned with saving the station and the unknown whereabouts of Scrivener and Donahue. A long night of dangerous fighting was still ahead. Meanwhile, their collective thoughts were united on the mission.

Scrivener had been wandering around in the dark for what seemed like hours, looking for Donahue. It hadn't been even ninety minutes before she spotted Donahue's mangled body collapsed in the brush where she had landed unconscious. Scrivener was so focused, she had lost sense of time, defensive training, her radio, and even the lack of awareness of combat that no longer was around her.

It was just a still Texas night as she frantically searched for Donahue. All she was aware of was the sound of the brush breaking under her feet crackling as she searched. Scrivener wasn't even sure why she was so intent on finding her, but she was.

Oh God, there she is. You poor thing.

"Kristen, It's Leah. I am here to get you out and take you home. Can you hear me?" Leah whispers into the expressionless face of Kristen Donahue.

Oh, man, you are really banged up.

Leah began her physical exam on her very first patient as a medic. She was bruised all over and had several broken limbs. Her right foot was twisted at the knee completely backward. Her head and face were extremely swollen. She had an obvious compound fracture of her right arm and anyone observing would have assumed internal bleeding or other additional injuries.

Kristen was still slowly breathing, but it was labored and shallow. Her pulse was only fifty. *She is dying and I don't know what to do!*

"Can you hear me? Kristen, are you in there?" *Shit, I don't know even where to start. NONE of this was in the videos I watched.*

She has no open wounds, no bullet holes, nothing. She's just unresponsive.

"I don't know what to do," Leah says almost in defeat under her breath.

What would Kevin do? She asked herself. Then she heard Kevin's strong voice plain as day. "Pray and ask God for His help."

I don't know how to pray... I have never actually prayed aloud before. I don't even really remember ever praying. I'm not even sure there is a god at all.

"Then pray that." This time Kevin's response was echoing in her head.

Oddly, Leah didn't even question the voice she was hearing. But she just knew that was the very first step. She was beyond desperate for direction, so she took it.

"God, honestly, I don't even know if you are up there. But I need some help. My friend here is hurt really bad, and I don't know how to help her. I just know I should. But I don't know how. My friend Kevin says you are the maker of all things, which I guess means people too, so you must know how to fix her. Will you please help me help Kristen? Show me what to do... er, AH... men."

Seems like a pretty silly prayer, Leah thought to herself.

Chapter 26

Darkness Falls

Richmond, Virginia –1500 miles east of the Texas Substation
"Sir, you should wake up. Something is going on out here,"
comes an anxious voice from one of the team leaders.

Tal Jordan jumped to his feet, now fully awake. In a low voice,
he asks "What's going on?"

"Well, the lights just went out. And I mean OUT. It looks like
everywhere, all over the city. But more than that, there is no more
radio, no more television, all our cell phones have no service, even
the internet is down!" reports the team leader.

"COMMS, do we have COMMS?"

"We do, –those are on battery."

Tal fumbles awkwardly to get his comms unit into his ear and
powers up to check in with the security teams.

"Security Team One, –SITREP," then Tal looks directly at the
Team Leader next to him. "Get everybody up and into their
defensive positions. I don't like this."

"All clear and quiet out here," reports Security Team One.

"Security Team Two, report," Tal says into his mic.

"Very quiet, and dark. Not a light on anywhere," reports
Security Team Two.

"Team Three, SITREP." Tal requests.

"No immediate movement in the perimeter. As far as the eye
can see everything has gone dark. I can see some cars on the
highway, lit up, some light here and there, coming from a building
or two. But otherwise, it weirdly dark."

"How far out from you does the light begin?" asks Tal growing
more concerned.

"Nowhere, I can't see any buildings, houses, parking lots, stores. Nothing. Just cars on the highway and a few cars on the streets. It's city-wide, maybe more," reports Team Three.

Team Three is in an Overwatch position which has the highest vantage of all the teams. "Remaining Teams, SITREP?"

"Team Five, all is quiet, no movement."

"Team Four, all's Quiet."

"Team Six, ditto. Dark and Quiet."

"Roger that –sit tight and report any activity. I'll get back to you," replies Tal.

"What's going on?" asks Colin as he entered the makeshift command center.

"Well, I am not sure. The power is out, which is the first move of a typical attack. But our security teams report no contact of any kind. Even odder, this power outage seems to be wider than just our local area, or downtown Richmond. It's the whole city. Even the TV and radio stations are down. So is the internet," reports Tal.

"So, I've put everyone in defensive positions while I am trying to determine exactly what's happening."

"Could it just be a city-wide power outage that has nothing to do with us?" asks Colin, trying to help in the brainstorming process.

"It could be just that, but we can't count on it," Tal answers,

"Sir, the Captain of the State Troopers wants to meet with you," interrupts another man.

"He'll need to wait," replies Tal. "I need to figure this out."

"I'll go see what he wants," says Colin.

"I think he was asking for you anyway, sir," replies the man.

"Well, there you go," says Tal to Colin. "Take a radio with you."

Colin smiles briefly and grabs a radio from the charger and heads out of the tent with his companion straight toward the Statehouse entrance. A couple of long pensive minutes later, Colin approaches the front door. As he cautiously opened the door, he was surprised to find the remaining State Troopers and all the civilians waiting in the lobby area of the great building, with all their belongings gathered, waiting patiently like they simply wanted a ride home.

As Colin crosses the threshold of the grand, oversized doors, the Captain of the Virginia State Troopers, stood and walks toward him. "We have been ordered out."

"Excuse me," replies Colin caught off guard.

"My Commander has ordered us to leave the building and return to headquarters. So, I want to see if you will allow the civilians to leave. I am only concerned with their safety at this point," details the Captain to Colin.

"You have always been free to leave. You are not a prisoner here. I only ask that you leave your long guns here and keep your sidearms holstered as you exit the complex. I just don't want any misunderstanding to arise, and someone to get hurt. Otherwise, you are free to go, you always have been," instructs Colin.

"Fine. Can we go then?" responds the Captain with a bit of an attitude.

"Sure. Let me call you an escort," continues Colin.

Colin picks up his radio: "Command, our guests have decided to leave. Can you send me an escort for them?"

There was a momentary pause, then came the reply. "Roger that, they will be there in two mikes." It was Tal's distinctive voice responding.

"Okay, gather up your stuff everybody. They will be here to escort you out in a couple of minutes."

While pointing to the polished walnut table in the foyer, Colin then says to the Captain: "Have your men leave their long guns and ammo on the table there."

The State Troopers complied and organized themselves in a protective detail to escort the remaining legislators to 'safety.' Moments later a three-man escort team arrived and met the Troopers at the door. Two of the men took the lead, the third took up the rear of the column as they began their short trek to the perimeter of the statehouse compound. As they left the building for the last time the captain had several thoughts that he kept to himself.

This is the first time I have ever been commanded to surrender. I do not like it. Only three in an escort? We could have taken them easily.

As they walked through the Statehouse Compound, he was trying to analytically determine the insurrectionists' defensive posture.

They have a strong defense parameter. No automatic weapons or explosives. They all look competent, some are fat and hillbilly like, but most look trained. This would be a hard defense to break for any police force. We need the National Guard in here. We have a long walk ahead; I hope these civilians can make it.

Colin stood at the top of the stairs and watched as the Troopers and civilians were escorted to the perimeter of the Statehouse compound and then one of the lead escorts shook the hand of the Captain of the State Troopers and warmly greeted them goodbye. Colin also noticed that there was a fourth escort he hadn't seen before. The whole event was being recorded by a videographer, including the handshake.

Oh, that was a good idea. Making sure this was recorded for posterity's sake. I bet it was Tal that thought of that.

"Security Teams, Command. The remaining State Troopers and civilians are departing the Statehouse. Please report any contact they may have. Beware that they should be getting transport out, do not interfere."

"Acknowledged." Each team replied in unison.

Colin stood and watched them for a while, and noticed they didn't remotely slow up, but just continued their deliberate escort down the city street, then turned a corner and disappeared out of sight. *Weird. You would have thought they would have had an MRAP pick them up and get them out of the area. They must be picking them up out of the immediate firing range of our defense.*

Then Colin turns and heads back to Command. Glancing at his watch. *Three twenty a.m., a few more hours before daylight.*

As Colin enters the Command Center, he overhears Tal's orders to a recon team.

"Get me a report on the situation in the Statehouse building. Check it for IEDs, provisions, armaments, and suitability for housing and command," Tal Orders.

"Command, we have some lights coming on," reports Security Team Three.

"Whereabouts? Neighborhoods, downtown, —what?" Colin asks over his radio.

"No, it's sporadic buildings. According to the map, it looks like a couple of hospitals, nearby, and the Police Headquarters. Then, some other buildings further out," replies Security Team Three.

"Ten-Four. Those would be buildings with backup generators," replies Tal. "Everything else remains dark?"

"Roger," came the swift reply.

Then Colin, queries, "Did our State Troopers get a ride?"

"Negative, they are still bugging out on foot."

"Roger that." *I guess nobody is coming to get them.*

Then Colin turns to Tal and asks, "so, what do we know?"

"The power seems to be completely out throughout the entire city, maybe further. They have gone into some strict emergency mode, like a natural disaster. The only movements we have seen are car lights heading into places like hospitals, and police headquarters. All of which seem to be within a disaster protocol."

"The power is selectively connected to the radio stations and local TV, who are on a message loop, while we have no civilian communications or cell phones. We are now regularly checking HAM frequencies and commercial air traffic. So far, not much there," replies Tal.

"Are we under attack?"

"I'm not sure, I don't think so. Our security teams have seen no significant movement, aggressive behavior, or threats from either military or law enforcement of any kind. It's almost as if they pulled back to their respective stations. Which makes me think this is a disaster posture, not an engagement with us."

"At first, the abrupt departure of our guests in the statehouse had me concerned. But the fact that nobody came to pick them up, makes me believe there were simply no resources available to pick them up. And, if you think about it, that is unprecedented. They are leaving the lawmakers on their own to make it home. Something is going on beyond us."

"But what?" asks Colin.

"That I don't know. But we will know by daybreak. If it's what I think it is, all hell will break loose beginning in a few hours."

"What do you think it is?" Colin pushing now.

"It's a disaster of some sort, a regional blackout, coming weather event, war? I don't know. But it's not about us anymore."

"If it is one of those, shouldn't we send everyone home now?"

"Probably, but we might be sending them into a trap, everyone thrown into prison for the rest of their lives, without being overrun by force. If we break up now, we could just be playing into their trap. Let's just hold tight and see what daylight brings."

"What if we are stuck here even longer than we planned? What about provisions, fuel, transportation, and electrical power? If this is a full-blown power outage, there will be a run on supplies," Colin said, thinking ahead.

Tal, pondering that thought, "You have a point there. Something we better get ahead of. If the power stays off for even a few hours into the day, there may be rioting and looting. We had best plan on bettering our supply situation while we can."

Just then the Statehouse Recon Team came in to give their report.

"Sir, The Virginia Statehouse is as pristine as the day she was built. No IEDs. And there are provisions, a commercial kitchen, a big conference room, offices we could use for barracks, a lot of resources. Plus, a BIG BRAND-NEW GENERATOR that we can use to light up the whole building and ancillary buildings and grounds."

"Perfect!" exclaims Tal.

"Here is what I need you to do. First, I want you to get a team to get that building ready for our use. The conference room should be set up like a hospital, etc. At the same time, I want you to pull together a provisions team, a big one. Use personal vehicles and go commandeer some needed resources and relocate the contents of Walmart and Home Depot down the street, over here. Think through everything we need for a year and get it here before daybreak. Once this city slowly wakes up, they will be looting anything and everything if the power stays off, and we won't be able to stop them."

"Roger that. Consider it done," replies the recon leader. With a salute, the men straight away exited the Command Center to attend to their missions.

"And what if we send everyone home?" asks Colin.

"Well then, the looters can find their loot up here after we leave. But if we don't get ahead of this situation now, the decision will be made for us, and we could starve due to the lack of provisions, and our tyrant Governor will then win." Tal answers bitterly.

"I am afraid that with the new day, comes a new life for us all."

★★★

1600 Pennsylvania Avenue, 3:50 a.m. Local Time

Knock, knock... "Ms. President, Ms. President," as the Secret Service Agent frantically burst through the door. "Ma'am, we need to get you to the PEOC."

"Don't call me Ma'am!" replies POTUS groggily. "Why are we going to the Presidential Emergency Operations Center?"

"We are under attack," replies the Agent as he grabs her under the arm and forcefully lifts her to her feet. He grabs her robe and shoves it into her free hand. As they cross through the bedroom door there was a team of agents to swiftly escort her down the hall and into the elevator and down to the PEOC, where the National Security Team was attempting to meet on very short notice.

"What the hell is going on!" asks POTUS loudly.

Director Helle of Homeland Security responded first interrupting the National Security Advisor, who should have been the one to give the briefing.

"Ma'am, we are under attack here on US soil. The power station, relay 'switching stations' on this map have been destroyed, shutting down all the electrical grids here, here, and here... showing on the map that the power is down everywhere, except the middle part of the United States."

"Was it an EMP?" she asked demandingly, looking at the General sitting to her right.

Helle interrupted again, "No, Ma'am, they were targeted by several groups of unknown assailants in a coordinated attack at each of the power stations separately."

"That's correct Ma'am. There was no EMP burst, confirms the four-Star General.

"We would know about it if there was an Electro-Magnetic Pulse. It would have taken several EMP's dropped from high altitude to take out the entire grid, and we would have not only detected the planes but taken action to remove the threat. Additionally, there has been no indication of an EMP on our sensors, anywhere," continued the General.

"Okay, it wasn't an EMP, then who was it?" Presses POTUS, looking back at Helle.

★★★

"Well, Ma'am."

"STOP RIGHT THERE!" interrupted POTUS. "When are you group of misogynists going to learn to put aside your privilege and STOP CALLING ME MA'AM?" yells POTUS.

The room sat in awkward and stunned silence. After thirty seconds, Helle began again, not wanting to lose the lead. "Understood, Ma'a... er... Ms. President."

"As you know," she didn't know. "As you know we seized the files from Director Johnson's office."

"Traitor Johnson," replied POTUS annoyed.

"Yes, Traitor Johnson," continued Helle.

"And we discovered he had been working on a suspected plan of forging terrorists that infiltrated the southern border into Texas. He was working with the Texas Rangers..."

"The what?" interrupted POTUS again.

"The Texas Rangers," replied Helle.

"What the HELL is the Texas Rangers?" asks POTUS. "I think that is their baseball team," interjected the Chief of Staff.

"So, the Traitor at the FBI, the Traitor that you all let get close to me..." pointing at every person in the room... "was working with a group of baseball players to detect foreign terrorists crossing our southern border? Where do you guys get this stuff, from comic books? I mean you just can't make this shit up," sighs, POTUS infuriated.

"But I guess you IDIOTS can!" POTUS was now yelling again.

"No, Ma'a..." began Helle again, before getting an icy stare from POTUS.

"No, Ms. President the Texas Rangers are an elite group of investigators that have been a sort of State Police in Texas since about the 1880s," *if memory serves*, "they have been tracking twenty foreign nationals in a suburb of Dallas and seem to have been in coordination with the FBI."

"You mean with Johnson?" asks POTUS without even looking up.

"Yes, with Director Johnson of the FBI," replies Helle.

"You mean Traitor Johnson?" again, interrupts POTUS.

"Yes, I mean, Traitor Johnson," Helle replies resolutely.

"I noticed by your little map up there, the only place in the whole country that has power is the middle part… the Red States?" asks the President.

"I bet that one station there on your map in Texas, is the one that powers all of those Red States, right?" she continued without pausing or waiting for a response.

"And, those elite comic book characters, those Rangers, the ones who were coordinating with the Traitor Johnson, Mr. Ghost Patriot himself, somehow, miraculously protected their station from these 'foreign attackers' but not any other state, not a single one… like over here in California."

She stood and pointed to the map. "Not **one** of these others could protect their own stations… just Texas?"

"Well, Ms. President…" Helle tried to explain.

"Or is it just a SUCCESSFUL plot by a bunch of White Supremacist red necks, that have coordinated with the Ghost Patriot himself to take this government down? Shit —people are you really that stupid, that you would think that the peace-loving Muslims, would send hundreds of terrorists into the United States, to attack us? And they did it by hiding among the freedom-loving migrants, our 'precious jewels', who we have graciously been embracing as they seek refuge from the tyranny of dictators from around the world. Even though we have been successfully attacked repeatedly by these White Supremacists in the last few months. Come on, man," dismissively argues POTUS.

Helle, seeing exactly where the wind was blowing shifted with it. "Yes, Ms. President that was the conclusion at Homeland as well."

The remainder of the room nodded in agreement. The President and Chief of Staff smiled broadly. "GREAT, we are in agreement then. So, what are our next steps to punish these bastards and get the lights on for our citizens?" demands POTUS.

Texas, 3:50 a.m. local time

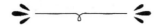

Kinum was peering intently through his infrared binoculars, spotting for targets. Alverez, lying next to him was focusing on locating visible targets in the brush and firing every few minutes. *We are in trouble now. These guys have melted into the night and it's very, very hard to see them.*

"Alverez, what is the range of an RPG?" asks Kinum.

"It's around five hundred to six hundred and fifty feet, to be accurate."

"So, it goes without saying that we need to kill these vermin before they get within seven hundred feet?" asks Kinum.

"Yep, that's what I am trying to do. But it's not easy to spot them, and I am the only Overwatch." *Except for the other guy, whoever he is.*

"How many do you think are left?" asked Kinum.

"It's hard to say, twenty to twenty-five maybe. I don't know how many got out of the vans. It'll only take seven good shots with those RPGs to destroy this station. If each guy has three rockets and they are proficient with those weapons, which I presume they are, that means with as little as a 10% target efficiency, we're screwed," replies Alverez dismally frank and matter-of-factly forthright.

Before Alverez could finish his thought, the first rocket of the night was fired from about 750 feet away. It went way high over the station exploding in the plains behind them.

"That was close," says Kinum.

"Not really," replies Alverez as he locates the shooter in his scope and squeezes off just one round to find its target.

In reply, two rockets almost simultaneously came flying directly for the sniper nest where Kinum and Alverez were hiding. The first one exploded just below them against the structure, causing it to shutter violently. The heat and burning gas, was almost unbearable as it immediately rose from the explosion.

But it was the sound, the ear-piercing shrill that shook Kinum to the core. Kinum dropped his binoculars and cupped his ears. "Damn! Are we still alive?" begged Kinum.

Alverez, unflinching, was looking to target the two men who launched the rockets. "Your first RPG round, I take it?"

"Where did the other one go?" asked Kinum as he rolled back onto his stomach. And quickly grabbed the binoculars again.

"It went high," Alverez responded as he killed one of the two who had targeted them. "They know where we are, we need to get out of this spot," recommends Alverez.

"There is no higher or more commanding position," Counters Kinum.

Alverez lifts his head from his rifle and looks right at Kinum. "It won't matter how high we are. As soon as they get a bit closer, they will blow us right into little pieces."

After the last near miss, it didn't take much convincing.

"Let move," says Kinum. Alverez began to hastily fold up his stock and grab his gear when he heard another RPG fire. He recognized that distinct **fisswhoosh** sound of an RPG launcher. It was much closer.

"Oh, shit, –hang on!" Alvarez cried.

They both hunkered down trying to be as flat and invisible as possible, waiting for their own destruction. But the explosion never came. They waited for maybe five seconds, then heard the report of a big bore long gun way off in the distance to their west.

"Move, move!" commanded Alverez.

As Kinum lifted his head and headed for the ladder leading down to the stairs, he saw the RPG rocket they both heard launched spinning widely in the night sky.

"What the hell happened?" asked Kinum as he bounded down the ladder landing firmly on the stairs.

"I think our guardian angel out there in the desert is back. He killed the bastard before the rocket had even left the launcher."

Alverez was correct in his assessment. O'Brian had positioned himself in a perfect location to flank the Power Station and had secured an unobstructed linear site on the combatants. With his superior scope and the lie of the terrain, he could see a couple dozen of them clearly as they moved forward into range to fire. As soon as he settled in and assessed the wind, humidity, and range, he started doing some real damage to the advancing combatants.

Daniels and McConnel had set up their SAWs behind the line of fighters and were set to deliver hundreds of rounds downrange on the clueless Muslim combatants who didn't know what was about to come their way. Oddly, they had not left a rear guard. So, for now, they lay hidden until the break of daylight.

Daniels looked at his watch. *Thirty-seven more minutes to sunrise.*

Another shooter popped up to fire at Kinum and Alverez's last known position, but before he was able to stand fully erect, O'Brian had killed him. Then a few seconds later came the report of the shot. This had a damping effect on the Hajjis who by now had become very reluctant to emerge from their cover. So, they sat and waited.

McConnel thinking it through whispered into his COMMS. "What are they waiting for? If the sun comes up, they'll be fucked. Everybody will be able to see them. The Rangers, us, and God Himself."

There was a pause. Then came the reply, "I have movement behind me," whispered Daniels. They all froze. Then, O'Brian swung his weapon twenty degrees.

"We got more party crashers," O'Brian says into his COMMS. "Looks like twenty men have come up on your six, smooth and quiet."

Hearing them now, McConnel asks, "Fight, evade?"

"No, I got you. Just become invisible. They do not have night vision and should move right on by you. —Radio silence."

Daniels and McConnel quietly grabbed their SAWs, tucked them up under themselves, and dissolved into the grassy brush around them. It was a tense few minutes as the group, who was spread out widely and sporadically, moved right past Daniels and McConnel.

The last two men of the group who took up the rear came upon Daniels. Something got their attention. They paused, aimed their AKs at what appeared to be a log on the ground then hesitantly kicked it.

Swoopth —came the sound of O'Brian's bullet, —straight through the chest of the first man, the 'Kicker.' His body violently lurched forward, and blood sprayed all over, blinding the second more hesitant man. The log suddenly sprang into a vertical position, and in a hard sideward thrust, lodged his USMC KA-BAR directly into the temple of the hesitant man.

Daniels then grabbed his victim and gently laid him down in the dried grass, where he had been lying. Now there were what appeared to be three logs on the ground.

Boom –In the distance, came the loud report of O'Brian's gun, which caused the remaining men to take cover. Everyone lay still for several seconds and then rose slowly to their feet and began to move, never missing the two dead men in the confusion.

"Okay, you are clear," reported O'Brian over the COMMS.

By then, all the men had moved past Daniels and McConnel a good fifty yards. The two men rolled into a prone position and leveled their SAWs at the fighters directly before them.

"Wait for my command." Daniels looked again at his now bloody watch. Sunrise was just fifteen minutes away.

Answering, after he felt his phone vibrate, "Kinum here."

"Kinum, it's O'Brian. Here is our SITREP. I am about 800 yards to your west in Overwatch. Daniel and McConnel are directly behind the enemy with two SAWs to take them out at the knees. They are going to attack just before daylight. When they do I want you and your men to fire everything you have. Your Overwatch team and mine will do as much damage as possible, then when the Hajjis turn to run, my guys will close the lid. Got it."

"Roger that," replies Kinum.

"Good. Oh, by the way, we found your Hajjis from Plano. They walked in. There are somewhere in the range of 40-45 combatants now. Tell your follow team, thanks for the heads-up... —they SUCK!" O'Brian disconnected the call.

As predicted, in the darkness, at the quietest hour of the morning, the station lit up like a Christmas tree in a coordinated attack of RPG explosions and gunfire. The attackers would first pop up five at a time and launch their rockets.

Alverez and O'Brian would eliminate two sometimes three before they would cover up again. Continuously the other combatants, the group from Plano, were keeping the Rangers' heads down. On that group, O'Brian did the most damage, as they would move around a lot and when they did, O'Brian had the best vantage point to one by one send each to his maker.

This firefight was one of the most sustained and intense firefights in O'Brian's long career, lasting well over thirty minutes as O'Brian, Alverez and the Rangers worked hard to protect the

Station. While the tempo of the firefight slowed, due to the sheer numbers of combatants being systematically reduced, their ferocity didn't. The terrorists knew that as soon as the sun got rising, they would be easy targets for the Overwatch teams. They also seemed to strategically switch up their tactics as the Plano team focused on Alverez and Kinum, and the RPG teams targeted the facility itself. And this was having a devastating effect.

Then it happened, as the station went completely dark, so did the plains around them. The darkness gave the advantage to the attackers as full darkness fell across the surrounding area, making them no longer visible to the Rangers. The RPG fire now came fast and heavy. Kinum noticed that two of the critical areas of the station were now burning and the attack seemed to be refocused on the other five crucial areas.

Meanwhile, the attackers had systematically moved up for better targeting. *It's only a matter of time now before we lose the station and our lives,* thought Kinum.

O'Brian was feeling the sheer exhaustion of the firefight from the strenuous long physical day, and the lack of sleep. The number of rounds he was able to put down range had now been cut by nearly a third, and his accuracy showed it. They were losing the battle and defending the station had become futile.

The explosions, the sun beginning to grey the sky and the COMMS chatter all drew Paul O'Brian back into his nightmare. Every target started looking like that woman in the Burka from Iraq, so many years ago and why was Emma walking next to her? This time he was so deeply lost in his dream, that he couldn't hear the calls from Daniels.

"Overwatch, we are ineffective here. The Hajjis have moved so close to the station that we are out of range. Is it clear for us to move up?" asks Daniels.

No response.

"O'Brian? Respond!" Daniels asks again.

Still no response.

"I think he may be injured or worse," says McConnel. "I haven't heard a firing report from that area of the desert for some time now. No matter. We need to move up and get in a better position before the sun lights up everything."

"Yeah, let's end this thing," Daniels says, in a way that only Daniels could say it.

O'Brian never heard the request of Daniels. He never heard anything, including Abdula, the leader of the Plano team, and his comrade who had silently crept across the Texas landscape in a wide arch to eliminate the lone sniper who was keeping them from their objective. They had been working their way through the night, through the familiar terrain of Texas, which they found similar to their desert home.

O'Brian never remotely saw what was about to happen, as he got caught up, lost in his nightmarish vision, bordering on delirium, he ended up lying prone, slumped down with his head turned away from the scope of his weapon resting on its stock, tears flowing, streaming down his face as he sobbed, muttering… "Emma, Emma, Nooo."

Abdula and his comrade had moved quietly up in a flanking position to O'Brian and then raised their AK-47s to their shoulder and without a sound took aim. Like a lamb before his shearers, O'Brian never moved. He just wept.

Far off in the Texas Plain, McConnel and Daniels froze in shock and stared to their west. They could see the muzzle flash and the repeated reports of semiautomatic gunfire in the darkness of the night.

There was a pause, a moment of what that meant, and then a terrible resolve.

"FUCK!" is all Daniels had to say.

Then came the clarity of McConnel. "Let's just end these bastards. Right here and right now!" He declared with finality.

The two men slowly and quietly crawled forward 150 more yards and covertly placed their weapons down. McConnel found a small outcropping of rocks while Daniels used a small dirt bump on the desert floor. It was just enough to give them a clear line of fire across the landscape.

And it was just in time too, as the sun eliminated the night sky, enabling them to see every Hajji lying against the long berm of the desert terrain, as all of their attention was focused in the opposite direction toward the electrical station and the firefight in which they were actively engaged.

Daniels and McConnel finished the last details of set-up and conferred briefly over COMMS.

"Let's work from the middle out," states McConnel.

"Agreed, I want us to kill as many of these fuckers as we can… that means either 'til my last breath or theirs."

"Agreed," replied McConnel … "To the death."

"Three. Two. One. –FIRE!" commands Daniels. The two squad automatic weapons made a horrifying report as they sent hundreds of rounds into the cluster of Hajji fighters in the center.

Literally, bodies were being dismembered as they both fired directly on the same point from different angles, then quickly and deliberately moved the barrel, one to the right and the other to the left. Within sixty seconds of sustained fire, it appeared nearly forty men had been slaughtered, and left strewn about in every direction.

"What the hell was that?" begs Alverez. He was completely surprised, –as much as the combatants were at the roar of fire that came upon them.

"I don't know, but let's help them," replies Kinum. "Target the right –their right and left flanks, –they are still out there."

Then Kinum barked the same orders over the Rangers COMMS. "Do not fire on the automatic weapons, protect their flanks… there are friendlies out there!"

Daniels and McConnel had been so focused on their targets they didn't see the counter engagement that was forming from the Plano team scattered about. Fortunately, Kinum and the other Rangers did and put an immediate end to their lives, just in time.

Then it all went quiet.

"I think they're all dead," says one of the Rangers over the COMMS.

"Stay in position until ordered otherwise," replies Kinum. Each Ranger held their position for a good ten minutes until the sun was fully in the sky.

"Any movement?" asks Kinum over the Ranger COMMS.

"Negative," each of the nine Rangers who were not dead or wounded in the battle replied.

"Alverez?" Kinum asks of the man next to him.

"Just those two to the west of us," replied Alverez.

Pointing with his left hand, Alvarez asks "Where?"

Kinum located the two men about six hundred yards walking away slowly but deliberately carrying their SAWs. Daniels swiveled on his heels to check their six as they walked. McConnel and Daniels were walking toward their fallen friend. Kinum immediately recognized them.

"I don't see anybody," replied Kinum mischievously, as he stood to his feet, with a grin.

"Roger that," replied Alverez.

It was never spoken of again between the two of them, and they were never mentioned in a single report to the brass either.

"Stand down Rangers. I think this thing is over."

Minutes later Captain Clayton and four more helicopters of Rangers were touching down at the desert station. One chopper was an air ambulance for the critically wounded. They also brought along the engineer to assess the station's damage.

"Glad to see you're still vertical," says Clayton, as he hugs his protégé.

"It was a long hard night. Many of us didn't make it. Some are wounded," replied Kinum.

"Your face is all blistered," Clayton notices.

"Medic!" he hollers and looks to see where the medics are.

"No sir, I am fine. Take care of the others first. They are much worse."

"Were we successful?" asked Kinum, already knowing the answer.

"The lights of Texas went out at 5:48 a.m. this morning. Sorry, son," said Clayton, looking disappointedly at his feet.

"Shit," is all Kinum could say.

Clayton smiles. *I have never heard him cuss.*

★★★

Chapter 27

Saying Goodbye and Hello

Richmond, Virginia – 10:00 a.m. Local Time

The Virginia Protestors had put their top IT guy, Chang, an Asian American, in charge of all communications, making him their Communications Chief. To that end, Chang brought a small handheld AM radio into the Command Center. "Sir, you should hear this. The President is about to address the Nation over the Emergency Broadcast System." Absolute quiet fell over the Command Center as the radio was placed in the middle of the table.

"Any update on commercial flights?" asked Tal of Chang.

"Just moments ago, the FAA ordered all commercial flights to cease take offs."

"So, everybody was diverted to nearby airports? Like during '9/11'?" asked Colin

"No, more like grounded. Once planes reach their destination, all flights are canceled. All airports seem to be bringing their birds home for good," replied Communication Chief Chang.

"Stand by for the President of the United States of America," was heard over the loud voice-over.

"My fellow Americans, only a few times in history has our country come under direct attack. The last time in our history it was the aggression of the Southern States, who desired to keep human beings as chattel which led to the Civil War as we patriots from the northern states rose to defeat them and their evil ways. And today the ancestors of these bigots, those same White Supremacists have attacked the sovereignty of this great country again.

Last night all across this country, her very own citizens have taken up arms in an overwhelming attack against our power

grid, destroying the main power stations that give you light and heat. The power that pumps your gas and provides food to each home in each state. It's a devasting blow to every American.

Therefore, we have defunded the FBI and tried to thwart their attack. It became apparent that the Traitor Jim Johnson, the 'Ghost Patriot' as he calls himself is the leader of these White Supremacists, these murderers. The poison was so deep we had to close the FBI to get to the bottom of the corruption. But it was too little too late and their evil plot was enacted against each of you. Make no mistake, they hate our way of life, they hate you and want to see this tolerant loving nation come to its end.

But you can have hope. Hope knowing that our military is protecting our borders and the interests of this great country from any foreign nation taking advantage of our vulnerable situation. The department of Homeland Security, along with the Department of Energy is working around the clock with our state and local partners to reestablish the power grid. To get the power back to your homes and businesses.

But until that happens, I have ordered all, but the most essential services closed. The airports are closed, the banks are closed, and I am declaring Martial Law across the country. Until further notice, all citizens will be required to be in their homes from 7:00 p.m. until 8:00 a.m. every day.

Your movement will be restricted to within three miles of your home, until further notice. I am federalizing all National Guard units to take over the security and relief efforts in every major city. The state and local police in your hometown will be sent home to attend to their families until we can bring safety to our streets and can determine exactly who is involved in this terrorist plot.

Make no mistake this was a systemic domestic terror plot, and the federal government will not rest until every one of these..." The President paused and choked up for effect. "These evildoers are punished.

But most importantly, I am asking the good citizens of this great country to cooperate with these orders. They are in place for your own good and the safety of your family. With your cooperation, this emergency will end soon, and we will be able to return to our normal everyday lives in a matter of weeks.

For now, while under this Martial Law, the press will be suspended. But I promise to address the nation every day at this hour over the National Emergency Broadcast System to keep you informed and feel comforted knowing that I am in charge and will never let anything happen to you.

Thank You for listening. And may God bless America. May her face shine once again upon our great nation."

The Command Center sat in stunned dumbfounded silence. "I think our illustrious President just took over as dictator," Tal stated, as a matter of fact.

"I am afraid you're right. In the very first volley, she dismantled all the law enforcement, suspended the free press, and took control over all the citizens," Colin replied.

"What's next, suspending the other two branches of government and the Judiciary?

"Well, what are we going to do now?"

"I'm not going to let her have it," said Tal.

"Have what?" asked Colin.

"Virginia," Tal replied with ferocity.

1500 miles west in Texas –at the same hour as the President's broadcast

Daniels and McConnel had made their way intently through the plains to where they approximated Paul O'Brian had fallen. They were determined to find his body and place it in a body bag. Then with what strength they had left, hike him out to the extract.

"What are we going to do about the two women?" asked Daniels bringing his concern back to his girlfriend.

"Oh, we have all day to look for them. Somehow knowing that senseless Scrivener chick, she probably survived all of this," McConnel states wryly.

"HEY, ARE YOU TALKING ABOUT ME BEHIND MY BACK?" Leah's head popped up with a grin, from behind the little knoll where O'Brian had been shooting from.

"What the hell?" Daniels turning towards the voice in utter amazement.

"See I told you," McConnel says as he strained his legs awkwardly to climb to her position. As they breached the small summit, there was Leah and O'Brian, just sitting up sipping some Gatorade and munching on a protein bar.

"I thought you were dead!" exclaimed Daniels in complete shock. The first one to lay eyes on them both.

McConnel right behind Daniels laughs out loud, ironically, "I didn't expect, —well, **both** of you to be alive."

"Oh no, we're fine. Just relaxing here waiting for the two of you," says Leah, kind of gleefully and almost smirking.

"Why didn't you answer over the COMMS?" asked McConnel.

"Mine was sort of shot up," replied O'Brian.

"I lost mine... somewhere out there." As Leah points whimsically out into the desert appearing slightly confused.

"Shot up?" asks McConnel for the first time noticing the IV in O'Brian's arm.

"Are you hurt?"

"No. No. Thanks to Leah," replies O'Brian with a bit of relief and a dash of pride.

"I got to hear this," says McConnel as he plops down to rest and rehydrate.

"Wait, what about Kristen? Where is she?" Daniels asks, still getting over the shock of finding them.

"Resting comfortably back in the same area where she was stationed," replies Leah.

"Okay, tell it," McConnel sensing a back story.

"Well, I was here working, to eliminate the Hajjis..." started O'Brian hoping to cover for himself.

"No that's not totally true, not when I found you." Corrected Leah.

"Okay, you tell it."

Leah took a deep breath and began happily telling her story.

"Well, once I found and treated Kristen, I got her stable and realized you guys must have gone off without us. I gathered my stuff and started walking down the road. In time, I figured out where Paul must be positioned, because I could hear his weapon firing. So, I just headed that direction." She took another deep breath wearing a puzzled look remembering the different events from the previous night.

"Then I heard a noise off to my left and realized some bad guys were coming, so I hid until they passed. They were being real sneaky in heading towards Paul. So, I followed 'em."

Leah paused and took a long drink, making sure she had everyone's attention for the 'good part.' After all, she was a journalist, and a good one.

"I watched them crawl over to the area where Paul was shooting from and waited. All was quiet, so I figured Paul must have known they were there. But just in case, I held my AR-15 in a ready-to-fire-position like LT taught me."

"Then suddenly, these mopheads popped up to their feet and aimed their AK's! So, without any thinking I took them out… shot them dead before they could even react, just like LT made me practice every day in the shooting range back at the hunting lodge," picking up her AR-15 and holding it triumphantly, she continued, "He taught me well, you know – how to 'eliminate the threat' as you guys always say."

"Wait, what? You shot the Hajjis?" clarifies McConnel. "Where are they?" Almost as if he didn't believe her. He noticed O'Brian shaking his head in the affirmative.

"No way, where are the bodies?"

"Right here," says Daniels, as he took a couple of steps into the brush, bending down to pick up both AKs and move them out of reach of the dead men. Something Leah would not have thought to do.

"Holy shit!" exclaims McConnel. "You broke your cherry by saving our leader's life! And, with an AR-15 nonetheless! That is hilarious."

Leah didn't find the irony all that funny, but still reveled in the moment.

Satisfied with the story, Daniels asks, "What about Kristen?".

"She was hit by one of the speeding vans. She's banged up pretty bad but stable. We really shouldn't try to move her though," replied Leah.

"And Paul, was he hit?" continued Daniels.

O'Brian interrupted, "I'm fine," hoping to end the conversation before his mental state was revealed.

"No, –he wasn't fine. He wasn't fighting back because he had passed out. His COMMS took a round because those bad guys had him targeted. I just interrupted, by killing them." Leah grinning.

"Passed out?" asked McConnel.

"Yeah, I think he was dehydrated. That's why I gave him the IV."

She covered for me. Looking at Leah. Leah just glanced and smiled back.

"Wow, what a story! Now, what are we going to do to bug out of here?" asked McConnel.

And as if on cue, in the distance, they could hear the steady *'thump, thump'* of Ace's HELO coming low and fast right towards them.

"I called for a ride," Paul said flatly as he jerked the needle from his arm, "let's go get our sister, Kristen, and load her up,"

Ace landed just out of sight of the power station, which caused the four to make a good jog to the LZ, but they somehow found the energy. They were going home after all.

Paul was first to climb in. "Ace, we have one more to pick up."

"Roger that. I brought an EMT friend. I couldn't get a doctor on such short notice. Things in town are in kind of a mess," responded Ace.

The EMT greeted Paul and immediately began to check out his vitals. Then peered down, reached in his bag and stuck another IV in Paul's arm.

"You're dehydrated," is all he said.

After a quick hop to Donahue's location, all four jumped out of the chopper and carefully lifted Kristen onto a gurney. Only Paul was ordered to stay in the HELO by the EMT. Minutes later they were in the air again, flying low and fast under the radar.

Daniels gave the EMT and Leah some time to examine her, after which they inserted a fresh IV as Leah got her to slowly sip some water.

"How is she doc?" asked Daniels of the EMT.

"She is pretty banged up. It's actually a miracle she is still alive. Somebody up there has plans for her," replied the EMT.

Leah just smiled to herself.

"Straight to Methodist," says the EMT to Ace.

"Roger that," replies Ace. *I hope I'll have the fuel for it.*

★★

Two Months Later

Ace once again is putting down on the front lawn of the Kinum Hunting Lodge in the same helicopter.

"Ready to go on holiday?" Ace asks Paul as he climbs in.

"Holiday?" asks O'Brian.

"Sure! Compared to the last time I picked you up, this has got to be a holiday," answers Ace in his jovial way.

"Oh, yeah. Right. It's a holiday of sorts," answers O'Brian.

The whole team, even Donahue on crutches would not miss this trip. They were headed back to Battle Mountain to see their friend Kevin and pay their utmost respects to Momma and Pop. The rumor is that every single Lost Boy is headed to the top-secret funeral on the Timmons Ranch.

This will be something to see. Thought Paul as they lifted off for the shorter flight to Addison Texas Airport. Ace was forced to use the smaller local airport, due to the grounded Southwest Airlines Fleet at Love Field.

It took only twenty minutes to touch down and change aircrafts. Leah was quick to disembark and noticed Ace's jet. The very first flight they flew on when coming to Texas was on this jet.

She was anxious to see Kevin and hold him again. Of course, Kristen was moving very slowly, with Daniels protective attentiveness to her every move. He wanted her to stay and recuperate in Texas. But she wasn't having any of it. *She's a tough old bird and stubborn.* Daniels thought as he gently helped her up the stairs into the Cessna Citation jet with its plush leather seats and interior layout.

"Are we it?" asked Daniels of Ace as he cleared the entrance.

"No. We have another load coming," replied Ace as he did his preflight.

Soon, up pulled Glenn Kinum and four other men. One, Paul recognized as the EMT from the helicopter. He took the copilots seat next to Ace.

Glenn was the last to enter. He found a comfy seat next to Leah.

"We're all here," stated Glenn to Ace up in front.

★★

"Let's head home," Ace said sadly.

"Hi, I am Kristin," greets Donahue to one of the new men who boarded the plane.

"No introductions, PLEASE!" responded Glenn Kinum loud enough for all to hear.

"Oh, that's right," replied Donahue. "Sorry." The new man just waved to Kristin.

"Why can't we meet the new people again?" asked Leah looking to her neighbor Glenn.

"Momma and Pop took in so many men over the years we actually, well, no one person knows all of them. Each of us knows at least one, or two of the Lost Boys. It's like a chain. What we don't want is to create a leak but rather, to keep the anonymity of the group secure as a whole. That way if one of us gets caught, the whole group will not be compromised," answers Kinum.

"Oh, that makes sense," answers Leah, not really understanding.

As the plane became airborne, Leah gazed out over Dallas. "Hey, the power is on. Everything is so... normal!" exclaimed Leah with eyes in the sky glancing over the city like her first time on a plane.

"Oh, you hadn't heard. We were able to put our station back together in a matter of days. All the power has returned to normal in the middle of the country. In the end, what you did ... really made a difference ... a big difference to millions of families."

"But how was it repaired so quickly?" asked Donahue.

"It turns out we were able to protect most of the station. Even though she took a hard hit, she was recoverable and with around-the-clock effort, they were able to repair her," continued Kinum.

"Shit, –I know that feeling" smirked Kristen looking at her leg.

"The other stations in the country didn't fare so well. The power still remains out everywhere else in the country and much of Canada."

"So, how long until they get it fixed?" asked Leah.

"Months," Kinum responded flatly.

"The other stations were flattened, and the lack of power, logistics, and this God-forsaken Martial Law Order has everything at a standstill. People are not allowed to work together; the bureaucrats seem to be running everything. It's all B.S."

All three just sat and thought about the implications of the state of the nation for the remainder of the flight.

Timmons Ranch 11:00 a.m. the next day

The Pastor humbly took to the small stage in the barn at the Timmons Ranch as he began the memorial service. The service itself wasn't all that remarkable- it was simple. It was the attendance that was so noteworthy and distinguished as it was filled with brilliantly accomplished Americans in every walk of life.

There were well over one hundred and fifty people attending, by Glenn's estimation. Every one of the Lost Boys and their families had made it but one, fifty-two in total. The one man, the one he was most eager to talk to, Jim Johnson, was missing. He didn't make it, and no one had heard from him. His absence was conspicuous, and he was missed by everyone.

What was even more remarkable than the attendance was the testimonies of the men as each stood and told their own private personal stories. Stories of growing up on the ranch, how Momma, Pop, and Jesus saved them, and the funny stories between "brothers" about the many sorted pranks they pulled. Even stories from the children – the "Grandbabies" as Momma liked to call them, as they stood and shared their feelings of how they'll miss Grandma and Gramps.

It lasted for hours. Leah wanted it to go on. But finally, Kevin stood, and leaving Leah's side for just a few moments, he addressed the crowd with his hat in hand.

"I want to thank all of you for coming, but the BBQ is going to be too well done if we don't get to it. May I suggest we move outside and 'get to eating' as Momma would always say. Also, please remember to pay your respects at the graves out under the Cottonwood trees… Oh hell, you know where they are." Kevin almost made it through without getting choked up.

Then Mark Fenton saved Kevin from a fate worse than falling off a colt.

"Excuse me, pardon me all," as he stood up abruptly.

"Lost Boys and The Patriot Team, please circle back here when you've had your fill of all that good Timmons beef. We want to all visit together for a bit, just us, please. This may be the last time, the only time to do so. And remember—no names and no introductions please."

On the hill just above the Ranch, in almost the exact spot where the Homeland Overwatch lost his life, lay two ex-FBI agents laying quietly in the Nevada sun taking pictures and writing notes.

"I knew it!" says Hernandez, the lead investigating agent. "That's the Governor of Florida. And that one is a Congressman."

"Oh, shit that is Sheriff Gillette from Las Vegas!" contributes Titus, the female agent.

"I knew this was going to be a treasure trove. Just hold the shutter button down and get every face," says Titus, as she takes detailed notes.

"How, do these people all know these Ranchers way up here, what are the odds?" rhetorically asks Hernandez to no one.

"Oh, get those three, the three men there. She points at O'Brian, McConnel, and Daniels. They look like military!" Titus says excitedly while looking at Hernandez.

They look like operators if I ever saw one. "Which one of you were riding the Harley back in April?" says Hernandez under his breath.

"I'm sorry, what? –I wasn't listening," replies agent Titus.

"Never mind. Just get good notes."

The Timmons Barn

Each of the Lost Boys slowly filed in, except for O'Brian, McConnel, and Daniels and the two women, Donahue, and Scrivener, who were already there. Some were still eating pensively, and others came with a beverage in their hand. Each of the Patriot team was sitting up front and together next to Kevin.

Congressman Fenton stood and addressed the group first as the barn doors shut. Outside the women began to clean up as the children organized a game of hide-and-seek together. A favorite of Pop's.

"Gentlemen… and ladies," addressing Scrivener and Donahue, "I wanted to give you a quick update on the state of the States, or, what we used to call the United States of America. As you know, most of the country remains in darkness and is under Martial Law. Mountebank, who I refuse to call President, has the country in a stranglehold and under the heavy weight of the various department heads of his Cabinet. He has shut all the communication systems down and is working hard to stop the various HAM operators from communicating. And yes, you heard me correctly when I said 'HE' –I refuse to play the pronoun game with him."

The Barn fell deafly silent, the only sounds Fenton could hear were the children giggling outside as each of his audience pondered that idea.

Fenton continues, "And the commercial airlines are grounded, but not civilian or Military Aviation. The good news is that most of the Nationalized Federal Troops are localized in the cities, and specifically along the coasts."

"Where their donors are!" shouted one of the men in the crowd loudly.

"That leaves most of God's country free to govern and police as they see fit. In most cases, the local Sheriffs have taken the lead in recruiting ex-police, ex-military, and many from local militias to bring order and relief to their communities. Thanks to the brilliant law enforcement measures of the Texas Rangers and several of our Lost Boy Brothers in cooperation with the valiant heroics of the Patriot Team here, the Power Switching Station in Texas was **the only** station saved and now restoring power to the middle of the country."

"Well done, Rangers, Lost Boys and Patriots!" came shouts from around the room.

"But what about the conditions in those cities whose power wasn't restored on the Eastern and Western Seaboard?" asked another man.

"It's bad, –really, really bad. There is widespread hunger, soon-to-be starving conditions. No septic, trash is taking over the streets. It's the end of the world stuff."

"The looting and riots lasted for the ninety-six hours as the models showed. Only, then did the Troops move in and restore order. It was like they waited until after the rape, death, and damage of the riots occurred. It's like that in nearly every city. They allowed complete anarchy rampage to run wild in the cities until all their steam ran out. Then and only then, the troops moved in and cleaned up."

"They began to shoot any looter and curfew breaker. Anyone outside three miles from their home, no matter what the reason is shot on the street. If you are out after 7:00 p.m. and before 8:00 a.m., you are shot where you stand. Hell, they are not even picking up the bodies. They are claiming it's a deterrent to the others."

"What about, the Congress and Senate, the Judiciary?" asked another.

"Mountebank has the entire city of DC in lockdown, No one, even on official business can get to their office. Plus, he is making it clear that if you violate the curfew orders, even the other members of government, their staff, will be shot. We believe he will attempt to suspend the Constitution in a matter of days. Then will suspend all other branches in government."

"Just like Hitler did in 1933," said one of the older men there.

Fenton nodded to his elder. Then continued, "Mountebanks end goal is to bring a not-so-new kind of Marxism. They call it Social Democracy."

One of the older men interrupted, "Is there anyone resisting? Is there anyone fighting back?"

"Yes, yes there is," Fenton replied.

"The group of Patriots that took the Virginia Capital, remember them? Well, they stood their ground and brought order to their city. They actually teamed up with the Richmond Police Department – what was left of it – and stopped the looting and rioting. Then they organized the city into wards and got all of them working together."

"What about the troops?" came another.

"They didn't want to have anything to do with any of those three thousand and growing armed red necks, so they stayed out of that city."

"Any others? Any other city's out of her grip?" squeaked Leah among all those big confident male voices.

"There are many. Many who stopped the Troops from entering their town, most of those are in the center of the country, where the lights are on. Heck, those areas are actually organizing relief efforts with food and water into the more populated areas, the starving areas. That's where all the food is grown, and they are trying to get some to the hungry."

Leah whispered into Kevin's ear, "That's amazing. After all the spiteful hate the coastal elites spew at the 'country bumpkins' in the Red States, they want to forgive them and help keep them from starving. If the shoe was on the other foot. I promise you they would let all of them die."

"Any other local militia or community protection groups?" asked Leah, as her reporter instincts started coming to life.

Fenton grins at Leah. *She doesn't realize how rude she can be, does she?*

"Yes, ironically, I heard a story that in South Central Los Angeles, the Southsiders, a notorious street gang has filled the Vacuum of LAPD pulling out and being dismantled. Apparently, they have things running smoothly in that area, their hood. I guess they are extremely protective and territorial."

"That gives me an idea," says McConnel to himself thoughtfully. *Tribal Leaders. Just like in Afghanistan.*

"So, what are we going to do to take our country back?" asked Kevin, getting angry, and feeling very helpless.

"Well, Kevin that is what we are going to spend the remainder of the night discussing. But first I want to take a brief break. I need to see a man about a horse." *One of Pop's old sayings.* Laughed Mark to himself and recognizing that many others got the reference.

"Kevin, can we talk to you a moment?" asked Fenton casually as a couple of the other men joined them while the group took a pause, stretched their legs, and talked amongst themselves. "Kevin, this is the Lost Boys Lawyer, and he has some papers for you to sign."

The Lawyer began to address the news that Kevin wasn't sure he wanted to hear. "Kevin, we all met and made some decisions that would directly affect you…"

"I know you want me off the ranch. Are you going to sell it or something?" responded Kevin resolutely.

The Lawyer paused and looked at Kevin, then over to Fenton.

"No, we are giving you the ranch, lock stock, and barrel. That's cattle, operating capital, equipment, land, and buildings. All of it."

Kevin looked up and just blankly stared at the three men standing there. The third one he realized was the Pastor who led the service. Then the Pastor broke the silence.

"There is only one stipulation…"

"Stipulation?" asked Kevin still in a shocked daze.

"Condition," continued the Pastor. "You must continue the ministry that Momma and Pop blessed so many others with."

"You want me to take more boys in and help them? Is that the condition? Well of course I will, I want to do that, yes, yes, yes. I want others to be loved like I was, how you have all been. Loved in Jesus' name. Yes, I want this kind of legacy! Just like Momma and Pop!" Kevin is beyond excited now.

Leah came trotting over, smiling, "What's all the happy about?"

Kevin sat down and began to explain what the papers were they just gave him. "They even gave me a SAT Phone." Leah was most happy about the phone.

Across the room, Paul O'Brian had walked up behind Lost Boy, Sheriff Gillette from Las Vegas Nevada. Paul tapped him on the shoulder.

"Sir, may I ask you something?" Paul began. *I cannot believe I have been running and hiding from this man all these months and now here he is standing in front of me, and I am going to ask him for a favor.*

"Sure, young man. What can I do you for?" asked Gillette with a broad smile.

"My ex-wife and my little daughter live in Vegas. Can you get someone to check on them for me?"

"Sure son. What is their address?" the Sheriff responded.

Paul wrote down the address and handed it to Gillette. "Here you go."

Gillette looked at what was written. "Oh, this is a bad neighborhood. Young man, it's even worse now since the riots. We need to get them out of there right away," the Sheriff says firmly with obvious concern.

"But how?" asked Paul.

"I'll take care of it. You're riding with Ace, right?

"Yes, we are headed back tomorrow."

"Good, I'll have Ace swing by Las Vegas and pick her up. They'll be sitting right next to you on the plane to wherever you're going. I'll take care of everything."

"Are you sure? My ex can be really stubborn, maybe she won't go."

Laughing, Gillette said, "I'll send my chief negotiator," patting Paul on the shoulder, Gillette continued, "My guys will talk her into it, I promise."

"Sir, I have just one more question," asked O'Brian

"Sure son, what is it?"

"Did you ever figure out how that thing got started in Bunkerville? I mean who fired the first shot?" asked Paul O'Brian with earnest.

"Nobody," says the Sheriff.

"Nobody? How can that be? Someone must have pulled the trigger to start all of this," presses Paul O'Brian.

"Weirdly, it was a backfire from the highway. That's what set this all off, **it's what led us here today, a simple backfire**." Sheriff Gillette said wryly, as he turned to walk away.

"Wait. What kind of Backfire? A car, a truck?" hating what the answer may be.

"I am pretty sure it was a Harley," and Gillette walked away into the crowd.

Oh, no. I did this. I started all this.

Paul's knees went weak.

★★★

A Question from the Author

Our World and Nation is facing hard times now. All the incidents in Ghost Patriot are torn from the headlines of actual events. The characters of course are fictional, and the scenarios are only one storyline synopsis of how these events could play out. But I wonder did you figure who was the Ghost Patriot?

Was it …?

- Paul O'Brian, who when confronting Leah said he would be like a Ghost, to exact revenge and protect their secret?
- Jim Johnson, who assumed the role of Ghost Patriot to distract from the others under investigation?
- Momma and Pop Timmons, who put into place by providential design a leadership cell of Patriots - the Lost Boys?
- Ranger Glenn Kinum, who recognized the threat of foreign terrorists and acted?
- Congressman Mark Fenton, who works behind the scenes to make the governmental changes needed?
- Joshua Cooper, who sees the manipulation of the FBI in extracting information and will not comply?
- Amos Cloyden, who rallied citizens from around the country to resist the overreach of the government?
- Sheriff Gillette, who worked to hold accountable only the guilty in the Battle of Bunkerville, regardless of who they are?
- John McConnel, Patrick Daniels, and Kristen Donahue, who willingly risked their lives and livelihood to protect freedom and their countryman?

★★★

- Kevin Linfield, who faithfully recognizes that God just keeps putting him in certain situations to make a positive impact on the outcome of people's lives?
- All the Rangers (law enforcement) who work every day to protect the citizens of Texas?
- Dr. John Jackson, who keeps his promises?
- Colin Johnson, who stands on his principles regardless of the personal costs?
- Tal Jordan, who loves Virginia and his country and is willing to die for liberty daily?
- How about Leah Scrivener, is she a Patriot in the making?

Throughout this book there are principled patriots, taking action in small and large ways, some boldly and others quietly behind the scenes to save their country. No one person is the "Ghost Patriot," but instead they are all patriots, working in their own quiet ways to preserve freedom, liberty, their Nation, and their way of life. Of course, as you close the pages in this book, it is my hope that you too will be willing to take your role, whatever it may be, in preserving the civil liberties, justice and religious freedoms of your country.

Will you be a Ghost Patriot?

Please log on to social media and let us know with this hashtag: #GhostPatriot, then take action.
Buy extra copies and ask your friends to read this book and share it with others.

- **Mike**

Author's Biography

Michael Stickler is a highly gifted best-selling author, producer, ex-felon, philanthropist, horseman, and internationally sought-after conference speaker. His best-selling book, Cliven Bundy American Terrorist or Patriot? quickly made the best-seller's list, revealing the truth of what is extensively and publicly known as the "Bunkerville Standoff." Mike's most recent book, Life without Reservation is widely acclaimed in the Christian community.

Read More of Mike's Books @ MikeStickler.info

Cliven Bundy American Terrorist Patriot

MikeStickler.info

Life Without Reservations

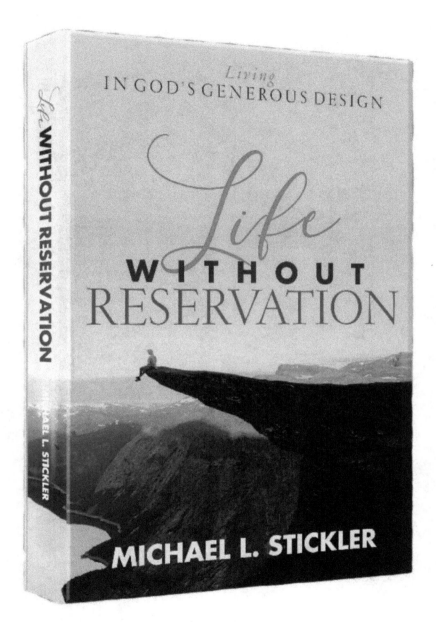

MikeStickler.info

CPSIA information can be obtained
at www.ICGtesting.com
Printed in the USA
BVHW050345110122
625923BV00018B/490/J

9 ‖781951‖648046‖